# THE BROODING DOC'S REDEMPTION

BY

## KATE HARDY

MILLS & BOON

*To Maggie Kingsley and Margaret McDonagh—*
*in loving memory of dear friends who were taken too young.*

First published in Great Britain 2013
by Mills & Boon, an imprint of Harlequin (UK) Limited.
Harlequin (UK) Limited, Eton House, 18-24 Paradise Road,
Richmond, Surrey TW9 1SR

© Pamela Brooks 2013

ISBN: 978 0 263 89876 7

Harlequin (UK) policy is to use papers that are natural, renewable and recyclable products and made from wood grown in sustainable forests. The logging and manufacturing process conform to the legal environmental regulations of the country of origin.

Printed and bound in Spain
by Blackprint CPI, Barcelona

**Dear Reader**

This is a story about forgiveness, and how love can give you a second chance.

GP Laurie thinks she's settled and has the perfect life with her daughter and her dog in a little country town—but she's missing something. And Marc needs to forgive himself for the past before he can move on and learn to be happy again.

Working together on a project to help their patients means they're thrown into each other's company—and, although neither intended to fall in love, that's exactly what they end up doing. But it takes a shock for them both to overcome their pasts and admit it…

This book's set in my part of the world, and I can honestly say that the bluebell woods Marc and Laurie visit are even more magical in real life. It's definitely one of the most romantic places in the world, and I'm lucky in that my research assistants are always happy to come with me. (Except the dog, because sadly dogs aren't allowed—otherwise he'd be there, wagging his tail alongside us.)

I'm always delighted to hear from readers, so do come and visit me at www.katehardy.com

With love

*Kate Hardy*

# CHAPTER ONE

THIS was ridiculous. Anyone would think that Marc was five years old and about to start his first day at school, not thirty-five and about to start his first day as a GP at Pond Lane Surgery.

He shook himself. There was absolutely no reason for him to be nervous. If Sam, the senior partner at the practice, hadn't thought that Marc would fit into the team, he wouldn't have offered him the job. Marc had spent ten years working in a busy practice in London. Working in a sleepy country town would be different, but he'd wanted different. Something to help him leave the memories behind.

He took a deep breath and pushed the door open.

The middle-aged woman at the reception desk smiled at him. 'It's a bit early for appointments, I'm afraid. We're not quite open yet.'

'I'm not actually here for an appointment,' he explained. 'My name's Marc Bailey.'

'Oh, our new GP! Welcome to the practice.' She shook his hand. 'I'm Phyllis—well, obviously I'm the receptionist. Sam's expecting you. I'll take you through to his office.'

A friendly face on Reception was a good start. Hopefully the rest of the day would match up to it.

Phyllis rapped on the open door. 'Sam? Marc Bailey's here.' She smiled at Marc. 'I'll leave you to it. If there's anything you need, just let me know.'

'Thank you.'

Sam shook his hand warmly. 'Welcome to Pond Lane. I hope you don't mind, Marc, but I'd like you to work with Dr Grant for the first half of the morning. I know you're perfectly capable of settling in by yourself, but it always helps to have someone teach you the horrible little quirks of a computer system that's new to you.'

'Uh-huh.' Marc wondered where this was leading. Was having someone shadowing him his new boss's way of making sure that he'd made the right decision in offering Marc the job?

'And you'll be helping her at the same time. Laurie works part time at the surgery. She's halfway through qualifying as a GP trainer, and it'll be useful for her to sit in on consultations with someone she hasn't worked with before.'

Marc gave him a wry smile. 'It's been a while since someone observed me in a consultation.'

'Laurie won't bite. She's a sweetie, and she makes the best lemon cake ever,' Sam said with a chuckle.

'Right.' Marc imagined a doctor in her mid-forties, the motherly type, who wanted to enrich her career by teaching new doctors.

'Oh, and I should warn you—she has this pet project. Given your experience in sports medicine, she might ask you to help out.'

Marc wasn't sure whether to be more intrigued or concerned. 'Noted,' he said.

'I'll take you through to Laurie.' Sam shepherded him through to Laurie's room. 'Marc, this is Laurie Grant.

Laurie, this is Marc Bailey, our new GP.' He patted Marc's shoulder. 'I'll leave you to sort things out between you.'

'OK.'

Laurie was nothing like Marc had expected. She was in her early thirties, a couple of years younger than himself, he'd guess, but what he really noticed were the dark corkscrew curls she'd pulled back in a scrunchie, her piercing blue eyes, and the sweetest-looking mouth he'd ever seen.

Which was terrible. He shouldn't even be noticing this sort of thing about her. She was his new colleague, and for all he knew she could be married.

Worse still, he found himself actually glancing at her left hand, to check.

No ring. Not that *that* meant anything.

She didn't seem to notice, and simply held out her hand to shake his. 'Welcome to Pond Lane, Marc.'

When his palm touched hers, it felt like an electric shock.

This really couldn't be happening.

But either it wasn't the same for her, or she was a bit better than he was at ignoring the zing of attraction, because she said, 'It's really good of you to let me sit in on consultations with you this morning, especially as it's your first day here. Leigh, the practice manager, is off today, but she left me all the details so I can set you up on the computer.' She laughed. 'Sam has this mad idea that because I'm the youngest doctor in the practice, it means I'm the one who's best with computers.'

'Are you?' Marc asked.

'Only because my brother's a computer consultant and taught me a lot, to stop me ringing him up and wailing down the phone to him every time I got stuck when I was a student,' she said cheerfully. 'Shall we grab a coffee, then go to your room and make a start?'

'Sure.' Marc found himself warming to her. She was efficient and bubbly, with an overlay of common sense: it was a good combination, and he'd just bet her patients adored her.

They headed for the staff kitchen, and Laurie switched the kettle on. 'Do you prefer tea or coffee?'

'Coffee's great, thanks.' Instant coffee, he noticed. A couple of years ago, he would've been a bit sniffy and insisted on bringing in a cafetière and a special blend of ground beans; and his suit for work would've been a designer label, his shirts hand-made. Nowadays, he knew there were more important things in life. And how he wished he'd been less shallow when he'd been younger. That he'd appreciated what he'd had.

'Milk or sugar?' she asked.

'Just as it is for me, thanks.'

She added a large slug of milk to her own mug, then shepherded him to his consulting room. Which looked incredibly bare: the only hint of colour was the plant on the windowsill. Compared to hers, which had had a child's paintings on the walls and framed photographs on her desk, the room looked impersonal and slightly daunting.

He'd have to change that, to help put his patients at ease. Though, even if all his photos hadn't been packed away, he couldn't quite face putting a photograph on his desk. This was a new start for him. No memories.

There was also a state-of-the-art computer on his desk, he noticed.

'It's probably very similar to the system you used before, but this one does have a couple of quirks.' She switched it on, and fished a note out of the file she carried. 'This is your username and password.'

And he noticed that when she talked him through the system, she let him press the keys rather than rattling through it and expecting him to watch what she did and take it all in. 'You're very good at this teaching stuff.'

'Thank you. It's something I like doing.'

'Is that why you're doing GP training?'

She nodded. 'Sam believes in job enrichment. Ricky—have you met Ricky yet?' At his shake of the head, she said, 'He's not in today, but he has ALS training. We all have our special interests. One of my friends suggested being a GP trainer, because I was always good at explaining things when I was helping others revise for exams. I looked into it and talked to Sam, and an opportunity came up last year to start a course. It means fitting things about a bit—I'm at the university one morning a week in term-time—and my hours are a bit odd, but I'm enjoying it.'

'Sounds good.'

Marc had a lovely voice, and Laurie hoped his manner with patients lived up to it. The last locum at the practice had been terrible, speaking to patients as if they were five years old, and they'd all complained to Phyllis and asked not to have any more appointments with him.

Though Marc was permanent rather than a locum. Given that he was moving here from London, Laurie had expected someone in his late forties or early fifties, wanting to exchange the bustle of life in the city for the much calmer pace of life in a small Norfolk town. Marc looked as if he was in his mid-thirties, a couple of years older than herself. And he was very easy on the eye, with hazel eyes behind wire-framed glasses, and dark hair, cut very short, which stuck up slightly on the top.

She damped down the surge of attraction. This was ridiculous. So what if he happened to remind her slightly of a TV star she'd had a crush on for ages? He probably wasn't single anyway; and, even if he was, she was very careful about relationships nowadays. No way was she giving Izzy a series of 'uncles' flitting in and out of her life in place of her absent father. Her little girl came first. Always would.

Besides, given what had happened with Dean, she didn't want to repeat her mistakes. Being single suited her just fine.

'So who's on your list this morning?' she asked.

He glanced at the screen. 'My first patient's Judy Reynolds.'

'Ah.'

Marc looked at her, frowning. 'Is there anything I need to know?'

'Only that she's on my mental list for my pet project.'

'Sam mentioned that.'

'I thought he might.' She smiled at him. 'I'd better not make you late starting on your first day, but maybe we can talk about my project at break?'

'Sure.'

He pressed the button to call in his first patient, and a few moments later there was a knock at the door.

'Come in,' he called.

A middle-aged woman walked in, and her eyes widened as she saw both Laurie and Marc sitting there.

'Hello, Judy,' Laurie said with a smile. 'I hope you don't mind me sitting in on your appointment with Dr Bailey?'

'Is this all to do with your GP training thing?' Judy asked.

'Yes.' Laurie smiled. 'If anything, Dr Bailey's senior to me—he's been a GP for longer than I have.'

'That's fine. I don't mind you sitting in.'

'Thank you. Just pretend I'm not here,' Laurie said.

Judy looked at Marc. 'So you're not another locum, then?'

'No, I'm here permanently.'

'Right.' She blew out a breath. 'That last locum was terrible—he spoke to you as if you were a toddler.'

Laurie didn't say a word—the practice manager already knew how everyone felt about that particular locum, staff and patients alike—but she wanted to see how Marc dealt with the situation.

'I'm sorry you had that kind of experience with him. But I'd like to assure you that that's not the way I do things, Mrs Reynolds,' Marc said. 'How can I help?'

'I'm probably wasting your time and I'm making a fuss over nothing, but I'm just—' She sighed. 'Well, I'm tired all the time. That locum sent me for blood tests, but I never heard anything back.'

Marc looked at the notes on the screen. 'I can see he checked you out for an underactive thyroid. Can I ask how your periods are?'

'A bit on the heavy side,' she admitted.

'That can make you a bit anaemic, which in turn can make you feel tired,' Marc said.

She grimaced. 'I'm almost looking forward to the menopause so I don't have to put up with them any more.'

'You don't have to put up with heavy periods now, either. It might be another five years before you're menopausal, but periods can often be a problem in the lead-up to menopause. I can give you something to make them a bit more manageable.'

Laurie liked the way he'd got straight to the point without any fuss or embarrassment.

Marc looked at the screen. 'Your blood results tell me your thyroid is working properly, but given that your periods are a bit heavy I'd like to take some blood and check your iron levels, if that's OK?'

Judy nodded.

'In the meantime, you might find it worth taking a supplement with B vitamins and zinc. That often helps with energy levels. Have you been under any extra stress lately?' he asked as he took the blood sample.

Judy shrugged. 'No more than any other mum who's got kids with exams coming up in a few weeks and they have to be nagged into revising.'

'Are you waking up at all in the night?'

'Not that I remember. I sleep like the dead.' She gave him a rueful look. 'Though my husband's been complaining about my snoring, and the kids say we do synchronised snoring.'

He returned her smile. 'And I bet they told you where it'd embarrass you most.'

'In the post office, where everyone could hear them.' She rolled her eyes. 'Yes.'

'It could be that you have sleep apnoea.'

'What's that?' Judy asked.

'It's where the soft tissues in your throat relax when you're asleep and block your airway for a few seconds, which brings your body out of deep sleep. It's so short you won't remember waking up. Even though you might think you've had a good night's sleep, you're not actually getting enough deep sleep to restore your energy levels.'

Laurie liked the way he'd explained it: concisely, and in layman's terms, while putting Judy at her ease. Marc was definitely going to be an asset to the team.

Judy looked worried. 'Do many people get it?'

'It's pretty common. About one in every fifty women of your age get it,' he said. 'But I need to ask you a few more questions to narrow things down a bit more, if you don't mind?'

Marc's manner was as nice as his voice, Laurie was pleased to discover, and he got a lot of information from Judy while keeping his questions relaxed and sounding concerned rather than aggressive.

'Do you have hay fever or anything like that?' he asked finally.

'Well, I often get a bit of a sniffle this time of year.' Judy flapped a dismissive hand. 'But it's nothing I'd bother a doctor with.'

'Any symptom's always worth checking out. That's what I'm here for,' he reassured her. 'I'd like you to have some tests, because from what you've told me I think you might well have sleep apnoea. I'll need to get in touch with the local sleep clinic, but what'll happen is that they'll give you a monitor to wear overnight to measure the oxygen in your blood and your breath, plus your heart rate, and then they'll analyse the data. It'll take me a couple of days to arrange, if that's OK? I'll get Phyllis to ring you as soon as I have some news.'

'Thank you.' Judy looked surprised. 'I'd never even heard of sleep apnoea before.'

'It might not be that,' he reassured her, 'but I think it's a possibility and it's worth checking out. If nothing else, we can cross it off the list of potential causes of your tiredness. You can do some things to help yourself in the meantime. I'm pleased you don't smoke or drink heavily, as that tends to make sleep apnoea worse, but losing weight would help you. So would sleeping on your side rather than your back.'

'How do I do that?' she asked.

'The easiest way is to put a tennis ball in a sock and pin it to the back of your nightie, so it's not comfortable for you to lie on your back.'

'Oh, very sexy,' she said with a grimace. 'My husband's going to wet himself laughing.'

'You said he's snoring, too. If it disturbs you,' Marc said, 'then you can do the same thing to his pyjamas. And tell him it's on your doctor's advice.' Mark smiled.

'I'll do that.' She smiled.

'Now—your periods. It says here you're not on the Pill.'

'No. John had the snip after our son was born.'

'OK. Have you had any problem with taking any tablets with progesterone in the past?'

'No.'

'Good. It's oestrogen that's making your periods heavy, and the progesterone will help balance that out a bit. You take the tablets for twenty-one days and then stop for seven, and you should find that your periods are a lot more manageable.'

'Thank you.'

'Losing weight,' he said gently, 'would help you with that as well. Your body produces more oestrogen when you're overweight.'

Judy looked upset. 'It's not as if I sit there watching TV all night, stuffing my face with doughnuts and burgers.'

'No,' he replied carefully, 'but your body's less efficient as you get older, so every year after you hit forty you'll need to exercise more and eat less to stay at the same weight. Which is totally unfair, but I guess at least it happens to all of us.'

'Can I suggest something?' Laurie asked. At Marc's nod, she continued, 'I'm about to set up a project for some of our patients who are having problems losing weight. It's not a judgemental thing, it's looking at ways we can support you better and help you. Would you like to come along and see what's on offer?'

'After all the diets I've been on, it's worth a try,' Judy said. 'All right.'

'Great. I'll put you down on my list, and I'll get in touch with more details later in the week,' Laurie said.

Marc printed out the prescription, signed it and handed it to Judy. 'I'll get Phyllis to ring you and make an appointment as soon as I hear back from the sleep clinic.'

'Thank you, Dr Bailey.'

'Pleasure. And I meant what I said. If you're worried about something, no matter how silly you think it is, come and see me. If it's something you don't need to worry about, I can tell you so you can stop worrying—and if it *is* something to worry about, then by telling me we've got a better chance of catching it early, which in turn means that treatment will be easier for you.'

'I will.' She looked relieved. 'Thank you, Dr Bailey.'

'My pleasure.'

Marc saw the rest of his patients up to the mid-morning break, then glanced at Laurie. 'Dare I ask if I passed muster?'

She rolled her eyes. 'It wasn't a test. It was a chance for me to observe how you do things, and maybe learn from you. But, since you asked, yes, you have the skills I'd want my trainees to have. You put patients at their ease, you talk to them in layman's terms, and you're a definite improvement on that locum.'

'Thank you. Though, from what I've heard this morning, just about *anyone* would be an improvement on that locum.' He raised an eyebrow. 'So how did Mrs Reynolds know about your training?'

'This is a small town, Marc. Everyone knows everything.'

'Right.'

He sounded slightly tense—wary about living his life in a goldfish bowl, maybe. She smiled. 'It's not being nosey, it's *caring*. It's being part of the community. Talking of which, my pet project might be useful for you. Obviously you don't need to lose weight, but it'll be a quick way for you to get to know a lot of people in the town.'

'So what does it involve?'

'Let's grab a drink, and I'll explain.' In the staff kitchen, she made them both a coffee, then chose a corner chair. 'We have quite a few patients on the obesity register. I'm looking at trying to stop them developing diabetes or having a CV incident. It's not all about diet—a few of them have brought in food diaries, and they've already made all the simple switches and are eating sensibly.'

'What about exercise?' Marc asked.

'That's what I think the problem is. They already have work and family commitments, and they put their own needs way down the list and they don't think they have the time to exercise.'

'So we have to change their mind sets first.'

'Exactly. A friend of mine at the university is doing a study on the effects of diet and exercise in people over thirty-five. He can lend us activity monitors, so we can get our at-risk patients to wear them for a week and we can show them a baseline of what they actually do, and then we look at how they can boost their activity, when and where.'

'Sounds good.'

'I thought we could repeat the monitoring at three-month intervals to see how the activity patterns of our patients have changed, and tie that in with weight, blood glucose and cholesterol checks. It's a win-win situation. My friend Jay gets people in his target group for his study, and we get to help our patients. And the monitors won't cost anything, so Leigh won't be on my case about budgets.'

'Ah, the joys of budgets. The key to getting people to do regular exercise is to find out what they actually enjoy doing,' Marc said.

She was pleased that he'd hit the nail on the head. 'That's why I want to get the local gyms and sports clubs involved, to set up taster sessions and beginners' classes. Once our patients find out what they enjoy doing, then we talk them into having an exercise buddy who goes with them to whatever the activity is.'

'So they feel they can't let their friends down and they stick to a programme,' Marc said. 'That's a really good idea.'

'Sam says you have an interest in sports medicine.'

'Yes.' Though Marc didn't volunteer any information about himself or what experience he had in sports medicine, Laurie noticed. Clearly he preferred to keep himself to himself. OK. She could work with that. She'd seen how he was with patients, and that was more important.

'So would you like to be involved in the project?' she asked.

'I can't really say no, can I?'

'Of course you can. I understand if you're too busy.'

He looked thoughtful, and for a moment she thought he was going to say no. Then he nodded. 'OK.'

'Thank you. When's a good time for you for a meeting?'

'After surgery?' he suggested.

Not when she had a pile of paperwork and then had to take the dog out and do the school run. 'Is there any chance you could make an evening meeting at my house?' she asked hopefully.

'Your house,' he repeated.

'Because I'm a single mum,' she explained. 'It'd be a lot easier for me to discuss work with you at my place after Izzy's gone to bed. If that's a problem for you, never mind—I'll ask my mum to babysit.'

Something in her tone told Marc that wasn't her preferred option. 'But you'd rather not?'

'Mum helps me out quite a bit as it is,' Laurie admitted. 'I try not to ask her unless it's really desperate, because it's not fair to keep relying on her.'

Discuss the project at her house.

*A family home.*

It was something Marc had shied away from for the last couple of years; since the accident, he'd quietly cut himself off from friends who had children. But right now it didn't look as if he had much choice in the matter. Given that Laurie had already explained why she didn't want to ask her mum, he'd feel mean if he pushed her into getting a babysitter. And he didn't want to explain why children were difficult for him, outside work. That was his business. His burden.

'If it's a problem for your partner,' she added, mis-

reading his silence, 'then she—or he—is very welcome
to join us. We won't be discussing individual patients, so
we wouldn't be breaking any confidentiality.'

*His partner was welcome to join them.*

Marc just about managed not to flinch.

'I don't have a partner,' he said, struggling to keep his
voice even. It was something he'd just about come to terms
with over the last two years. But he still couldn't forgive
himself for Ginny's death.

Laurie grimaced. 'Sorry. You must think I'm being
horribly nosey. I guess that's the problem with growing
up in a small town—you know everyone and everyone
knows you, and if you don't know something you tend to
come straight out and ask. It wasn't meant maliciously.'

He understood that—he'd already worked out that
Laurie Grant was warm, bubbly and incredibly enthusiastic—but he didn't want people knowing too much about
him. If they knew the truth about his past, they'd despise
him as much as he despised himself. 'Uh-huh,' he said
neutrally.

'How about this evening?' she suggested.

'That's fine. What time's good for you?'

'Izzy goes to bed at seven. So any time after that.' She
shrugged. 'Unless you'd like to come for dinner? It's nothing fancy, just pasta and garlic bread and salad, but there's
more than enough if you'd like to join us.'

'Thanks, but I'll take a rain check if you don't mind.'
He didn't want to be rude to his new colleague; but he was
also guiltily aware that in other circumstances he would've
loved to share a meal with her. There was something about
Laurie that drew him; she wasn't a conventional beauty,
but there was a warmth and brightness about her, and her
smile made the room feel as if it had just lit up. Though,

for his own peace of mind, he knew he needed to keep himself separate. And in any case he'd guess that, as a single parent, her life would be complicated enough without adding someone like him to the mix.

'No problem.' She scribbled down her address on a piece of paper, added her phone number and handed it to him. 'Just in case you get held up. See you later.' She smiled. 'Enjoy your first morning, and welcome to Pond Lane Surgery.'

The rest of the morning surgery went fine. Marc went home for a sandwich and ate it in the kitchen. He stayed out of the dining room, because it contained a stack of boxes he hadn't been able to face unpacking. Boxes full of memories he couldn't handle.

Maybe he should've taken up his sister's offer of help, instead of being too proud and telling Yvonne that he was fine and he'd be able to sort it out. Because he wasn't fine. And he couldn't sort it out.

Still, he'd brushed her offer aside, so he'd have to live with his choice. The boxes couldn't stay there for ever, so he'd have to make himself do it room by room.

One step at a time.

# CHAPTER TWO

MARC wasn't in the mood for cooking when he got home from an afternoon of house calls. He made himself a salad and ate it listlessly—food nowadays was fuel, rather than a pleasure—then looked up Laurie's address on his satnav. Her house was totally the other side of the town from his, far enough to justify using the car rather than walking.

When he parked his car outside and walked up the path to her front door, he wished he'd thought to bring her some flowers or something. OK, so this was a work meeting rather than a social event, but it was still being held at her house, and he felt uncomfortable turning up without anything. Then again, would flowers be making the wrong kind of statement?

He shook himself. Oh, for pity's sake. He needed to be professional about this. But he was horribly aware that this whole situation was throwing him. He was about to walk into just the kind of home he could've had if the accident hadn't happened. A family home. One with children.

But the accident *had* happened. He had a bachelor pad, not a family home. And he only had himself to blame.

He knocked on the front door. There a brief woof and a 'Shh!', and then Laurie opened the door. A chocolate Labrador with a wagging blur of a tail was desperately trying to barge past her. There was a smudge of flour on Laurie's face and several of her dark corkscrew curls had escaped from the scrunchie she used to hold her hair back. The whole effect was unbelievably cute, and he found himself wanting to tuck the stray curls into place and brush that smudge of flour from her skin.

Which was incredibly dangerous. He didn't need that kind of contact. Didn't want it. His heart had been broken, he was still trying to patch it up, and no way was he ever risking any kind of relationship again, other than on a strictly colleagues basis. He even kept his family at a distance nowadays, because it was easier. If he didn't let himself feel, he wouldn't hurt.

Misinterpreting his sudden stillness, she pushed the dog back behind her. 'Sorry, Cocoa's a bit over-friendly.' Within a nanosecond, the dog was trying to push past her again. 'I forgot to ask if you're OK with dogs. I can put him in the utility room, if you'd rather.'

'No, it's fine. I like dogs.' It had even been part of his and Ginny's plans. A baby, and then a dog. A house with a garden.

Ginny would've loved the old cottage he'd found to rent in the small Norfolk town. She would've loved the duck pond on the green, the ancient flint church with its round tower, the gentle undulations of the countryside around them. But because of his own stupidity he had nobody to share it with. Nobody to love. Nobody to love him back.

He pushed the thoughts away and held out his hand for the dog to sniff, then scratched the top of the dog's head. There was a look of sheer bliss on Cocoa's face and he leaned towards Marc.

'He'll be demanding a fuss from you all night,' Laurie warned with a smile. 'Come in. I hope you don't mind, but I'm waiting for some stuff to come out of the oven, so we need to stay in the kitchen. Can I get you a coffee, or maybe a glass of wine?'

*Definitely not wine.* That had been one of the causes of his downfall, and he hadn't touched a drop since the funeral. 'Coffee would be lovely, thanks,' he said politely.

'Come in and sit down.'

It was clearly a family kitchen. There were several paintings held on the fridge with magnets, obviously the work of a young child. And if that wasn't enough proof, there was a cork board on one wall covered with school notices and photographs of a little girl, varying from babyhood to what looked like about five years old.

Marc couldn't help thinking how his own child would've been eighteen months old now, toddling every-where and starting to chatter away. A boy or a girl? It had been too soon to tell.

He dug his fingernails into his palms, and the slight pain was just enough to stop him thinking and ripping the scars off his heart.

On the worktop, there was a plate full of cupcakes cov-ered in very pink icing, along with lots of sparkly sprin-kles—and there were almost as many on the worktop as there were on the cakes. A pile of washing-up was stacked up next to the sink and a batch of cookies sat on a cool-ing wire rack next to the oven. Clearly Laurie was in the middle of a baking session.

She followed his gaze when she turned round from the kettle and winced. 'Sorry, it's a bit untidy. I meant to clear up properly before you got here, but then Izzy wanted me to read her bedtime story a second time, and—' She spread her hands. 'Well, you know how it is with kids.'

Not personally. And he never would now. He didn't

deserve to have a family. 'Yes,' he said, as neutrally as he could.

Cocoa sat at Marc's feet and rested his chin on Marc's knee; absently, Marc rubbed the top of the dog's head.

'Would you like a cookie with your coffee?' Laurie asked.

'Thank you. But I hope you didn't go to all this trouble for me.'

'No, of course n—' She winced, cutting the word off as she put a couple of cookies onto a plate. 'Sorry, that came out the wrong way. I didn't mean you weren't worth taking any trouble over. I'm baking because it's the PTA coffee morning tomorrow. Izzy decorated the cakes.'

Laurie's little girl. Which explained the sprinkles, and probably most of the mess.

'Obviously I don't get a chance to actually go to the coffee morning because I need to be at the surgery for my shift, but I try to do my bit to help. I always make them some cakes to sell, give them a raffle prize and leave them money for some tickets. If they draw my name out, they choose something for me and send the prize home with Izzy.'

Laurie was clearly very involved with village life. Not only was she a GP, she was also a mum who did things to support the local school. Would Ginny have been like that? he wondered. Probably. As a teacher, she would've been involved with the school, either because she worked there or because their child went there. Though she would've been a bit less chaotic than Laurie. Their house in London had never been as untidy as this.

'So did you enjoy your first day at the practice?' she asked.

Work. He could talk about work, he thought gratefully. Not personal stuff. That was good. 'Fine.'

'Good.' Laurie put a mug of coffee in front of him, along with the cookies, then added milk to her own coffee and sat down opposite him. 'I've been thinking about the easiest way to tackle this. I thought we could maybe brainstorm all the different kinds of exercise we can think of, then I'll list all the people within a five-mile radius who can offer each one, and we can divvy up the calls between us and ask them if they'd be prepared to do a taster session for us.'

'Sure. That sounds reasonable.'

She looked relieved. 'Great. One tiny thing: would you mind if I asked you to deal with Neil Peascod? He owns the gym and swim place at the other end of the town.'

'Do I take it he's likely to be difficult?' Marc asked, wondering why she didn't want to deal with the guy.

'Not exactly.' She flushed. 'He was a bit, um, persistent with me last year. I guess he didn't like to think that someone might actually say no to him.'

'He asked you out?' Then Marc realised how rude that sounded. 'I apologise. I didn't meant it to come out like that.'

Laurie didn't look in the slightest bit offended. She simply laughed. 'Don't worry, I'm under no illusions that I'm the next supermodel. I'm thirty years old, I'm a mum, I have lumpy bits, and I have days when my hair needs stuffing under a hat so nobody can see how frizzy it looks.' She smiled. 'And I also have days when I look utterly fabulous. But they're the rare ones. Dog-walking isn't exactly the time or place to wear a little black dress and high heels.'

At the W-word, the Labrador deserted his post at Marc's

feet, rushed over to Laurie, put his paws on her knee and licked her face hopefully. She rolled her eyes and petted him. 'No, Cocoa, I didn't mean *now*. You know as well as I do that walkies is when I get home from work and before I collect Izzy from school.'

Marc couldn't help smiling. He liked Laurie. She was warm and bubbly, yet at the same time she was very down-to-earth.

'Sorry about that.' When she switched her attention back to him, he noticed just how blue her eyes were. Almost as bright as the forget-me-nots in his garden. 'Neil. No, he's not *difficult*. He just thinks that he's the answer to a desperate single mum's problems.' She wrinkled her nose. 'Yes, I'm a single mum but, no, I'm not desperate, I don't necessarily need a man in my life to make it complete, and I'm doing just fine, thank you very much.'

She didn't sound bitter, but as if she was simply stating the facts. Or was that a gentle warning to him? Marc wondered. He'd told her that he was single. Perhaps this was her way of telling him that even if he might be interested, she wasn't.

'Noted,' he said drily. He took a bite of the still-warm cookie. 'This is very nice.'

'Thank you. And please don't let Cocoa con you into sharing with him. They're bad for his teeth, and he's very far from being a poor, starving hound.'

The dog looked up at him with mournful eyes, and Marc couldn't help smiling. 'Not according to him.'

'He's an old fraud.' She smiled back. 'Sam said you were interested in sports medicine. Is that what you did in your last job?'

'It was more of a spare-time thing, really. I worked with the local rugby club.'

'Oh. Do you play?' she asked.

'Not any more.' Marc found himself volunteering information; he hadn't expected that and it unnerved him slightly. 'I was injured.'

'Knee?' she guessed.

'Shoulder. Dislocation, then a rotator cuff tear.'

'Ouch.' She looked sympathetic. 'I'm not surprised you stopped playing. In your shoes, I wouldn't want to risk doing that again.'

'Believe me, after three months of doing nothing but triage calls because my arm was out of action, I'd never risk it again.' And he wished with all his heart that he hadn't given in to the frustration he'd felt at having to give up the game he loved. Because then maybe he could've stopped the chain of events that had wrecked his life and robbed him of everything else he loved.

'I guess rugby and football probably wouldn't be the best kind of exercise for our group anyway,' she said.

'I'd say no to squash as well,' he said.

'Very sensible. And we'll ban them from jogging. We're trying to improve their circulation, not give them shin splints.'

'Or overdoing it in the first flush of enthusiasm and giving themselves a heart attack.' He looked thoughtfully at her. 'Badminton's a possible.'

'And swimming. As well as low-impact exercise classes and circuit training,' she suggested.

'Maybe martial arts—kick-boxing doesn't have to be fast and furious.'

She smiled. 'I've always fancied trying that one myself.' She took a laptop from a drawer in the huge pine dresser. 'Let's start getting this down.' The computer whirred and made a couple of protesting noises, and she rolled her eyes. 'Sorry, this is a bit old. I'm afraid it takes ages to boot up.'

His own was state of the art and would've been ready to go by now. As a single mum, Laurie would have to juggle her finances, and a new computer probably wasn't top of her priorities, Marc thought.

They made a list together. Halfway through it, the timer on the oven beeped.

'Sorry, do you mind if I sort this out?' she asked. 'The topping works best if you do it when the cake's hot.'

'I take it that's for school?' He grinned.

'Yes.' She smiled. 'But, if you're good, I'll make a cake for the surgery later in the week.'

It smelled wonderful, and Marc ignored the fact that this was the first time he'd been interested in food in a very, very long time. 'I'm good,' he said. 'If you can talk at the same time as you do whatever it is you're doing to the cake, I'll take over the typing.'

'Excellent. Thanks.'

Marc surreptitiously watched her as she took the cake out of the oven, pierced the top with a skewer and spooned the contents of a bowl over it. She looked up and caught him looking at her. 'It's lemon and sugar.'

The citrus scent made his mouth water. 'Is this the one Sam told me about?'

'Yes. It's his favourite. So, are you going to do some typing or just hoping for cake, like Cocoa is?'

He couldn't help smiling. 'I'm typing. Start talking.'

Within twenty minutes they had a good list. They worked through it again and weeded out some of the more unlikely suggestions they'd come up with.

'This looks good to me. I'll work my way through it

and put in the contacts, and then give you your half of the list tomorrow,' Laurie said.

'That's fine,' Marc said. 'And I guess I'd better let you get on.' Especially as he felt way too comfortable here. And that unnerved him.

She smiled at him. 'Thanks. Sadly, the washing-up won't do itself, and it'd be a bit self-indulgent to have a dishwasher when there's only Izzy and me living here. Are you sure you don't want another coffee before you go?'

'I'm sure, but thanks for the offer. See you tomorrow.'

There was something lost about the expression in Marc's eyes, Laurie thought when Marc had gone. Had he been through a bad divorce? That might explain why he'd come here from London. Maybe she could find a tactful way of talking to him and help him understand that it did get better eventually.

OK, so she hadn't actually been married to Dean, but the break-up and then sorting out everything afterwards had been tough. The only thing missing had been the fight in court; the rest of the acrimony and guilt had been there.

Just as Marc had left, she'd wanted to put her arms round him, hold him close and tell him not to worry because everything was going to work out just fine. Which was crazy. She barely knew the man. And she certainly wasn't looking for any complications in her own life.

Then again, she'd been lucky. She'd had people there for her when her own life had hit the skids. And she had the strongest feeling that Marc didn't. He was a stranger to the area. He could do with a friend. OK, so when she'd come home she'd been far from a stranger—but she knew what that felt like, to need a friend. So it would be mean of her to back off and ignore him... Wouldn't it?

# CHAPTER THREE

On Wednesday morning, Marc walked into his surgery to find a plate on his desk containing a cupcake exactly like the ones he'd seen in Laurie's kitchen the previous night, along with a printed copy of the table he and Laurie had made together, detailing the different exercise providers and which of them was going to call each one, with space to scribble notes.

That cake gave him an odd feeling. Was this the sort of thing his own child would've done with Ginny, making cakes and decorating them haphazardly and sending him off to work with one? A little thing, made with such love...

He shook himself as he heard a rap on the door, a nanosecond before it opened. Sam, the senior partner, leaned round the door. 'Morning, Marc. How are you settling in?'

'Fine, thanks.' Marc summoned up a professional smile, not wanting Sam to see how much the cupcake had thrown him.

'I meant to say yesterday, Ruth said you're very welcome to come to ours for lunch on Sunday. It's not much fun having weekends on your own and it takes a while to settle into a small country town, especially when you're used to the city.'

Marc appreciated the overture of friendship but he'd

learned that, once people knew about his past, any friend-ship tended to come tempered with pity. He had quite enough pity for himself without needing it from others. 'Thanks. That's really kind of you, but I have a few things to sort out.'

'Sure. Well, you know where we are if you change your mind. Just turn up.'

'Thanks. I will.' Though Marc had no intention of doing so. He didn't deserve such kindness. Not after the way he'd messed up.

Sam glanced at the cupcake and smiled. 'Oh, good. I hoped we'd get some of the leftovers from the PTA baking session. Laurie's cakes are wonderful.' He laughed. 'Even if Izzy does put half a ton of sprinkles on every single one.'

Marc carefully sidestepped the subject of children. 'Laurie and I brainstormed the project last night.' He waved the table at Sam. 'She's added the contact details, and we're splitting the calls between us.'

'Excellent.' Sam looked pleased. 'I can see you're going to fit right in. We definitely made the right choice, ask-ing you to join us.'

'Thank you. I hope I live up to that.'

Marc didn't get the chance to see Laurie during surgery as she was busy on house calls and, because she worked part time, she finished earlier than he did. After he'd seen his last patient for the day, he looked at his watch. Laurie's place was on his way home from the surgery. He knew he probably ought to call her first and make arrangements to discuss the project, but he couldn't resist the impulse to drop in and see her.

And he didn't want to analyse the reason too closely.

'Oh, Marc.' She looked flustered when she opened the front door.

'Sorry, is this a bad time?'

'No, but my house is chaos city at this time of day, so I'll have to ask you to ignore the mess. Izzy's drawing pictures at the kitchen table. Come in, and I'll put the kettle on.' Her smile brightened back into a welcome.

And that was half the reason he was here.

Because that smile drew him. Made him feel that the world was a better place.

Marc followed Laurie into the kitchen, where a little girl was sitting at the kitchen table. Cocoa was sitting patiently by the child's feet, clearly hoping for a share in the cake that sat on the plate beside her. He wagged his tail at Marc, but didn't leave his position or break his eyeline from the table.

'Izzy, this is Dr Bailey. He's come to work with me at the surgery and he's just popped in to see me about a project we're working on together.'

The little girl looked up at him. 'Hello, Dr Bailey,' she said shyly.

'Marc, this is Izzy, my daughter.'

'Hello, Izzy.' He looked at Laurie. 'She's very like you.' She had the same wild dark curls, though they weren't tied back neatly like Laurie's hair was; and Izzy's eyes were a deep brown rather than a piercing blue.

'I've got a new friend at school,' Izzy said. 'Her name's Molly. She moved here last week and she only started in our class yesterday. I said she could play with me and Georgia at playtime so she won't be lonely.'

Taking the new girl under her wing—just as Laurie was taking him under her wing, Marc thought. Like mother, like daughter. 'That's very kind of you,' he said.

'Me and Mummy made some cakes. Would you like one?' Izzy asked.

'No, thank you.'

She nodded sagely. 'Because you don't want to spoil your dinner.'

Marc was torn between wanting to smile—he'd just bet that particular phrase came from Laurie—and panicking. He wasn't used to this. He'd kept himself separate for so long; contact with a child, outside work, spooked him slightly.

'That's right,' he said. 'But your mum brought some of your cakes into work this morning and I had one then. It was very nice.'

She beamed at him. 'Did you like the sprinkles?'

No. He'd scraped them off, along with most of the icing; it had been a little too sweet for his taste. 'They were delicious,' he said, not wanting to spoil it for her.

'I like sprinkles.'

He couldn't help smiling. He'd already worked that one out for himself.

'Would you like a glass of milk?'

She really was her mother's daughter—warm, sweet and generous. And it scared the hell out of him.

'Thank you for the offer but I'm fine, thanks.'

'Grown-ups normally have coffee or tea, Iz,' Laurie said, putting her arms round her daughter's shoulders and resting her face against her little girl's.

It was just how Marc had imagined Ginny would be with their child, and it sent a shockwave through him. He really, really wished he hadn't given in to that impulse to call in and see her. If only he'd waited until this evening, or had called her first to arrange a time when Izzy would be in bed…

'But I'm not allowed to use the kettle. I'm too little,' Izzy pointed out.

'I know, sweetheart.' Laurie kissed her. 'Do you want to do another drawing for me? I need to talk to Dr Bailey about work. We won't be long, I promise.'

He was eating into Laurie's family time, and that wasn't fair. And seeing Izzy, the love between parent and child—something he'd wanted so badly and would never have now—made him want to back away. Fast.

'Did you want a coffee, Marc?' Laurie asked.

'No, thanks, I'm fine. I only called in because I was passing and I thought it'd be just as quick to drop in as it would be to ring you later.'

He looked nervous, and Laurie didn't have a clue why. 'Good idea,' she said.

'I wanted to let you know that I've had a good response already from the calls I've made. But do you have a slot booked on a regular basis in a hall or something, or will our patients need to go to a different place each week?'

'I thought we'd try and keep everything in the same place, because then there's less chance of any confusion and also no excuses for not turning up,' Laurie said. 'I'm waiting for a phone call to confirm it, but I'm pretty sure we've got the village hall on Wednesdays at eight. Sam says we can use the surgery's waiting room for the talks from the cardiologist, diabetic specialist and nutritionist, if we need to, but obviously it's not a suitable space for an exercise class. Even a small one.'

'Great. I'll call my contacts back to pencil in some dates, then. Oh, and I hope I haven't stomped all over your toes, but I drafted a letter to the patient group over lunchtime. Do you want me to email it to you, so you can see if I've missed anything or there's something you think needs changing?'

'That'd be great, thanks. It's probably easier to send it here than to the surgery. Do you have my email address?'

'No.'

She scribbled it down on a piece of paper and handed it to him. For a second, their fingers touched, and awareness surged through her; she damped it down swiftly. This wasn't appropriate. Wrong time, wrong place. And probably wrong man; she didn't exactly have a good track record in that department.

'Thanks. I'll, um, see you tomorrow. And I'll email you that letter when I get home.'

'OK.'

'Bye, Izzy.' Though he didn't go over to the little girl or so much as look at her drawing, let alone comment on it.

Not that Izzy seemed upset by it. She was too busy colouring in her picture. 'Bye bye, Dr Bailey.' She smiled at him, and Laurie's heart clenched with love for her daughter.

Was it her imagination, or had Marc gone very, very still?

Imagination, she decided, and saw him out.

But over the rest of the evening, she wondered. Did Marc have children and his divorce had been so acrimonious that he didn't have access to them? Then again, she had a fairly good instinct about people, and she didn't think Marc was the unreasonable type that would make any solicitor wary of allowing him access. Maybe it was something else, she thought. Something sadder, because Marc had definite shadows in his eyes.

Just before afternoon surgery the next day, there was a rap on Marc's consulting-room door. Expecting it to be

Sam, he looked up with a smile, and felt his eyes widen as he saw Laurie.

Which was ridiculous. She was his colleague; she'd made it clear that she was perfectly fine being single; and, even if she had been in the market for a relationship, Marc knew he was too damaged to be able to offer her anything.

'Hi. You OK?' she asked.

'Sure.'

She waited, and he sighed. 'No.'

'Tough morning?'

He nodded. 'Something like that.'

She came into the room and sat on the chair his patients used. 'Want to talk about it?'

'I can't dump it on you. Anyway, it's nearly time for us to see our next patients.'

'True.' She looked at him. 'If you're not busy tonight, you could come over and tell me then.'

'Dr Fixit?' he asked.

'That's what I do,' she said lightly. 'What you do, too.'

'Not in this case.'

She reached over to squeeze his hand, and the contact made his skin tingle. 'Marc, we all get patients where we can't make everything all right for them. Nobody else would be able to fix it either, so don't blame yourself.'

Easier said than done. He blamed himself for a lot of things.

And then she gave him that light-up-the-room smile. 'I could give you my trainee pep talk. Which would be immensely cheeky of me, given that you're more experienced than I am.'

'It would,' he agreed. But that smile had done a lot to ease his soul.

'Up to you. I'm not busy tonight—well, once I've read

Izzy a bedtime story or six. So if you want to talk about it, come over.'

'Why are you asking me?' He grimaced. 'Sorry. That was ungracious.'

'But a fair comment. I'm asking you because I do the same job as you. Unless you have family or friends who do, too, they won't really get what you're feeling right now and why. Plus you're new around here, and could maybe do with a local friend.'

Friendship. That was what she was offering. 'Thank you.' He felt incredibly humbled.

She smiled at him. 'I actually came to say that letter you wrote was perfect. I'll do a mail merge and send them all off today,' she said.

'Great.' And how ridiculous that her approval pleased him so much. She was his colleague. He knew he was good at his job. He didn't need approval from her. But it still warmed him. 'Your daughter's very like you.'

And why on earth had he said that?

'The spit of me at that age, but with brown eyes,' Laurie agreed with a smile.

'I didn't mean just in looks. It's the way she is. Warm and open.'

Oh, now, he *really* hadn't meant to come out with that. He didn't want her thinking that he was pursuing her, the way the gym guy had last year. Because he wasn't pursuing her. Was he?

Her smile widened. 'Thanks. I'm trying to give her the best view of life and other people—and I don't want her to think it matters that she doesn't have a dad.'

'Of course it doesn't.'

Though Marc couldn't help wondering what had gone

wrong with the marriage. He couldn't imagine anyone being daft enough to let Laurie go.

And that was an even more dangerous thought. Laurie Grant was sweet and warm and chaotic, and she most definitely didn't need any more complications in her life. Especially a complication like him. 'My patient's here,' he said, gesturing to the screen on his desk. 'Better not keep him waiting.'

'No.' She got up and walked to the door. 'See you later, maybe.'

Marc couldn't stop thinking about Laurie all afternoon. And he found himself going over to her place later that evening. Izzy was in bed, to his relief, and Laurie had tidied up. He wondered if she'd done it specially.

'Yes,' she said, 'I did tidy up in case you came over.'

He groaned. 'I'm sorry. Did I say that aloud?'

'No, but it was written all over your face.'

He felt the colour seep into his cheeks. 'I'm sorry. I wasn't criticising you.'

'I know, but it was chaos city here and it'd gone beyond even *my* mess tolerance levels.'

She made coffee, and ushered them through to her living room. There were pictures everywhere, more even than he could remember Ginny having in their house. 'So tell me about your patient.'

'She's about our age, and had cysts on both ovaries. The surgeon couldn't save them. And now she wants a baby and can't have one without help.' He sighed. 'I really feel for her.' Especially as it had ripped the top off his own scars. Elaine Kirby had said how much she wished she'd starting thinking about a baby earlier, instead of leaving it until her career was settled and she'd saved up enough to extend her maternity leave. And how Marc wished he and Ginny hadn't waited so long either...

'IVF?'

'Her husband isn't keen—it's not the money, it's the emotional upheaval and what she'd have to go through physically. And she's not sure about adoption—even though it's the being there that makes you a parent, not the biology.'

'That's very true.'

He grimaced. 'Sorry. That wasn't meant to be a pop at you.'

'I know.' She brushed it aside. 'Poor woman. That's a tough situation. But you can't fix everything, Marc.'

'You try,' he pointed out.

'Yes, and I always will. But you have to be realistic. Some things you can't fix.'

'I'm sending her for counselling.'

'Which is exactly what I would've done, too.'

'It doesn't feel like enough.'

He sounded so miserable. And Laurie wanted to cheer him up. 'Maybe not now, but these things take time.' She looked at him. 'I have an idea. Something that will make you feel better.'

'Dr Fixit again?'

'Absolutely.' And the fact that Marc Bailey was utterly gorgeous...well, that had nothing to do with this. A relationship wouldn't be a good idea for either of them. But friends she could do. 'Are you busy on Sunday?'

'Why?' he asked, sounding wary.

'Because,' she said, 'you're new to the area and there's something special you probably don't know about but you need to see, and it really has to be *this* weekend.'

His eyes narrowed. 'What does?'

'Something,' she said softly, 'that I always came home for at this time of year. Even when we were really busy at the practice in London.'

He blinked. 'You lived in London?' He sounded surprised, as if he hadn't expected that.

'I haven't always worked in a small town.' She smiled to take the sting from her words. 'I trained in London, and I worked as a GP there after I qualified. I decided to come back home when Izzy was born. It was probably a bit selfish of me, but I needed my family's support, and I'm glad I made that decision. So, shall I pick you up at nine on Sunday?'

'You don't know where I live.'

'No, but you're going to give me your address.'

Marc could say no, but he had a feeling that Laurie wouldn't accept it. What was it she'd said about the gym guy not taking no for an answer? She could give the man a real run for his money. Knowing he was beaten, he gave in and scribbled his address on a piece of scrap paper.

She stuffed it in the pocket of her trousers. 'Great. By the way, depending on how much rain we get over the next couple of days, you might need wellies. It can get a bit boggy. If you don't have any, I can borrow Joe's.'

Joe—was that Izzy's father? he wondered.

The question must have been written over his face, because she explained, 'Joe's my big brother.'

'The computer expert?'

She looked pleased that he'd remembered. 'That's him.'

'I have wellies.'

'Good. I probably won't see you before the end of surgery, so have a nice day.' She smiled. 'See you on Sunday.'

Marc had no idea what he'd agreed to. And he really wasn't sure whether he was more intrigued or terrified. Whatever, Sunday was going to be *interesting*…

# CHAPTER FOUR

ON SUNDAY morning, Marc was half expecting Laurie to be late, given how chaotic her house was. But she was dead on time, pulling up outside his house in an estate car—which *was* chaotic inside—with a child seat in the back containing Izzy, and a dog guard behind that so Cocoa could sit in the very back of the car without wriggling over into the back seat next to Izzy.

The little girl beamed at him as he opened the passenger door. 'Hello, Dr Bailey.'

Formality didn't sit easily with him. 'You can call me Marc, if you like,' he offered.

'Marc.' Her smile widened; she clearly loved the thought of having a grown-up friend. And Marc was torn between being charmed and wanting to back away.

'So where are we going?' he asked.

'You'll see,' Laurie said, at the same time as Izzy burst out, 'To see the bluebells!'

'Bluebells?' Marc asked.

'Just outside the next village is one of the last patches of the ancient woods of England,' Laurie explained. 'And this weekend of the year is when the bluebell carpet in the woods is at its best. They're proper English bluebells, with a scent, not the hybrids you get in stately homes and what have you. It's always packed, so we come to see them early, before the crowds get there.'

She smiled at him, and his heart actually skipped a beat. Oh, help. He didn't trust himself to say a word; all he could do was hope that she didn't think he was being rude.

'And you definitely don't get this in London, I can tell you,' she said.

When they got there, the car park, to his eyes, looked more like a bog. No wonder she'd said to bring welling-ton boots. But Laurie didn't seem to be bothered by the mud. She simply changed Izzy's shoes for a pair of bright red wellies, then changed her own for bright purple boots covered with large white polka dots.

Marc hid a smile. He'd known Laurie Grant for a week, but he already had a fair idea of what made her tick and he wasn't in the slightest bit surprised that she'd picked something so exuberant. They suited her right down to the ground. His own wellies were much more boring, plain and black. Which he supposed suited him, too: dull and boring.

Laurie clipped the lead onto Cocoa's collar, and the dog jumped out of the car, wagging his tail. Izzy held onto Laurie's free hand, then looked at him with a slight frown. 'This is the first time you've been here, so you might be a bit scared.'

She gave him a bright smile; she was definitely her mother's daughter, he thought.

'You can hold my other hand, if you like,' she suggested. 'That'll make you feel brave.'

Marc's first instinct was to say no. The idea of holding the little girl's hand, looking as if they were out together on a family outing—when he knew damn well he didn't *deserve* a family—made him feel slightly sick.

But then Izzy smiled at him again and something felt as if it had cracked inside him. 'Thank you. I'd love to hold your hand.' To his ears, his voice sounded rusty. He glanced at Laurie for direction—was he doing the right thing?—but she was behaving as if absolutely nothing was out of the ordinary.

Together, hand in hand, they walked through coppiced woodlands. Marc could see the odd patch of primroses, and some white flowers he vaguely recognised but didn't have a clue what their names were, but there were no bluebells.

Then Marc caught his breath as they turned the corner and he could see bluebells absolutely everywhere. He'd never seen anything like it before. Deeper into the wood, in dappled sunlight, there were more patches of deep blue. 'That's stunning,' he said. 'A real bluebell carpet.'

'Isn't it just?' Laurie said softly. 'Though I always think they look more like drifts of bluebells at the side of the path. Like blue snow. Wait until we get there and you can catch the scent.'

Marc had never seen anything so lovely—and it was so different from London. Instead of the noise of traffic, all he could hear was birds singing. He didn't have a clue what birds they were, but their songs sounded beautiful.

And then, as they drew closer, he caught the scent of the bluebells. Delicate and sweet, like a slightly softer version of a hyacinth. The epitome of a late English spring.

'So, are you glad I nagged you into this?' Laurie asked softly.

'Very,' he admitted. 'I wouldn't have missed this for the world.'

'I told you it was special.'

Yes. And so, Marc was beginning to realise, was she.

'Would you mind holding Cocoa while I take some pictures of Izzy for her grandparents?' she asked.

'Sure.' He loosened his hand from the little girl's so he could take the dog's lead from Laurie, and wasn't sure whether he felt more relieved or bereft. This whole thing was stirring up memories and dreams for him, the good mixed up with the bad and the unthinkable, all blurring into one.

'Izzy, darling, come and stand here so I can take your picture for Nanna and Granddad—remember not to squash the bluebells, so other people who come to see them can enjoy them, too,' Laurie said. She took a camera from her handbag and crouched down so she could take pictures of her daughter with the bluebells in the background. 'My parents used to do this with my brother and me every year,' she said, 'and it's lovely to look back on the pictures and see how we change from year to year.'

How his own parents would've loved a picture of their first grandchild among the bluebells, Marc thought. A little girl or a little boy in red wellington boots, just like Izzy was. He had to swallow the sudden lump in his throat. To distract himself, as much as anything else, he suggested, 'Why don't I take some pictures of you both with Cocoa?'

'Would you mind? Oh, that'd be lovely. Thank you, Marc.' Laurie's smile was sweet and piercing, widening the crack round his heart.

Marc had to hide a smile when he heard Izzy tell the dog very solemnly to be careful not to tread on the bluebells—she really was a carbon copy of her mother—but the Labrador was on his best behaviour and sat perfectly still, his mouth open as if he were smiling.

'Mummy, can you take a picture of me with Marc, please?' Izzy piped up.

Help. This wasn't what he'd signed up for. But, even though it made him feel slightly uncomfortable, he didn't have the heart to refuse to have his photograph taken with her.

Izzy insisted on seeing the photograph on the screen on the back of Laurie's camera.

'Perfect,' she said in satisfaction. 'Mummy, can we print it out and put it up in the kitchen with all the other photos? Marc's our new friend, so he should be there with everyone else.'

'Yes, darling, of course we can,' Laurie said with a smile.

*Our new friend.* Izzy had accepted him so easily, just as she'd clearly accepted the little girl who'd just joined her class and had made her into a friend. Marc felt a complete fraud. If either of them knew what he'd done, he was pretty sure they wouldn't want to have anything to do him.

'I'll print out a copy for you, too, Marc,' Laurie added.

'Thank you.' He hoped he didn't sound as grumpy and ungrateful to her as he did to himself. He didn't mean to be. It was just that this whole thing made him feel all mixed up again.

To his relief, once Laurie had finished taking photos, they walked on. Izzy didn't stop chattering to him, but she didn't seem to worry that Marc wasn't quite as communicative as her mother.

As they walked on, the sky was getting darker. And then Marc heard a loud rolling boom. 'Was that a plane?' he asked.

Laurie glanced up at the sky. 'No. It looks like a thunderstorm over there, and it's heading this way.' She grimaced. 'Rats. They mentioned it on the weather forecast this morning, but I hoped it would hold off until this afternoon. If we don't get back to the car before the storm reaches us, I'm afraid we're going to get a little bit wet. Sorry about that.'

'I really don't mind if we get wet,' Marc said, meaning it. 'It'll be worth it for seeing the bluebells.'

There was another rolling boom. This time, Marc timed it. 'That was eight seconds. So does that mean the storm's eight miles away?'

'No, it's one mile for every second between seeing the flash and hearing the thunder,' Laurie explained. 'The thunder always seems to last longer out here; I guess the sound rolls around more, as the land's so flat.'

Then the first drops fell, slow but huge spatters of rain.

'We're going to have to make a run for it,' Laurie said. 'Marc, do you want to run with Cocoa or with Izzy?'

'Me!' Izzy piped up. She took Marc's hand, but with her legs being so much shorter than his she simply couldn't keep up with him as he ran.

Marc had no choice. He couldn't let the little girl get soaked or fall face first onto the boggy ground, could he? So he scooped her up and ran behind Laurie, carrying her in his arms.

Just as he would've done with his own child. If he'd had the chance.

He forced himself not to think about that and concentrated on following Laurie back to the car and not dropping Izzy.

They were all soaked by the time they got back to the car. Laurie unclipped Cocoa's lead and put him in the back while Marc helped Izzy into her seat. But the buckle defeated him. 'Sorry, I don't have a clue how these things work,' he admitted.

'You don't have any nephews or nieces?' Laurie asked.

'No, my sister's five years younger than I am and she's single,' he said, then winced, hoping that Laurie didn't think he was making a comment about her situation.

But she didn't seem in the slightest bit fazed by his words. She had the harness clipped in place within seconds. Izzy was shivering, and Laurie kissed her. 'I'll put the heater on, darling, and we'll go home now so you can change into some dry clothes. We won't be long, I promise. OK?'

'OK, Mummy.' The little girl's teeth were chattering. 'Love you.'

'Love you, too.'

Again, time seemed to shift in Marc's head. Ginny would have been exactly like this with their child—warm, loving, comforting.

If only.

Laurie drove back to her place. 'Do you mind if I get Izzy into dry clothes before I drop you home, Marc?' she asked.

'Don't worry about giving me a lift. I can walk back from here.'

Laurie frowned. 'Your place is a good couple of miles away from here. And it's still raining.'

He shrugged. 'It doesn't matter. I don't mind walking.'

'Look, if you want to stay for lunch, you're very welcome. It's nothing fancy—only soup and a sandwich, because Mum's cooking for us all tonight,' she offered.

It was so very, very tempting. But Marc couldn't let himself do it. He needed to be back at home. In safety. Where he could repair his barriers again. 'No, I'll be fine—but thanks for the offer. And thank you for taking me to see the bluebells.'

'Pleasure. But if you won't let me drop you home, at

least stay until the rain dies down and have a cup of tea,' Laurie urged.

He shook his head. 'I'm already wet, so a bit more rain isn't going to make much difference. See you later. Bye, Izzy.'

'Bye, Marc!' The little girl waved madly at him.

And he was gone.

He'd bolted, Laurie thought as she helped Izzy change into dry clothes. What had scared him most, her or Izzy? He didn't seem entirely comfortable around children; and yet he'd held her little girl's hand, and carried her back to the car when it was raining. So was it her? Did he think she'd been coming on to him? OK, yes, she found him attractive—especially when she saw one of his rare smiles—but she hadn't intended to do anything about it. Had she been giving out the wrong signals?

Marc Bailey was a puzzle. And she didn't have a clue how to start working him out.

Laurie didn't see Marc at the surgery on the Monday or Tuesday, but on Wednesday he left an email for her on the surgery system: *Can we have a project update this evening?*

*Sure. What time?* she typed back, sent the message, and called in her next patient.

When she was writing up her notes after the consultation, her computer beeped to signal a message from someone in the practice. Marc again: *Is 8 OK?*

*8 is fine*, she replied. Izzy would be in bed, asleep, so they'd be able to get everything sorted without interruptions. But she also wondered whether maybe Marc was avoiding the little girl, too, given the way he'd dashed off on Sunday.

'Focus on your work. On your patients. Whatever issues Marc Bailey has, they're none of your business,' she told herself sharply.

All the same, she couldn't help wondering.

Marc was perfectly polite when he turned up at her house at exactly eight o'clock. But he also threw her by giving her a huge bunch of glorious red tulips.

'Oh—how lovely! Thank you.'

'These are to say thank you for Sunday,' Marc said. 'And because I feel guilty that you've been the one doing all the hospitality—you've supplied all the cake and the coffee.'

'Only because it's easier for me if we meet here. And it's been costing you petrol,' she pointed out, hoping that she didn't sound as flustered as she felt.

When was the last time someone had bought her flowers, other than her parents or her brother?

Though he hadn't given them to her in a romantic sense, she reminded herself crossly. This wasn't a date. This was work. He was just being polite.

But it still flustered her. Especially because she loved the glossy showiness of the flowers; they were exactly the sort of thing she'd buy herself as a treat at the end of a hard week.

'Come through into the kitchen and sit down. I'm going to put these gorgeous flowers in water before we start.'

She put the tulips in a vase of water, placed them on the kitchen windowsill, then made them both a coffee and sat down at the kitchen table with him. 'All righty. Jay—my friend at the university—is letting me have twenty monitors. We have a diabetic expert, a nutritionist and a cardiologist who've agreed to do a talk for us, and we've got the village hall for an hour at eight on Wednesday evenings.'

'We have ten yeses so far,' he said, taking out a folder to show her the replies they'd received. 'I'll give it until Friday and then, if we still have fewer than twenty, I'll start ringing round and talking them into filling up the spaces.'

'Great. We can always spread the monitoring, if anyone else wants to join in a bit later,' she said. 'What about our exercise providers?'

They worked through their list, and within forty minutes had worked out a schedule including badminton, ballroom dancing, martial arts and circuit training, as well as toning exercise.

'Obviously the swimming and the aqua aerobics will have to be at the pool,' she said, 'and the walking group is obviously going to be outdoors, but we've got a good mix over the next three or four months.' She smiled at him. 'Thanks for all your help on this. It would've taken me ages to do everything on my own.'

'No problem. And you'll be pleased to know that Neil Peascod wasn't, um, persistent with me.'

'Funny guy.' But she liked the fact that Marc was teasing her. It meant he felt more confident in her company, and maybe that he felt accepted as part of the team at the practice. 'I'm glad you came round this evening.'

Marc went very still. She'd wanted to see him? Why? 'Oh?' he asked carefully.

'Because I was wondering if I was a problem for you.'

Oh, no. Please don't let her be that perceptive. 'How do you mean?' he asked.

'On Sunday,' she said, 'you couldn't wait to leave. I

wasn't sure if the problem was me or Izzy but I figured that, as you held her hand in the woods and you carried her back to the car, it was probably me.'

He blew out a breath. 'No, it's not you. It's me.'

'I'm guessing,' she said softly, 'that you came to Norfolk to get away from London—and you left someone special behind.'

Yes, he had. But not quite in the way she was obviously thinking.

'Divorce is always hard, even if it's amicable—and most of the time it's not that,' she said. 'But it does get better. Or, at least, easier to comes to terms with, in time.'

'You think I'm divorced?'

She shrugged. 'You have a white line on the ring finger of your left hand.'

Yes, because he'd taken off his wedding ring the day before he'd moved out of London, in an attempt to try to move on.

'I used to have one of those myself,' she said.

'I'm not divorced.' There was a lump in his throat, but he needed to get the words out. To stop Laurie making any more assumptions. He owed her at least some of the truth. 'My wife died.'

She reached over the table to squeeze his hand. 'I'm sorry, Marc. That's rough on you, to lose your wife so young.'

She didn't know the half of it. All of a sudden, it was too much for him and he couldn't handle it. 'It was all my fault,' he said tonelessly. And then, because there was nothing else he could say, and he couldn't bear to sit there being polite over coffee when all he wanted to do was curl into a ball and howl at the memories filling his head, he pushed his chair back and walked out.

* * *

Laurie stared after him, too stunned to call him back.

How could his wife's death possibly be Marc's fault? No way could she believe that. Marc Bailey was a good GP; she'd heard on the grapevine that their patients were more than happy with him. And he'd been good with Izzy, letting her chatter on to him and not cutting her off impatiently.

No way could a man like that be to blame for anyone's death.

Poor guy. She'd made assumptions, jumped in with both feet and pushed him way too far.

They needed to talk. Sooner, rather than later. But she couldn't leave Izzy alone in the house, and this wasn't the sort of conversation you could have on the phone or by text. So she'd have to leave it until tomorrow.

But there was one thing she knew always made people feel better. Something that helped them to talk. 'We have work to do,' she told Cocoa, and got out the ingredients to make one of her lemon cakes.

# CHAPTER FIVE

LAURIE walked into her consulting room the next morning with a tin of cake, intending to tackle Marc and sort things out between them before he saw his first patient. But she stopped when she saw a square box on her desk, neatly wrapped and tied with a ribbon; an envelope was sticking out from the parcel.

Who would leave something like this on her desk? It wasn't her birthday and it couldn't be a present from a grateful patient; Phyllis would've explained to anyone who'd brought in a gift that medics weren't allowed to accept anything from patients, but a communal jar of coffee for the practice kitchen or a donation to their charity of the month instead would be very much appreciated.

Surprised, Laurie opened the envelope, read the note swiftly, and realised that Marc had beaten her to it.

*Sorry. I shouldn't have said what I did last night. Can we talk, please? M*

He had bold, confident handwriting—and yet Laurie was pretty sure that, deep inside, Marc was neither. He was torturing himself, and although he'd left London behind he clearly hadn't been able to leave his demons there.

Laurie hadn't slept well last night, unable to stop thinking about what he'd told her. Any attempt to guess at what he'd actually meant would've been wild speculation, because she didn't have a clue, but one thing she was convinced about was that he was punishing himself unnecessarily.

She untied the ribbon and removed the wrapping paper. The box contained a gorgeous selection of chocolates—expensive ones, she recognised. To get them on her desk this morning before her shift, Marc would've had to make a special trip to the supermarket five miles down the road to buy them.

He'd made a real effort.

Now it was time for her to do the same. She picked up the phone and dialled his extension.

He answered on the second ring. 'Marc Bailey.'

'Marc, it's Laurie.' She paused. 'You really didn't have to buy me chocolates, you know.'

'I did, actually, because I felt bad. It's an apology. I shouldn't have said what I did and walked out on you. It really wasn't fair to dump that on you. And I'm sorry.'

'It was my own fault, for pushing you too hard. And I'm sorry for that. So let's call it quits.' She paused. 'I feel horribly guilty about taking these posh chocolates.'

'They're for *you*, Laurie. Not for the surgery,' he said quietly.

She knew what he meant. If she put them on the table in the staff kitchen, everyone in the practice would start speculating about who had bought Laurie a gift like that. In a small town, secrets didn't stay secret for very long; they'd soon find out that he was the one who'd bought them. And the last thing Marc needed was people talking about him. Given that he was a widower at such a young age, he'd probably had more than enough pity and sympathy at his last practice. That was probably why he'd moved here, she realised: to make a new start. Where there weren't any memories and wouldn't be any unwanted pity.

'You really didn't have to buy them, but thank you,' she said softly.

'Can we start again?' he asked carefully.

'Of course we can. Actually, I made you a cake as a peace offering.'

He gave a wry chuckle. 'You fix everything by cake, don't you?'

'Don't knock it. Cake goes a long way towards fixing an awful lot of things.' She paused, and decided to take a risk. 'Do you want to grab a sandwich from the patisserie at lunchtime with me and eat it by the duck pond?'

'That'd be good.'

'I only get twenty minutes for lunch,' she warned. 'Because I'm part time, I have paperwork to do and then I'm on phone triage before I take Cocoa out and pick Izzy up from school.'

'I'll make sure I'm on time,' he promised.

'Good. I'll leave the cake in the staffroom, then. Sam will think I made it for him, and we won't disillusion him.'

'Agreed. And thank you,' he said softly.

It was a busy morning at the practice, but both Marc and Laurie finished their surgeries on time.

She smiled at him. 'Right. Time to introduce you to my favourite bad habit—as in the best bread I've ever tasted.' She took him to the patisserie in the middle of the high street.

'Let me see. It's Thursday. So would that be a sweet chilli chicken salad wrap and a bottle of sparkling water to go, Dr Grant?' the woman behind the counter asked Laurie with a grin.

'I might just have the special today, Tina,' Laurie said.

Tina just snorted. 'Yeah, right, Laurie. Any day with a Y in it, you order a sweet chilli chicken salad wrap.'

'Tut. And just when I was going to introduce a new customer to you,' Laurie teased. 'You'll put him off.'

Tina just laughed. 'He'll be just like everyone else—one taste of my mum's bread, and you're hooked.' She smiled at Marc. 'Hi. I'm Tina. Nice to meet you.'

His answering smile was slightly wary. 'Marc Bailey.'

'My new colleague,' Laurie added. 'So be nice, Tina.'

'I'm *always* nice. What can I get you, Marc?'

He looked slightly lost. 'Um—what do you recommend?'

'Are you a vegetarian?'

'No, I eat most things.'

'Crab salad, then,' Tina said. 'The fish man was here this morning, and they were freshly caught at Cromer. And a strawberry tartlet—Karl brought in the first batch from the new season's crop this morning, so I couldn't resist making them, and my pastry is much better than *hers*.' She indicated Laurie.

'But *my* lemon cake trumps *hers*. By miles,' Laurie retorted.

'In your dreams, sweetie.' Tina sorted out their order. 'Laurie, Georgia's been plotting play dates with Izzy. Is it OK with you if she comes over for tea and a play at our place after school on Monday?'

'She did say something about that to me the other day, so I'm sure she'd love to,' Laurie said. 'And she's been talking about Molly, the new girl.'

'So has Georgia.' Tina smiled. 'I'll catch Molly's mum in the playground today and see if Molly can come, too.

But either way I'll pick Izzy up from school for you on Monday.'

'Thanks. And how about I pick Georgia up the Monday after, for tea and a play at ours?' Laurie said. 'And if you see Molly's mum before I do, invite her to mine that day as well.'

'Will do.' Tina finished wrapping their sandwiches for them and took the money. 'Catch you at school this afternoon.'

'So they know you pretty well at the patisserie, then?' Marc asked when he and Laurie were settled on the bench by the duck pond.

'I grew up here, so I went to school with some of the staff,' she said. 'We lost touch a bit when I went to university, but I've got to know some of them better in the playground while we're waiting to pick up the kids from school. You've probably already worked out that Tina's daughter Georgia is Izzy's best friend—and, although Tina teases me like mad, we get on really well, too.' She smiled. 'I've been really lucky in that everyone's accepted me back here for who I am. Nobody's given me a hard time for making a mess of things in London.'

Laurie was a bit chaotic, Marc knew, but that wasn't the same as making a mess of things. 'I can't imagine you making a mess of things.'

'Don't you believe it.' She gave him a wry look. 'There's my relationship, for starters. I'm usually a pretty good judge of character, but Dean sneaked under my radar. Looking back, I should never have gone out with him, let alone got engaged to him and bought a house with him.'

'It's easy to be wise in hindsight.' Marc surprised himself by asking, 'Was the break-up a long time ago?'

'It probably started the day I did a positive pregnancy test,' she said. 'But, for all I know, there could've been other affairs before then.'

He blinked. 'Your fiancé had an affair?'

'He was with a patient when I was in labour with Izzy.' She paused. 'That's not as in treating an emergency, by the way, because he's a dermatologist. That's *with* with.'

He blew out a breath. Was the man crazy? Why on earth would he cheat on a woman like Laurie? 'I don't know what to say.'

Her smile held no mirth whatsoever. 'Most people have plenty to say. Starting with Dean being a cheating scumbag and me being an idiot for not spotting how unreliable he was. But he wasn't really a scumbag.'

'No?' Marc couldn't help the question.

'No. He just didn't do responsibility. It was different at work—he's really good at his job and he'd never, ever let a patient or a colleague down—but he couldn't cope with responsibility at home. He left everything to me to deal with.' She shrugged. 'I should've worked that out for myself and not expected more from him than he was able to give.'

'That's very forgiving of you.'

'I wasn't very forgiving at the time. I left him, because no way was I going to let him cheat on me again.' She bit her lip. 'And the one thing I still can't forgive him for is the fact that he hasn't seen Izzy since the day I left him. When she was a week old and I found out about his affair. He's never shown the slightest bit of interest in her, and in the few days when we both lived with him, he never once changed her nappy or offered to give her a bath, and he certainly didn't make a move towards her if she cried. It was as if she didn't even exist.' She sighed. 'OK, Izzy wasn't actually planned, but it takes two to make a baby. She's his *daughter*. And I really don't understand how he could ignore her.'

'I take it he wasn't happy about you being pregnant, then?'

'You could say that. When we found out that I was pregnant, he suggested that I could have a termination.' Her voice was dry.

Marc felt anger surge through him. Whatever was wrong with the man? The day he and Ginny had found out that she was pregnant had been one of the happiest of his life. With the injury to his shoulder, he hadn't been able to pick his wife up and whirl her round in joy, but he'd bought his wife the biggest bouquet of flowers that the florist could arrange for him. And he'd made sure Ginny had felt loved and supported all the way. He'd been overjoyed at the idea of making a family together.

And then he'd wrecked it all with his selfishness.

Which, he supposed, really made him no better than Laurie's ex.

Laurie didn't seem to read anything into his silence, and he guessed that most people reacted the same way. Anger, disbelief, and not having a clue what to say.

'Dean just doesn't want to be a father,' she said. 'Which is ironic, really, as Izzy has at least two half-siblings—to my knowledge, anyway.'

'Two?' Marc didn't follow. If the man had wanted Laurie to have a termination, how come he'd gone on to have two more children?

'Neither of them were planned. One of them was the patient he was, um, *with* when I was in labour. When that came out, he had to pass her case to a colleague. And then he did the same to her as he had to me. The second he found out she was pregnant, he lost interest in her and started seeing someone else.' Laurie shook her head. 'It's weird, really, because his parents are ever so nice and they're still involved in Izzy's life. He really can't blame the way he is on having a dysfunctional upbringing.' She shrugged. 'Or maybe his parents gave him a bit too much. He was an only child, they had him quite late in life, and maybe they wrapped him more in cotton wool than the average parent would've done.'

'You mean, they spoiled him.'

'Sort of, but when they found out why I'd left him they didn't try to pin the blame on me or make any feeble excuses for his behaviour. They were really angry with him and threatened to disown him. I had to persuade them out of it.'

'That's very forgiving of you,' he said again. 'I'm not sure I could've done that, in your shoes.' Forgiveness was a tricky thing. He couldn't forgive himself. Ginny's parents couldn't forgive him either. And he knew that they were right. He should've taken better care of his wife and their unborn child.

'Dean's their only child. Expecting them to cut him out of their life because he'd made a bad decision—well, that wouldn't be fair on them. What he really needs is a good shake and to learn to face up to responsibility. And to learn how to make a proper commitment to someone.'

'Would you take him back if he did?'

She shook her head. 'I don't love him any more. We did have some good times, and I'll always be grateful that he gave me Izzy, but it wouldn't work out between us now. And I'm really glad I didn't marry him. It was a bit of a mess to sort out the house, but it would've dragged on much longer if we'd had to go through a divorce as well.'

She sighed. 'I feel so sorry for his parents, because Izzy's the only one of their grandchildren that they actually see. They live the other side of the country, so they don't see Iz as often as they'd like to, but I email photographs to them every week—like the ones I took at the bluebell woods—and she draws them pictures so they don't feel completely left out.'

'I'm impressed that you're so—well, balanced about it.'

'It wasn't their fault that I broke off my engagement to their son, and you're not meant to be impressed.' She ate a bite of her sandwich. 'Life's very short, and what's the point of making things harder than they need to be, or hurting people? I don't want Izzy growing up seeing only the dark side of things and the negatives. Sure, not everything in life is going to work out absolutely perfectly, but you can always make the best of what you have.'

Pollyanna. And, given what she'd just told him, he could understand her needing that kind of defence mechanism. To see the best in things and block out the bad stuff, at least in front of her daughter.

'You're a fixer, aren't you?' he asked. He knew she was doing exactly that with him. Taking him under her wing, because he was a newcomer to the area and didn't know anyone. Just the same as when she and Tina had been planning a play date for their children and they'd included the new little girl Izzy had talked about.

'It's why I'm a doctor.' She looked at him. 'And why you are, too, I'd guess.'

He sighed. 'Yeah. Though I couldn't fix the one important thing.' And he definitely couldn't tell her the whole of it, especially after what she'd just told him. He had a nasty feeling that she'd think as badly of him as she thought of her ex.

'For what it's worth,' she said softly, 'I don't believe a word of what you said last night. You're a good man. You've gone above and beyond the call of duty with my pet project, you've been patient with Izzy even though close contact with children obviously isn't comfortable for you, and our patients think you're the best thing since sliced bread. And that really doesn't fit with what you're accusing yourself of.'

He shifted awkwardly on the wooden bench. 'I guess I owe it to you to tell you the truth.'

'You don't owe me anything, Marc,' she corrected. 'But if you want to talk to me, I'll listen and it won't go any further than me.'

'Thank you.'

Though he couldn't get the words to come out. He couldn't frame them in the right way. He knew she was going to think badly of him when she knew the truth. OK, so it was his just deserts; but he *liked* Laurie and he didn't want her to despise him.

Then again, the truth would come out eventually. It was better that she heard it from him, and better that she knew sooner rather than later.

'That rugby accident I told you about—I didn't cope very well with it,' he began.

'Not many people would. A rotator cuff tear is pretty painful.'

'Yes, but what I hated was not being able to move easily, not being able to do everything I'd always taken for granted, and having to rely on other people to do things for me. I couldn't play the game I'd loved since I was a kid, and watching it…' He grimaced. 'That was a really poor second best. When you watch a match, it's nowhere near the same as the buzz you get from playing in it. And I hated the fact I'd let the team down.'

'It wasn't your fault that you got injured—and, to be honest, you know it's a "when" rather than an "if" that you're going to get injured when you play contact sports,' she reminded him.

'I still felt I'd let the team down. And it was even worse when I realised how much damage I'd done to my shoulder—it wasn't just that I'd be out for the rest of the season. I was never going to play again.'

'Couldn't you have switched to, I dunno, coaching or something?' she asked.

'Not properly—talking someone through a move isn't always enough, and showing someone how to do something would've risked more damage to my shoulder.' He sighed. 'Work was bad, too. With my arm out of action, I couldn't even examine patients properly. The only thing I could do until I was healed was phone triage.' He grimaced. 'I could manage a phone, as long as it was on loudspeaker, and I could type up my notes one-handed, but I didn't feel I was doing a proper doctor's job.'

'Phone triage isn't so bad,' she said. 'You get to reassure people, and that's worth something.'

Still seeing the positive, Marc thought. He hadn't been able to see that kind of positive in his job; at the time, he'd only been able to focus on what he hadn't been able to do. 'When it's for a morning a week, as part of a rota, triage is OK—but when it's the only thing you can do, it's unbearable.'

'Was it the shoulder of your writing hand that you damaged?' she asked.

'No, my left. Which is my gear-changing hand, and my car's manual rather than automatic, so I couldn't drive either.' He grimaced. 'I was disgustingly sorry for myself and I behaved really badly. I started drinking a bit too much in an effort to cope with it—and when that didn't work, I drank more to blot out how I felt.'

She said nothing and there was no censure in her gorgeous blue eyes, but Marc still found himself squirming.

'I can understand why people drink too much, now I've done it myself,' he said. 'I didn't actually become an alcoholic but, looking back, I can see I could've gone down that road so very easily.'

Had it not been for the accident. That had stopped him in his tracks. He hadn't touched a drop of alcohol since.

His mouth went dry again. 'My wife... We lived in London, so Ginny hadn't bothered learning to drive. There was no real need, with public transport being so good. But we'd thought about moving out of London, so that would've meant not having such good public transport and needing to drive, so she decided to have lessons. She passed her driving test a couple of weeks before my accident. I'm not one of these men who can't stand to be driven by a woman, and I was glad that she had a chance to get more experience driving because I was out of action, but...' He shook his head. 'I leaned on her too much.'

'If you couldn't drive, what else was she supposed to do? Let you struggle? Make you change the car for an automatic?'

Fair point, he thought. But Laurie still didn't get it. So he had to be honest with her. Tell her the worst. 'We went to a party. My arm was better by then, so I was supposed to be driving us home. But, as I said, I'd got into the habit of drinking. I had two or three glasses of wine without even thinking about it. Then I realised I was over the limit, so Ginny was going to have to drive us home.'

'She hadn't been drinking, too?' Laurie asked.

'No.' Because of the baby. But he couldn't quite bring himself to tell Laurie that. 'On the way back, we collided with another car. It wasn't Ginny's fault—it was the other driver's. He was concentrating on his mobile phone instead of where he was going, and his car was on the wrong side of the road.' Marc closed his eyes. 'She didn't even have time to beep her horn at him to warn him we were there. She drove round the corner and he was just there, heading straight for us.' His breath hitched. 'And I got out of that car without a single scratch. No bruising, no blood, no whiplash, nothing. But Ginny... Her side of the car took the brunt of the impact. She was killed instantly.'

*Along with their baby.* His whole life had shattered like the windscreen of their car.

Laurie took his hand. 'I'm so sorry. But, Marc, you weren't to blame. The other driver was on the wrong side of the road.'

'But if I hadn't been so selfish, so self-indulgent, and drunk too much, I would've been driving, like I was supposed to. Maybe we would've gone home by a different route. Maybe we would've gone home at a different time. Maybe I could've avoided the accident.'

'That's a lot of maybes,' Laurie said. 'And has it occurred to you that maybe if you had been driving, you would've been the one killed in the crash and Ginny would've been left to cope on her own?'

Yes. But it hadn't made him feel any better. 'It was my fault,' he repeated.

'Tell me,' she said softly, 'if a patient told you what you've just told me, would you be blaming him for his wife's death?'

'I…' He shook his head. This was too close to the bone. 'I can't answer that. I don't know.'

'I don't think you would. I think you'd be telling your patient that it was an accident—that it was something outside his control and it wasn't fair to beat himself up over it.'

'Maybe. But I can't forgive myself, Laurie. And neither can her parents. I let her down. And I hate myself for what I did.'

'When did it happen?' she asked softly.

'Two years ago.'

'That's a long, long time to hate yourself.'

He sighed. 'I know. I did try counselling, but…' He shrugged. 'Maybe I just wasn't a good fit with that particular guy and someone else could've made me see things differently. But he told me that I was the only one who could forgive myself, and I'd have to come to terms with it in my own time.'

'He sounds like our awful ex-locum,' she said. 'Yes, you *are* the only one who can forgive yourself; but counsellors are supposed to help you find the tools to do that. He clearly didn't.' She squeezed his hand. 'I'm not going to patronise you or tell you what to do. But what I can tell you is that our patients like you and you really fit in at the practice. Sam would never have offered you the job if he thought you wouldn't take proper care with the patients. And all that means you're a better man than you think you are.'

'Maybe.'

'Definitely.' She glanced at his sandwich. 'If you've finished with that, I know some ducks that'd be very interested in the crusts.'

Feeding the ducks. Something he'd been looking forward to doing with his child. How could he do this now?

But Laurie had saved bits of her wrap for the ducks, and it seemed churlish not to join her. Especially as she hadn't judged him anywhere near as harshly as he deserved.

And Marc discovered that, actually, feeding the ducks on a sunny lunchtime was fun, watching them splashing and diving for the scraps of bread.

'I do this with Iz on Saturday mornings,' she said. 'We buy a couple of rolls from the patisserie, especially to feed the ducks. Though don't tell Tina or I'll be toast.' She paused. 'You're welcome to join us this weekend, if you like.'

'Thanks, but…' He couldn't think of an excuse, and just gave her an awkward smile.

'I knew you'd say that.' She spread her hands. 'Well, it's an open invitation. If you change your mind, that's fine. Just call me on Saturday morning and I'll tell you what time we're going to be here. Oh, and you'd better eat that strawberry tart, because Tina's going to ask you what you thought of it next time she sees you.'

'She is?'

'And not necessarily in the patisserie. You'll probably bump into her in town at some point, and she'll ask you then.'

He looked at her. 'People actually do that?'

'Welcome to life in a small town, Dr Bailey,' she said with a grin. 'I assume you've only ever lived in a city?'

'London,' he confirmed. 'I grew up there, I trained there, and I worked there.'

'London. Where nobody really gets the chance to know anyone. It's very different here.'

Marc wasn't sure if it was a promise or a warning. He'd

spent the last two years keeping himself separate—keeping himself sane. And it seemed that it was going to be much harder to do that here. That he was going to be part of the community, whether he liked it or not. In London, he'd never so much as seen his patients outside work. Here, he was living among them.

She smiled at him. 'I'd better get back to my paperwork. It's up to you if you want to stay and talk to the ducks for a bit or if you want to come back to the practice with me.'

Again, there was no censure in her face, no judgement. Just her down-to-earth smile and good humour. He glanced at his watch. 'I'll stay with the ducks.' Try to get his head back together. 'But thank you, Laurie. For listening.'

'No worries. And it's not going any further than me,' she reassured him. 'See you later.'

# CHAPTER SIX

LAURIE wasn't too surprised that Marc didn't ring her on Saturday or join her with Izzy in feeding the ducks. Now he'd told her about the accident, he was probably worrying that she'd judge him and find him wanting as a human being. Apart from the fact it wasn't true, she thought that Marc had already done more than enough judging of himself. Unfairly so.

She didn't really get to see him until their first session with their patients on the following Wednesday evening. She wasn't sure whether Marc was actively avoiding her or just busy. In the end, she'd had to resort to using the surgery email to ask him if he wanted to do the talk to the patients at the surgery on Wednesday evening.

*It's your project, so I'm happy for you to do it, if you want to. I'll give you whatever support you need. M*

It was nice that he wasn't trying to take charge, the way Dean probably would've done if she'd worked on a project with him. Even so, Laurie had the distinct feeling that Marc was avoiding her—and she had a pretty good idea why, too. Because she knew the truth about him.

How could she make him see that it hadn't changed anything? The past was the past. It had been a tragic accident. And he was being totally unfair to himself.

\* \* \*

Laurie was already in the surgery waiting room at half
past seven when Marc arrived.

'Hi, there.' She looked up from one of the chairs she
was rearranging.

'Leave that. Let me do the heavy stuff,' he said.

She raised an eyebrow. 'You mean a mere woman can't
move a chair?'

'A woman's perfectly capable of moving a chair,' he
said, 'but it makes sense for the person with the bigger
muscles to lift the heavier stuff, whether that person's
male or female.'

She grinned. 'OK. I'm pleased to say that you've just
passed the sexism test, Dr Bailey.'

'Good. What do you want done and where?'

'Chairs there, and a couple of tables—one at the front
for the speakers, and one for refreshments, please.' She
looked at him. 'I'll be in the kitchen.'

'Where you'll make much better tea than I do. Ginny
always says that mine's too strong.' And then he caught
himself. Using the present tense again. Would he ever
get used to it?

But Laurie didn't make a comment. She just smiled at
him. 'I didn't make any cake for tonight. I thought it might
be a bit tactless, given that we're talking about weight loss
and sensible choices.'

'Fair point,' he said, and made himself smile back.
'Where's Izzy?'

'In bed. It'd be way too late for her to stay up if she
came with me, especially as she's got school tomorrow.'

Of course. Why hadn't he thought of that? Probably because he wasn't used to children. And he'd avoided them
in the last couple of years.

'Not to mention being incredibly boring for her, even
if I'd brought pens and paper. Mum's babysitting for me,'

she said. 'She's going to babysit for me on Wednesday nights during the project, so I can come along to the sessions. And I'm going to treat her to a spa day at the weekend to say thank you.'

Clearly Laurie was close to her mother, just as Ginny had been close to her parents. Marc was guiltily aware that he'd put a huge distance between himself and his own parents since the accident. Moving out of London had been just another step in that direction. Maybe he'd call them tonight when he got home. Just to say hello and let them know that he'd settled OK.

By the time he and Laurie had finished sorting things out, their speakers had arrived.

Laurie greeted Mike the cardiologist, Sally the diabetes expert and Lisa the dietician with a formal handshake and a warm smile, before introducing Marc to them; but Marc noticed that Jay, the guy in charge of the exercise project at the university, received a warm hug.

Marc was shocked and surprised to feel jealousy prickling down his spine. This was ridiculous. He didn't have the right to be jealous. He wasn't in any kind of relationship with Laurie. She'd simply taken him under her wing because she was a fixer, and he'd be stupid to think it could be anything more than that. She'd made it very clear that she wasn't in the market for a relationship. Maybe, Marc thought, that was because she was already in a relationship. With Jay. 'Friend' had probably been an understatement.

He switched into professional mode; as the patients arrived, he helped serve coffee and tea. Laurie gave a brief talk, introducing the experts, and then let them do the rest of the talking.

Jay talked about his research and how to use the monitor—using Laurie as his model to show exactly how to wear it, Marc noted wryly. 'You'll be wearing it for a week. I'll use the numbers to show the range of results in my research, so nobody will be able to identify any of you personally from my report. But I'll also be able to give you all a personal profile so you can see for yourselves exactly how much activity you do and when,' Jay explained. 'That'll help you see where you have an opportunity to add in some exercise, or maybe change the way you do some things.'

The cardiologist, the diabetes expert and the dietician did their talks, and Marc could see from the expressions on everyone's faces that they were all much more motivated to look at their lifestyles and see where they could make changes. Laurie's pet project was getting off to a great start. And when she handed out the schedule for the exercise taster sessions, there was a real buzz in the room as everyone discussed the options and the things they'd never even thought about trying before.

He slipped out quietly into the kitchen and sorted out the washing-up, while Laurie saw the patients out and said goodbye to the experts.

She came in when he was putting everything away.

'Oh, Marc, I'm sorry. I didn't mean to leave it all to you. You should've waited for me so I could do my fair share.'

'It's not a problem. Did your friend get off OK?' He hoped he sounded more casual than he felt.

'Jay, you mean?' She smiled. 'Yes. It's a shame they couldn't get a babysitter, or Fiona would've come too. His wife's my best friend from university. She met Jay after we graduated, and by lucky chance she ended up moving here with him, which means I get to see her a lot more often than we did just after we qualified. He's a nice guy, a real sweetheart—it's not just surface charm.'

The way it had been with her ex? Marc thought, reading between the lines.

'I think our patients liked him, too. And they were all chatting about the project as they went out, sounding really keen and enthusiastic.' She beamed at him. 'You know, I think this really might make a difference, Marc. The ones who've been struggling with their weight, the ones who are heading towards a higher risk of a heart attack or stroke and developing insulin resistance or even diabetes—we're giving them a real chance to do something about it and change their lives for the better.'

'Yes.' And now Marc felt a total fool, not just for that unexpected surge of jealousy but because it had been totally unnecessary in the first place.

'Thanks so much for your help on this. I would say let's go to the pub and I'll buy you a drink, but I guess you might not want to do that.' She squirmed. 'Sorry, that was really tactless. I didn't mean to put my foot in it.'

'You didn't. It's OK,' he reassured her. 'You guessed right: I don't drink now. Though you don't necessarily have to have alcohol in a pub.'

She brightened. 'So you'll let me buy you an orange juice or whatever in the King's Arms?'

He really ought to make an excuse. But his mouth had other ideas. 'Or you could have a coffee at my place, seeing as you've provided all the hospitality so far.'

'You're actually inviting me into the bat cave?' She slapped a hand over her mouth. 'Sorry, sorry, sorry. I can't even use a sugar rush as an excuse for letting my mouth run away with me, because there was no cake to-night. I apologise.'

The bat cave. Marc felt something bubbling inside him he hadn't felt for heaven only knew how long—laughter—and it felt good to let it out. It sounded rusty, but he was actually laughing.

Oh, wow.

Marc had only ever given Laurie the most guarded smiles before, even when they'd gone to see the bluebells. And now, seeing him laugh was a revelation. It made him look younger, much more approachable—maybe more like the man he'd been before his life had imploded in tragedy.

He was utterly, utterly gorgeous, and his mouth was beautiful. Laurie went hot as she caught her thoughts and realised she was actually wondering what that mouth would feel like on her skin. Oh, help. This was the last thing he needed. And she ought to make some excuse to put some distance between them.

Yet he'd invited her back for coffee. She guessed it was the first overture he'd made in a long, long time. Maybe even since the accident. So how could she possibly knock him back now?

'The bat cave.' He was still smiling.

'I've only seen your house from the outside,' she reminded him. 'It could be a bat cave inside.'

'I'll have you know, my house is spotless. No cobwebs, no spiders, no damp, and definitely no bats.' His eyes crinkled at the corners. 'And my coffee's excellent.'

'Sounds good to me.' She gave him a bright smile. And please let her common sense come back. Some time between right now and when they arrived at his place would be perfect.

Between them, they set the alarm on the surgery and locked up. She climbed into her car and followed Marc back to his place.

It was a beautiful old detached flint cottage, the kind of place she would've loved but couldn't afford—which was why she'd bought a modern townhouse on the new estate at the other side of the town.

'It's a lovely house,' she said as he opened the front door and ushered her inside.

'It's rented for six months,' he said. 'But I'll see how it goes. I might get a chance to buy it later.'

Meaning once he'd settled in.

And if he decided to stay. Laurie knew that his contract was initially for six months, and then he and Sam would agree on whether he'd stay with the practice or not.

She wasn't surprised that the décor inside was neutral. It was also very, very neat and tidy; again, that was understandable as it wasn't his own place. And yet there was nothing personal about it, nothing to give her a clue about who Marc was outside work.

She followed him into the kitchen. It was so different from her own kitchen: no important letters from school pinned to a cork board, and no photographs or children's drawings held to the fridge with magnets. It looked like a show home, a place that would be photographed in one of the glossy home and lifestyle magazines she'd used to read in the days before Izzy and Cocoa—the days when a pale carpet and white furniture wouldn't have been totally impractical.

And there was one other big difference. The worktops

were totally clear, apart from a gleaming and very expensive-looking coffee machine. So it hadn't been an idle boast when he'd said his coffee was excellent. Oh, help. And she'd given him ordinary instant coffee from a jar. Which was about the worst thing you could do to someone who was fussy about coffee.

'Proper coffee or decaf?' he asked.

'At this time of night, decaf, please—otherwise I'll be awake all night and yawning all over my patients tomorrow.'

'Sure.' He made them both a mug of coffee as expertly as any trained barista in a posh coffee shop. He even heated the milk and made a little pattern on top of the coffee, she noticed. A million miles away from her usual routine of pouring boiling water onto granules and sloshing in a bit of milk.

'Thank you.' She took a sip. 'This is really lovely. I think I should apologise now for giving you bog-standard instant coffee at my place.'

He smiled. 'It's OK. I'm not a coffee snob.'

'With a machine like that?' she scoffed. No way did she believe him.

'Busted, hmm?' His smile was tinged with sadness. 'Yes, well. I've learned that there are more important things in life than decent coffee.'

'Mmm.' She didn't have a clue what to say. And giving him a hug didn't seem appropriate.

'Let's go and sit down.'

The living room was just as neat as the kitchen. And just as clear. No pictures, no photographs, no books or music or films. Though, she supposed, he might keep everything as a digital copy. Less cluttered. Marc Bailey definitely wouldn't put up with the kind of chaos she lived in.

He gestured to her to sit down on the sofa, and took a seat next to her.

'So, have you settled in OK?' she asked brightly.

'More or less.' He glanced round the room and sighed. 'Well, I haven't finished unpacking.'

She could guess why, but she knew he needed space. So she waited.

'To be honest, I really can't face it,' he said. 'There are boxes in the dining room that I haven't even touched since the day the removal people packed them. I only really did the boxes for the kitchen and the bathroom. My sister Yvonne offered to come down from Glasgow to give me a hand, but I told her I was fine.'

'And you regret it now?'

'I was too proud,' he admitted. 'And I don't want to ask her now, because then she'll think…'

That there was a problem. He didn't have to say it. Particularly as there *was* a problem. Boxes filled with stuff that held too many memories for him.

'Sometimes,' she said gently, 'it's easier if someone who doesn't have any emotional involvement with the situation helps you. I don't mean to be pushy, and I won't be offended if you say no—but if you want a hand unpacking, I'd be happy to help you.'

'Dr Fixit?' he asked wryly.

'Absolutely. Plus, what goes around comes around.' She shrugged. 'My family and my friends all pitched in when I moved. Part of me wanted to be super-independent and tell everyone I could do it all on my own, but I had Izzy to think about. Also, physically, I wasn't really up to the

job. I had a bit of a rough labour and I ended up with a
C-section. I couldn't drive anywhere for a month after-
wards or lift anything heavier than the baby. For her sake,
I had to admit to my limits and accept help.'

She'd had a baby to think about. Unlike him. He just had
the yawning gap of might-have-beens.

'Mum and Dad said straight away that I could stay
with them while I was sorting myself out. And I really
appreciated it. After Dean agreed to buy out my share of
the house in London, when I bought my place, everyone
pitched in again to help me move in and build the flat-
pack furniture and what have you. But I grew up here, so
I know everyone. You don't, yet.' She paused. 'But if you
let them close, people will be there for you.'

That was the problem. The idea of letting people close
again—and then maybe letting them down...

No. 'I don't des—' he began.

She put her mug of coffee down, reached across and
pressed her finger against his lips to stop the word coming out. Every nerve-end tingled where she touched him.

'Yes, you do,' she said softly. 'Everyone deserves a
second chance.'

If only he could believe that.

Right now, he felt more lost and confused than he ever
had in his life. And he was horribly aware of the sweet
vanilla scent she wore. The softness of her skin against
his. The warmth in those stunning blue eyes. And, oh,
God, he wanted her. He really, really needed to feel her
close to him.

Unable to help himself, he caught the tip of her finger
between his lips.

Her eyes widened, and a hectic flush spread across her cheeks.

He ought to stop this. Right now.

And yet he found himself curling his fingers round her hand, moving it so her palm was against his lips, and pressing a kiss against her soft, soft skin. He folded her fingers over the place where he'd kissed her, still keeping his gaze locked with hers. And when her lips parted slightly, it was too much to resist. He leaned forward and brushed his mouth lightly against hers.

His lips tingled even more, and he couldn't help doing it again. And again. Until her arms slid round his neck and she started kissing him back.

It was only the sound of a car horn that shocked him back into common sense. And Marc was horrified when he realised that he was lying flat on the sofa, Laurie was sprawled over him, and he'd untucked her shirt and was stroking the bare skin on her back.

He closed his eyes. 'Laurie. I'm so sorry. I…' Oh, help. He didn't have a clue what to say.

'Me, too.' She wriggled off him, and restored order to her clothes.

'I shouldn't have done that.' His head and his common sense were firmly back in control, though his body was urging him not to listen to them and just yank her back into his arms.

'It was both of us,' she said.

Which was more generous than he deserved.

He dragged a hand through his hair. 'I hope this isn't going to make things awkward between us at work.'

Colour stained her cheeks. 'Because I jumped you, you mean?'

'That's not fair. I started the kissing business.'

'I touched you first,' she pointed out.

'OK. I guess we're both feeling guilty and embarrassed about this.'

She nodded.

'And we're both going to behave sensibly in future,' he said.

'Absolutely.' But then she reached forward to pick up her mug at the same time as he did, and their fingers touched. The tingle spread right through his body; and he could see it was the same for her, because her pupils went absolutely huge.

'Or,' she said softly, 'we could…admit something.'

All the air went out of his lungs.

Was she saying that she was attracted to him?

Well, Laurie Grant might be a fixer, and he'd noticed that she hugged people and was warm with everyone, but he didn't think she went around kissing people like this.

'You and me?' he asked, the words a hoarse whisper.

She lifted her chin. 'Just so you know, I don't make a habit of this sort of thing.'

He cupped her cheek with his palm. 'You didn't have to tell me. I know that's not you. Me neither.' She was the first since Ginny. The first woman he'd kissed like this, other than his wife, in more than ten years. Which made him feel incredibly guilty. This was wrong, wrong, wrong.

She turned her face to press a kiss into his palm, then gently removed his hand from her cheek and folded his fingers over the kiss, the same way that he'd done to her. 'So what are we going to do about this, Marc?'

What his body was urging him to do was to scoop her up and carry her upstairs to his bed.

His common sense was still in charge. Just. 'Neither of us needs any extra complications in our lives.'

'Absolutely,' she agreed.

'This—this *thing* between us would be a complication.'

'Indeed.'

Just as his common sense was doing a mental high-five and a victory dance, his libido fought back. 'But I want to.'

She moistened her lower lip. 'Me, too.'

The action undid him, and he leaned forward to kiss her on the mouth. It was meant to be a sweet, gentle, exploring kind of thing, but desire flared between them and the kiss turned much deeper and much, much hotter than he'd intended. By the time he broke the kiss her mouth was really reddened—and he was pretty sure his was in the same state.

'OK. So we've established that I like you and you like me,' he said. Because she deserved nothing less than honesty.

'Yes. And this is just between us. Nobody else needs to know about it.' She was still staring at his mouth, and it took all his strength not to wrap her back in his arms and kiss her until they were both dizzy.

'I thought you said everyone knew everything in a small town.'

'Not straight away. And we can be colleagues at work. Professional. Discreet.'

He stole another kiss. Making it quick, because he dared not linger. 'I'm not thinking discreet right now. I want to carry you to my bed.'

'Yes.' Her voice was husky, sexy as hell, and he very nearly did just what he'd just suggested.

But his common sense had some more ammunition. 'I feel guilty about this.'

'So do I. My mum's babysitting my little girl because I was doing a work thing this evening. I ought to be getting home and taking over from her.' She blew out a breath. 'But all I can think about right now is ripping your clothes off.'

Oh, yes. That worked for him. 'Laurie. My control's hanging by the thinnest of threads,' he warned. 'But we have to be sensible. I don't have a condom.'

'Me neither.' She gave him a rueful smile. 'Which makes things a little bit tricky for us.'

'There are other things we could...' He stopped himself. 'Laurie. No. Go home. Now. Please. Before we both start behaving as if we're teenagers.'

She laughed. 'I think we already did that.' She indicated his sofa.

And how. The question burst out of him because right now he really, really needed to know. 'When could your mum babysit for you again?'

'Next Wednesday night, when we drop in to the village hall to see how the first exercise taster session is going.'

He swallowed hard. 'And we'd need to talk about it afterwards. Work together on a report. And here would be... quieter. More private.'

She shivered. 'I feel like a teenage girl planning prom night. Planning to...' She shook her head and closed her eyes for a moment. 'This is going to be a disaster.'

She'd changed her mind? Disappointment closed round his heart like a mailed fist. 'You're right. We should be sensible,' he said. 'Stick to being just colleagues.'

'I didn't mean that. I mean, it's been a while, for both of us. We're planning things. Expecting things. And I...' She paused and looked him straight in the eye. 'I don't want to disappoint you.'

It was the first time Marc had seen Laurie anything other than completely confident, and it shocked him.

But then he remembered that her ex had cheated on her. Including when she'd been giving birth to their daughter. That would've shattered anybody's confidence. And he guessed that Laurie was the type who'd smile to cover up her real feelings and pretend everything was just fine, even when it wasn't. Hadn't she said that you could always make the best of things? So her Pollyanna outlook was probably to stop herself getting hurt.

'You won't disappoint me,' he said softly. 'I like you, Laurie Grant. And that's a very good start.'

'Mmm-hmm.'

He took her hand and pressed it to the left side of his chest. 'There's your proof.'

Her eyes widened as she felt his heart thudding. 'Sorry. I'm being wet.'

'No apologies.' He stole the swiftest of kisses. 'No regrets. And no expectations. We'll see where this takes us, get to know each other.'

'Take it slowly,' she said.

Apart from the plans they'd made for next Wednesday night. Though he wasn't sure whether that thrilled him or scared him most. 'Yes.'

She nodded. 'I'll see you tomorrow at work, then.'

'OK.'

When he'd seen her out, he made himself another cup of coffee and sat down at the kitchen table.

He really hadn't expected this. A second chance. One that, despite what Laurie had said earlier, he still felt he didn't deserve.

He thought of Ginny.

'I don't love you any less,' he said softly. 'I'll miss you

for the rest of my life. And I'll never forgive myself for letting you down. But I'm lonely, Gin. Bone-deep lonely. I think Laurie is, too. We're both on our own. And maybe we'll be able to help each other. Make things better for each other. Make some sense out of—well, all the things that have gone wrong for both of us.'

He smiled wryly. No expectations, they'd said.

Yeah, right.

# CHAPTER SEVEN

THE following Wednesday couldn't come quickly enough for either of them. Although they managed to keep their relationship completely professional at the surgery, Marc was very aware of Laurie. He knew the second she walked into a room, even if his back was to the door. Every time he looked at her, he felt as if he was burning up.

And tonight, he thought—tonight they'd have the ultimate closeness. He couldn't wait to hold her. Touch her.

But halfway through the Wednesday morning, Laurie had a call from the school secretary, Renee.

'Izzy's not feeling very well,' Renee explained. 'She says she's got a tummyache. I felt her forehead and she's definitely got a temperature.'

'Oh, no—poor baby. She was fine this morning. I wouldn't have sent her in otherwise,' Laurie said.

'It's not your fault. There's a bug doing the rounds. Can you come and pick her up?'

'I'll call my mum. If she can't come now, I'll talk to Leigh and see if the others can take on my patients. Tell Izzy I love her and she'll be home soon—and I'll ring you as soon as I know what's going on.'

To Laurie's relief, her mother was only pottering in the garden and was able to go and collect Izzy and look after her until Laurie had finished her shift. She quickly rang Renee back to explain that Diane was on her way.

At her break, she caught up with Marc. 'Izzy has a temperature and a tummyache. Mum's picked her up for me so I can finish my shift this morning, but I'm sorry, I'm going to have to ask you to do the project class on your own tonight. I'm not going to be able to make it.' And she really, really hoped that he could read between the lines of what she was saying.

'No worries.'

'It's not an excuse,' she said softly as they both left the staffroom. 'I'm not backing out of seeing you.'

'I know,' he said, keeping his voice low. 'But you come as a package. Izzy needs to come first, and I accept that.'

'Thank you for being so understanding.'

He raised his voice back to normal tones. 'I'll collect the monitors from our patients. And it's the circuit training session, so it might be good for me to join in and do a class anyway.'

'OK.'

He lowered his voice again. 'And we'll take a raincheck on our other plans—until next Wednesday.'

Laurie's pulse spiked, and she went hot all over. 'Indeed.' And she flushed, knowing just how husky her voice sounded. And why. And because he knew why, too.

Part of her was aware how crazy this was. They didn't know each other that well. Neither of them was in the right place for a relationship—Marc was still grieving and blaming himself for his wife's death, and she was trying to keep life on an even keel for her little girl, which meant keeping any relationship under wraps until she was absolutely sure where it was going. Laurie didn't want to introduce a new man into Izzy's life until she was sure that it was what they all wanted.

And what she and Marc were planning to do…

Well, it wasn't a relationship, exactly. It was mutual attraction. And part of her really wanted to act on that attraction, to let her hair down for once and just enjoy it. Yet part of her worried that it was all going to go badly wrong. Had it been more than just an inability to take responsibility that had cracked her relationship with Dean? Or had that been his way of letting her down gently, and avoid having to tell her that she wasn't enough for him? If she let herself get close to Marc, would it go wrong?

She pushed the insecurities away. No. She had to look on the bright side, the way she always did. She liked Marc and Marc liked her. They were keeping this quiet to take the pressure off, for both of them. And they were just going to keep it light. Put a bit of fun and brightness into their lives. What was wrong with that?

Izzy still had a tummy ache when Laurie got home, but Laurie's mother had given the little girl a dose of infant paracetamol and put a cool cloth on her forehead, so her temperature was down, and the little girl was fast asleep.

'I read her a few stories from the princess book until she nodded off,' Diane said. 'Renee told me there's a bug going around. There were four other little ones waiting to be picked up when I got there.'

'Poor little mites. It's miserable feeling like this, especially when it's sunny outside and they'd rather be out in the playground with their friends. Thanks for rescuing me, Mum.'

'Any time.' Diane hugged Laurie. 'You know I'd be happy to do more to help you. If you weren't so independent…'

Laurie smiled. 'I know, Mum, and I appreciate it. But I don't want to take you for granted.' She grinned. 'No pun intended, Mrs Grant.'

'As if. You're worse than your father,' Diane teased.

'Have you had any lunch yet?' Laurie asked.

'I waited for you. I made us a salad,' Diane said. 'And I had some cold salmon in the fridge from last night, so I brought that over with me.'

'Mum, that's wonderful. Thank you. And you spoil me.'

'That's what mums are for. No doubt you'll do the same for Izzy.' She paused. 'And for her brothers and sisters.'

Laurie shook her head. 'That's not going to happen, Mum.'

'Because you never do anything where you actually meet people, other than the mums of other children at school,' Diane said.

Laurie smiled. 'I'm hardly going clubbing at my age.'

'Anyone would think you were fifty, not thirty!' Diane rolled her eyes. 'I just wish you'd take some time for yourself and—well, I know Dean hurt you, but not all men are like that.'

'I know. You'll be ganging up with Fiona next,' Laurie said lightly. 'She wants me to be as happily settled as she is. But I'm fine as I am. Really.'

'Hmm. An only child's a lonely child.'

'No, she's not. Izzy has plenty of friends, plus she has me and you and Dad—not to mention her Uncle Joe, Aunty Rose and her cousins. It's fine, Mum.' Laurie smiled to take the sting from her words. 'Let's have some lunch.'

Marc wasn't surprised when Laurie wasn't at work, the next morning. He'd already seen a couple of children from Izzy's school, the previous day, and the tummy bug seemed to be lasting for about three days. It was unlikely that Laurie would be back until Monday.

Leigh, the practice manager, had arranged a locum to cover Laurie's shifts—thankfully not the one who'd upset so many patients before—and Marc grabbed a moment during his morning break to call Laurie.

'How's Izzy doing?'

'Still feeling rough, poor love. I'm giving her lots of sips of cool water, and hopefully she'll be able to manage something at lunchtime.'

'How are *you* doing,' he asked softly.

'I'm OK. You?'

He took a risk. 'I missed you last night.'

'Me, too.'

Funny how that quiet little admission sent a thrill all the way through him.

'How was the class?' she asked.

'Surprisingly fun. I think our patients enjoyed it, too.' He paused. 'I collected all the monitors. Do you want me to drop them off to your friend Jay?'

'No, it's OK. I was going to drop them at his place rather than his office—it's a good excuse to see Fiona and the baby. If Izzy's up to it, I was planning to do that on Saturday after we've fed the ducks. And I should be back at work on Monday.' He noticed that she didn't ask him to feed the ducks with her this week. She'd admitted that she'd missed him, but was she also having second thoughts about what they were planning, confused about whether they were doing the right thing? He was, too. And yet she still drew him.

Izzy was much better on Saturday, so Laurie rang her best friend. 'Fiona, I need to get these monitors back to Jay.

Izzy's been off for the last couple of days with a bug; she's OK now, but I can just drop them off and not come in, if you like, to make sure the baby doesn't pick up any germs.'

'Don't be daft,' Fiona said. 'It'll be lovely to see you both. What time can you come over?'

'After we've fed the ducks? I promised Iz some fresh air.'

'Great. You can stay for lunch. Jay's out playing squash, so we can have a girly chat and Iz can draw me one of her fabulous pictures.'

After she'd taken Izzy to feed the ducks, Laurie picked up some sweet-scented stocks from the florist in the middle of town, then drove over to Fiona's with the monitors she'd borrowed from Jay.

Fiona greeted her with a hug, and made them both coffee after she'd seated Izzy at the table with a glass of milk, paper and crayons. 'I hear the new doctor in your practice is very dishy,' she said.

'He's a nice guy,' Laurie said carefully. 'He fits in well in the practice, and he's helping me with my pet project.'

Fiona raised an eyebrow. 'Is he single?'

'Mum's already given me a lecture this week about dating, and that's more than enough. Don't you start, too,' Laurie said with a groan.

'Your mum has a point,' Fiona said. 'It might be good for you to meet someone. You're a great mum to Izzy, but you need some time for you as well.'

'I'm fine.' But Laurie could feel the betraying heat in her face.

Fiona looked interested. 'You're blushing, Laurie. Anything you want to tell me?'

'No.' Even though Fiona was her best friend and Izzy's

godmother, Laurie didn't want to say a word to her until she was sure where this thing with Marc was going.

Fiona smiled. 'Jay said he was a nice guy.'

'Jay,' Laurie said, blowing out a breath, 'is stirring.'

Fiona gave her a hug. 'Sorry, I know I shouldn't tease you—but it'd be so nice to see you having some fun in your life.'

'I do have fun.'

'I know you do, with Izzy, but you know what I meant—you deserve someone who's going to treat you better than That Man did.'

Laurie shrugged. 'I'm doing OK. Really. Now, is Eve asleep or do I get the cuddle I've been looking forward to all week?'

To her relief, Fiona allowed herself to be distracted by the baby and dropped the subject.

On the Wednesday evening, Diane was looking after Izzy, as arranged, and Laurie went to the kick-boxing taster session at the village hall. She arrived early, in case anyone had questions for her, and she was pleased to see that everyone in the group turned up to give it a try.

'I don't think it's for me—I'm never going to be like that Jackie Chan,' Russell Parker confided, 'but my son said I ought to come along and give it a go, and it might not be as bad as I think it is.'

'And he's absolutely right,' Laurie said with a smile.

Several other patients came over to chat to her and say how much they were enjoying the taster sessions—and that they'd been surprised by the sheer range of exercise available. Some had even talked their partners into being their exercise buddies, once they'd found something they wanted to do again.

Laurie was really glad that it was working out how she'd hoped it would, but at the same time she was desperate for the class to be over. After this, she'd arranged to call in to see Marc to discuss how the session had gone, and then...

She felt hot all over. She'd actually arranged to meet him in the full knowledge that they would be going to bed together, and it made her feel scared and excited all at the same time. Did he feel as mixed up as this, she wondered, wanting so desperately to do it and yet worrying that it was all going to go wrong?

After the session, everyone helped clear up. Several of the patients sounded enthusiastic about doing a beginners' martial arts class in the future, and the class leader took their names with a smile.

Finally, the village hall janitor arrived and locked up. And then Laurie drove to Marc's house. She parked outside and just sat there for a moment, her pulse hammering. What if he'd changed his mind? Was she about to make an enormous fool of herself?

Her mobile phone rang and she jumped. She grabbed it from her handbag, just in case it was her mother and there was a problem with Izzy, but Marc's name was on the screen.

She answered the call warily. 'Hello?'

'Are you going to sit there in your car all night, Laurie, or do you want to come in?' He sounded amused, but she could hear the tension in his voice, too. So he was as worried about this as she was. Thinking about what could go wrong. How awkward it could become at work.

And, paradoxically, that made her feel better. 'I'm on my way,' she mumbled.

He opened the front door to her. 'So how did the session go?'

'It was good fun. I did a few of the moves with them, and I might be tempted to go along to the beginners' class myself. Everyone turned up again, so we must be doing something right.' She grimaced. 'Sorry, I'm talking too much. I'll shut up now.'

He closed the door behind her and smiled. 'Does it help if I tell you that I'm nervous, too?'

'Yes.' She swallowed hard. 'So it's…' Her throat dried. 'It's still on?' she finished.

'Unless you want to call a halt.'

'I haven't been able to stop thinking about this all day,' she admitted huskily.

'Good, because neither have I—and I've been on a slow burn all week, remembering what it feels like to kiss you.'

His eyes were very dark, and his words melted her. She said nothing, just tipped her head back. He gave her a slow, sweet smile, and then wrapped his arms round her. And it felt like heaven. He brushed his mouth against hers, teasing and enticing and demanding all at the same time; she slid her fingers into his hair and kissed him back.

When he broke the kiss, they were both shaking. Laurie couldn't remember the last time she'd felt this burning need.

Marc took the scrunchie from her hair and let her hair fall around her shoulders. 'Your hair's amazing.' He twined a curl round his finger. 'Soft, like silk.' His voice deepened. 'And I'm dying to know what your skin feels like.'

'Me, too. Yours, I mean, not mine.' Her words sounded croaky, but he didn't laugh at her; he just gave her an intense, smouldering look, took her hand and led her up-stairs.

He paused at a doorway. 'Give me two seconds.'

Laurie could hardly breathe, knowing that she was going to walk through that door into his bedroom, take her clothes off, and make love with him.

They barely knew each other. She was going to have sex with a near-stranger. This was totally shocking. Totally un-Laurie-like behaviour.

Yet, at the same time, they'd spent enough time together to know what damage the other had been through. She knew they'd be careful with each other. This would be *safe*.

So why did it feel so dangerous?

Marc reappeared in the doorway. 'Just so you know, I rented this house furnished. And I bought all new linen and soft furnishings when I moved.'

She knew exactly what he was telling her. The bed they were about to share he hadn't shared with anyone else. There were no memories for him, and she didn't need to worry that he was going to compare her to anyone. And she really appreciated that reassurance. 'Thank you.'

He rubbed the pad of his thumb gently along her lower lip. 'You're very welcome.'

He led her into his room. It was quaintly old-fashioned with a four-poster bed, a polished wooden floor and a fireplace that clearly wasn't used because the place for the firebox was filled with dried flowers. He'd lit scented tea-light candles on the mantelpiece, and the soft light made the room incredibly romantic. And at last Laurie stopped feeling faintly cheap and grubby.

'So, Dr Grant.' Marc leaned forward and stole a kiss. 'What now?'

He was wearing a formal shirt, but without a tie and with the top button undone. Not saying a word, Laurie reached up and undid all the rest of the buttons, before untucking the soft cotton from his waistband and pushing his shirt off his shoulders.

His eyes glittered. 'What a good idea.' He did the same with her shirt; Laurie could hardly breathe as he undid the buttons and his fingers brushed against her skin.

Slowly, wordlessly, they undressed each other down to their underwear.

She felt ridiculously shy, like a teenager all over again.

As if he understood, he whispered, 'Close your eyes.'

She did so, and felt him unclip her bra. And then he scooped her up.

Laurie opened her eyes again. 'Marc, what about your arm?'

'It healed a long time ago. And lifting you onto my bed isn't going to do any damage,' he reassured her. 'It's not as if you're a rugby prop forward who's built like a brick outhouse and I'm just about to collide with you at speed.'

She relaxed and let him lift her onto the bed.

There were cool, smooth cotton sheets against her back, and her head rested on the softest of down pillows. She felt the mattress dip slightly as he climbed onto the bed beside her. She was glad he'd opted for the softer lighting when she realised that he'd already removed his underpants and was curling his fingers round the elastic of her knickers. She lifted herself from the bed so he could peel them down

She wanted this so badly, yet at the same time it made her panic. She could still remember the mechanics of what they were about to do, but she hadn't remembered the feelings; that sudden rush of desire was overwhelming.

He kissed her lightly. 'If you're having second thoughts, that's fine. We'll stop.'

'It's just… Well, it's been a while,' she said, 'and it feels like the first time all over again.'

He smiled at her. 'Technically, it *is* the first time. For us. If it makes you feel any better, I'm terrified that I'm going to be rubbish—I don't know where and how you like being touched, what pleases you, anything.'

'Same here.' She bit her lip. 'Maybe we should just be brave and explore together?'

'That,' he said, 'is a brilliant idea.' He dipped his head to kiss her, then shifted so he could kiss his way down the side of her neck.

'That's nice,' she whispered.

Emboldened by the way he was touching her, she began to explore him, stroking his back. She knew she'd found a place he liked when he arched against her and sighed with pleasure.

He kissed the hollows of her collarbones, then along her sternum, and she arched up to him. He cupped her breasts, took one nipple into his mouth and sucked. Laurie felt herself grow wet with desire, and rocked against him slightly. 'More,' she whispered.

Marc toyed with her other nipple, then finally slid one hand between her thighs. He stroked and teased until she was close to whimpering. She pushed herself against his hand, and then finally he eased one finger into her; she gave a sigh of relief.

'Better?' he asked.

She nodded. 'Sorry.'

'No apologies,' he reminded her. 'I'm exploring and finding out what you like.' He circled his thumb on her clitoris as he continued pushing inside her.

Laurie was shocked by the speed of her orgasm; within only a few seconds she fell apart in his arms.

'I wanted that first time to be for you,' he said softly, 'and now I think you're ready.'

She heard the rip of a foil packet, the snap as he rolled the condom on. And then, oh, bliss, he was kneeling between her thighs, fitting himself to her entrance and slowly, slowly easing into her. She reached up to jam her mouth over his, mimicking with her tongue what he was doing to her with his body.

Unbelievably, she felt her body tightening all over again. This was crazy. She shouldn't feel so in tune with him Shouldn't the first time be messy and awkward and a bit embarrassing?

And then she stopped thinking as she climaxed again, and felt his body surge in answer against hers.

He held her close until both their heart rates had slowed back to normal, then gently eased out of her. 'I'd better deal with the condom.'

When he came back from the bathroom, she'd pulled the sheet over herself, feeling shy. He was still completely naked. He stopped short as he saw her, his eyes widening.

'You're beautiful,' she said.

'So are you. Under that sheet.' He joined her underneath it, and held her close with her head pillowed on his shoulder. 'Thank you.'

'Thank you.' She shifted so she could press a kiss against his chest. 'That was pretty amazing.'

'So what now?' he asked.

'No expectations, we said.'

'And no regrets.' He drew her closer. 'I liked being a teenager all over again.'

'So you're saying you want to do this all over again?'

He shifted so that he could look her straight in the eye. 'Do you?'

'I asked first.'

He stroked her cheek. 'Yes. I know it's complicated, I know you come as part of a package, and I know I'm an emotional mess. But I still want to do this again. With you.' He paused. 'And you?'

She nodded. 'But I'm not ready to go public, Marc. Not for a while.'

'Uh-huh.'

'Not because I don't like you—I do, or I wouldn't be here, because I don't go off and have hot monkey sex with just *anybody*—but I have Izzy to think about.'

'Of course you do.' He kissed her lightly. 'Speaking of her, you need to get back before your mum starts worrying about you.'

'I did tell her that I was going to see you before I came home, talk about the project with you.'

'And you did.' He grinned. 'Just not for very long.'

'I guess we both got a little bit distracted.'

'Hot monkey sex. Hmm.' He stole another kiss. 'So is this going to be same time, same place, next week?'

'It's your turn to do the class next week,' she pointed out. 'And I can't offer you anything more than coffee afterwards.'

'OK. Just coffee. I'll take the offer.' The corners of his eyes crinkled. 'Even if it is instant stuff out of a jar.'

'You're such a coffee snob,' she teased back.

He kissed her lightly. 'I'll get you a fresh towel so you can have a shower. And, much as I'd like to, I'm not going to join you. Otherwise you'll have to explain to your mother why your hair's wet. And I'm not sure how she'd react to the idea of you having hot monkey sex in a shower.'

She couldn't help smiling. 'You like that phrase, don't you?'

'You're the one who used it first,' he reminded her, and stole another kiss. 'See you downstairs. I'll leave a fresh towel outside the door.'

'Thanks.'

It felt strange, showering in someone else's bathroom, and Laurie got herself ready in double-quick time. Her clothes were slightly rumpled, but hopefully her mother wouldn't notice.

Marc gave her a lingering kiss goodbye. 'See you at work in the morning, Dr Grant. And if you're good I might even buy you a sweet chilli chicken salad wrap from the patisserie and feed the ducks with you at lunchtime.'

'That,' Laurie said with a grin, 'is a date.'

# CHAPTER EIGHT

Marc and Laurie headed for the patisserie on Thursday lunchtime to buy sandwiches—running the gauntlet of more good-natured teasing by Tina—and ate them in the sunshine on the bench by the duck pond.

There was nobody around to hear him, but Marc lowered his voice anyway. 'Right now, Dr Grant, I'd really like to kiss you. Like I did last night.'

Laurie went deliciously pink. And then he remembered how she'd looked as she'd climaxed, her eyes wide and her skin flushed like that, and went decidedly hot under his own collar.

'Marc,' she said in a warning whisper.

'I'm not going to do it—at least, not in the middle of the town where anyone could see us and start gossiping,' he reassured her. 'Besides, we don't want to scare the ducks.'

To his relief, she smiled back. 'Absolutely. Otherwise I'll have to give them double rations next time I come.'

'Saturday morning?' he asked.

'Not this week—I checked the weather forecast and it's going to be glorious, so I'm taking Izzy to the beach.' She gave him a sidelong look. 'How are you on rock pools and crabbing?'

'Rock pools and crabbing?' he echoed, mystified.

She shook her head and tutted. 'You're such a Londoner! I was wondering, would you like to come with us?' When he said nothing, she added softly, 'No strings.'

Well, he knew she came as a package. And he wanted to see more of her. So he'd just have to shove all the guilt back where it came from, and make an effort to get to know Izzy, too. 'I'd like that. Thank you.'

'Shall I pick you up at nine?' she suggested.

'Or I could pick you up.'

She shook her head. 'Izzy's seat is already in my car. Besides, I wouldn't want to get yours messy.'

'I'm not that much of a neat freak,' he said.

'No?' she teased.

'No.' He couldn't resist leaning closer and whispering, 'And you can ruffle me any time you like, Dr Grant.'

'Marc!' But she was laughing.

'What do I need to bring?'

'Nothing—I have the bucket, spade, beach towels and sun cream. So just yourself.'

'Is Cocoa coming, too?'

'Dogs aren't allowed on the beach in summer, so Mum and Dad are going to pop round to let him out. It'll be just the three of us.'

Just the three of us.

He was being given a second chance at a family.

Did he dare to take it?

On Saturday morning, Laurie knocked on Marc's front door at nine. She was wearing cut-off faded denim shorts, a bright pink T-shirt and espadrilles, and looked adorably cute. He itched to kiss her but he knew that he couldn't, not with Izzy there. Before they went public, she'd need to talk to Izzy. And, given how Laurie's relationship with

Dean had ended and the way the man had destroyed her trust, Marc knew that it would take a while until she was ready. Giving her time to get used to the idea worked for him, too; he wasn't entirely sure that he was ready for this. Though he did know that he wanted to see more of Laurie.

The little girl greeted him with delight when he got into the car. 'Hello, Marc. Mummy says you're coming crabbing with us.'

'Yes.' He made an effort. 'I've never done it before.'

She smiled shyly at him. 'I have. Three whole times.'

'So can you teach me how to do it?'

She looked thrilled at the idea. 'You bet I can!'

This time, he felt much more at ease with her, less panicky than he'd been the day they'd gone to the blue-bell woods, and he even found himself joining in with the songs that Izzy and Laurie sang in the car, with a bit of prompting from Izzy.

Laurie parked on the cliffs at the edge of the town. 'I thought it'd be nice to walk down the cliff path to the sea-front,' she said.

Marc fell in love with the old Victorian seaside resort, with its promenade and its pier with the lifeboat house on the end. 'This really isn't what I expected,' he said. 'I thought Norfolk was all really huge flat beaches?'

'You're thinking of Wells and Holkham, the ones that tend to be used as film sets,' she said. 'We have cliffs too, here at Cromer and then the stripy ones out at Hunstanton. They found a mammoth in the cliffs just up the road a few years ago.'

He looked at her, intrigued. 'So does that mean we can go fossil hunting?'

'This particular beach isn't quite in the same league as Lyme Regis or Whitby when it comes to fossils,' she said with a smile, 'but we can look. And even if we don't find an actual fossil, there are lots of pretty pebbles.' She ruffled Izzy's hair. 'The tide's in, so shall we go crabbing first?'

She led them onto the pier, where they hired a line and bucket and bought some bait. Izzy showed him how to wind out the string, and how to wind it up again. It took them half an hour to catch a single tiny crab, but Izzy was delighted.

'And now we have to put it back, so it can grow big and its mum doesn't worry about it,' she said.

When they'd returned their crabbing equipment, they stopped to buy ice creams. Marc was quietly amused to notice that the little girl liked sprinkles on her ice cream as well as a chocolate flake, and he let her choose the topping for his own cone. How many years had it been since he'd last eaten one of those? he wondered as he tasted the sweet, creamy mixture. How many years since he'd felt as carefree as this, with the sound of the waves lapping at the shore, the tangy scent of the sea in his nostrils, huge white gulls shrieking above, the sun warming him and white streaky clouds scudding across a deep blue sky?

By the time they'd finished their ice creams, the tide had gone out enough to leave shallow pools around the rocks. Several families were already there, peering into the clear water and pointing things out to each other.

'Can we go 'sploring, Mummy?' Izzy asked.

'Of course we can, darling. But remember what Granddad said about not having bare feet on the rocks?'

'In case you get cuts on your feet,' Izzy said solemnly.

Laurie rummaged in her beach bag and retrieved some flip-flops. Izzy took her trainers off and changed into the flip-flops; Laurie tucked her shoes and Izzy's back into the bag.

Marc removed his trainers and rolled his jeans up above his calves before following them onto the beach. The wet sand felt beautifully cool against his feet. He was amused to notice that Laurie's toenails were painted a very bright pink; he hadn't noticed that on Wednesday when she'd been in his bed, but then again he hadn't exactly been looking at her feet. He'd needed to touch her and taste her and lose himself in her.

He thoroughly enjoyed poking around the rock pools with Izzy. They found more tiny crabs, and the highlight for the little girl was when they found a sea anemone and a starfish. Laurie was watching them both, and Marc shared a complicit smile with her; the little girl's delight was infectious.

When Izzy had had enough of the rock pools, Marc helped her to make a big sandcastle with a moat. They decorated the towers at the corners with seaweed, and then Marc took her to the water's edge to fill her bucket with water so she could tip it into the moat. The sea was cool but delicious against his skin.

Izzy tipped the water from her bucket into the moat; it drained away quickly, but stayed for just long enough for Laurie to take a picture of Marc and Izzy together with their moated castle.

Marc couldn't remember the last time he'd felt this relaxed or had had such fun. Was this what it would've been like with his own child? He pushed the thought away. Now wasn't the time or the place.

They ate fish and chips sitting on one of the benches on the seafront; a line of gulls perched on a nearby wall watching them with beady eyes and waiting for one of them to drop a chip or some fish so they could swoop on it.

'This is fabulous,' Marc said.

'Didn't you live near a seaside where you lived before?' Izzy asked.

'I lived in London so, no, there isn't a beach. There used to be a little one by the Tower of London, but that was a lot of years ago, when my granddad was tiny.'

'So that's why you never went crabbing before?' she asked.

'That's right. But I really enjoyed today, and I hope we can do this again later in the summer.'

Izzy glanced at her mother, waiting for her nod before saying, 'Yes, please!'

As they walked back up the cliff path to the car park, Marc noticed that the little girl's steps were flagging. She was clearly tired, He could leave it to Laurie to deal with the situation. Or he could make an effort—the way Laurie had when she'd invited him to share her day. He could do what any other man would do in this situation when a friend's child was tired and his friend had her hands full. Even though it felt scarily like taking things another step forward.

'Would it be OK for me to give her a piggyback?' he asked Laurie quietly.

Laurie looked concerned. 'What about your shoulder?'

'My shoulder's fine—really—and Izzy's not exactly heavy. I can carry her.'

'If you're sure, thanks.' Laurie gave him a grateful smile.

'Izzy, are your legs tired?' he asked.

At her reluctant nod, he said, 'How about a piggyback?'

'Like the ones Granddad gives me?' At his nod, she beamed. 'Oh, yes, please!'

It warmed him that Laurie trusted him with her most precious possession, and Marc was careful to make sure that Izzy was comfortable and that he was holding her securely as he gave her a piggyback up the cliff path.

'That was brilliant. Thank you,' Izzy said as they got to the car and he set her down.

She fell asleep in the car on the way home, and Marc couldn't help feeling antsy on the way back. Today had been a revelation. A joy. Yet, at the same time, it scared him witless how easy it was to get close to Laurie and Izzy.

*Too* close.

He hadn't expected it to be like this, and he wanted it to stay like this and he wanted to back away in equal measures. Laurie had said that her parents were going to drop round to let Cocoa out. Would they still be there? Had Laurie said anything to them about him? He really wasn't ready to make their relationship public.

But when they got back to the village Marc was relieved to note that there was no car parked outside Laurie's house. So meeting her parents was something he didn't have to face just yet.

'Do you want me to carry her in?' he asked when Laurie parked the car.

'Thanks, that'd be good. We've tired her out.' She smiled. 'I think I'm just going to put her to bed as she is. She can have a soak in the bath tomorrow to get the sand out.'

He carried Izzy upstairs, following Laurie into the smaller bedroom. He wasn't in the slightest bit surprised that Izzy's bedroom was full of pink and purple and sparkly things. Laurie pulled the duvet back and he laid the little girl down gently on the bed. Izzy stayed fast asleep while Laurie gently removed her flip-flops and drew the duvet over her. And the look of sheer love on her face as she kissed the little girl's cheek made Marc's stomach clench. Loving someone like that was dangerous. It meant you had everything to lose. And he'd learned that the hard way. Losing everything wasn't something he'd risk. Ever again.

'Do you want to stay for a coffee?' she asked when they went downstairs.

'That'd be lovely.' He could put up with her awful coffee for the sake of spending more time with her.

'Go and sit down. Put some music on, if you like.'

He didn't, though he did look through her CDs and found out that she liked pop music rather than the mixture of classic rock and classical music that he favoured.

When she brought the mugs in, he was surprised to discover that she was actually giving him proper coffee, with a layer of *crema* on top. Then again, he knew that some brands of instant coffee mimicked the effect. He sniffed the brew experimentally and smiled. This was definitely proper coffee. And he realised that she'd done this especially for him.

'Did you go out and buy a coffee machine?' he asked.

'Nothing like as fancy or as expensive as yours,' she said. 'It's just one of those French presses—the one where you push a plunger down in a glass jug.'

'It does the job.' He tasted it. 'And that's a very nice coffee blend, Dr Grant.'

'It's Italian roast—though I'm afraid it's from the supermarket, not the kind of posh deli a coffee purist like you would get yours from,' she teased.

'I'm not that much of a purist. And this is a million times nicer than the last coffee you made me. Thank you.'

He noticed the dimple in her cheek when she smiled. It was the same as the dimple in Izzy's cheek when she'd seen the starfish.

Funny, a month ago he would've run a mile from this. He still wasn't entirely comfortable with the situation, still felt those prickles of guilt, but there was also a warmth and a lightness in his soul that he'd never expected to feel again. 'Thank you for asking me to go with you today. I enjoyed every second of it.'

'Me, too,' she said softly, and her cheeks went adorably pink.

'Laurie, I know that, here and now, I can't do with you what I really want to do—it's not appropriate, with Izzy asleep upstairs—but can I at least hold you?'

She nodded, put her coffee down and went over to join him. Marc scooped her onto his lap and held her close. Funny, just being with her made him feel better.

The dog had clearly decided that he wasn't going to be left out, and sneaked up onto the sofa next to them.

Laurie looked at the dog and sighed. 'Cocoa, you know you're not supposed to be there.'

The Labrador gave her a guilty wag of his tail, and looked up at her with big, pleading brown eyes.

'Oh, you impossible dog! All right, I neglected you today, so you can stay put. As long as Marc doesn't mind you huffing all over him.'

'I like dogs.' He scratched the top of the Labrador's head. Weird how this felt so much like being at home. The centre of a family. Everything he'd always wanted—everything he'd cut himself off from because he knew he didn't deserve it.

'I'm probably not as strict with him as I should be,' Laurie admitted.

'Would I be right in guessing he's a rescue dog?' Marc asked.

'Well—yes. He was six months old when he came to live with us. Everyone said I shouldn't take him in, because Iz was a toddler and you never know how dogs are going to react, but all he needed was some love. He adores Iz, and he's the gentlest dog I've ever met. Completely daft, but gentle.'

*All he needed was some love.* Dr Fixit had seen that straight away, and the dog had clearly responded in kind.

She wrinkled her nose. 'I suppose I do spoil him a bit, but how can you resist those gorgeous big brown eyes?'

Marc made his eyes as wide as possible and gave her a soulful look over the rim of his glasses, and she burst out laughing. 'It's not quite the same, Marc. Your eyes aren't brown. There's green and gold mixed in there, too.'

'I can do the eye thing. Cocoa will teach me—won't you, boy?'

The Labrador's tail thumped.

Marc kissed her lingeringly; then he was content just to sit with her, holding her close.

'I got some fabulous photos from today. I love that one of you and Iz with the sandcastle. I'll email it to you when I've transferred the pictures to my laptop.'

'That'd be nice.' He kissed the top of her head. 'I've never met anyone who takes quite so many photos.'

'I like photos.' She gestured to the line of frames on the mantelpiece.

Even though he hadn't met her family yet, the likeness in the portraits was obvious—her parents, her brother— and what struck him most was that every photograph was filled to the brim with what he'd been missing since the day Ginny died.

Love.

And he stuffed the thought immediately in the box in his head marked 'Do not open'.

Reluctantly, at the end of the evening Marc took his leave and kissed Laurie goodnight. 'I'll see you on Monday morning,' he said softly.

The next morning, he opened his email to discover the photographs from Laurie, and he was stunned. It was the first time he'd seen himself without shadows in his eyes since the day of Ginny's funeral. He actually looked happy.

He thought about it and realised that he *was* happy, and it was Laurie who'd taken the weight off his shoulders. She'd made him really think about the burden of guilt he'd been carrying. He knew it would never go completely, but it had lightened. Though he felt guilty about that, too.

Maybe it was time he tackled some of the unpacking he'd been avoiding.

He replied swiftly to Laurie's email, thanking her for the photographs, then closed his laptop, headed to the dining room, slit the packing tape on the first box and opened it.

Over the rest of the day he worked his way steadily through the boxes. He put his books on the shelves in the living room, along with his music and films. So much of this had been shared with Ginny, but depriving himself of it wasn't going to bring her back or make him feel better. Maybe Laurie was right and it was time to remember the good stuff instead of looking at the might-have-beens.

But the one thing he couldn't quite bring himself to unpack was the box he knew was full of photographs. He needed to wait just a little longer before he could cope with that.

Wednesday it was Marc's turn to go along to the taster class; this time it was the ballroom dancing class, and although he enjoyed himself he wished that Laurie had been there with him. He would've liked to hold her, dance with her. And nobody would've speculated about them being together, because he and Laurie were both there for the sake of their patients.

He called in to see her afterwards, to update her on how the evening had gone.

'It's a shame you didn't come along. We learned how to do a social foxtrot.' He smiled. 'I danced with all the women in our group. It was great fun.'

'You're such a flirt, Dr Bailey,' she teased.

'The teacher was really nice. I think some of our patients are going to take it up—and apparently doing the cha-cha and the quickstep, if you do a whole hour's dancing, is nearly as good as doing a cardio class.'

'Except it doesn't feel like exercise—and if it's something they can do with a friend or their partner and it's good for their social lives as well as their fitness levels, so much the better,' she said.

They sat on the sofa with Laurie on Marc's lap and Cocoa curled up beside him.

'Do you fancy doing something together this weekend?' he asked.

'What were you thinking?'

'What sort of thing does Izzy like doing?'

'We could go to the park. She loves the swings and slides, and we could kick a ball around. Or the cinema, if you don't mind sitting through an animated movie—I should warn you now that she adores princesses, so it'll be a really girly animated movie.'

'I guess it depends on what's showing and what the weather's going to be like. And maybe we could go out for a meal afterwards.'

'That would be lovely. There's a nice American diner that Izzy likes—we sometimes go there with my parents.' She paused. 'My parents are planning to have a barbecue on Sunday. You could come with us.'

Meet her family. Admit that they were a couple. Marc wasn't quite sure he was ready for that. 'I'm sure your family is as charming as you are,' he said softly, 'but are you ready to be outed yet?'

'No,' she admitted, to his secret relief. 'I'm enjoying having you all to myself for the moment, and I'd rather wait a little longer and talk to Izzy about it first before we go public.' She stroked his face and there was a look of mischief in her expression when she said, 'But I do have another idea.'

'I'm all ears.'

'Izzy's going to Molly's after school on Monday. For tea. I don't have to pick her up until half six.'

He nuzzled her cheek. 'Which means you'd be free to come and have an early dinner with me.'

She looked surprised. 'You can cook?'

'How does it go? Let me think. Pasta, garlic bread, salad, nothing special…' He grinned.

She laughed back. 'That's my line. Actually, that sounds wonderful. I'd love to.'

# CHAPTER NINE

On Saturday afternoon, Izzy looked pleased to see Marc when he turned up at their house. 'Are you coming round to have a play date?' Izzy asked.

'Sort of. I thought maybe we could go out somewhere, like that day we had at the seaside. So I was wondering, would you like to go to the cinema or the park?' he asked.

'With Mummy, too?'

'With your mum, too,' he confirmed.

The little girl thought about it. 'The sun's all shiny and nice, so can we go to the park, please?'

'Sure. That sounds like fun.'

'And will you play ball with me?'

'Of course I will.'

Marc was surprised to discover how much he enjoyed their time in the park. Once they'd played piggy-in-the-middle and he'd taught Izzy how to dribble a ball, they went over to the play area. Marc pushed Izzy on the swings, making her shriek with joy as she went higher; he lifted her so she could swing on the monkey bars, but kept close enough so he could catch her if she lost her balance; and he timed her on the slide to see how fast she could go.

He'd just finished timing her third go on the slide when

she said, 'Look, it's Georgia!' She beamed and ran over to her best friend, then hugged her tightly.

Tina came over to join them. 'Fancy seeing you both here. Together.' She looked meaningfully at Marc. 'I didn't know you had children, Dr Bailey.'

'I don't,' he admitted.

She raised an eyebrow. 'So you're here with Laurie and Izzy, then?'

Marc exchanged a glance with Laurie. Was she ready to tell her friend the truth about their burgeoning relationship, or would she want to keep it quiet and just between the two of them for a bit longer?

'We're being very boring and talking shop,' Laurie said. 'It's hard to find enough hours in the day. You know that Marc's helping me with my project—we're taking the chance to catch up with that.'

It wasn't a *total* fib, Marc thought with a throb of guilt. They probably would discuss it at some point during the day. And he felt even guiltier about being relieved that Laurie wasn't ready to go public yet.

'I'd heard about that—well, actually, Mum did, in the shop,' Tina said. 'She's been talking to Judy Reynolds, who says it's brilliant and Wednesdays are now her favourite day of the week.'

'I think we can safely say that's a result, Laurie,' Marc said with a grin, giving her a high five.

'Mum asked me if I could have a word with you about adding her to it,' Tina said. 'She says she's getting terrible middle-age spread and she's trying to eat sensibly—she never even tastes the stuff she makes at the shop—but she just hasn't got time to do an exercise class.' She grimaced. 'Well, she *says* she hasn't got time, but I think it's because she doesn't like it. She really hated that new dance class she did with me a couple of months ago. She said it was too fast and she couldn't follow most of the moves, and I guess she was right.' Tina sighed. 'I've tried asking her to come to the gym with me, but she won't—even though I told her there are plenty of other women there her age and she won't be out of place.'

'We had a ballroom dancing session last week,' Marc said, and 'I think there's going to be a beginners' class set up some time very soon, if she wants to try that.'

'I bet she'd love it, but talking Dad into being her partner and going with her...' Tina looked wistful. 'That's so not going to happen. She says she only just persuaded him to dance at their wedding, and she had to nag him like mad to dance at mine!'

'If she went on her own, there'd be someone there she could dance with,' Laurie said. 'Or there's aqua aerobics.'

'That's mainly resistance work,' Marc said, 'so it's not going to make her feel as wiped out as a more advanced dance class or doing high-impact aerobics, but it'll still give her a good workout and get her heart rate up safely. The water's a supportive environment, so it'll be kind to her joints, too.'

Tina looked thoughtful. 'I did aqua aerobics as an antenatal class and really enjoyed it. I'll suggest that to her.'

'Or tell her to come to the village hall on Wednesday at eight,' Laurie said. 'I'm not sure if I'll be able to get her on to the monitoring side of the project—that depends on whether or not my friend Jay still has some gaps—but there's no reason why your mum can't do the taster sessions with everyone else. I can email you the schedule so she can see if there's anything she fancies trying.'

'That'd be great. Thanks, Laurie.' Tina hugged her. 'Georgia, honey, we need to go—we've got to pick up some shopping for Nanna and Granddad. See you later, Laurie. Marc.' She smiled at them.

'That was a close call,' Marc said when Tina was out of earshot and Izzy was back on the slide. 'Do you think she'll say anything?'

Laurie shook her head. 'Tina knows I juggle things and multi-task like crazy—and that you're working on the project with me. And it wasn't a total fib about us talking shop.'

'No.' He paused. 'What if she did say something?'

'I hope she doesn't. I'd rather Izzy heard it from us,' Laurie said. 'Don't take this the wrong way, Marc, but it's still early stages. I'm not ashamed of what we're doing, but I'm also not ready for Izzy to think we're anything other than just friends.'

He really wasn't ready to go public. And if Laurie had been…everything would have started to unravel. He wasn't ready for that either.

'That's fine,' he said lightly. 'And you're absolutely right—it's still early stages. We're taking things slowly.'

When they'd finished at the park, they headed back to Laurie's to let Cocoa out and for Izzy to wash her face and hands, then went out to the American diner Izzy liked.

'They have a special ice-cream machine here where you make your own sundae,' Izzy told him, and pointed out the line of people queuing up to make their own sundaes. 'Can we?'

Marc looked to Laurie for guidance; at her nod, he said, 'Sure, if you have room after your dinner.'

When they'd finished their main course, Izzy looked expectantly at them both.

'Sorry, I don't have room for a pudding,' Laurie said, patting her stomach.

Izzy's face fell. 'Oh.'

'I do.' Marc smiled at the little girl. 'How about you and I make a sundae together and share it?'

She beamed at him in reply.

Five minutes later they'd reached the head of the queue for the ice-cream machine. Marc turned out to be very adept at swirling the ice cream round so it made a huge mountain. Izzy added plenty of rainbow-coloured sprinkles and mini chocolate flakes, and together they went back to join Laurie with their creation.

Marc nearly teased Laurie for being predictable when she took a photograph of him and Izzy with their spoons poised just above their dessert, grinning conspiratorially.

When they'd finished, Izzy gave him a spontaneous hug and said, 'I'm glad you're my friend. You make the most brilliant ice-cream sundaes, and this is one of the *best* times I've ever been here.'

'Me, too,' he said easily.

'It's the *only* time you've ever been here,' Izzy pointed out.

'It's still the best,' Marc told her with a grin.

Though he didn't quite dare meet Laurie's eyes, not sure what he'd see there. And not wanting to think about what he'd like to see there. He really wasn't ready to take this another step forward, and he was pretty sure she wasn't either

To avoid the awkwardness, he turned the conversation back to ice cream and favourite flavours. And only then he did look at Laurie, relieved to see that she was laughing and her expression was light rather than intense.

* * *

Late on Monday afternoon, Laurie's phone beeped, signalling a text message.

*Am home now. Come round any time you like.*

A thrill ran through her. It was crazy, but Marc made her feel as if she was eighteen years old again. And she'd even dressed up a little, the way she would've done for a date in her teens.

Because this counted as a date.

And Marc obviously noticed, because he kissed her lingeringly when he closed the front door behind her. 'You look gorgeous—not that you don't usually, but…well, I'm not used to seeing you in a skirt.' He kissed her again. 'And you have very nice legs, Dr Grant.'

Pleased, she smiled at him and kissed him back. 'Thank you.'

'Would you like some coffee? Or something cold?' he asked.

'It's baking out there. Something cold would be lovely, please.'

He fetched them both a glass of chilled sparkling water with ice and slice of lime.

'Perfect.' She took a grateful sip.

'Come and sit down.' He ushered her into his living room.

She looked around, frowning slightly. 'Something's different about your house, though I can't put my finger on it. Hang on, do I spy things on your shelves? Clutter? Tut, tut, what happened to Dr Neat Freak?' she teased.

'I just unpacked a few things.'

She raised an eyebrow. 'Indeed. You have books, you have films, you have music…' She browsed along his shelves. 'So you're a big sci fi fan.'

''Fraid so,' he teased.

'When did you do all this?'

'Last weekend.' He touched the backs of his fingers to her cheek. 'Spending the day with you and Izzy gave me a bit of backbone, and I finally felt brave enough to face it—all except one box,' he admitted.

'One box?'

He swallowed hard. 'Photographs.'

She took his hand. 'And would I be right in guessing that they've been packed away since well before you moved?'

He nodded. 'We used to have nearly as many photographs as you do around the house, but after Ginny died I felt bad every time I saw them. I packed them away to stop myself going crazy with guilt. I put them in a box quite a while before I decided to move away from London, and I haven't looked at them since. Which also makes me feel bad.' He sighed. 'I know I'm going to have to face them eventually.'

'How about now? When you've got someone to keep you company?'

'I can't ask you to do that.'

'Of course you can.' She reached up to kiss him. 'It's not just about the hot monkey sex, you know. We're friends, too. And you'd do the same for me.'

He thought about it. 'Yes.' And, because it put the moment of reckoning off for just a little longer, he asked, 'Do you have pictures of Izzy's father around the house?'

'That's a bit of a tricky one.' She sighed. 'If Dean had wanted to be part of Izzy's life—well, I guess we wouldn't have split up in the first place, because he wouldn't have run away from his fear of being a father by having an affair and then leaving it to me to make the decision to end our relationship. But if he'd simply fallen out of love with me and in love with someone else, and had still wanted to be part of Izzy's life, then obviously for her sake I'd still have pictures of him around the house.' She shrugged. 'But he doesn't want to be part of her life. So, no, I don't have pictures of him around.'

'Does Izzy ever ask about him?'

'Thankfully, no. I guess I'm a bit of a coward, because I still haven't worked out how to tell her that he doesn't want to know her. I don't want her to feel rejected or abandoned. I want her to know that she's loved very, very much—but it's a hard thing to do, to tell a child that one of her parents just doesn't want to know. I did think about telling her that he died when she was a baby—but that wouldn't be fair, because then I'd have to tell her the truth when she's older, and a lie that big would do an awful lot of damage to her.' She bit her lip. 'Right now, she's too young to understand just how complicated people are, so I fudge the issue, and luckily I'm not the only single parent in the school so she doesn't feel that she's different.'

'From what I can see, you're doing a great job,' Marc said, meaning it. 'And I'm in the camp that thinks Dean needed his head examined. A talented, caring, lovely woman like you and a beautiful child—he was a fool to let you both go.'

And, although Marc still hadn't worked out how to tell her the whole truth about the accident, he was talking from experience. As a man who'd been every bit as much of a fool and had let everything good in his life go.

Maybe working through the photographs with her would help him find the right words to tell her the rest of his past.

'Are you sure you don't mind helping me?' he asked again.

'Of course I'm sure.'

He fetched the last box from the dining room, and carried it into the kitchen. Once he'd set it on the table and sliced open the tape, he stopped. Unpacking his life. His memories. All the things he'd lost.

He felt slightly sick.

'Marc, remember the story about Pandora?' she said softly.

'No.' Well, he sort of did. Half-remembered. But at that precise moment his head felt as if it had frozen and he couldn't think of anything.

'She opened a box. It was full of scary stuff. But, right at the bottom, there was hope.'

Hope.

That was what Laurie was offering him. A future even.

He undid the flaps of the box.

Right at the top was a photograph from his wedding day; the silver frame was slightly tarnished and needed polishing. The sight of it sent a throb of guilt through him.

As if she guessed what was wrong, she said softly, 'A silver polishing cloth will sort that out in a couple of minutes. Don't beat yourself up about this.' She smiled at him. 'Ginny was a gorgeous bride.'

His voice sounded rusty as he replied, 'Yes.' Ginny was classically pretty, with blonde hair she'd worn in an elegant chignon and clear grey eyes. There was a huge lump in his throat as he stared at the photograph. 'We'd only known each other for six months when we got married.'

'A whirlwind romance,' she said lightly.

'Something like that. We met at a party, a friend of a friend, and we just hit it off.'

He took the next photo out of the box: one of Ginny sitting reading in their garden when he'd called her name and she'd looked up at him over the edge of her book. It was one of his favourites, the one he'd kept on his desk at work in his old practice.

'She looks nice as well as beautiful,' Laurie said.

'She was. Everyone who knew her liked her. She was the sort who never had a bad word to say about anyone.' He smiled. 'I'm not going to say we never had a fight—that'd be totally unrealistic—but they were never bad fights. They were always over something little and stupid, and we made up quickly.'

When he took the next photo frame out and set it on the table, Laurie said, 'They look so much like you, they have to be your parents.'

'Yes. This one was taken at the wedding. My dad's a chemistry teacher, a bit of a mad professor type. Getting him in an ordinary suit takes a lot, and to get him into morning dress…' He gave her a rueful smile. 'Well, Ginny talked him into it.'

Next was a woman in a graduation photo. 'Your little sister?' Laurie guessed.

'Yvonne. Vonnie. Yes. She's up in Glasgow.' She swallowed. 'She's a primary school teacher. I haven't seen her for months.' He sighed. 'I really ought to make the effort and go up to see her.'

'But it was easier to keep your distance from people who'd known Ginny and would bring back all the memories?' Laurie asked softly.

How could she understand that so easily? 'Yes.'

He took a photo album out of the box, but he couldn't quite face opening it and seeing all the memories on the pages.

And then a loose folder slipped out of the album onto the table.

It was small, square, glossy and white, and Marc knew that Laurie would realise exactly what it was. He sucked in a breath. He was going to have to tell her now, even though he wasn't ready and didn't have the right words.

And it felt as if someone had just opened his chest, reached in and was squeezing his heart.

## CHAPTER TEN

LAURIE recognised the type of folder instantly. She had one of those herself, tucked into Izzy's baby book.

Marc hadn't said anything about having children.

But now she had a horrible, horrible feeling that she knew why. And why he'd been so antsy around Izzy at first.

*Because he must have lost a child.*

And, difficult as it was to face, she knew they both had to face it. Pussyfooting around the truth would be the quickest way to let misunderstandings happen. 'That's a scan picture,' she said softly.

'Yes.' Marc closed his eyes. 'I should have told you before now. I just didn't have the right words to tell you the worst bit.' He blew out a breath. 'So I guess I owe you the whole truth this time. I'm sorry I didn't prepare you better. And I'll understand if...' His voice tailed off as if he couldn't bear to say any more.

But she knew him well enough now to be able to guess what he meant. He'd understand if she didn't want to see him any more.

'Don't build a bridge to trouble,' she said.

He opened his eyes again, looking tortured. 'Ginny was...' He stopped, as if the words were choking him, and his voice was hoarse when he resumed. 'She was pregnant when she was killed. We'd only had the dating scan three days before.'

So he hadn't just lost his wife, he'd lost his unborn child as well, Laurie thought. She remembered her own scan with Izzy; she'd been alone because Dean hadn't wanted to be there. Part of her had been thrilled to see the new life growing inside her, and part of her had worried that Dean would never come to terms with it. And he hadn't; he'd missed out on everything because he wasn't interested. Whereas Marc had been there at the scan for his baby; he'd missed out everything because it had been taken from him. Her heart ached for him.

'We hadn't told anyone about the baby. We wanted to wait until Ginny was at least twelve weeks and we'd had the scan. It felt like tempting fate to say anything before then,' Marc said. 'We'd planned to have both families over to our place the following weekend. We told them it was just because it was summer and we thought it'd be nice to get together. And we were so looking forward to telling our parents that they were going to be grandparents.' He dragged in a breath. 'But Ginny never got to do that. She never got the fuss she deserved from her mum and dad. I took that from her.'

Marc looked as if he was drowning in misery, and Laurie felt guilty for pushing him. He hadn't wanted to face the photographs, and now she could see why. It had clearly ripped the top off all his scars, and he was hurting again as if it had only just happened.

She wrapped her arms round him and held him close. 'It wasn't you that took it from her, it was the accident. Nothing about this was deliberate. And the accident took the baby from you, too. As well as the woman you loved. You're just as much a victim of this as she was.'

'I just wish I'd taken better care of her.'

'Nobody can change the past,' she said softly. 'You've been holding onto this for two years, Marc. Don't you think it's time you let go of the bad feelings and forgave yourself?'

He said nothing.

'Ginny loved you as much as you loved her, right?'

He nodded.

'So would she want to see you ripping your heart out like this?' Laurie asked. 'Would she want to see you drowning in misery and guilt?'

'I suppose not.'

'Exactly.' She paused. 'And you could always try looking at it the other way round. Supposing you'd been the one behind the steering-wheel when that other driver was on the wrong side of the road? Supposing you'd been killed and she'd walked away without a scratch? She would've been left to bring up the baby on her own. A single parent. Don't get me wrong—I don't regret having Izzy for a minute, not a single second, and she brings such joy to my life. But being a single parent isn't easy. Even if you have close family who'll support you and help out with babysitting, at the end of the day all the responsibilities are yours, and yours alone. You don't have someone to share the worries with, someone to talk over decisions with. You just have to hope that you're doing the right thing and then try not to beat yourself up about it if it turns out that you did the wrong thing. You have to recognise that you did your best at the time, and that expecting more of yourself in hindsight just isn't fair to anyone.'

He swallowed hard. 'I guess so.'

'On top of all that, would you have wanted Ginny to grieve for you for the rest of her life, forgetting all the good times you had together and only focusing on the stuff you didn't have time to do together?'

He was silent for a long, long time. 'No, of course not. I'd want her to be happy. To find someone else who'd love her as much as I did.'

'I didn't know her, but I'd guess that you married someone with as generous a spirit as you have. You need to forgive yourself, Marc, for her sake. Let yourself remember the good times without torturing yourself with might-have-beens.'

'I don't even know if we were going to have a boy or a girl—it was too early to tell—and...' He blew out a breath. 'He or she would've been a toddler now. Twenty months. Walking, just starting to chatter.'

'That's why you find it hard to be around children, outside work?'

He nodded. 'But your Izzy...she's so like you. Warm and sweet and accepting. And what she said on Saturday night...'

Laurie held him close. 'She meant it. She really likes you.'

'That's why I didn't want to get close to anyone. Because I'm terrified of making another mistake like that, letting someone else down.' He looked her straight in the eye. 'I'm scared of letting *you* down.'

'I've already been there,' she said, 'and I can tell you now that you're nothing like Dean. If anything, you're too far the other way and you're holding yourself responsible for things that nobody else would hold you responsible for.'

'Ginny's parents do,' he said. 'They blame me. They

said I should've been driving—I knew she was pregnant, and I should've looked after her better.'

'That's grief talking. Pain. And you were there with her at the end, so that makes you the one it's easiest for them to lash out at,' she said.

'I took their only child away from them. Their grand-child. Their future.'

'Not you. The accident,' she said again. 'There's a dif-ference. And I only wish I could make you see it.'

She stared at him, feeling frustrated and helpless. He was so unhappy, blaming himself and not letting himself see what he still had left in his life. Not letting himself see the hope. How could she reach him, make him realise that it wasn't his fault?

She reached up to kiss him, and the kiss turned heated as Marc responded, clearly needing the warmth that she could give him.

Laurie wasn't quite sure how they'd got there—whether he'd carried her or they'd stumbled together, still kissing and wrapped in each other—but the next thing she knew they were in his bed, skin to skin, and her arms were tightly round him as he entered her.

Afterwards, he held her close. 'I'm sorry, that wasn't fair of me.'

'Don't feel guilty. I was with you all the way.' She pressed a kiss against his bare shoulder.

'What's that noise?' he asked, frowning.

She listened, and recognised the tone instantly. 'The alarm on my phone. Which means I need to go and col-lect Izzy from Molly's mum.'

'Oh, help, and I didn't cook dinner for you as I prom-ised. I'm sorry. I've been really selfish.'

'No, you haven't. It's OK. I'm not desperately hungry,

and I can make myself an omelette or something later.' She touched his face and smiled. 'I think there was something else we both needed a little more than food.'

'Thank you. For understanding. For not judging.'

'Of course I'm not going to judge you. I'm not perfect. Nobody is.' She kissed him lightly and scrambled out of bed. 'I'd better get dressed. I'll see you tomorrow. But you can't change the past, Marc. You can only learn from it and make the future better. And remember what I said about Pandora. There was hope left in the box. You still have that. You just need to let yourself see it.'

On Wednesday evening, Laurie came home after seeing Marc.

'Did you have a good evening, Laurie?' Diane asked.

'Yes. Tonight was badminton.' She laughed. 'There are people who can do racquet sports, and then there's me, so although I joined in I was pretty rubbish. But some of the patients seemed to enjoy it, so I'm crossing my fingers that the badminton club might set up a beginners' league for them.'

'That's good.' Diane paused. 'How was Dr Bailey?'

'Fine.'

'So it was a good debriefing meeting, then?'

Laurie felt her eyes narrow. 'Is something wrong, Mum?'

'No. But your eyes are very sparkly tonight, love.'

Laurie frowned. 'No, they're not.'

'And you've been smiling an awful lot more lately,' Diane mused.

'I have no idea what you mean.'

Diane looked thoughtful. 'In fact, anyone looking at

you right now might think that you've recently been very thoroughly kissed.'

Laurie's hands flew to her face. She could feel her cheeks heating and knew that her face was bright red—and not from the badminton session either. 'I don't know what to say.'

'You're entitled to have some fun in your life, love. And Izzy likes him.'

Laurie gave up trying to pretend that she didn't know who her mother was talking about. 'How do you know?'

'She was telling me about him today—how he's your friend from work and he's new, like Molly in her class, so you're being kind and letting him go out with the two of you and Cocoa. Apparently, Cocoa likes him, too.'

The dog wagged his tail, as if to confirm it.

Laurie squirmed. 'Mum, I don't date loads of men and introduce Iz to a new "uncle" every week.'

'I know you don't, love.'

'And Marc's a nice guy.' Laurie took a deep breath. 'As far as she's concerned, we're just friends. Like her and Molly.'

'He lost his wife, didn't he? That's so sad, to lose someone so young.'

'Mmm,' Laurie said noncommittally. She wasn't going to betray any of Marc's confidences.

'So are your father and I going to meet him?'

Laurie blew out a breath. 'Mum, we're not dating officially.'

'Just unofficially.'

'We're taking it slowly,' Laurie said.

'All right. This Sunday. Lunch at one.'

'He might not be free.'

Diane smiled. 'I think he will be. Talk him into it. And

if that doesn't work, kiss him into it. It's what I do with your father.'

Laurie groaned. 'Mum, that's way too much information!'

Diane just laughed and hugged her. 'It's time you met someone nice. Someone who'll treat you a lot better than Dean did. And children and dogs tend to be good judges of character. If Izzy and Cocoa like him, that's a good thing.'

'And that's not enough for you?' Laurie asked helplessly.

'No. I want to meet him properly.'

The following morning, Laurie sent Marc a text: *Houston, we have a problem. Need to talk.*

His reply came straight back: *Duck pond at lunch?*
Perfect.

Tina raised her eyebrows at them in the patisserie. 'Lunching together again, Dr Grant and Dr Bailey? People will start to talk, you know.'

'We're discussing the project,' Laurie said loftily. 'Talking of which, did you give your mum the schedule?'

'Yes. And thanks for that; she's cheered up a bit. I think she's going to come on Wednesday night, though she's—well, she's being totally daft. She's worried about being the new girl.'

Laurie smiled. 'She'll know absolutely everyone there, so she won't count as new. Trust me, she'll enjoy it.'

They paid for their sandwiches, then headed for the duck pond.

'So what's the problem?' Marc asked.

'We've been rumbled,' she said.

He frowned. 'How do you mean?'

'Mum guessed. Last night. She, um, said that I looked as if I'd been kissed. Very thoroughly.'

'Ah. So we need to cool it?'

'Not exactly. But she's expecting you to arrive for Sunday lunch at one o'clock.'

For a moment, she thought he was going to make an excuse.

Then he nodded. 'OK. I'm driving. I'll pick you up at… how far away do your parents live?'

'Ten minutes from me. Your side of the village.'

'Twenty to one, then. To give us some wriggle room.'

'OK.' She could guess exactly why he wanted to drive; it would give him an excuse not to drink, without having to explain why.

Laurie felt incredibly nervous on the Sunday—more so even than the first time she'd taken Dean to meet her parents. This was going to be an important milestone. What if they didn't like Marc? She was pretty sure that wouldn't be the case—Marc had nice manners, plus he was genuinely one of the good guys—but, even so, the worry was there.

He arrived at twenty-five to one, and she put Izzy's seat in the back of his car.

'No, Cocoa, you can't come with us because you know Smudge won't like it,' Izzy told the dog solemnly.

'Who's Smudge?' Marc asked.

'Nanna and Granddad's cat. She's called Smudge because she's white and she has a big grey smudge across her nose.'

'Ah, right.' Marc handed Laurie a gorgeous bouquet of flowers.

'How lovely,' she said.

He smiled. 'Sorry, Dr Grant, they're not actually for

you—but I was hoping perhaps you could look after them while I'm driving.'

He'd thought to buy her mother flowers. Laurie's heart swelled. Yes, this was going to work out. Even though right at this moment he looked even more nervous than she did. 'She'll love them,' she said softly. 'And she'll like you.'

Marc didn't look convinced, and climbed into the driving seat.

Laurie directed him to her parents' house. As Izzy ran down the garden path to knock on the front door, she said softly, 'I'm sorry about this. I don't want it to be an ordeal for you—and we can leave any time you like. Give me the nod, and I'll do a fake call on my phone and say it's a patient.'

'Thank you.' He gave her a wry smile. 'Ginny's parents loathe me, but I guess they have a reason—yours don't.'

'Yet' was written all over his face.

She squeezed his hand briefly. 'It's going to be fine.'

Her parents were already at the door, waiting for them.

Laurie introduced them swiftly. 'Mum, Dad, this is Marc, my new colleague at the practice and brilliant co-coordinator of my pet project. Marc, these are my parents, Diane and Roderick Grant.'

Marc handed the flowers to Diane and a bottle of wine to Roderick.

'How lovely—thank you, Marc. Come and sit down,' Diane said, 'while I put these in water.'

'I'll come with you, Mum—Izzy and I made some cakes,' Laurie said.

'Can I get you a glass of wine, Marc?' Roderick asked.

'No, thanks—I'm driving,' Marc explained. 'But coffee or a soft drink would be lovely—whatever's easiest.'

'Fair enough.' Roderick looked approving, clearly relieved that Marc wasn't going to put his daughter and
granddaughter at risk.

When they sat down in the living room, the cat came
over and sniffed at him, then curled on his lap.

Diane stared at him in surprise. 'Smudge doesn't usually go anywhere near men except Roderick. She was
badly treated as a kitten. But she obviously likes you.'

'So does Cocoa—so do I,' Izzy piped up.

'And I like you and Cocoa too, Iz.' Marc made a fuss
of the cat and smiled. 'So Smudge is a rescue cat? Now
I know where Laurie gets her rescuing tendencies from.'

The conversation was easy over lunch, and Diane allowed Marc to help clear the table, though she shooed him
out of the kitchen. 'You don't have to wash up. That's what
dishwashers are for.'

They sat in the garden after lunch. Marc wasn't that
surprised when Laurie's brother Joe, sister-in-law Rose
and their children dropped in during the middle of the
afternoon, saying that they were 'just passing'. He'd expected to be under scrutiny by the whole family—and he
could understand why. Laurie had been hurt in the past
and they'd want to be sure that whoever she was seeing
would treat her properly.

But the atmosphere stayed relaxed and easy, and Izzy
had a whale of a time running around the garden with her
cousins. Marc was surprised to discover that he was enjoying himself, too. But at the same time it scared him. This
was almost too perfect, too good to be true. Laurie's family were accepting him as easily as Ginny's family had.
And yet it had gone so badly wrong with Ginny. What was
to say that this wasn't going to go wrong, too? Part of him
wanted to back away before that could happen.

And yet Laurie had already been badly let down. He didn't want to hurt her. He was going to have to be very, very careful.

When Marc drove Laurie and Izzy home later that evening, her phone beeped several times. He didn't ask, and she didn't look at the texts; but he could make an educated guess who they were from and what the subject was.

'Marc, will you read me my bedtime story tonight, please?' Izzy asked.

He knew he ought to make an excuse. Back off. Yet how could he resist those big brown eyes and that hopeful smile?

She persuaded him into reading her three stories, and then Laurie came up to kiss her goodnight.

'One more story? Please?' the little girl asked hopefully.

'No. You've had lots of stories from Marc already tonight. It's time to go to sleep now, or you'll be too tired at school tomorrow to play with Georgia and Molly,' Laurie said.

Izzy thought about it, then nodded and wriggled back under her covers. Though not until she'd had a kiss goodnight from both Laurie and Marc.

'I hope today wasn't too much of a trial,' Laurie said quietly when they went downstairs.

'No. Your family's lovely. They're very like you,' Marc said.

'They liked you, too. That's what the phone barrage was about.'

'I thought my ears were burning,' he said drily.

She laughed and kissed him. 'Mum says you're a sweetie, Rose says you're a keeper, and my brother wants to know your secret because the cat will never let Joe pick him up but was all over you.'

'So does that mean we're going public now?'

'Not quite—I've asked them to keep it to themselves for the time being. Though Mum will no doubt be talking to Fiona.' She rolled her eyes. 'Actually, I'm a bit surprised that she and Jay didn't "accidentally" call in as well as Joe and Rose this afternoon. Mum and Fiona have been having this campaign for months to make me date someone.' She laughed. 'They were even going to sign me up on a dating site until I had a hissy fit on them.'

'Hmm.' Marc paused. 'I guess you could meet my family. If you liked.'

She nodded. 'I'd like that.'

'It's time I invited them down. Maybe you could come for Sunday lunch?'

'That'd be great.' She kissed him. 'I just hope—well, that they won't mind me being a single parent. And that they won't think I'm using you.'

'They won't. And once they've met you and Izzy... Well, I think you'll bring as much of a sparkle to their lives as you do to mine.'

She held her breath. Was Marc about to declare himself?

She knew how she was beginning to feel about him, and she hoped that he felt the same way. That the fears about it all going wrong were starting to fade and he could see a potential future with her.

But when he moved the conversation onto a different topic, Laurie knew that she'd just have to stay patient for a little longer. Until he was ready.

# CHAPTER ELEVEN

'THE project,' Marc said when he and Laurie were eating their sandwiches by the duck pond on Monday lunchtime, 'might just have notched up its first success.'

'Who?'

'Mrs Reynolds. I saw her about her results today, and she's going to try exercise and lifestyle changes and review it again in a month. Obviously she gave me permission to tell you this.' He smiled. 'She's signed up to join the gym.'

'Neil's?'

He nodded. 'She, um, has similar views about him to yours. But apparently they offer one-to-one personal training sessions and some of the trainers are female. She's booking in appointments on the way home from work so it makes her turn up for it, and she had her induction session last week.'

'That's brilliant news.'

'And she says she would never have done it if you hadn't asked her to go along to the Wednesday sessions.'

'I'm so pleased. This is the sort of thing that really makes our job worthwhile, knowing we've actually made a difference,' Laurie said, beaming at him.

'That's what I told her, Dr Fixit,' Marc said with a smile. 'And I said you'd be as pleased as I was.'

'I'm so going to give her a hug on Wednesday,' Laurie said. 'That's made my day.'

'It's a lovely house. Ginny—' Peggy Bailey stopped short and looked nervously at her son.

'Ginny would've loved it,' Marc finished. 'The garden, the fact it's old and full of character, the view.'

She looked at him in wonder. 'You actually said her name.'

'I can do that now.' It still made him ache inside, and he knew that he'd never quite stop missing her, but he was ready to move on.

'So you're really happy here?' Peggy asked.

'Your mother's worried about you,' Donald said. 'Because you moved a hundred miles away, among strangers. At least in London you knew people.'

'And I had too many memories,' Marc said gently. 'Here, it's a new start for me. I like the people I work with, I like the people around here, and I'm really enjoying my job.'

'That's good. All you need is—' Peggy bit back the words. 'Sorry. I won't say it.'

Marc smiled. 'It's OK, Mum. I know what you're going to say. All I need is to meet someone. Not to forget Ginny, but someone who'll help me move on.'

'Well, yes.' She gave him a hug. 'I'm sorry. I know you're thirty-five, not five, and you're very clever and you're capable of doing anything you choose—but I'm your mother. I can't help worrying about you.'

Just as Laurie worried about Izzy. 'I'm not going to give you a hard time about it, Mum.'

'I notice you've got your photographs up. You haven't had them out since—well...' she finished awkwardly.

'Since Ginny's funeral, when I took them down because I couldn't face them. I know. And I shut you, Dad and Vonnie out afterwards. I'm sorry.' He blew out a breath. 'It was the only way I could cope and keep myself going.'

'You do look happier here,' Donald said.

'I am,' Marc said. And they'd meet the reasons why, very shortly.

He finished showing them round the house.

'The table's set for five,' Peggy noted as they reached the dining room.

'I was coming to that. I've invited a couple of people round—people I'd like you to meet.'

Peggy's eyes widened. 'Marc, are you seeing someone?'

'Yes, but it's complicated. Laurie and I are keeping it quiet at the moment. Not because we're ashamed of what we're doing, but because we're taking things gently and because she has her little girl to think of.'

'A little girl.' There was a film of tears in Peggy's eyes.

'Mum.' Marc hugged her. 'I know. But Izzy's older than…' He couldn't quite bring himself to say the words. 'She's five. And she's a sweetie. I'm pretty sure you'll both like them.'

'Do you love her?'

'I'm not ready to answer that one yet, Mum,' he said gently. 'But we'll see how it goes.'

A quarter of an hour before lunch, the doorbell rang. Marc ushered Laurie and Izzy inside and introduced them swiftly to his parents. 'Laurie, Izzy—these are my parents, Peggy and Donald Bailey. Mum, Dad, this is my friend and colleague Laurie Grant and her daughter Isobel—though everyone calls her Izzy.'

'We made you some special cakes for tea,' Izzy said.

'With lots of sprinkles, I hope,' Marc said.

She nodded. 'Lots and lots and lots. I did one with an M on it, 'specially for you.

He ruffled her hair. 'Thank you, sweetheart.'

Laurie had some idea of how nervous Marc had been about meeting her family, because she felt the same about meeting his. Although she'd always got on well with Dean's family, this was different, and she really hoped that Marc's parents wouldn't compare her to Ginny.

But Peggy and Donald turned out to be really easy to talk to. And they were naturals with children, she thought; Peggy asked Izzy about school, and taught her how to draw cats—a skill that Laurie knew Izzy was going to love sharing with Georgia and Molly.

'So you work together?' Peggy asked over lunch.

'Yes, and Marc's helping me out with my pet project— preventative medicine. It's aimed at people who are at risk of developing diabetes and heart conditions. We've been setting up taster exercise sessions and talks from experts, and so far the project's going really well. Even though the summer holidays are coming up, everyone's making an effort to be there on Wednesday nights.' She smiled at Peggy. 'That cat you drew for Izzy was amazing. Obviously I had to draw some diagrams, to get through med school, but it's not my strongest suit.'

'I was an art teacher, before I retired,' Peggy said.

'I like art,' Izzy chipped in. 'We made pottery hedgehogs at school. They're being cooked in a special oven at middle school next week, and then we're going to paint them. We all had to think of names starting with H. Mine's called Horatio.'

At teatime, Peggy and Donald were impressed with

Izzy's sparkly cupcakes, and Laurie had to promise to email Peggy the recipe for her lemon cake.

Laurie was surprised at how quickly the time went. 'We have to go, young lady,' she said to Izzy.

'Already?'

'Yes, because I need to wash your hair tonight, and you know it takes ages to dry. Plus you've got school tomorrow.'

Izzy nodded. 'I've had a lovely time. Thank you for having us, Marc,' she said politely.

'My pleasure, Iz. And thank you for the cakes. Especially for my one.'

'My pleasure,' she echoed. 'It's the holidays soon, and Mummy says we can go to the beach and go swimming lots and lots.' She hugged him. 'Will you come crabbing with us again?'

'Sure I will. Come on, I'll give you a piggyback to the car.' He bent down so she could climb onto his back. 'Ready—one, two, three!'

When Laurie and Izzy had gone, Peggy said, 'They're lovely, both of them. And they both clearly think a lot of you.' She paused. 'Can I tell Vonnie?'

'I'd rather do that myself,' Marc said. 'I was thinking about inviting her here in the school holidays.'

'She'd love that,' Donald said.

'And I'm so glad to see you with a smile in your eyes again,' Peggy said. 'I missed that. And anyone who can put the smile back in your eyes is more than OK with me.'

Marc called Laurie later, after his parents had left. 'You made a hit with my parents.' He paused. 'I was thinking about asking my sister to stay in the school holidays. Would you be OK about meeting her?'

'Of course, and you're being nice and letting me meet everyone gradually. I'm afraid you got the whole lot of my family at once.'

'Well, they live nearby. Mine live a long way away.'

'I liked your mum and dad. So did Izzy; she says your mum has nice hair.'

He laughed. 'I'll tell her; she'll be pleased. I'll see you at work tomorrow.'

The middle of the month saw the twelve-week point of the project.

'Today's not so much an exercise session as a time to review how things are going and sort out another week of measuring your exercise levels and how they've changed,' Laurie said with a smile. 'Marc and I will be checking your weight, your blood pressure and taking a blood sample so the lab can tell us your cholesterol levels. Next week we'll be able to give you the overall group results, as well as giving you a private letter with your personal results.'

'And then it's the last week of the project,' Marc said. 'Which I guess might make it easier for some of you, as it's almost the end of term.'

There were general groans. 'Can we extend the project?' Frank Riley asked. 'Because I'm really enjoying this and I don't want to stop.'

'Me neither,' Judy Reynolds agreed. 'I'm feeling much better than I was three months ago. And I'm definitely doing more exercise.'

'I'm walking my neighbour's dog for her,' Peter Jackson chipped in.

'And I'm eating better. I did a food diary, and I couldn't

believe how much I was eating between meals. I don't now,' Carrie Baker said. 'And I eat a lot more fish. I didn't think I liked fish, but once you've used a few herbs and spices…well, it's not so bad.'

'Carrie, I've got a really good recipe for sweet chili salmon,' Judy Reynolds said. 'I'll write it down for you and bring it next week.'

'They've really gelled as a group,' Laurie said when she and Marc were packing everything away at the end of a session. 'I love the way they're swapping recipes and encouraging each other.'

'And they want to continue,' Marc said.

'There was some research I read, a couple of years back, that it takes just over two months on average to form a habit—obviously it depends on what the habit is, because some things in the study took longer and some took a lot less. I guess we've got them into the exercise habit. But it'd be a shame to pull the support away now,' Laurie said. 'Would you mind keeping it going for a bit longer—say, until the end of the school holidays?'

He stole a kiss. 'That's fine with me, Dr Fixit.'

'Great. I'll sort out the hall booking tomorrow.'

'And then maybe next week we can find out which of the activities they liked best and see if we can get those people back for more sessions,' Marc suggested.

'Good idea.' She smiled at him. 'I've really loved doing this. It's made a difference.'

'And we work well as a team.' Marc held her gaze. 'We're good together, Laurie.'

And she had the distinct feeling that he didn't just mean professionally. Which was good, because that was how she was beginning to feel about him, too. It was scary, thinking about trusting someone—but she knew he wasn't Dean. He wouldn't let her down. Wouldn't abandon her.

But she wouldn't push just yet. Taking it slowly was working just fine for both of them.

The following week, they collected in the monitors.

'I've got your individual results here,' Laurie said, 'but I'd like to tell you how you've done as a group. On average, you've lost more than ten pounds each, your blood pressure has improved by ten points, your resting pulse is down by five beats a minute and your cholesterol levels are down one and a half points. Obviously, that's an average, but I don't want any of you to feel disappointed with how you've done, because *all* of you are showing an improvement in your health.'

'And we're happy to keep the sessions going until the end of the summer holidays, if you are,' Marc said.

'Absolutely!' Judy Reynolds said with a grin. 'And we really appreciate it, Dr Bailey.'

'Good, because now we want to know which activities you enjoyed most, so we can get people back again,' Marc said. 'And, if enough of you are interested, we might be able to get some beginners' classes sorted out for the start of the new term.'

The summer, Laurie thought, was one of the best she could ever remember. The sun seemed to shine every day; being school holidays, she was able to spend more time with Izzy, and sneak in more time with Marc as well.

Yvonne, Marc's sister, came to stay with Marc for a week; Laurie liked her instantly, and Izzy adored her to the point where she asked if Yvonne could come to be the new teacher at school, because Mrs Richards was leaving to have a baby.

It was the happiest Laurie had ever been. Now Marc had opened up to her, she was falling in love with him. She loved his dry sense of humour, his willingness to spend time with Izzy, the way he was good with her dog and her parents' rescue cat.

Marc Bailey was the kind of man she'd always dreamed of being with. Patient, kind and loving. Her family liked him, and his family liked her.

Perhaps it was time to talk to Izzy, to see how she'd feel about Marc taking a bigger role in their lives. Time that she stopped being a coward and worrying that it was all going to go wrong.

Because what could go wrong?

The following week, when term had started again, Laurie felt a bit queasy. She knew there weren't any sicky bugs doing the rounds; Izzy seemed fine, so it probably wasn't anything she'd eaten or Izzy would've been complaining of feeling sick, too. And there was a metallic taste in her mouth.

Or maybe it was the pine nuts she'd had in the pesto the other night. She'd had a couple of patients coming in saying that everything tasted awful, and one of them had brought in an article about 'pine mouth'. It seemed that the taste disturbance occurred a couple of days after you'd eaten pine nuts and lasted for a couple of weeks, but other than that there was no lasting harm. Well, she'd just avoid pine nuts for a while and put up with it.

But the day after that her bra felt uncomfortable and her breasts were sore.

If it wasn't for the fact that Laurie had had her period as normal last month, she'd think she was pregnant.

Which was totally ridiculous. She and Marc had used condoms. Of course she couldn't be pregnant.

Or could she? Now she thought about it, her last period had been a bit on the light side. And there had been one time where a condom had broken; she'd meant to do something about the morning-after pill, but had forgotten.

Oh, help.

Izzy hadn't been a planned baby either.

Just supposing…?

She couldn't get the idea out of her head all day. No way could she get a test from the pharmacy attached to the surgery; she didn't want anyone to know about this. In the end, she drove five miles away to the supermarket; and, just to make sure she didn't see anyone she knew who might glance into her basket and see what she was buying, she covered the test with a newspaper until she reached the self-service tills, and ran the test over the bar code reader as quickly as possible.

Luckily Tina had invited Izzy and Molly to tea with Georgia, so Laurie didn't have to wait until Izzy was asleep before doing the test. She drove home, went to the bathroom, did the test, and waited.

One blue line appeared in the test window, to tell her it had worked.

She kept looking at the window, with one eye on the second hand of her watch to check the time. After two minutes there was no second line. She breathed a sigh of relief. Of course she wasn't pregnant. This was obviously some weird kind of bug.

She turned away to wash her hands, then took some

toilet paper to wrap round the test, intending to bury it at the bottom of the bin.

She stopped dead.

Somehow, when she'd looked away, another blue line had appeared on the test.

How? How could it just have appeared out of nowhere?

Especially as it wasn't even a faint line—it was a wide, strong line.

The test was positive. Very, very positive.

She was pregnant.

# CHAPTER TWELVE

LAURIE went cold.

Pregnant.

She closed the lid on the toilet seat and sat down, wrapping her arms around herself, but the cold feeling wouldn't go away.

Pregnant.

And this wasn't a planned baby.

This was where her life had all gone wrong last time. When she'd found out that she was accidentally pregnant, it had signalled the end of her relationship with Dean.

OK, so Marc was nothing like Dean; but she knew he had issues about children. He'd looked broken inside when he'd told her about the unborn baby he'd lost in the accident. Would the news of her pregnancy bring everything back to him and make him crumble? Was she putting her trust in someone who wouldn't be able to cope with a baby—the same mistake she'd made before?

Marc seemed to have grown close to Izzy, but that was different. This was a pregnancy. It would bring back difficult memories for him—memories of the scan he'd gone to with Ginny, the accident, and everything he'd lost. Laurie couldn't help panicking that everything was going to go wrong when he found out.

She had to find a way to tell him. But right at that moment she had absolutely no idea how to break the news. How to soften it. How he'd react.

She made excuses to avoid him at work; and on the Wednesday night she claimed she had a headache, saying that she needed an early night and maybe they could catch up on the project later.

And please, please, let her find the right way of telling him that she was pregnant with his baby.

Something was wrong with Laurie, Marc was sure. He wasn't the paranoid sort, but she was definitely avoiding him, both at work and outside.

He didn't have a clue what was wrong, and his imagination was working overtime. Was she ill? Maybe she didn't want to worry him?

Or had she decided that she didn't want to take their relationship any further, and was slowly freezing him out? Though he didn't think that was her style; Laurie was direct about everything. She hated people pussyfooting about, and said that was the quickest way for misunderstandings to happen and cause problems.

When she'd made the excuse of yet another headache on the Friday night, Marc decided that enough was enough. He went to the supermarket and bought the nicest bouquet available: pink gerberas; purple sweet-scented stocks; white carnations; and white roses with the most delicate pink edging. Flowers he knew she'd adore. And hopefully they would persuade her to talk to him.

He knew Izzy would be in bed at this time of night. He didn't want Cocoa to bark madly and wake the little girl, so instead of knocking on the front door he rang Laurie's mobile.

She sounded wary. 'Marc?'

'We need to talk,' he said. 'I know Izzy's asleep, so rather than me ringing the bell and making the dog bark his head off, can you let me in?'

'Where are you?'

'Outside. In my car. And I'm not budging until you let me in and talk to me.'

He heard her sigh. 'OK.'

He'd locked his car door and was waiting outside by the time she undid the front door. He handed her the flowers.

'They're lovely, but you didn't need to buy me flowers.'

'Yes, I did,' he corrected. 'Something's wrong, Laurie. I don't know if it's something I've done or said, or something I've omitted to do or say—but something's wrong and I'm totally clueless about it. Talk to me. Tell me what's wrong, and we can fix it.'

She bit her lip. 'It's not exactly something you can fix.'

He felt his eyes widen. 'You're ill?'

'No.'

He blew out a breath. 'Thank God for that. I was worried you were sick. Though, obviously, if you were, I'd support you and do whatever I could to help.'

She shook her head. 'It's not that.'

He had to face this head on. 'Or that you'd changed your mind about us and didn't want to see me any more, except as a colleague.'

She bit her lip. 'No-o.'

Her expression and the tone of her voice didn't bode well. He took a deep breath. 'OK. Hit me with it.'

'Come and sit down in the kitchen while I put these in water.'

He noticed that she hadn't offered him a drink, and that definitely wasn't usual behaviour for Laurie. She was clearly nerving herself to tell him something but what, he had absolutely no idea. She'd said that she hadn't changed her mind about them—or had she changed her mind and didn't know how to tell him?

He waited until she'd finished fiddling with the flowers.

And then, finally, she sat down opposite him. Not next to him or on his lap, he noticed, but opposite him.

This wasn't going to be good.

'There isn't an easy way to say this, Marc.'

Right. So she *was* breaking up with him.

He did his best to keep his voice neutral. 'So don't try to make it easy. Give it to me straight.'

She took a deep breath. 'I'm pregnant.'

*Pregnant?*

*With his baby?*

Marc felt as if someone had just punched him hard in the gut, and he couldn't breathe.

She was pregnant.

The last time he'd had news like this, he'd been thrilled to bits. He and Ginny had tried for a baby for six months, and Ginny had been worrying that maybe something was wrong because several of her friends had fallen pregnant the first month they'd tried. He'd been so pleased. So looking forward to having their baby, seeing the first smile and hearing the first giggle and the first word.

And then his life had gone into meltdown.

This wasn't the same. It wasn't remotely the same. He and Laurie weren't married—they weren't even a couple, as far as most of the outside world knew—and they hadn't been trying for a baby. There was no reason to think that his life would be hit by the same tragedy twice over.

But right now all he could see was the car coming towards them. Hear the crash. Glass splintering. The scrape of metal on metal. Ginny's head going forward. Everything echoey and muffled, as if he was under deep water. All in slow motion, as if he was living through it all again and this time he was even more powerless because he knew exactly what was going to happen and he couldn't do a thing to stop it.

Bile rose in his throat. He couldn't deal with this. Not here. Not now.

'I need some air,' he said, pushed his chair back, and left.

Laurie was too numb to move. But she heard the front door close quietly behind Marc.

*He'd gone.*

And she'd made the same mistake all over again. She'd fallen for a man who couldn't commit to her. She'd fallen for a man who didn't want a child. Who'd walked out on her.

True, Marc wasn't Dean. He hadn't been unfaithful to her or ignored Izzy.

But he'd still abandoned her as soon as she'd told him that she was pregnant. Just as Dean had when she'd told him the news. Yet again she'd put her trust in the wrong man.

'I'm such an idiot,' she said.

Cocoa put his paws on her knee and licked her face.

That was when the tears finally came. Laurie wrapped her arms round the dog, buried her face in his fur, and sobbed.

She'd known that Marc would find the news difficult to take. He'd lost his unborn child in the accident, along with Ginny, so of course the idea of a new baby would bring all that grief to the forefront.

Though she'd thought—*hoped*—that he'd be able to push it aside and focus on the fact that they were having a baby. That they could have a future together, as a family. Izzy had bonded with him, her family liked him, and his family liked her. They had a real chance of making this thing between them work.

But obviously Marc was never going to get over the past. Not that she would ever expect him to sweep his memories of Ginny into a mental box, never to be opened again—that would be wrong, because he'd loved his wife and she was part of his past, part of what had shaped him as a man. Laurie had really hoped that he could find it within himself to move on. That he felt enough for her to be able to leave his sadness behind and just remember the good bits about his past.

The night air wasn't cool. It was sticky and cloying, and Marc felt as if he was choking as he leaned against his car. No way could he walk back inside that house and give Laurie the reassurance he knew she needed.

He knew he was behaving badly. He was being a total and utter jerk. Dean had abandoned Laurie practically from the moment she'd told him she was pregnant with Izzy—and here he was, doing exactly the same thing.

Not that Marc intended to abandon Laurie. He'd do the right thing by her. Of *course* he would.

But he really needed to get his head round the situation and be able to think straight before he could talk to her.

And, to get his head round it, it meant he finally had to come to terms with the past.

He reached for his mobile phone. *I'm sorry.*

And then he stopped tapping in the text message. What could he possibly say? He couldn't make this all right. He couldn't walk in and tell her that everything was going to be fine, because right now he was a wreck and he couldn't think straight. He'd say completely the wrong thing and make the situation even worse. He knew he needed to reassure her, but the words wouldn't come. His brain felt sealed up with panic.

Thank God that it was Friday night and he didn't have to struggle through work tomorrow. If it took him the whole night, sitting up and thinking, he'd find the right words. And then he'd talk to her.

He climbed into his car. But instead of driving back to the cottage, he found himself going to the garage to fill his car up with petrol. And then he headed for the place he knew he really needed to go to sort his head out.

London.

He knew he could ring his parents and ask for a bed for the night, but it was going to be late by the time he got to London and it would be unfair to disturb them. Plus, if he was honest with himself, he didn't really want to talk to anyone about the situation with Laurie. He just needed to be alone with his thoughts.

He pulled into the next lay-by, rang one of the roadside hotel chains and booked a room over the phone with his credit card.

Laurie couldn't sleep. Every time she closed her eyes, she saw the shock on Marc's face as she'd told him about the baby, followed by the distress and the way he'd almost gagged.

*I need some air.*

Except he hadn't come back. And his mobile phone was switched off. He'd made it very, very clear that he didn't want to know.

What was she going to do? How was she going to explain to Izzy that Marc was out of their lives now? She'd just made the mistake she'd always promised she'd never make, and now her daughter was going to pay for it. Laurie knew that the little girl adored Marc, and she'd be devastated about not seeing him again.

What a mess. Worse still, it wasn't fixable. And somehow she was going to have to find the words to explain to her daughter that Izzy was going to be a big sister, but the baby's daddy wasn't going to be there for any of them.

She curled into a ball, her hands cradled round her stomach. 'I'm not very good at picking daddies,' she said softly to the tiny life inside her. 'But I promise you I'm going to be the best mum in the world to you, and Izzy's going to be the best sister ever. You're not going to miss out on any of the love or any of the things your father can't give you. Because we'll be there.'

If only Marc could've been there for her…

Marc barely slept. Every time he closed his eyes, he saw the accident again. Or the misery on Laurie's face as she told him the news. And no matter how many times he turned over in bed, or pummelled his pillow, he couldn't get comfortable. He couldn't find the words he needed either.

Early the next morning, he went to the open-air market near his old house, knowing that it would be another hour or so before the shops opened and not wanting to wait that long.

To his relief, the florist on the market stall was able to make him a hand-tied arrangement with its own water supply. And when he walked into the churchyard and saw the fresh flowers in the vase on Ginny's grave—proof that her parents had visited very recently—he was glad he'd thought of something that didn't need a vase. He didn't want to displace anything of theirs; he just wanted to give his late wife something of his own.

He placed the flowers on the grave, and sat down cross-legged next to them. 'Freesias, irises and delphiniums. They were always your favourites,' he said softly. And then it was as if a dam had broken and the words spilled out. 'I know I haven't visited you for a while, but I needed to move away, to make a fresh start where I didn't start every day in a black hole thinking that you were just in another room in the house and you'd walk through our bedroom door any second—and when you didn't it was like losing you all over again. And I haven't stopped thinking about you, even though I'm more than a hundred miles away from London.' He paused. 'Gin, I could really do with some of your common sense. I've been given a second chance of happiness, and I've really messed it up.'

He sighed. 'I've met someone. It doesn't mean I'm going to forget you—you're always going to be part of me—but if I were you and you were me, I wouldn't want you to be on your own. I'd want you to meet someone who'd make you happy again and love you as much as I do. And I know that's how it is for you, too.' He stared at the headstone. 'I wanted to make a family with you so much. I should never have left it so late. And I'm sorry I didn't look after you better.'

The brightness of the early morning had given way to clouds. Well, he didn't care if it rained and he got wet. He needed to talk to Ginny. Sort this out in his head.

'You'd like Laurie,' he said. 'In another life, you would've been friends and you'd probably have taught her little girl. Maybe our little girl or boy would've been best friends with Izzy. But that life never happened. We didn't have that chance. And I never thought I'd find love again.'

And then it hit him.

That was exactly what he'd found.

*Love.*

He really did love Laurie.

He'd fallen in love with her sweetness, her kindness, the dimple in her cheek when she smiled. And she made him feel as if the world was a different place. A better place.

It shocked him to the core. All these weeks he'd been telling himself that they were just having a good time together, that his heart wasn't involved and his barriers were still in place.

Wrong, wrong, wrong. Without him even noticing, they'd melted away, as softly as early-morning mist when the sun came out.

He wasn't sure if it made him feel more exhilarated or terrified. He loved Laurie. They could be happy together. A future full of warmth and laughter and having someone to share the tough bits. It could be wonderful.

And it could all disappear in a second.

Was love worth the risk?

But it was too late to put his barriers up again now. She was in his heart. Along with Izzy. And he knew with rushing certainty that he wanted to be a family with them, and their new baby, and Cocoa.

Or had he just lost that chance?

He raked a hand through his hair. 'I don't know how it happened. *When* it happened. We were just friends. And then…suddenly she was more than that. She's not a replacement for you. She's—well, she's just herself. She has her own place in my life.' He blew out a breath. 'Except I've really messed it up. And I'm not sure if it's fixable.'

He could almost hear Ginny's soft voice telling him to go on.

'It's not tactful telling you this in the circumstances— but you're the one who needs to know,' he said. 'Laurie's going to have a baby. My baby. We didn't plan it. And I've been so selfish and left her waiting, because I don't know what to say and I can't quite get my head around it.'

Why? What was stopping him? The questions echoed in his head as clearly as if she was actually talking to him.

He had to be honest with himself, too. 'It scares me stupid that I could lose her and our baby, the way I lost you, and bits of me think maybe I shouldn't take the risk.' He sighed. 'And bits of me… I want to make a family with her, Gin. I want Izzy to call me "Dad". I want to take the chance of happiness with both hands and hold it close.' He paused. 'I know I didn't take care of you the way I should've done. This is like a second chance for me. Is it so bad of me to want to take it?'

Silence. Well, of course. How would he get an answer?

'I love her, Gin. It's not the same as it was with you. I'm older, we haven't known each other for so long, and there's still a lot about her that surprises me. But I know I'll be happy with her. And I know that you'd love her too. I want to spend the rest of my life with her. *If* she'll have me.'

The sun came out and shone straight into his eyes. It was almost, he thought, as if Ginny was giving him her blessing.

'Thank you,' he said quietly. 'I might not come and see you here that often, but you're not just here in the church-yard. You're here, too. Always.' He placed his hand over his heart. 'And I'll grow delphiniums for you in my garden and think of you when they bloom.' He stood up, pressed his fingers to his mouth and then to her head-stone. 'God bless.'

Back at his car, Marc called Laurie. When her landline went through to the answering-machine, he hung up. This wasn't something he could say in a message. He needed to say it to her.

Was she out, or was she call-screening? He wouldn't blame her if it was the latter. But he tried her mobile anyway.

For a moment, he thought it was going to go through to voicemail. But then she answered. 'Hello?'

She sounded terrible, her voice cracked and strained by lack of sleep. Which was all his fault.

'Laurie, it's Marc.' Stupid. She'd already know that from his name flashing up on the screen of her phone.

'Where are you?' she asked.

'In London.' Honesty compelled him to add, 'I've just been to Ginny's grave.'

'Oh.'

'We need to talk.'

'Right now,' she said, 'I'm not too sure if I want to talk to you.'

'I don't blame you. I've been a complete idiot, and I'm so sorry. But I'm not Dean. I know I walked out on you last night, and I shouldn't have done that. I panicked. I'm completely in the wrong. And I want to apologise to you properly.'

She said nothing, but he heard a tiny sob, quickly muffled.

'Laurie, I'm sorry. I reacted badly. I don't have an excuse, but I needed to get my head around—well, several things. I'm driving home now. And I know I deserve absolutely nothing from you, but right now I really want to hold you. To make things right between us. Can I come and see you?'

She gulped. 'Yes.'

Should he tell her how he felt about her right now? Or should he wait so she could see his face and know he meant it?

He decided to wait. 'I'll see you soon. And everything's going to be all right, Laurie. I promise.'

'Don't make promises you can't keep.'

'This one I can definitely keep,' he said softly.

'Drive safely. Don't—don't take any risks.'

'I won't. Take risks, I mean. I'll be home as soon as I can.'

The traffic was terrible, but eventually he made it back to Norfolk and parked outside Laurie's house.

'Where's Izzy?' he asked when she opened the door.

'With my parents. I didn't want her overhearing any of this.'

'You look terrible.' Her eyes were red and swollen, and she'd obviously spent much of the night crying.

She lifted her chin. 'I told Izzy—and my parents— that I had a cold.'

Guilt flooded through him. She was pregnant, and he should've taken care of her, not left her to get on with it and be miserable.

'I'm so sorry.' He touched her cheek with the backs of his fingers. 'Do you want me to get you a cold flannel for your eyes?'

'No.' Her mouth thinned. 'You said we needed to talk.'

He exhaled sharply. 'We do.'

'You'd better come in.' She stepped to the side, and her body language was screaming, Don't touch. And even

Cocoa was looking at him reproachfully, rather than wagging his tail and insisting on having his tummy rubbed.

Marc knew it was what he deserved. He followed her into the kitchen; when she sat down, he did the same.

'Firstly, I'm sorry about last night. I panicked.'

'I noticed.'

'I'm not making an excuse. What I did was unfair to you. And I'm scared I'm going to say the wrong thing now and hurt you. I don't mean to.'

'You don't want to know about the baby. You've already made that clear.'

'No. That's not it at all.' He blew out a breath. 'I owe you total honesty, Laurie. Some of it might be painful. But I guess this is a warts-and-all conversation. Will you hear me out?'

She was silent for so long that he thought she was going to tell him to leave.

And then she nodded.

'I've been here before, Laurie. The thrill of knowing that I'm going to be a dad, all the plans and the love and the joy. And then the black hole when I lost Ginny and the baby. And last night... It just brought everything back. The crash. How I felt. The yawning emptiness. I panicked. That's why I walked out. Not because I don't want you or the baby or Izzy—I do, I want *all* of you—but because that potential of loss scares me stupid.'

'There's always a risk of losing something. But if you stand on the sidelines and you never take that risk, then you've lost it all anyway,' she pointed out.

'Yes. You're right. Last night, I should've pushed all of that out of my head. And what I should've told you—'

'No.' She shook her head. 'Don't say anything you don't mean. I've been here before.'

'No, you haven't. Not with me. Laurie…I love you.'

She stared at him, looking shocked. 'You love me?'

'I have done for ages. Probably since I first met you, but I've been in denial about a lot of things so I can't be sure of that. But I've definitely loved you all summer. Maybe since Izzy and I made that ice-cream sundae together.'

Her eyes were suspiciously shiny, and he knew she was close to crying. 'Oh, Marc. I love you, too. Except…I'm scared,' she whispered.

'I know. But I'm not Dean. I know I left last night, because I was overwhelmed and I was selfish and put my needs before yours. But I want to make that right now. And I can assure you that I'm not planning to dump you. Or to go off with any of our patients.'

'I know you wouldn't be unfaithful. You're not the type.' She lifted her chin. 'But are you going to walk out on me every time it gets tough? Because if you are, I'm better off without you. I'm not putting Izzy on a roller-coaster like that. Or the baby. Or me.'

He deserved that, he knew. 'No, I'm not. I can't prove it to you, but last night was different. This morning I got my head together, I'm ready to move on from the past. It still scares me stupid that I could lose you and the baby, but you're right—it's worth the risk.'

'Are you sure?'

'I'm sure. And it doesn't matter that we didn't plan to have this baby,' Marc said. 'I want to be a family with you and Izzy and her little brother or sister. And it's not to replace Ginny or the baby I never got to meet, before you start thinking that. This is *our* baby. And I want the three of you—and Cocoa—more than you'll ever know.'

This time the tears spilled down her cheeks. 'Oh, Marc.'

He went round to her side of the table, scooped her up

and settled her on his lap. 'We need to go public now,' he said. 'I want the world to know I'm your partner. And I want to be Izzy's dad.'

Her eyes brightened with hope. 'Really?'

'Really. It isn't about being a biological parent, it's all about being there—and I'm going to be there for all of you. You, Izzy, our baby, Cocoa. I'm going to be there.'

'Oh, Marc.' She rested her head on his shoulder and wept.

He held her close. 'Don't cry, honey.'

'It must be hormones.' Her voice was shaky. 'I'm never this wet.'

'I know. You've had to be strong and independent for so long—but now you can share the worries with me.' He stroked her hair. 'I should be doing this in a fancy restaurant or under the stars or when the sun's setting over the sea—but I don't want to wait to ask you. If Izzy gives me her permission, will you marry me?'

She cried even harder, and Marc panicked.

'What's wrong? Don't you want to marry me?'

'Yes, I do—of course I do—but you're going to ask Izzy.' She dragged in a breath. 'You care about her feelings.'

'Of course I do. It's a big thing for her. She's had you all to herself for her entire life, and having to share you might be hard for her. I want to reassure her that she's not sharing you, she's getting me as well. And if Izzy wants me to be her dad, I'd be hugely, hugely proud.' He kissed her gently. 'And then I guess I need to ask your dad's permission.'

Laurie's smile was slightly wobbly, but it made him feel as if the sun had come out. 'I have a feeling you'll get it.'

* * *

The next day, Marc took Izzy to feed the ducks.

'You're my friend, right?' he asked.

She nodded, beaming. 'You're one of my best friends.'

Now for the big question. 'How would you like to be my daughter as well as my friend?'

She looked thoughtful, and was silent for a long, long time, just throwing bread to the ducks. 'No,' she said eventually.

Marc felt sick. He'd thought that he got on well with the little girl; but if he didn't have Izzy's blessing there was no way he could marry Laurie. It just wouldn't work. 'Why not?' he asked, careful to keep his voice neutral.

'It's not because I don't like you,' she said, 'but I don't want to leave Mummy and live with you. She'd be lonely without me, even though she has Cocoa.'

Marc nearly dropped to his knees in relief. He smiled. 'You don't have to leave your mum, Izzy. What I mean is that I'd like to marry your mum and make you my daughter, so you'd be Izzy Bailey rather than Izzy Grant. Your mum would be Dr Bailey, like me. And we'd all live together with Cocoa.'

'So you'd be my real daddy?' she asked.

'If you want me to be, yes.'

'And I could—' Her eyes widened. 'I could call you Daddy?'

He wrapped her in a hug. 'I'd love that. I'd be so proud to be your dad, Iz.'

She hugged him back. 'Does that mean I'll have a little brother or sister? Matthew in my class, his mum got married last year and now he's got a baby sister.'

'I'll see what I can do,' Marc said. He and Laurie had agreed to wait a little while before telling Izzy about the baby, but he could reassure Laurie now that that particular worry was out of the way. 'Shall we go and tell your mum the good news?'

'You bet!'

Laurie's family, predictably, was delighted to hear the news. So was Marc's. As the news spread in the village, Laurie was overwhelmed with good wishes from everyone.

But there were still shadows in Marc's eyes, and she had a pretty good idea why.

'I think,' she said softly, 'we need to call in a favour from my parents and get them to look after Iz for the weekend.'

'Why?'

'Because you need to make your peace with Ginny's parents.' She took a deep breath. 'And there's something I need to do. A promise I need to make. To Ginny.'

Marc held her close. 'You're amazing. Do you know that?'

'Keep telling me. I'm happy to hear it.' She kissed him. 'You're amazing, too. And this is going to work out just fine.'

# CHAPTER THIRTEEN

THE following weekend, Marc and Laurie visited Ginny's grave together.

She knelt down by the grave. 'In another life, we would've been friends and our children would've played together,' she said softly. 'Marc's always going to love you. I promise I'll never take that away from you, but love isn't a fixed thing. It expands and grows, so he has room in his heart for me and Izzy, too. And our baby. And if it's a girl, maybe you won't mind if we name her after you. If I were in your shoes, I'd like to think that that's how he'd remember me.' She dragged in a breath. 'I just want you to know that I'll look after him. That I'll do my best to make him happy. And that we'll make the most of having a second chance.'

She left Marc to make his own peace with Ginny, waiting for him on the bench outside the churchyard. Finally, he came to join her, and his eyes were slightly red.

'Are you OK?' she asked.

'No.' His voice sounded choked.

She hugged him. 'Sorry. I know that was hard for you.'

'It isn't that.' He held her close. 'Laurie Grant, you're an incredible woman and I really, really love you. My world's changed so much since you've been in it.'

'I love you, too,' she said softly.

'Come on. I'll take you to my parents, and then I'll go and see the Frasers.'

'Are you sure you don't want me to come with you?'

He nodded. 'Maybe they'll agree to meet you once I've talked to them. But this is something I have to face on my own.'

'Even if they won't talk to you, Marc, remember that love stretches. You're not doing anything wrong, and you're not pushing Ginny out of your life.'

'I know.' He held her for a moment longer. 'Let's go.'

Walking up the path to Ginny's parents' house brought back a flood of bad memories for Marc. Of the way they'd screamed at him. The way they'd refused to forgive him.

Two years ago.

Time was meant to be a healer. But would time have changed Carol and Stephen Fraser's attitude towards him?

There was only one way to find out.

He took a deep breath, and rang the doorbell.

Carol Fraser opened the door and stared at him in seeming disbelief. 'What are *you* doing here?' Her lip curled with bitterness.

'I need to talk to you,' Marc said quietly.

She shook her head. 'I don't want to talk to you.'

'I don't blame you for hating me,' he said. 'Believe me, I've hated myself.'

Stephen joined her at the door, clearly having overheard the conversation. 'Our daughter's dead.'

'And nothing I can do can bring her back. I wish I could. I wish things could've been different.'

'I wish you'd been driving and it had been you,' Stephen said, his face suffused with colour.

'For a long time, so did I,' Marc said. 'I need to talk to you both. Please may I come in?'

They just stood there in silence, giving him a bitter stare, and Marc thought that they were going to refuse. But finally Carol nodded. Saying nothing, she and Stephen stepped aside and let him.

Marc followed them into the living room and waited for them to ask him to sit down. When they didn't, he remained standing.

'It's been more than two years now,' he said. 'I'll always love Ginny, but she wouldn't want me to spend the rest of my life on my own.'

'You're asking our permission to see someone?' Stephen asked, his tone full of disbelief.

'No. But I'd rather you heard this from me than from someone else. I've met someone. We're going to get married.'

Carol's eyes narrowed. 'Why are you telling us?'

'Because,' he said, 'I've learned something. Love stretches. It's not a thing that you ladle out into bowls for a while and then the pan's empty. Ginny loved you very much. Before she was killed—'

'Murdered,' Stephen cut in.

'Killed,' Marc repeated gently. 'It was an accident—and it's taken me two years to come to terms with that. Yes, I should've been driving. But there are so many variables. If we'd left earlier or later, if we'd taken a different route, if the other driver had paid attention to the road instead of to his mobile phone—but they're all ifs. And they didn't happen. We've lost Ginny, and we have to come to terms with that.'

'I'll *never* come to terms with that. Do you have any

idea what it's like to lose your only child?' Carol demanded.

'Actually,' he said, 'I do. And every day I think how old our little one would be, and wonder what he or she would be doing now. I've avoided children for two years because I couldn't handle it—and that's the baby I never got to meet. But you had thirty years of loving Ginny. Thirty years of memories. And maybe it's time to hang onto the good stuff and let the bad go.'

'How do you think we'll ever get over it?' Stephen asked.

'I don't know. But—look, before the accident, we all got on well. You know I loved your daughter, and I would've done anything for her.'

'But you didn't, did you?' Stephen's lip curled. 'You didn't look after her enough.'

'I made one wrong choice. And I have to live with that every day of my life,' Marc said softly. 'But I've learned from what happened. And I'm asking you for a second chance. If I'd been the one who'd died in the crash, I'd like to think that Ginny would've moved on with her life, found someone who loved her as much as I did and would make her happy. And I'd like to think that she would've stayed in touch with my parents, too, still looked on them as part of her extended family.'

There was a long, long silence and Marc thought maybe he'd gone too far.

'That's what you're asking from us?' Carol asked.

'Yes.'

'Ginny was all we had,' Stephen said.

'I know. But, when I married her, you had me as well.' He paused. 'You still have me. If you want that.'

'How can we bear to see you with someone else in our daughter's place?' Carol asked.

'That isn't how it is. Laurie isn't in Ginny's place. She's not pushing Ginny out of my life. I'll still have Ginny's photo up with all the others, and...' He blew out a breath. 'Well, hey, I can't make things any worse than they are, so I might as well tell you the rest. We're going to have a baby. It wasn't planned, but we're thrilled about it. And so is Laurie's little girl. If we have a daughter, we'd like to call her Ginny—so your daughter's memory is still going to live on with us.'

'Call *your* child after *our* daughter,' Stephen echoed, shaking his head.

'In another life,' Marc said, 'if Ginny and I had moved to Norfolk, I think she and Laurie would've been friends. I would've known Laurie through work and Ginny would've known her through school. And you would probably have met her at our house and liked her.'

'And yet you're putting her in our daughter's place,' Stephen said.

'Not in Ginny's place. In her *own* place in my life,' Marc said gently. 'Laurie doesn't look anything like Ginny, but she has that same warmth, that same caring spirit. She's a doctor—that's how I met her. At work. She's taught me that love stretches, that even when life is rough you can still make the best of what you have. And I hope that you'll find it in you to do that with us. It's not going to be the same—of *course* it's not—but this way you still get to have that extended family.'

'And she's OK with this?' Stephen asked.

Marc nodded. 'We've talked it over. She came with me to Ginny's grave this morning. To tell Ginny that she'd look after me and make sure her memory lives on.'

Carol looked thoughtful. 'Where is this Laurie now?'

'With my parents. I didn't think it would be fair to bring her to meet you without talking to you first. Just so you know, my parents like her very much. They've welcomed her into the family.' He paused. 'It's your decision now. If you'd like to meet her, we'd both be delighted about it. And if you meet her it might reassure you that Ginny's not going to be packed away and forgotten about.'

They said nothing.

'I'll give you some time to think about it. We're going to be in London until about four today. If you'd like us to meet you somewhere today, just call me and tell me where and we'll be there. Otherwise I'll leave it to you until you feel ready.' He swallowed hard. 'I'll go now. And I'm sorry. I should've tried harder to talk to you, a long time before now. I should've looked after you better, the way Ginny would've done with my parents.' Even though the Frasers had made it very clear they hadn't wanted anything to do with him and would always blame him for Ginny's death, Marc knew he could and should have tried harder, for her sake. 'I'll see myself out. But I hope from now on that we can maybe come to some kind of understanding. Some kind of peace. For Ginny's sake.'

They still said nothing.

And he had nothing left to say right at that moment. Though he would try again, he thought as he left. Maybe next time he'd try a different tack.

He was almost back at his parents' house when his phone beeped to signal a text message. He let it wait until he'd parked the car, then fished his phone out of his pocket. He'd half expected the text to be from Laurie—but it was from Carol, saying she'd like to meet Laurie.

*Thank you. What time and where?* he texted back.

It was a while before she replied, and he was just getting out of his car when his phone beeped again. *The park opposite our house, two o'clock.*

It would be tight, but it was doable.

Laurie and his parents met him with a hug. 'How did it go?'

'It was fairly awkward,' he admitted. 'They still blame me—and they were pretty shocked when I told them about you and the baby.'

'It can't have been easy for you either,' Laurie said.

'It wasn't.' He paused. 'But they've had time to think about it, and they've just texted me. They want to meet you.'

By the time two o'clock came, Laurie was incredibly nervous. This would be Marc's second chance from his in-laws. What if they decided they didn't like her, and changed their minds?

As if Marc could guess what she was thinking, he squeezed her hand. 'Don't worry. This will be fine. Just be yourself.'

She gave him a wry smile. 'Hey, well, this was my idea. I can't chicken out now.'

But as they drew nearer to the couple sitting on the park bench, she felt sick. Please, please, let them like her. Let them give Marc the second chance he deserved.

Marc introduced them swiftly.

'Thank you for agreeing to meet me.' Laurie said. 'I didn't know Ginny, but Marc talks about her, and in her photographs she looks like a really lovely woman. I know this must be really hard for you, seeing me with Marc. And you had such a terrible loss, your only child—I can't even begin to imagine what it would be like to lose my little girl.' Even the thought of it made her blood freeze. 'I think I'd be beside myself.'

Carol swallowed. 'Marc said you had a little girl.'

'Izzy. She's five.' Laurie took her phone out of her handbag and showed Carol one of the photographs.

'She looks very sweet.' Carol looked misty-eyed. 'I remember Ginny at that age. She used to chatter away all the time.'

'So does Izzy. And she loves decorating cupcakes— you wouldn't believe how many different coloured sprinkles she uses.'

'Ginny loved doing that, too.' Unchecked, a tear trickled down Carol's face.

Laurie hated to see her distress. Unable to hold back any longer, she hugged Carol. 'I'm not your daughter, Mrs Fraser. I can never even begin to take her place, and I wouldn't ever be so insensitive as to try, but you're still part of Marc's family. And I hope that maybe one day you'll be able to consider yourself part of mine, too.'

Carol was shaking. 'Marc says you're having a baby.'

Laurie nodded. 'And if she's a girl, we'd really like her to share your daughter's name—so Ginny's memory is still going to live on with us.'

Carol broke down completely, holding Laurie as tightly as Laurie was holding her. 'Marc was right—you do remind me of my Ginny. You look nothing like her but you've got that same caring way about you.' She dragged in a breath. 'Ginny was a teacher.'

'I'm a doctor, so I guess it's a similar thing—we look after people.'

Carol pulled away so she could look Laurie in the eye. 'And you're not going to push Ginny out of Marc's life?'

'Of course I'm not. She'll always be there in his heart,

and she'll always have a picture up in our house. And you'll always be welcome there, too.' Laurie felt the tears spill over her own eyelashes.

Awkwardly, Marc patted her shoulder and Stephen rested his hand over Carol's.

Carol turned to Marc. 'You're right. The accident wasn't your fault. Yes, you should've been driving, that night, but you weren't the one on the wrong side of the road.' She swallowed hard. 'I blamed you because it was easier having someone to be angry with—something to fill the hole Ginny left behind.'

'Better to fill that hole with love than with anger,' Laurie said. 'Love and hope. Because there's always something good to find about the world.'

Stephen stared at her. 'That's—that's the sort of thing Ginny would've said. She…she would have liked you.' He looked at Marc. 'That second chance you talked about? I think we all need that. Carol and I haven't been fair to you. And you lost her, too.' He held his hand out for Marc to shake. 'Maybe we should focus on the good memories, like you said. Celebrate her instead of missing what we never had a chance to share. And I hope—' His breath hitched 'I hope you two will be happy together.'

'Thank you,' Marc said, and shook his hand.

# CHAPTER FOURTEEN

LIFE, Laurie thought, didn't get any better than this. Preparations for the wedding were in full swing; the church was booked, the reception was going to be at the local hotel, and Tina's mum was making the wedding cake. Yvonne, Fiona, Izzy, Georgia and Molly were bridesmaids; Joe was the best man; and she knew that Marc was relieved that the Frasers had actually accepted their invitation to the wedding. Laurie and Izzy had rented out their house and moved in with Marc, and Marc had had the news that morning that the landlord was happy to sell them the house.

It was all working out perfectly.

Laurie was on her way to some house calls at the care home at the outskirts of town, singing along to the radio, when a cat ran out in front of her. Not wanting to hit the animal, she braked hard—but then she felt a jolt, heard a bang, and the car was careening out of her control and heading toward a wall.

Time seemed to slow down and speed up all at once.

Emergency stop. Right. She needed to put her foot on the clutch and combine it with short, sharp pumps on the brake so it didn't lock up. Praying as she did so, she pumped the brake.

And then the car hit the wall.

The seat belt locked, holding her away from the steering-wheel, and Laurie felt a sharp pain across her abdomen.

Oh, God. *The baby.* She struggled to take some deep, even breaths, aware that she was shaking. The baby needed oxygen. And she had to calm down; stress wasn't good for the baby.

She couldn't feel any wetness between her legs, but that didn't mean anything. If the accident had caused her to have a placental abruption, there wouldn't necessarily be any blood yet. The bleed could be masked by its position, and she would just start to have symptoms of shock as the bleed grew.

She wanted Marc. Right now.

Though, at the same time, how could she ring him and tell him she'd crashed the car? The last time she'd brought all his nightmares back, the night she'd told him she was pregnant, he'd walked out on her. Would he let her down again?

For the baby's sake, she hoped not.

And she wasn't sure what scared her most. Marc's reaction or her situation.

She had to sort this out. Right now. And, please, please, let her really be able to rely on Marc.

She was shaking even harder as she pushed the switch on her hazard lights and tried to release her seat belt. It took her several goes before she managed it; then she reached down into the passenger footwell to grab her handbag. She misdialled Marc's number twice, but finally his phone started to ring.

'Marc?'

'No, it's Phyllis. He's switched his mobile through to the surgery reception.'

Of course he had. He'd be with a patient. Laurie couldn't think straight. She took a deep breath. 'Phyllis, I need to speak to him. I wouldn't ask if it wasn't urgent. Please.'

'Are you all right, love?'

Yes. No. She didn't have a clue. All she knew was that she wanted Marc. 'I need Marc.'

'All right, love. Hang on in there.'

Marc's phone beeped, and he frowned. Phyllis would know from the practice computer system that he was with a patient and shouldn't be interrupted. So she'd only be calling him if it was something important.

'I'm sorry, would you mind if I take that?' he asked his patient.

'Sure, go ahead.'

'Marc, I've got Laurie for you,' Phyllis said.

His frown deepened. Laurie worked here herself, so she'd never normally interrupt him when he was with a patient. He knew she was out doing some house calls; but if she wanted a second opinion on a patient's condition, she'd leave a message for Phyllis to grab him between patients, and wait for him to call her back. What was going on?

He suddenly had a nasty feeling something was seriously wrong.

'Laurie? Are you all right?'

'I— Marc, I'm all right, at least I think I am, but I had an accident.' Her voice sounded wobbly.

He thought of Ginny and felt sick. No. This couldn't happen all over again. It just *couldn't*. He struggled to sound calm. 'What happened?'

'I had to brake hard and I think I must've hit a pot-hole. I slid over the road, and I think my tyre blew.' She was sounding more and more scared. 'The car hit a wall. I don't think I can drive it any more.'

'Where are you?' he asked urgently.

'The other side of town from the surgery. I was on my way out to Whitegates Care Home.'

'I'll come and get you.' He clenched his fists, forcing himself to stay calm. 'Can you smell petrol?'

'I don't think so— Oh, my God, I'm using my mobile phone and the car might be leaking!'

'It's OK. Don't panic. You would've blown up by now if there was a problem.' He hoped he sounded much more cool and casual than he felt, and that injecting a bit of dark medic humour would calm her down. 'OK. Deep breath and put your hazard lights on, honey.'

'Done it already.'

'Good. You're safest to stay in the car, so don't move. I'm leaving now.' He put the phone down and turned to his patient. 'I'm sorry, I would never normally ask you to come back later or to wait to see another doctor, but I really have to go right now—this is an emergency.'

'I was trying not to listen in, but it sounded like you were talking about an accident. Is it Dr Grant?'

'Yes.'

'Oh, dear. I hope she's all right.'

So do I, thought Marc. So do I. 'Thank you. I'll get Phyllis to book you in.' He ushered his patient out of the consulting room then gave Phyllis a quick rundown of the situation.

'You go, love. I'll sort out the patients, and I'll ring Diane to ask her to pick Izzy up from school,' Phyllis said. 'Give Laurie my love, and keep me posted, OK?'

He nodded. 'Thanks. I will.'

He drove out of town in the direction Laurie had taken, and blanched when he saw her car ploughed into the wall. It brought back way too many bad memories of the accident that had taken Ginny from him.

Please, please, don't let Laurie be taken from him, too.

But right now he had to put her feelings before his. She needed him, and he wasn't going to let her down ever again.

He parked behind her, switched on his hazard lights and waited just long enough for the car behind him to overtake them. Seconds later he had Laurie's car door open and his arms wrapped round her.

'Are you OK?' he asked.

'I think so. Shaky. But OK.'

'I'd better check you over.' He took her pulse. 'OK. I'm happy with that. And it's probably better than mine is right now.' Her blood pressure, too, was normal. That was a good sign. And she wasn't showing any symptoms of hypovolaemic shock. 'Did you black out or anything?'

'No, and I didn't hit my head. I'll probably have a bruise from the seat belt, though,' she said ruefully. 'I called the police to tell them I had an accident but nobody else was involved, and I called the insurance company. They're sending a pick-up truck out to fetch the car. They won't be long.'

'I'll drive you home,' Marc said. 'Call them on the way and tell them I'm taking you home and then I'll be back. You need to rest—and I think you ought to have tomorrow off. Actually, I might call in the big guns and get Diane to babysit you.'

She shook her head. 'There's no need. I was pretty

scared when it happened, but it was just the shock and the speed of it. I'm fine now. Marc, you're overreacting.'

'No, I'm not,' he said firmly. 'I'm not going to risk anything happening to you, Laurie. Don't argue.'

Laurie knew why he was worrying. Because of the last accident he'd had to deal with. But he was here. And he'd put her needs first without a moment's hesitation.

She wrapped her arms round him. 'You really don't have to worry. But I get why you are.'

'Yeah. And you'll rest?'

'I'll rest,' she promised.

And although she thought he was definitely overreacting, she agreed to take the next day off work.

She was pottering around the garden when it struck her that something was odd. Something was missing.

When she worked out what it was, she went cold. *She hadn't felt the baby move for quite a while.* She knew that the baby was well insulated, but supposing the accident had done more damage than she'd thought?

No.

It was unthinkable.

She drummed her fingers on her belly, hoping to persuade the baby into kicking back.

No response.

She sat with her hands pressed again her stomach, praying for the baby to kick hard enough for her to feel it.

Still nothing.

Maybe she was panicking over nothing. She had a definite bruise from the seat belt, so maybe that was the problem. Maybe her body could only concentrate on one feeling at a time. Besides, she'd only just started to feel the baby's movements—earlier than she had with Izzy.

But her worries grew all morning.

Marc rang her during his break. 'Everything OK?'

'I...' Laurie dragged in a breath and tried to keep the sobs back, but she failed.

'Laurie? Laurie, what's wrong? Talk to me, honey, tell me,' he demanded.

'Marc, I can't feel the baby move, and I'm—I'm—I'm so *scared!*' she burst out.

'I'm on my way.'

He was with her in five minutes, and she knew he'd broken every speed limit on the way. He'd brought the hand-held Doppler ultrasound machine from the surgery with him. He pressed the transducer to her stomach and they both listened to the built-in speaker, but there was none of the clop-clop-clop they were both desperate to hear, the rapid beat of the baby's heart.

'Don't panic,' he said. 'This thing looks as if it came in with the ark and it's probably too old to be working properly. Or I've put it in the wrong place.'

He tried again.

Still nothing.

He'd already lost one baby, with Ginny. And now they couldn't hear the baby's heartbeat—so the chances were high that he was going to lose another. Laurie didn't think she could bear it.

He held her tightly and kissed her. 'I'm going to call the hospital, OK? Try not to worry.'

After a quick conversation he put the phone down. 'I've spoken to one of the midwives in the maternity unit and they're going to give you a scan at the hospital. Come on, I'm driving.' He gave her a hug. 'It's going to be fine. It's probably because you're worried, and maybe a bit bruised, so you're not feeling things the way you should be. And it's still early to be feeling the baby kick, in any case.' He tried to convince himself.

'You feel it earlier with the second one,' she reminded him.

'And the surgery definitely needs a more up-to-date Doppler. It's a machine error, OK?'

She knew he was trying to reassure her, but it wasn't working. She swallowed hard. 'I can't bear the idea of losing our baby,' she whispered.

'You're not losing our baby.'

'If I hadn't had that accident…'

'That's my line,' he said, and kissed her. 'Come on. Breathe. I'm here, and everything's going to be just fine.'

Laurie was really relieved to be able to lean on Marc, even more so than when she'd called him from the car accident. She'd worried that he might crumble and leave her to deal with it, unable to face a similar situation to the one that had wrecked his life before. But he was just brilliant—calm, reassuring and completely in charge. There wasn't even a hint of panic in his eyes. He was there for her. For the baby.

She was numb throughout the drive to hospital and couldn't concentrate on a thing. Marc parked the car, then held her hand all the way as they walked to the maternity unit.

Her name was written on a whiteboard, under the word 'Emergency'. Laurie went cold at the sight.

He kept his hand tightly wrapped round hers. 'You know as well as I do what that means. It's "Emergency" because it isn't a scan that's been booked in as routine by the midwives. *Breathe,*' he said, making her take deep breaths in and out. He fetched her a plastic cup of water and made her sit down in the waiting room. 'Sip this slowly,' he said. 'I'm going to let the receptionist know that we're here.'

It could only have been a few minutes but it felt as if a lifetime had gone by when one of the obstetricians came in and introduced himself.

Marc filled him in on the details. 'Laurie's sixteen weeks pregnant. It's her second baby. She had a minor car accident yesterday; she didn't think she was hurt, but she can't feel the baby move today. I used the surgery's Doppler to hear the heartbeat but I couldn't get a result—I think the machine was playing up, but obviously we need a bit of reassurance.'

'OK. Try not to worry.' The obstetrician smiled at them. 'We'll do our best to see what's going on. Come through with me, and we'll get the portable scanner going.'

Laurie lay on the bed as the doctor directed, lifting her top up. He placed conductive gel on her stomach. In theory, this was just like the twelve-week scan she'd had the previous month, when she and Marc had been thrilled to see their baby on the screen—but this felt much, much scarier.

Laurie couldn't see the screen and she knew that Marc couldn't either.

Panic seeped through her. Was the doctor keeping the screen turned away from them because it was bad news and he was trying to work out how to break it?

Her hand tightened round Marc's. This was unbearable.

The doctor was frowning and moving the transceiver on her stomach, and the seeping panic turned into a flood. Please, please, *please*, don't let them lose their baby. Please, don't let Marc have to go through this again.

But then the doctor smiled at them both and turned the screen round so they could see it.

'I'm pleased to say that here we have one baby. Kicking very happily, even though you can't feel it. So there's absolutely nothing to worry about.'

Laurie felt her face crumple, and then she sobbed with relief.

Marc was shaking, and when she looked at him she could see that his eyes were wet, too.

'You can see the heart beating, here. It's very strong, and there's absolutely nothing to worry about,' the doctor said again. 'What I'd recommend is that you go home now and try to get some rest.'

'You bet she will,' Marc said. 'I'm going to wrap her in cotton wool.'

Laurie felt her eyes widen. 'Marc, you can't do that.'

'No? Fine,' he said. 'I'll call your mum. And mine. And if they don't make you rest, I'll call in Fiona, Tina, Phyllis—and, actually, yes, I think Carol as well. And she'll be really strict with you. You don't stand a chance.'

Laurie knew when she was beaten. And she was so, so grateful that he was taking care of her like this. 'OK, I get the picture. I'll behave. I'll rest.'

'Good, because I'm not risking anything with you.' He held her close. 'I love you, Laurie Grant. And I want you right as rain on our wedding day. So, to my way of thinking, that means you have four weeks of rest, starting from this very second—and I'll run any errand you ask of me.'

'Even if it's fetching me chocolate ice cream from the twenty-four-hour supermarket at two in the morning because I have a craving?' she tested.

'Yes.'

'Or running the bridesmaids over for a dress fitting?'

'Yes.'

'Checking the flowers?'

'Anything you like, as long as you rest,' he said, and kissed her.

Four weeks later, it was the sunniest November morning Laurie could ever remember. The day when she was going to become Dr Bailey.

She and Izzy had stayed overnight at her parents' house, because Marc had gone superstitious and insisted on observing all the traditions. The senior bridesmaids were all ready, and the three junior bridesmaids were all thrilled to be allowed to wear nail polish as well as have flowers in their hair.

'Ready, love?' Roderick asked.

'I'm ready.'

Diane arranged her veil in place. 'You look lovely, darling.'

'Mummy, you look like a princess,' Izzy sighed happily. 'And Daddy's going to be a prince.'

'Definitely my prince charming,' Laurie said with a grin. Even if he was forever nagging her to sit down and put her feet up, and she knew he'd make her pace herself in the dancing.

And she loved every second of her wedding day. Driving in the old-fashioned car with her father to the church; walking up the aisle on her father's arm towards Marc; the first kiss with her new husband; the hugs and warm congratulations of all their guests, including Dean's parents and Ginny's.

But Izzy stole the show when she gave her speech. 'Uncle Joe and Granddad have already said welcome to the family,' she said, 'but I want to say it too. Because Marc's really special and he makes my mummy smile. He's my daddy now they're married, so I don't have to call him Marc any more.' She ran over to him and hugged him. He lifted her up, resting her against his hip. 'I love you, Daddy,' she said, and Laurie had to blink back the tears.

'I love you too, Izzy Bailey.' His voice was slightly croaky with emotion. 'And I'd like to make a toast to the women in my new family. Laurie Bailey, my wife. Izzy Bailey, my daughter. And, according to the doctor at yesterday's scan, we have a third: Ginny Bailey. It's going to be another four months or so before we meet her, but I reckon she's going to be just as gorgeous as her mum and her big sister and I'm going to love her just as much. The Bailey women. Because they're amazing.'

'Amazing,' everyone echoed, lifting their glasses.

# EPILOGUE

*Twenty-four weeks later*

'MY LOVELY, lovely girls.' Marc couldn't remember ever feeling this proud and happy. Sitting on the side of his wife's hospital bed, with their day-old daughter in her arms, and their five-and-a-half-year-old sitting on his knee—he'd declared a long time ago that he didn't care that Izzy wasn't biologically his, because she was *definitely* his—he'd rate this as the best moment of his entire life.

'Ginny's a really pretty name,' Izzy said with satisfaction. 'A princess name. I'm going to read her all my princess stories. And she can wear all my dressing up clothes when she's big enough, because I'll be too big for them then.'

'That,' Marc said, 'sounds absolutely perfect.'

\* \* \* \* \*

# AN INESCAPABLE
# TEMPTATION

BY
SCARLET WILSON

First published in Great Britain 2013
by Mills & Boon, an imprint of Harlequin (UK) Limited.
Harlequin (UK) Limited, Eton House, 18-24 Paradise Road,
Richmond, Surrey TW9 1SR

© Scarlet Wilson 2013

ISBN: 978 0 263 89876 7

Harlequin (UK) policy is to use papers that are natural, renewable and recyclable products and made from wood grown in sustainable forests. The logging and manufacturing process conform to the legal environmental regulations of the country of origin.

Printed and bound in Spain
by Blackprint CPI, Barcelona

**Dear Reader**

My family and I had the pleasure of cruising around the Mediterranean last year and visiting some wonderful places. It was a great experience and there was nothing like waking up in a new port every day. We visited the ruins of Pompeii and the Château D'If—the prison that inspired *The Count of Monte Cristo.*

Imagine living that life every day. The crew we met were all hardworking, dedicated professionals, and I couldn't think of a better setting for a medical romance.

Gabriel is a gorgeous Venetian doctor. He's returned home to be closer to his family as his father is unwell. He comes from wealthy background and has a poor experience of women, who have frequently been more interested in his money than his heart.

Francesca is using the cruise ship as a safe haven while she waits for her visa to Australia. But what is she really running from?

These two had to work hard for their happy-ever-after, and I'm so glad that they get it in such a beautiful setting.

Please come and say hi at my website:
www.scarlet-wilson.com

*Scarlet*

## DEDICATION

My family are so lucky to have been blessed
with three beautiful babies in the last year.

Welcome to the world, Taylor Jennifer Hyndman,
Oliver Edward Nyack and Noah Alexander Dickson.

Wishing you lives filled with love, health and happiness.

xx

# CHAPTER ONE

'HELP!'

Gabriel turned his head, trying to figure out where the cry had come from amongst the bustling bodies at the port side. The Venezia Passegeri was packed—mainly with crew and harbour staff. Carts packed with passengers' luggage and an obscene amount of fresh food were being piled aboard the cruise ship in front of him, all blocking his view.

'Help! Over here. Someone help!'

The cry rippled through the crowd as heads turned and focused towards the shout. It only took Gabriel a few seconds to realise the cry was coming from the edge of the quay. He dropped his bag and pushed his way through the crowd. A woman was standing near the edge, her face pale, her breathing coming in rapid, shallow breaths. Her trembling hand was pointing towards the water.

Gabriel's eyes followed her finger. There, in the water, was a child—a teenager—struggling in the waves that already seemed to have a grip of him. He must have only just fallen in, but this part of the marina was right on the outskirts of Venice, nearest the sea, and the waves were picking him up and down as he coughed and spluttered, pulling him out to sea.

Gabriel didn't even think. He just dived in. Straight into the murky waters of Venice.

By now a few crew members had noticed the commotion and were shouting in rapid Italian. Gabriel swam quickly towards the boy. It only took a few seconds to wish he'd taken the time to remove his shoes and dress uniform jacket. They weighed him down almost instantly. His white uniform would never look the same again.

The boy kept sinking before his eyes, the waves sweeping over his head as he struggled for breath. Gabriel powered forward, anxious to reach him before he disappeared from sight again.

He got there in less than a minute but the boy had sunk under the waves. Gabriel took a deep breath and dived underwater, reaching down into the darkness. It was amazing how the strong Italian sun penetrated so little through the murky waters. Venice was renowned for its dirty canals. The cruise ship terminal was situated on the outskirts near the edge of the Adriatic Sea, where the deep-keeled ships could dock. And although the waters were marginally better here, they still looked nothing like the clear blue seas depicted in the travel brochures. His fingers brushed against something and he tried fruitlessly to grasp it. Nothing.

Frustration swept over him. His face broke the surface of the water and he gasped for air, trying to fill his lungs. Beneath the waves he shucked one foot against the other. It was a move he did every night in the comfort of his penthouse flat while sitting on the sofa, but struggling to stay afloat it was so much more awkward. Finally he felt a release as the five-hundred-euro hand-made leather shoes floated down into the murky depths. Now he would find the boy.

He dived beneath the waves again, reaching out, trying to circle the area beneath him. This time he felt something bump against his hand and he grabbed tightly before kicking his burning legs to the surface. The two of them burst above the waves, the teenager's flailing legs and arms landing a panicked punch on the side of Gabriel's head.

He flinched. His brain switching into gear. The woman at the quayside had shouted in English.

'Stay still,' he hissed at the boy. The sun was temporarily blinding him as the water streamed down his face.

He could see the jetty. Figures shouted towards him but he couldn't hear a word. The current was strong here and he could hardly believe how quickly they'd moved away from the quay.

The glistening hull of the luxury cruise ship seemed so far away. He'd been standing before it only a few minutes earlier.

He put both hands around the boy's chest and pulled him backwards against his own chest, trying to swim for both of them in his version of the classic lifesaving manoeuvre.

But the boy couldn't stop panicking. The waves were fierce, the water still sweeping over the top of them, causing the boy to writhe in Gabriel's arms as he struggled for breath. A shadow loomed behind them.

His arms were aching as he fought to keep their heads above the water. How on earth was he going to get them back to the quay? Again he could hear the boy coughing and spluttering, choking on the waves that kept crashing over their heads.

He'd never done a sea rescue before. Last time he'd seen one he'd been watching TV. It had all looked so much easier then. Didn't the lifeguards on TV always put people on their backs and pull them towards shore? It didn't seem to be working for him. And they had that strange red plastic thing to help them. Where were the lifebelts here? Shouldn't every port have them?

What on earth was he doing? This was madness. Being a cruise ship doctor was supposed to be easy. It wasn't supposed to kill you the first day on the job.

The irony of this wasn't lost on him. He'd known this job was a bad idea right from the start. A cruise ship doctor was hardly the ideal role for a paediatrician.

But family came first.

And this had been the first job he'd been able to find at short notice. Close enough to Venice to be here when needed but far enough away not to attract any unwanted media attention.

His father's health was slowly but surely deteriorating. And the call to the family business—the one he'd never wanted to be part of—was getting louder and louder. Being a fourteen-hour flight away was no longer feasible. Then again, finding a position locally in his specialist field hadn't been feasible, either.

Timing was everything. If he'd applied for a paediatric post six months previously, with his background and experience he could almost have guaranteed his success. But all the desirable posts had been filled and it would be another six months before slots were available again.

This was a compromise. Only the compromise wasn't meant to kill him.

He saw a small boat in the distance. It seemed to be moving very slowly, creeping around the huge hull of the cruise ship as if it was crawling towards them like a tortoise. Every muscle in his body was starting to burn. His arms were like blocks of lead. The figures on the jetty were still shouting towards them and the shadow appeared again.

Gabriel struggled to turn his head as the brick wall loomed above them. All at once the danger became apparent. The sweeping current was taking them straight towards it and with Gabriel's hands caught tightly around the teenager's chest there was no opportunity to lift his hands and protect his head.

So much for being here to support his family.

And then everything went black.

Francesca was bored. Bored witless. Her mother's favourite British expression.

She smiled and nodded as someone walked past, shifting uncomfortably in the dress uniform. This was the one part of her job she hated. All the staff hated it. So much so, they drew straws each time the captain insisted one of the medical staff stand near the check-in desks in the terminal.

Standing in front of a pull-up banner of the *Silver Whisper* was not her idea of fun. The captain thought it made the medical staff look 'accessible'. She was going to have to talk to him about that.

She watched the passengers wandering in and looking in awe at the side view of the ship. As soon as they appeared the crew entertainment staff were all over them, thrusting brochures of trips the cruise ran at every port they stopped at. Francesca sighed and looked at her watch. This was going to be long day.

She glanced over her shoulder. None of the other senior staff were around. Who would notice if she slipped out for a few minutes? A smile danced across her lips. She crossed the terminal building in long strides, slipping out through a side door that took her down to the dock where the ship was moored.

The dock was jammed with suitcases and sweating crewmen struggling to load them on board. Her brain automatically switched into work mode—ticking off in her head who hadn't attended for their required medicals. She was going to have to crack the whip with the crew. Huge delivery crates of food were being wheeled up one of the gangways. It was amazing the amount of fresh food that was loaded at every port.

She wandered along the walkway, nodding greetings at several of the familiar crewmen, relishing the feel of the sun on her skin. Today, as every day, she'd applied sunscreen. But her Mediterranean skin rarely burned and the slightest touch of sun just seemed to enhance her glow.

This was the life. Working on a cruise ship had sounded like a dream at the time and a good sideways move. A chance to use all the skills she'd learned working in Coronary Care and A and E, along with the ability to use her advanced nurse practitioner status, and all in a relatively calm and safe environment.

But the long hours and constant nights on call were starting to wear her down. Thankfully she had a good supportive team to work with. A team that was slowly but surely helping her rebuild her confidence. The ship was a safe place to try and learn to trust her nursing instincts again. She'd once thought those instincts were good, but personal experience had taught her differently. It was time to start over and the ship seemed a good—if a little boring—place to start.

At the end of the day this was only supposed to be a temporary arrangement while she waited for her work visa for Australia to come through. But there had been delay after delay, with two months turning into three and then four. It seemed as if she'd been waiting for ever for the chance to spread her wings and go further afield. A chance to escape the memories of home.

'Nurse! Nurse!'

She turned swiftly towards the shout. It was at the end of the dock where a small crowd was gathered, pointing and looking out towards the sea. Francesca started running towards the shouts—one of the crew had obviously recognised her.

She could feel the adrenaline start to course through her veins. When had been the last time she'd dealt with an emergency? Would she be able to deal with one again? She'd started her staffing in a coronary care unit where cardiac arrests had been a daily occurrence. Then she'd moved to A and E to increase her skills. Expect the unexpected. That's what the sister she'd worked with had told her.

And she'd been right. From toddlers with a variety of household objects stuffed up their noses to RTA victims, she'd never known what would come through the door. Up until now she'd enjoyed the relative calm of the cruise ship. It could be a little mundane at times, dispensing seasickness tablets, dealing with upset stomachs and advising on sunburn. Maybe things were about to liven up?

She reached the edge of the dock and followed the pointing fingers to the two figures in the water. One looked like a child. She felt her stomach sink. The last thing she wanted was an injured child. A motorboat was approaching them and not before time. She winced as she watched the strong waves barrel them both into the port wall. Even though it was hundreds of yards away she could almost hear the crack.

The boat was almost on top of them and she watched

as they dragged the child on board then struggled to reach the man, who had slipped beneath the waves. One crewman jumped into the water to help. Her heart thudded in her chest. Were they going to find him? The child was older than she'd first thought—probably a teenager—but the man?

Yes! They'd found him.

Oh, no. He was dressed from top to toe in white—an officer's uniform—and they were dragging his lifeless body out of the waves.

She started pushing the others aside. 'Let me through.' The boat was heading towards them. She turned to one of the crewmen, 'Go on board to the medical centre. Tell Dr Marsh I need some help. Tell them to bring a trolley and some resus equipment.' The crewman nodded and ran off.

Francesca noticed a woman sobbing near her and elbowed her way through the crowd. 'Are you okay?' she asked.

'My son Ryan. He was running along the walkway and he slipped. I got such a fright.' She gestured around about her. 'I couldn't find anything to throw to him. I couldn't find any lifebelts. And he can barely swim. Only a few lengths in a pool.' She shook her head furiously. 'Never in the sea.'

Francesca nodded, trying to take in all she'd heard. 'Who's the man?' she asked gingerly, dreading the answer she was about to hear.

The woman shook her head again. 'I've no idea. He appeared out of nowhere and dived straight in. Ryan was swept away so quickly, then he disappeared under the waves.' She was starting to sound frantic again. 'That man had to dive a few times before he finally found him.' The woman turned to face Francesca, her voice trembling. 'But

what if he hadn't? What if he hadn't found my son…?'
Her voice drifted off and her legs were starting to shake.

Francesca put a firm arm around her shoulders. 'Just
hold on for a few minutes longer. Your son will probably be
in shock when the boat reaches us. The sun may be shining but the water out there is pretty cold. How old is he?'

'He's thirteen.'

Francesca's brain was rapidly calculating the drugs she
might need for an adolescent. It was always tricky to cal-
culate for kids—everything was generally based on their
weight as children came in all different shapes and sizes.
And from her experience, at a time of emergency the last
thing a parent remembered was their child's weight. It
didn't matter. It was worth a try.

'Do you know how much Ryan weighs?'

The woman shook her head. Just as she'd suspected.
If necessary, she'd have to make an educated guess when
she saw him. Hopefully by then the rest of the team would
have arrived.

Please don't let her have to resuscitate a child. She'd
done it a few times in A and E and had been haunted by
every occasion.

The motorboat was getting closer. Francesca recognised a few crewmen who must have commandeered some
poor unsuspecting local's boat. Fear crept through her. The
teenager was sitting at one side, a blanket flung around his
shoulders, his face pale and water dripping from his hair.
But the officer lay unmoving in the bottom of the boat—
never a good sign. One of the other crewmen was leaning
over him, so she couldn't see clearly what was going on.

The boat bobbed alongside them and she leapt over the
gap to the other craft. She took a few seconds to check
Ryan over. He was conscious, he was breathing and his

pulse was strong. How he looked was another matter entirely. 'Get him onshore and get one of the medical team to assess him,' she instructed, before pushing the others out of her way to get to the man.

She glanced at his face and noted the three gold stripes on his shoulders. Not only an officer—but a senior officer. The uniform was familiar but the face wasn't. Maybe he wasn't one of theirs?

She was on autopilot now, the adrenaline bringing back all the things she'd thought she'd forgotten. She knelt by him, putting her head down next to his, her eyes level with his chest looking for the rise and fall that was distinctly lacking. Her fingers went to the side of his neck, checking for a carotid pulse. Nothing. She tipped his head back and had a quick check of his airway. Clear.

She didn't hesitate. She could do this in her sleep. On some occasions she almost *had* done this in her sleep. Some skills were never forgotten.

She took two deep breaths, forming a tight seal around his mouth with her own, and breathed into him, watching for the rise of his chest. She pulled at the white jacket, ripping down the front, and gold buttons pinged off and scattered around the bottom of the boat, revealing a plain white T-shirt underneath. She wasn't going to waste time trying to remove it. The firm muscles of his chest were clearly outlined and she had all the definition she needed.

She positioned her hands on his chest and started cardiac massage, counting in her head as she went. She was frantically trying to remember everything she could about drowning victims—an area she had little experience in. It seemed almost absurd when she was working on a cruise ship—but most passengers never came into contact with the sea. Didn't they have quite a good chance of survival if they were found quickly enough? She knew that there had been newspaper stories about children with hypothermia being pulled from frozen lakes and resuscitated successfully. But although this man's skin was cold, he wasn't hypothermic. There wasn't going to be any amazing news story here.

She kept going, conscious of voices behind her and shouted instructions. There was a thud as the boat rocked and a pair of black shiny shoes landed next to her. Her heart gave a sigh of relief. David Marsh was here to help her but she didn't stop what she was doing, leaning over and giving two long breaths again.

'Throw me over a defib and a bag and mask,' came the shout next to her.

Francesca kept going, the muscles in her arms straining as she started cardiac massage again. David was more than capable of organising everything around them.

She was counting again in her head. Twenty-two, twenty-three, twenty-four... *Come on.* She willed him to show some sign of recovery.

The handsome Italian features weren't lost on her. The dark brown hair, long eyelashes, strong chin, wide-framed body and muscled limbs. This man could be very impressive—if he was standing up.

David was pulling up the T-shirt that had been underneath his officer's jacket. 'I don't recognise him.' He squinted. 'Who on earth is he?'

She shook her head, 'I have no idea. Somehow I think I would have remembered this one.'

He slapped the pads on the muscular brown chest that Francesca was desperately trying not to notice and turned to switch on the machine. Then, before her eyes, the lean stomach muscles twitched. 'Wait!' she shouted.

She held her breath for a few seconds and then he did it again. Twitched. And then coughed and spluttered everywhere. The Venetian water erupted from his lungs all over the deck around them and she hurried to help him on his side.

The monitor kicked into life, picking up his heart rate. His breathing was laboured and shallow. David read her thoughts and handed her over a cylinder of oxygen with a mask as he slipped a pulse oximeter on the man's finger.

Francesca bent over the man, blocking out the bright sunlight and shading his face from the nosy bystanders. She spoke in a low, calm voice. 'I'm holding an oxygen mask next to your face to help your breathing,' she said, praying he would understand because right now she had no idea if he spoke English. He opened his eyes. They were brown. Deep dark brown.

Wow.

But she must think purely as a professional. She must ignore everything about the Italian hunk they'd just pulled from the water. All the little things that would normally have sent shivers skittering down her spine.

She pulled her penlight from her pocket. This man probably had a head injury. She'd seen him being bounced off the port wall. She lifted his groggy eyelids and shone the light first in one eye and then the other. He gave the smallest flinch.

Pupils equal and reactive. She turned to David. 'We need to start proper neuro obs on this guy.'

He nodded. 'What happened?'

'He went in to rescue the boy. Once he'd got him the current carried them to the port wall and he was knocked unconscious. I think he was under the water for just over a minute.' Her hand reached around to the back of his head.

His dark brown hair was wet but she could feel some abrasions at the back of his head. She pulled her hand back—blood.

'Can you give me something to patch this before we move him, please, David?'

David nodded and handed her some latex gloves and a dressing pad. 'Stretcher will be here in a minute. We'll get him onto the trolley and see if we can find some ID.'

Francesca hadn't lifted her head. He was still groggy. In all the TV shows she'd ever watched, victims of a near-drowning seemed to get up almost as soon as they were revived and walk off down the beach into the sunset. Usually hand in hand with their rescuer.

The thought of walking off into the sunset with this guy was definitely appealing. Like something out a fairy-tale. If only he would come round.

As a child she'd always loved the childhood fairy-tales Cinderella, Rapunzel, Snow White and Little Red Riding Hood. Her father had read them to her over and over again. Those were some of her fondest memories of him.

She leaned in a little closer to the man. If she really wanted to do a set of neurological observations on this guy then she needed to try and elicit some kind of response from him, a response to a painful stimulus.

'Wake up, Sleeping Beauty,' she whispered.

# CHAPTER TWO

GABRIEL was in a dark place. Nothing. Nothingness. Then a sharp pain in his chest and the need to be sick. He coughed and spluttered, conscious that he was being pushed on his side but totally unable to assist. His head was thudding. His lungs felt as if they were burning. He heard a little hissing noise and felt a gentle, cool breeze on his face. What was that?

Someone tugged his eye open and shone a bright light at him. How dared they? Couldn't they see he just wanted to sleep? To be left alone for a few moments in this fuzzy place?

He felt a little pinch on his hand. Then another, more insistent.

'Ouch!' He was annoyed, irritated. Then he heard a soft, lilting voice with the strangest accent he'd heard in a while. 'Wake up, Sleeping Beauty. Are you with us?' Warm, soft breath tickled his cheek.

His eyelids flickered open. The sun was too bright.

Someone was trying to block the sunlight out.

Rats. It must be a dream. She was far too pretty for real life.

She was every guy's dream. A real-life modern-day princess. Mediterranean skin and dark eyes with tumbling brown curls. But something in this fairy-tale still wasn't working.

She spoke again. 'There we go, that's better.'

It was that accent. It didn't fit with his Mediterranean dream princess.

It confused him. Made his brain hurt. No—that wasn't his brain, that was his head.

He blinked again. The smell of the Adriatic Sea assaulting his senses. His skin was prickling. All of a sudden he felt uncomfortable. Something wasn't right. He was wet. Not just damp but soaked all over.

In the space of a few seconds the jigsaw puzzle pieces all fell into place. The young boy drowning, his attempt at saving him and the almighty crack to his head. He pushed himself up.

'Whoa, sailor. Take it easy there. You've had a bump on the head.'

'You can say that again,' he mumbled, squinting in the sunlight. 'And it's Doctor, not sailor.'

The princess's face broke into a wide perfect-toothed smile. 'Actually, I'll correct you there. On board, you're a sailor first, doctor second.'

David Marsh leaned forward, clutching some wet credentials in his hand. He held out his other hand. 'Well, this is an interesting way to meet our new boss. Gabriel Russo, I'm Dr David Marsh, your partner in crime. And this…' he nodded towards Francesca '…is Francesca Cruz, one of our nurse practitioners. But as you've just been mouth to mouth with each other, introductions seem a little late.' He signalled to the nearby crewmen. 'We're just going to get you on this stretcher and take you to the medical centre to check you over.'

Francesca felt a chill go down her spine at the name.

She recognised it but couldn't for the life of her think why. She stared at him again. Was he vaguely familiar? She was sure she'd never met him, and with features like those he wasn't the kind of man you'd forget.

Gabriel looked horrified and shook his head, water flying everywhere. 'No stretcher. I'm fine. I can walk.' He pushed his hands on the bottom of the boat and stood up, standing still for a few seconds to make sure his balance was steady.

His eyes found the thick rope securing the small boat to the quay before he stepped over the gap and back to the safety of solid ground. He spun round to face Francesca. 'How's the boy? Is he all right?' But he'd turned too quickly and he swayed.

She caught hold of his arm and gave him a cautious smile. 'He's on his way to the medical centre to be checked out. He was conscious, breathing but distinctly pale when he arrived. Now, how about I get you a wheelchair?'

'I don't do wheelchairs.'

She signalled over his shoulder. 'I can be very bossy when I want to be.'

Dr Marsh cut in, 'I can testify to that. Particularly if you think you're going to get the last chocolate. I should warn you in advance that's criminal activity in the medical centre.'

Gabriel felt pressure at the back of his legs as he thudded down into a wheelchair that had appeared out of thin air. 'I said I don't do chairs,' he growled.

'Let's argue about that later,' said Francesca as she swept the wheelchair along the dock.

The hairs on his arms were standing on end and he started to shiver—an involuntary action—a sign of shock.

A few seconds later a space blanket was placed around his shoulders.

He grudgingly pulled it around him, noting the efficiency of his new staff and the easy rapport and teamwork—all good signs. Within a few seconds his nurse appeared to have walked the hundreds of yards along the dock and was pushing him up the gangway.

This was a nightmare. The worst way possible to meet your new staff. Yet another reason he should never have taken this job.

She seemed to turn automatically to her left, heading toward the service elevators. Gabriel felt mild panic start to build in his chest. Could this day get any worse?

Then she quickly veered off to the right. 'Where are we going?' he growled.

'To the medical centre. We're already on Deck Four so it will only take a couple of minutes.' If she was annoyed by his tone there was no sign.

Gabriel heaved a sigh of relief and settled back in the chair. He'd be fine once he got something for this headache and was out of these wet clothes. Then he could get started.

The chair turned sharply into the modern medical centre. Consulting rooms, treatment rooms, in-patient beds and state-of-the-art diagnostics and emergency equipment. He knew the spec for this place off by heart—it was impressive, even by his exacting standards.

She wheeled him through to one of the rooms and pulled the curtains around the bed, pushing the brake on the wheelchair. She disappeared for a second and came back with a towel and set of scrubs.

Francesca's brain was whirring. Gabriel Russo. Why was that name so familiar? Then it hit her like a ton of bricks falling from the sky. She *had* seen him before. Only last time he'd been wearing a pair of white designer swimming trunks and been perched on the edge of a multi-million-pound yacht, his arm lazily flung around the shoulders of her bikini-clad friend Jill.

*The Italian stallion,* Jill had called him and that picture had adorned her flatmate's bedside cabinet until one night when a sobbing Jill had phoned Francesca at 3:00 a.m. to come and pick her up.

Francesca would never forget the sight of Jill in her sodden green designer gown, her hair plastered around her face and tears running like rivulets down her cheeks after Gabriel had flung her out of his penthouse flat.

Jill had been broken-hearted over his treatment of her and had taken a good few weeks to get over him—a long time for Jill.

And Francesca had waited a long time, too—to tell this man exactly what she thought of him. He was alive. He was breathing. His heart rate was sound. After a few general observations for head injuries he should be fine. There was a determined edge to her chin; it would be criminal to waste this opportunity. And she had absolutely no intention of doing so.

Something was wrong. Something had changed. He could sense it immediately; the tension in the air was palpable. Right now, all he wanted to do was climb into that pristine white bed, close his eyes and lose this thumping headache.

But the soft side of his Mediterranean princess had vanished and she was staring at him as if he were something she'd just trodden on.

Or maybe he was imagining it? Maybe the resuscitation and head knock had affected him more than he'd thought?

'You're Gabriel Russo.'

Gabriel's pounding head jerked in response to the sharp tone in her voice. He wasn't imagining it. 'I thought we had established that.'

'No, you're Gabriel Russo, *Italian stallion*.' She lifted her fingers in the air, making the quotation mark signs, wrinkled her nose and then continued, 'Stinking love rat. You used to date my friend Jill—until you threw her out of your apartment in London at 3:00 a.m. in the pouring rain.'

'No one's ever called me Italian stallion to my face before.' He felt almost amused. The nickname had been plastered across the press often enough. He wasn't used to being blindsided. Then again, he wasn't used to being resuscitated.

Jill. The name flickered through his brain. He'd certainly dated more than his fair share of beautiful women and he'd worked all over the world. Something fell into place. London. No. Let's hope she wasn't talking about *that* Jill. Just what he needed—a misguided, loyal friend. If his head wasn't thumping so much this could almost be funny. Not only that—Ms Misguided was a knockout. A beautiful work colleague would never be a problem. But an angry, venomous one would be. This was a small team. They had to work together. It could be badly affected by two people who didn't get on.

She wasn't finished. 'But I bet plenty of women have called you a heartbreaker before.'

'Have we met?' His eyes ran up and down her body and she felt a prickle of disgust—he'd almost mirrored her thoughts from earlier. 'I think I'd remember.'

A few minutes before she'd had nice thoughts drifting about her head about their new doctor. She'd thought he was handsome. She'd thought he was fit. She'd even thought... No. She hadn't. She couldn't possibly have.

He frowned. 'Jill? Who was she again? Remind me.'

Francesca felt rage build inside her. Arrogant so-and-so. The palm of her hand itched—she wanted it to come into contact with his perfect cheek.

'Six years ago. London. Blonde model. You took her on your yacht for the weekend.'

'Oh, *that* Jill.' His frown deepened, puckering little lines around his eyes. He turned away, pulling his muddied jacket and T-shirt over his head, and she sensed it was on purpose. She tossed the scrubs and towel onto the bed beside him.

'Yes, *that* Jill.' The volume of her voice increased in proportion to her rage. 'The one you dumped in the middle of the night in the pouring rain outside your flat. What kind of a man does that?'

He whipped around, the muddied jacket and T-shirt clenched in his fists, leaving his wide brown chest right in front of her eyes. The fury in her voice couldn't match the venom in his eyes. 'What kind of a man does that?' he growled.

She gulped. He was half-dressed, his shoulder muscles tense, his bare abdomen rigid. If they were shooting an action movie right now he would be the perfect poster-boy hero.

All of a sudden the room felt much smaller. Maybe it was the six-foot-four presence. All trembling muscle and eyes shooting fireballs in her direction.

She could feel every hair on her body stand on end. And she hated it.

Because amongst the repulsion there was something

else she was feeling—something more—and it went against every principle she had.

She pushed all those thoughts aside. If she ignored them then they weren't actually *there*.

He still hadn't answered. Probably because he was incoherent with rage.

'What are you doing here anyway? Aren't you supposed to be some billionaire-type doctor? You don't actually have to work for a living, do you? Why on earth would you be working on a cruise ship?'

He shook his head, almost imperceptibly. What a surprise. All the usual assumptions, misunderstandings and wrong conclusions. All the things he went to pains to shake off. Normally he wouldn't care what some stranger thought of him. But this stranger was part of his team *and* she was going to have to learn who was boss around here—hardly an ideal start. 'Some things you wouldn't understand.' He leaned against the side of the bed, and could feel the pressure inside his head increase.

'Try me.'

Something flashed across his face. He took a deep breath. 'How well do you know Jill?'

'She is my friend. She was my flatmate in London. We lived together for six months.'

'Six years ago?' There was an edge to his voice—almost as if he couldn't believe someone had been friends with Jill that long.

'Yes. We don't live together any more but we keep in touch.' She scanned her brain, trying to think of the last time she'd heard from Jill—maybe a week or more?

'And how many times did you have to pick her up heartbroken in the middle of the night?'

'Once.' Not strictly true. But he was beginning to look

too smug. There was a lot not to like. He was too handsome and too sure of himself. And she didn't like that look on his face—as if he knew something she didn't.

'Jill is a really good friend of mine. She helped me when I needed it most. Make no mistake about where my loyalty lies, Gabriel.'

Those words didn't even touch what Jill had done for her. When her father had died, Jill had dropped everything and flown straight up from London to Glasgow. She'd organised the funeral, dealt with the post-mortem, sorted out the insurance and the contents of the house—all things that Francesca couldn't possibly have dealt with. Jill had been her rock.

In the past their relationship had always felt uneven, as if Francesca was constantly running after Jill and taking care of her. But when the chips had been down Jill had more than risen to the challenge. Francesca couldn't have got through it without her.

'How long are you here for?'

'I haven't even done my first shift and you're trying to get rid of me?'

She shrugged.

'As long as I want. I took this job at short notice— someone had broken their contract—so I was pretty much offered what I wanted. It's up to me to decide how long I want to stay.'

Great. Who knew how long she would be stuck with him? 'You didn't answer the original question. Why would a billionaire doc like you want to be working on a cruise ship?'

He waved his hand dismissively. 'Family stuff.'

It was the first interesting thing he'd said.

Yip. The walls in the room were definitely closing in

on her. This was her worst nightmare. Working with this man every day was going to play havoc with her senses and her principles. She hated the fact that under other circumstances she might like him. She hated the fact she'd almost flirted with him.

'I know you'll have some clean uniforms in your quarters but how about putting these on right now?' She pointed to the scrubs. She wrinkled her nose at the ruined jacket and T-shirt, still in his hand. 'I don't care how good the laundry staff are here, they're not going to be able to save *those*.'

Gabriel stood up, his legs feeling firmer than before. He hadn't even considered his appearance. The pristine white uniform he was holding was covered in remnants of brown sludge. His body hadn't fared much better. From the port wall perhaps? She was right, no matter what the TV adverts pretended to show, no washing powder on the planet could sort this out.

He grabbed the towel to rub his hair, momentarily forgetting the reason he was there and wincing as the edge of the towel caught his wound.

'Easy, tiger.' Francesca pushed him down onto the edge of the bed. 'Let me do that.' She took the towel from his hands and gently dried around the edges.

'Stop fussing,' he muttered, trying to swat her hand away. 'I need a shower.'

Francesca was doing her best to push her anger aside. She had a job to do. Whether she liked him or not, he was a patient—one she'd just resuscitated and with a head injury. She was a good nurse. This was straightforward. She could do this. 'Right now I'm in charge—not you. You can go in the shower when I say so.' She stuck a tympanic thermometer in his ear. 'I'm going to do a full set of neurological observations on you, then clean that head wound and either glue or stitch it.' She glanced at the reading on the thermometer. 'You're still cold. We're going to heat you up a bit first.' She pulled a blanket from one of the nearby cupboards.

Gabriel sighed. At least she was an efficient nurse, even if she was smart-mouthed and hated his guts. 'Where's Dr Marsh?'

She peered around the edge of the door. 'He and Katherine are dealing with the teenager. Children get priority. I'm sure you'd agree with that.'

The child, of course. What was he thinking? There was a child to be attended to. 'I should go and check him over.' He tried to push his blanket off, but she laid her hand firmly on his shoulder.

The constricting feeling across his chest was almost instant. Paediatrics—children were his whole reason for being a doctor. There was no way he'd watch a child suffer. He couldn't stand the thought that there was a child in the next room requiring attention while he was being pushed onto a bed.

It made him feel useless. It pushed him into dark places imprinted on his mind. Memories of long ago. Of a child with a scream that sent shivers down his spine. Feelings he'd spent his whole professional career trying to avert.

He pushed himself off the bed again.

'Gabriel.'

Her face was right in front of his, her large brown eyes looking him straight on and her voice firm.

'Ryan is fine. David Marsh is more than capable of looking after a shocked teenager. Maybe—just maybe—if we were resuscitating him, like we did with you, I might let you go and assist. But this isn't an emergency situation. You're not needed. You're not even officially on duty. Right now you're a patient, not a doctor. And a cranky one at that. You'd better hope that your head injury is making you cranky because if that's your normal temperament you won't last five minutes in here.'

She was right. The rational part of his brain that was still functioning *knew* she was right. But his heart was ruling his head. He was cursing himself for not paying more attention to the port wall. He shouldn't have dived straight in, he should have taken a few more seconds to get his bearings. Then maybe he could have protected Ryan and stopped him from slipping from his arms.

They could hear rapid chatter next door. She obviously didn't realise his background in paediatrics. It was hardly surprising. Six years ago he'd been just about to pick his speciality and he'd dumped Jill before he'd made his final choice.

'You should stay where you are. I'm going to attach you to a monitor for a few hours. You, sir, are going to do exactly as I say—whether you like it or not.' She pulled the wires from the nearby monitor. 'I'm not the pushover Jill was,' she murmured.

Gabriel felt a weight settle on his chest again. For a second he'd seen a little glimpse of humour from her. For a second he'd thought maybe she didn't hate him quite as much as it seemed. This was the last thing he needed—some smart-mouthed nurse with a load of preconceived ideas him. How close was she to Jill? Hopefully she didn't have any of the same tendencies—that could be disastrous.

Every part of his body was beginning to ache and if he didn't get something for this headache soon he was going to erupt.

It was almost as if she'd read his mind. 'I'll give you

something for your headache in a few moments. I want to have a clear baseline set of neuro obs and I can't give you anything too strong—I don't want to dull your senses.' There was a hint of humour in her voice, the implication that his senses were already dulled crystal clear.

It was just about as much as he could take.

'Enough about me. What about you?' he snapped. 'What's with the accent? Where are you from?'

The unexpected question caught her unawares and she jolted. She put the unattached wires down and her brow wrinkled. She bent to shine her penlight in his eyes again, satisfying herself that his pupils were equal and reactive.

'I'm from Scotland.' She straightened up.

'You don't look like you're from Scotland,' he mumbled as he dropped the towel he'd been using to dry himself, revealing the taut abdominal muscles, and pulled the scrub top over his head. 'You look like a native. And what were you doing in London?'

'I could be offended by that,' she said quickly, placing one hand on her hip as she tried to drag her eyes away from his stomach. Was this his natural response? Was he normally so blunt? Or was this an altered response that she should be concerned about? She had no background knowledge on which to base a judgment. Should she just take for granted that he could be quite rude?

He'd paused, half-dressed, and was watching her. Watching the way her eyes were looking at his taut abdomen. She felt the colour flooding into her cheeks. There was no point averting her eyes, she'd been well and truly caught. She could be cheeky, too.

'Put those away. You'll give a girl a complex. And they'll need to go, too.' She pointed at his muddied underwear and handed him the scrub bottoms, averting her eyes for a few seconds to allow him some privacy. She slid her hand up inside his scrub top to attach the leads to his chest. His brown, muscled chest.

Time to change the subject. 'My parents were from Trapetto, a fishing village in Sicily. But I was brought up in Scotland. I'm a Glasgow girl through and through.' She waved her hand. 'And don't even try to speak to me in Italian. I'm not fluent at all—I know enough for emergencies and how to order dinner but that's it.'

'Didn't you speak Italian at home?'

His voice brought her back to reality. 'Rarely. There wasn't much call for it in Glasgow.'

Her eyelids had lowered, as if this wasn't a conversation she wanted to get into. Why was that?

Francesca picked up his dirty clothes. 'I take it you're okay if I dump these?'

He nodded and shifted on the bed, frowning at his attached leads. 'So what are you doing here, Francesca?'

She froze, a little shocked by the bluntness of the question. This guy was going to take a bit of getting used to.

She frowned at him, knowing her brow was wrinkled and it wasn't the most flattering of looks. 'What on earth are you talking about?'

There it was again, that little hint of something—but not quite obvious.

'I would have thought that was obvious. I'm here working as an ANP. Maybe I should check that head knock of yours again.'

His eyebrows lifted. 'I'm curious what a young, well-qualified nurse like you is doing here.' His hand swept outwards to the surrounding area.

She felt a little shiver steal down her spine. Nosy parker. She kept her voice steady. 'You mean here…' she spread her arms out and spun round '…in this state-of-the-art medical complex, in the middle of the Mediterranean, with a different port every day and a chance to see the world?'

She planted her hands on her hips and looked at him as defiantly as she could. She was stating the obvious. The thing that any website would quote for prospective job-seekers. It was a cop-out and she knew it. But she didn't like the way he'd asked the question. It was as if he'd already peered deep inside her and knew things she didn't want anyone else to know.

'I'm just curious. Your family is in Glasgow. And yet, you're here…' His voice tailed off. Almost as if he was contemplating the thought himself.

Something inside her snapped. Were all Italians as old-fashioned as him?

'My family isn't in Glasgow any more. Get a life, Gabriel. Isn't a girl allowed to spread her wings and get a job elsewhere? Maybe I'm trying to connect with my roots in Sicily. Maybe I was just bored in Glasgow. Maybe I want to see the world. Or it could just be that I'm killing time until I get my visa to Australia. I thought cruise ships would be fun. Truth be told, so far I've found it all a bit boring.' The words were out before she'd thought about it. Out before she had a chance to take them back.

She cringed. He was her boss. He was her *brand-new* boss, who had no idea about her skills, experience and competency level—probably the only things that could be her saving grace right now. How to win friends and influence people. Not.

She pushed the dirty clothes inside a plastic disposal bag, 'I'll get rid of these,' she muttered as she turned to leave.

This was going to be nightmare. This ship was huge.

Big enough for two thousand, six hundred passengers and
five hundred staff. But this medical centre? Not so big.
And the staff worked very closely together. Some days
the medical centre felt positively crowded.

And the last thing she needed was to be stuck with some
playboy doc. A pain shot through her chest. The last time
she'd been distracted by a playboy doc it had had a devastating effect on her family life, causing irreparable damage. She could *not* allow that to happen again, no matter
what the circumstances.

Every part of her body was buzzing. She hadn't even
had a chance to think about what had happened today.
She'd resuscitated someone.

Someone who could, potentially, have died if she hadn't
taken those actions.

The thought of dealing with a death again horrified her.
It didn't matter that she was a nurse. Her circumstances
had changed. Everything had changed.

Deaths weren't supposed to happen on cruise ships.
Working here was part of her safety net—keeping her away
from the aspects of her job she couldn't deal with any more.

And now him.

On top of everything else.

She leaned back against the wall. There was no two
ways about it.

This ship wasn't big enough for the two of them.

# CHAPTER THREE

FRANCESCA's fingers thumped furiously on the keyboard.

Hey babe!
You'll never believe who I'm working with right now—
Gabriel Russo. Yes, the very one. And he's every bit the
conceited billionaire boy that he was six years ago. It took
me a few minutes to work out who he was—probably because I had to resuscitate him first—but needless to say,
once I'd reminded him I was your flatmate you could cut
the atmosphere in here with a knife.

Cruise ships might look huge in real life but the reality is, when you can't stand to be around someone, they
seem very small.

Haven't seen you in a while, so hope you're doing well.
In the meantime living in hope he'll fall overboard,
Fran xx

'Busy?'

The voice, cutting through the dark medical centre in
the dead of night, made her jump. Couldn't she get any
peace from this man?

She could barely tolerate being in the same room as
him. What's more, he constantly appeared at her shoulder,

checking over what she'd done. And for someone whose confidence was already at rock bottom it was more than a little irritating.

There were always two crew members on call at night—one for the passengers and one for the crew. One week had passed and this was Gabriel's first official night on call and Francesca had drawn the short straw of babysitting him.

She spun around in her chair to face him. He had his black medical bag in his hand. 'I'm waiting for one of the crew members to meet me,' she said. 'She's complaining of abdominal pain.'

'Need a hand?'

Francesca bit her tongue to stop her saying the words that were dancing around her head right now. *Over my dead body* probably wouldn't go down that well with her boss.

'No, I'm fine, thanks.' She pasted a smile on her face and gestured towards his bag. 'You look busy enough anyway. Lots of passenger callouts?'

He nodded, rubbing his hand across his eyes. 'Three in the last hour. All for really ridiculous things. Please tell me this isn't a normal night.'

Francesca smiled. If it had been anyone else she would have told him about the 'cougar list' currently taped inside one of the cupboard doors in the treatment room.

The list of well-known passengers—mainly women in their forties and fifties—who developed symptoms requiring a cabin call whenever a new, young doctor came on board. She could bet in the last hour Gabriel had seen a lot of skin and satin negligees.

Not all the passengers changed every week or every fortnight. A certain select group seemed to spend a large part of their life cruising. It was not unusual to have the same passengers on board for four to six weeks at a time. Sometimes they swapped to another ship for a month and then came back to the *Silver Whisper* again.

The 'cougar list' had been started by Kevin, one of the nurses, after he'd noticed a sharp rise in callouts whenever a new doctor started. It was really just a warning list to give the person on call the opportunity to decide if they wanted to take the other crew member on duty with them. She would tell him about the list—really, she would—just not yet.

Francesca was sure that Gabriel could handle a few coy looks. After all, hadn't he spent his life chasing women, collecting them like trophies and then unceremoniously dumping them? This should be a breeze for him.

'Here, have a look at this.' She handed him the communiqué she'd been given requesting details about the rescue at Venezia Passegeri. Apparently the media were keen to run a story. 'They're a little late but maybe they were short of news.'

A dark shadow passed over his face as his eyes flew over the page. 'Absolutely not. No names. I don't want to talk about last week. Make sure the communications officer understands.'

She shrugged, a little surprised by his reaction. 'The cruise line probably wants the publicity,' she suggested. 'What's the problem? You're used to being in the news.'

'No!' He looked furious. He crumpled the piece of paper in his hand and threw it deftly into the wastepaper bin. She smirked. *Message received, loud and clear.*

Was this man temperamental? Maybe his snappiness after his head injury hadn't been the result of the accident. His questions to her had been a little blunt. He certainly wasn't exhibiting all the traits Jill had told her about of the flirtatious, playboy doctor. Gabriel Russo seemed to be a wolf in doctor's clothing. And the thought intrigued her.

Katherine had complained bitterly last week that Gabriel wasn't the best of patients—apparently she'd had to practically pin him to the bed to monitor his neuro obs overnight after his head injury. He'd been furious when Dr Marsh had insisted he be monitored overnight and it had been a relief to them all when he'd been given a clean bill of health the following morning and allowed to take on normal duties.

His pager sounded again and he sighed, picking up his medical bag and heading for the door. 'If I'm not back in an hour page me.' He hesitated for a second, his brown eyes connecting with hers. 'Please.'

Francesca couldn't help but smile. Maybe he was finally catching onto the cougar brigade.

She turned back to the computer and pulled up the file for the crew member she was about to meet.

The notes were limited. Elena Portiss, twenty-seven, from Spain, working on board as a bartender, with a declared past medical history of endometriosis.

She'd phoned ten minutes earlier saying her abdominal pain was worse than usual—bad abdominal pain was not uncommon in a woman with a history of endometriosis.

There was a noise behind her and Francesca stood up and flicked the switch, lighting up the medical unit.

'Elena?'

The young woman nodded.

Francesca was immediately struck by how pale the girl was. Her pale blue eyes were dull and lifeless, her normally tanned skin pallid and slightly waxy.

'Come in here.' Francesca walked into the nearby room and gestured Elena towards one of the examination trolleys. She worked quickly, checking her temperature, blood pressure and pulse. 'You have endometriosis?' Francesca spoke slowly, taking care in case there was any difficulty in language.

Elena nodded. Francesca noted that her hands were positioned carefully over her stomach, obviously trying to keep her pain in check. 'It was diagnosed last year after I had very painful periods.' She lifted her shirt and pointed to a little scar next to her belly button. 'I had a camera in there.'

Francesca nodded. If Elena had had a laparoscopy done and the diagnosis confirmed then it was likely that her symptoms were related to her endometriosis.

'Do you normally use painkillers?' Elena nodded and fumbled in her bag, pulling out a battered box with the name written in Spanish. Francesca took the box, looking at it and writing the name down in the notes. It was a commonly used non-steroidal anti-inflammatory drug that was effective in treating endometriosis.

'We will be able to give you something similar,' she reassured Elena, 'but the box may look a little different. Have you tried anything else?'

Elena pulled a second, slightly more battered cardboard box from her bag. 'I stopped taking these,' she said, 'as they made me feel unwell.' As she didn't recognise the name on the box Francesca opened it and pulled out the foil strip with the twenty-eight tablets enclosed. Around half were missing and she realised immediately what they were. Oral contraceptives were commonly used to treat endometriosis in women who weren't trying to start a family. They worked by regulating the hormone levels to stop the production of oestrogen in the body. Without exposure to oestrogen, the endometrial tissue could be reduced and this helped to ease symptoms.

'Do you remember when your last period was?' Francesca asked.

'I'm not sure. I had some bleeding yesterday and a little this morning, but it wasn't much.'

'I'm so sorry, but I'm going to have to get a urine specimen from you. Do you think you can manage to go to the toilet for me?'

Elena grimaced as Francesca helped her to the toilet. It only took a few minutes before she was back on the couch and Francesca reattached her to the blood-pressure cuff. BP was ninety over sixty. Hypotensive. Colour poor. Alarm bells started to go off inside Francesca's head.

The amount of pain that Elena was exhibiting was more than would be expected. Elena nodded, still clutching her stomach.

Francesca's spider sense was tingling. Her instinct—the thing she'd thought she'd lost.

This wasn't right. This didn't *feel* right. Elena's pain seemed too severe and too localised to be endometriosis. Francesca knew that endometriosis was a painful condition in which the endometrial cells that would normally be present within the lining of the womb could be deposited in other areas around the body. These cells were still influenced by the female hormones and could cause pain in various areas, particularly around the pelvis.

And she knew how painful it could be—one of her friends spent a few days every month doubled up in bed. But this just didn't add up.

She checked the urine sample for infection and it was clear. Francesca opened the nearby cupboard and pulled out another test. It was only a hunch and she could be wrong. Using a little pipette she dropped a few drops of urine onto the test and checked her watch. A little line appeared.

Her heart gave a flutter in her chest. She hadn't been wrong and for a second she felt almost elated. Then common sense pulled her back to reality.

She needed help. And no matter how much he irritated her, she knew who to call.

The pager sounded again.

Gabriel was annoyed. What would be the reason for this ridiculous callout? A stubbed toe? A grazed elbow? He was going to have serious words with the team in the morning if this was what they normally dealt with.

He glanced at the number on the pager. The medical centre. Francesca. Now, that *was* a surprise. She'd looked as if she'd rather set her hair on fire than ask him for help earlier.

And as for the media request…

It made his blood boil. His family were constantly in the paper—particularly in Italy. With the words 'tragic' usually appearing in the second sentence. Twenty-five years ago the media had been all over them and their 'tragic' loss. Every time they were mentioned in the press it was all raked over again.

The last thing they needed was more painful reminders.

Didn't they get that the loss of Dante was imprinted on them for life, seared on their very souls?

Gabriel had never once given an interview to a journalist.

Correction. Gabriel had never *knowingly* given an interview to a journalist. The ugly remnants of a faked past relationship by an aspiring reporter burned hard. That, and his experience with Jill and a few others like her, told him that women weren't to be trusted. Under any circumstances.

It only took him a few moments to reach the medical centre.

'What's wrong?'

Francesca was waiting at the door for him, some notes in her hands and a worried expression on her face.

She thrust the notes towards him. 'Elena Portiss, twenty-seven, severe abdominal pain, past history of endometriosis.'

'Have you given her some analgesics?'

'Not yet.'

'Why not?'

She hesitated just for a second. 'Because she's pregnant and she doesn't know it. I think it may be an ectopic pregnancy,' she said tentatively.

Gabriel's eyes skimmed over the notes in front of him. He'd no idea why she looked like a deer currently caught in the headlights. She'd done everything he would have expected. 'Let's find out.'

Francesca caught his arm as he walked past her. 'I haven't given her any indication about what I think may be wrong.' Gabriel caught the worried expression in her eyes. He understood completely. Endometriosis was frequently associated with infertility. To tell the patient that she was pregnant but that the pregnancy was ectopic would be a devastating blow. He strode through to the treatment room and spoke to Elena, who was lying on the examination couch, her face still racked in pain.

'Hello, Elena,' he said confidently, 'my name is Dr Russo. I'm one of the ship's doctors. Nurse Cruz has asked that I take a little look at you.' He shook Elena's trembling hand. As he placed his hands very gently on her stomach he noticed her visibly flinching. 'I promise you, I will be very gentle.'

He moved lightly across her abdomen, pressing gently with his fingertips from one side to the other. 'Where is the pain worse? Here? Here?'

Elena shook her head tensely, and then grimaced again in pain as his fingers reached her right side. The clinical signs were all present. She was pale, hypotensive, with lower abdominal tenderness and distension. That, together with a positive pregnancy test, gave an almost conclusive picture.

Francesca watched him from the corner of the room. Had she been wrong to mention her tentative diagnosis? Other doctors might have thought she was stepping on their toes to make such a suggestion.

But Gabriel hadn't even blinked. He didn't seem offended or annoyed with her suggestion. His only concern seemed to be for the patient.

Given the hostility between them it could have been a perfect opportunity for him to take her to task.

But apparently not. This man wasn't exactly how she'd imagined him to be.

'Okay, that's me finished.' He took his hands from Elena's abdomen and stood next to her.

'Do you know the date of your last period, Elena?'

She shook her head miserably. 'I have been bleeding on and off for several months. I can't say for sure. I was taking the Pill, too, but it made me feel unwell, so I stopped. Then I had some light bleeding yesterday. I'm not sure when my last period was.'

Gabriel nodded, 'That's okay'. He turned to Francesca. 'Can you check her BP and pulse again for me, please, and draw some bloods? I'll need her urea and electrolytes, but more importantly a full blood count, please.'

Francesca nodded and set the monitor to retake Elena's blood pressure while she opened the nearby drawer to find the blood bottles. Once the blood pressure had been recorded she removed the cuff and replaced it with a tourniquet to facilite taking some blood. It only took her a matter of seconds to locate a vein. 'Just a little prick,' she said to Elena as she gently slid the needle into the vein and attached the bottle to collect the blood samples. Francesca released the clip on the tourniquet, letting it spring apart, relieving the pressure on Elena's arm. She placed the needle in the nearby sharps box and gave Gabriel a quick glance as she left the room. 'I'll phone Kevin and get him to do the blood results for us.'

She wondered if he realised how quickly her heart was beating in her chest. Elena's blood count would be a good indicator of whether her diagnosis was correct or not.

It could also prove that her instincts were still completely off.

The medical centre was equipped with a wide range of laboratory equipment that allowed the staff to carry out many diagnostic tests that were essential to diagnosing and treating patients. Kevin arrived a few minutes later, hair mussed, took the blood samples and prepared them for testing. When she returned to the room Gabriel was sitting next to the examination trolley, talking to Elena. Francesca could see the serious expression on his face and watched as he gently took Elena's hand to explain her condition. Gabriel was surprising her. He was taking time to talk to Elena, to hold her hand and explain clearly what was happening. For some reason she found it almost the opposite of what she'd expected. This was a man who'd flung her friend out on the street at three o'clock in the morning yet here he was as a doctor, doing everything he should and showing empathy for his patient. In her head that just didn't fit. Her curiosity was piqued.

She listened quietly in the background.

'Elena,' he said gently, 'I think it is likely that you're having an ectopic pregnancy.' He noticed the complete confusion on her face, and realised she hadn't really understood. 'Your urine test shows that you are pregnant—but this is not a normal pregnancy.'

'But I can't be pregnant—I have endometriosis—it's not possible for me to be pregnant.' Her face was filled with shock.

'It is possible,' Gabriel continued carefully. 'Have you had sex in the last six weeks?'

Elena nodded numbly.

'Although your condition makes it difficult to conceive, it is not impossible. It is likely that because you were taking the contraceptive pill you've become unclear about when your next period was due. Your urine test is definitely positive. However, the pain and discomfort that you are feeling makes it likely that, instead of implanting in the womb, the fertilised egg has implanted in your Fallopian tube.' He picked up a nearby book with pictures of the female reproductive system and pointed to the various areas, showing her where the fertilised ovum had likely reached.

The medical staff often used these clear diagrammatic books to explain conditions to crew members of different nationalities. 'The embryo can't develop within this confined space and causes bleeding and pain. Sometimes the tube can rupture and that can be very serious. But in all cases the pregnancy can't continue.'

He waited for a moment, until he could tell that Elena

had processed the information he had given her. Elena started sobbing uncontrollably. Gabriel had been right. The news of a pregnancy, followed by the news that it was ectopic and couldn't produce a baby, had devastated her.

'What happens now?' she asked.

Gabriel stood up from the chair. 'We have to watch you very closely so we are going to admit you to our intensive care unit. I'll put up some fluids and give you some pain relief. One of our nurses will come and take some more bloods from you in the next few hours. I will have to arrange for you to go to hospital at the next port.'

Kevin appeared and handed Gabriel the blood results. Haemoglobin eight point seven. Gabriel glanced in Francesca's direction. No words were needed. They both knew that was much lower than normal for a woman of her age and more than likely an indicator of some internal bleeding.

Francesca felt the flush of relief rush through her system. She'd been right. For once her instincts had been good. If things weren't so serious for their patient right now she would run outside and breathe a big sigh of relief.

When had been the last time she'd felt like this? The last time she'd had real confidence in her abilities as a nurse?

After her initial meeting with Gabriel, she couldn't have blamed him if he'd ignored her instincts at all. But he hadn't.

He hadn't even really questioned her. He'd taken her at her word and just moved on. He hadn't even *doubted* her. Why?

This virtual stranger had more faith in her than she had in herself. Maybe there was more to him than met the eye.

Sure enough, they'd been mouth to mouth before, but he couldn't remember any of that—could he?

Francesca administered the analgesia and then moved through to the intensive care unit to set up the bed and equipment that would be needed.

Gabriel came over and placed a hand on her shoulder, his forefinger touching the delicate skin at the side of her neck. She felt herself flinch but not in displeasure, just at the electricity of his warm touch. The tingles running down her spine were making her lose her concentration. He leaned towards her with a wide smile, showing his perfect teeth. 'That was an impressive call, Francesca,' he praised. 'Not one that everyone would have recognised— and that includes medical staff. Her initial symptoms could easily have been written off as her ongoing endometriosis.' He nodded his head in appreciation. 'What made you think twice?'

'Instinct,' came the immediate reply, followed by a loose shrug of the shoulders. 'It just didn't seem right.' *Instinct.* The word had come to her lips so easily. Almost automatically. Too bad she hadn't always trusted her instincts. Maybe then she would still be in Glasgow.

Maybe then she would still have some of her family left.

Something else stirred inside her. He was praising her. He was giving her the credit for the diagnosis. And it spread a warm feeling through her insides. Maybe she should be more confident about herself—the way she used to be.

'I've spoken to the captain. We are due to dock in Piraeus tomorrow at nine. He's told me that if there are problems he will probably be able to arrange a quicker dock time, as long as we give him some notice. He could alter the speed accordingly as the actual physical sea miles could be covered more quickly if it was necessary. Who will be looking after the patient?'

'I will.' There was no way she wanted anyone else to look after Elena. She wanted to see this through.

The next port was in Athens, Greece, and although the actual distance between Venice and Athens was not huge, they often spent full days at sea. This gave passengers time to adjust to the feel of the ocean and a chance to find their way around the boat. They'd already circled the Med once and were repeating the journey again.

Kevin appeared at the door. 'She's complaining of shoulder-tip pain now, Dr Russo.' Gabriel crossed the room quickly. Shoulder-tip pain could be a serious sign. It could mean that there was internal bleeding into the abdominal cavity that was irritating the diaphragm. This was usually a sign that the ectopic pregnancy had ruptured and would require surgery—something they were not equipped to do at sea. He spent a few more moments examining Elena, while Francesca rechecked her pulse and blood pressure.

'Pulse one-ten, BP eighty-five over fifty.' Her hand reached automatically towards the intravenous fluids that were hanging next to the bed. 'Do you want these increased?' He nodded and she automatically adjusted the controls on the machine. It was clear from her symptoms that Elena's ectopic pregnancy had ruptured and she was bleeding internally. Her pulse had risen and blood pressure dropped, which meant she was going into hypovolaemic shock. Increasing her intravenous fluids would only be a minor stopgap in trying to treat her. She really needed surgery.

Gabriel stood up swiftly. 'I'm going to notify the captain and arrange an emergency evac.'

Francesca watched his retreating back. She was impressed by how calm he was. She hadn't been able to ascertain whether Gabriel had much experience of being at sea, but on more than one occasion she had seen other doctors panic at the thought of dealing with a surgical emergency on board. Most doctors were used to working in large general hospitals that had all the services they needed at their fingertips. Working at sea was entirely different. Making a wrong decision could cost a patient their life, but Gabriel appeared to be taking it all in his stride.

There was the tiniest flutter in her stomach. If, for any reason, they couldn't get Elena off the ship there was a possibility she could die.

Francesca pushed the thought from her mind. She couldn't even contemplate anything like that. She couldn't bear the thought of having to deal with the death of a patient. Not now.

She watched as he pressed the button on the phone to end his first call and start another. 'The captain will go with my decision. We can't wait to get to the port. I'm phoning the Medevac agency to arrange a suitable rendezvous point for the helicopter.'

'I'll get the Medevac checklist.'

Francesca started completing the essential checklist that would give the Medevac team all the vital information they needed to know about the patient. By the time she had finished Gabriel had put down the phone. He quickly checked Elena again, noting her BP and pulse and checking her IV fluids.

'Have you told her yet?' he asked.

Francesca shook her head. 'I wanted to wait until you had confirmed it with the captain. Do you want me to tell her now?'

Gabriel shook his head. 'Let me,' he said.

There it was again. Compassion for his patient. This from a man who had thrown her friend out on the street in the middle of the night. Some things just didn't add up. How long would it take Jill to answer that email?

He walked over to where Elena was lying and took her hand again. 'Elena? It's Dr Russo. I need to speak to you again.'

Her eyes flickered open at the sound of his voice. She was obviously still in pain.

'Elena, I think that the ectopic pregnancy has probably ruptured and caused bleeding into your abdomen. That's why you are feeling so unwell.' He pointed to the IV fluids hanging next to her. 'These can only help for a limited amount of time. You really need to have surgery to stop the bleeding.'

'But how can I?'

'We've made arrangements for you to be airlifted off the ship and taken to a nearby hospital. The helicopter will be here soon, we just need to make sure you are ready to be moved.'

She looked shocked at the prospect and twisted uncomfortably on the bed, her face still racked with pain. 'But where will it land?'

Gabriel spoke reassuringly. 'Deck Sixteen—the sports deck has room for the helicopter to land next to the jogging track. We'll arrange to take you up there once we have word they will be arriving.'

The phone rang in the nearby office and Gabriel came out. 'The closest largest town with medical facilities is Amaliada. They have a large general hospital that can deal with this. We're around ninety miles off the coast from Amaliada right now. That was the captain. He's cleared the landing site and ETA is in the next ten minutes. We better get a move on.'

Francesca produced some thick woollen blankets to

protect Elena from the wind and tucked them round her.
Gabriel finished casting his eye over the Medevac checklist
and signed it. He grabbed the nearest luminescent jacket
and pulled it over his uniform; Francesca and Kevin were
already wearing theirs. 'Are we good to go?' he checked,
and when they nodded in agreement he released the brake
on the trolley and started pushing it out of the door.

His hand and forearm were next to Francesca's and she
glanced up at him, wondering if he realised his hand was
touching hers. His head was down and he seemed totally
focused on his task, then, out of the blue, he gave her hand
a little squeeze and shot her a quick grin. Two other crew
members were waiting in the corridor for them to clear
the path to the nearest lift. Francesca watched Elena carefully. Her BP was still low and colour poor, but she could
already hear the hum of the approaching helicopter so it
wouldn't be long now.

The doors of the lift opened at Deck Sixteen and they
were immediately met by the biting wind caused by the
hovering helicopter. The noise was deafening.

'Let's stay in here until the helicopter lands,' shouted
Gabriel. They watched as four crewman wearing luminescent jackets like their own, and carrying paddles, signalled
the helicopter it was safe to land.

The helicopter touched down and they ran forward,
pulling the trolley between them and keeping their heads
down low. A Medevac team member opened the side door
of the helicopter and jumped out.

'Dr Russo?' he shouted above the din of the rotating
blades. Gabriel nodded and helped move Elena onto the
helicopter's own trolley, which could be easily lifted inside.
He bent his head next to the Medevac team member, hand-
ing over the checklist and shouting some extra instructions.

Francesca and Kevin pulled the medical centre trolley back towards the lift, moving out of the way of the crew-men who were ready to signal the helicopter to lift off.

Gabriel ran over to join them next to the lift and in a matter of seconds the door banged shut and the helicopter took off into the sky with a small wave from the Medevac team member. They watched as the noise dissipated and the whirring blades became a blur in the distance.

Silence fell over them. All that was left was the steady sound of the ship's engines, purring away in the dark of the night.

'Well,' said Gabriel, the serious expression leaving his face and a wicked glint in his brown eyes as he turned towards Francesca. He gave her a wink. 'A near drowning, a resuscitation and an ectopic pregnancy all in the space of one week. Who said this job was boring!'

# CHAPTER FOUR

'DID you know about this?'

Gabriel looked distinctly unimpressed. He was holding the pink piece of paper containing the 'cougar list' in his hand. The tape was still stuck to the top of the page and the cupboard door was lying open.

She smiled. 'Oops. Did I forget to mention that?'

'Yes. You did.'

For a second she almost felt guilty. But it didn't last long. He was scowling at her again. The thrill and adrenaline from last night was gone and they were back to the routine of her hating him and him watching her every move. This would be a long day.

He was still growling at her. 'Any reason you didn't tell me about it?'

*Because I think you're a snake and you deserved a bit of your own medicine.*

The words danced around her brain. She bit her lip to stop herself from saying them out loud. Why did he look so mad? Offended almost?

Was he currently reading her less than complimentary thoughts?

She tried to change the subject quickly. 'It's probably going to be quiet today—most of the passengers will dis-

embark at Piraeus to go on the sightseeing tours of Athens.'
Francesca picked up a crew list. 'Katherine is working too
this morning so it would probably be best if we tried to
cover as many of the crew medicals as possible.'

Gabriel glanced over the list, underlining a few names
in red. 'These are the ones I want to see.'

Francesca felt her lips tighten. The role of the advanced
nurse practitioner was one that some doctors struggled to
understand. Her job included most of the extended skills
that general nurses could do—cannulation, suturing,
venepuncture. But she also had advanced skills in reading X-rays, prescribing some general medications and diagnostic skills more equated with those of a junior doctor.

On a day-to-day basis these weren't always needed.
Most patients attended with minor illnesses, respiratory
and gastrointestinal infections, minor skin complaints and
fractures and accidental injuries that happened either on
board or ashore.

But the crew medicals could involve more intensive
work-ups and regular reviews of ongoing chronic conditions, and Francesca enjoyed doing them. Gabriel had just
underlined some of the patients that she normally reviewed
herself and it irked her.

'I normally see these patients.' She pointed to the few
he'd marked on the list.

His brow narrowed. 'And today I'm going to see them.'

Was he just being pig-headed? Did he think this a role
that only a doctor could fulfil? Or was he just doing this
to annoy her?

'But I've seen these patients on a regular basis. I understand them, and how they deal with their conditions. Surely
it would be best if they were reviewed by someone familiar
with their set of circumstances?' She was determined to

keep the annoyance out of her voice. She wanted to sound professional. She wanted to sound completely rational.

Gabriel seemed unmoved. 'Like I said, today I'm going to see them.' He picked up the list and started walking to his room. 'Sometimes it takes a fresh pair of eyes to look over a case to decide on the best plan of treatment for a patient.'

She could feel the hackles at the back of her neck rise.

She wanted to shout. She wanted to tell him he was condescending. She wanted to tell him to stop trying to find fault with her. Did he really think she was going to fall for that lame excuse?

She knew he was going to look over all her patient consult notes to see if he could find a reason to get rid of her. Did he have to be so obvious?

She turned and smiled sweetly, pasting a smile so sickly on to her face he would have no doubt what she was thinking. 'Whatever you think, Dr Russo.' She picked up her copy of the list and headed into the next room, sitting down in front of one of the computers and tapping furiously.

Her mind whirred. *I hate him. He's a superficial, condescending git. He has more money than sense. He flung Jill onto the street at 3:00 a.m. Who does that? How dared he? Does he think he can treat all women like that?*

'So what's with you and our hunky new Italian doctor? You can't keep your eyes off him.' Katherine had perched on the edge of the desk next to her.

'What?'

She smiled at Francesca and folded her arms. 'But I can't quite get what's going on between you two. When I say you can't keep your eyes off him—it's not in a good way. You look at him as if you're plotting fifty different ways to kill him and hide the body.' She shook her head knowingly. 'Now, that isn't the sweet-natured Francesca I know and love.' She bent across the desk, closing the space between them both and propping her chin on one hand. 'So what gives? Are you a lover scorned? Did you meet in a past life? Were you secret childhood sweethearts—?'

'Have you completely lost your mind?'

Katherine's face broke into a wide smile. She nodded her head, 'See? I knew it. I *knew* there was something there.' She couldn't hide the self-satisfied look from her face. 'So why do you hate him so much? Because, to be honest, after that one hellish night doing his neuro obs I've found him quite charming. And so has everyone else. And have you seen him with kids? The guy is *seriously* good with them.'

Francesca shook her head. She couldn't believe this. She couldn't believe the rest of the staff was fooled by his good looks and killer abs. She finished the notes she was inputting and turned to face Katherine.

'I think he's conceited. I feel as if he's constantly looking over my shoulder, trying to find fault.'

Katherine sighed. 'He's only been here just over a week. How can you possibly think that?'

Francesca held up the list. 'Look at this. He's taken all my usual crew members for review. He's checking up on me. He's trying to find fault.'

'Or maybe he's the new guy and he's trying to work out how we do things around here?'

Her words hung in the air. Francesca didn't like them. It made her look as if *she* was trying to find fault with him. Not the other way about.

'You honestly find him charming?'

Katherine nodded slowly, her gaze disappearing off into the distance. 'Yeah, he is kind of charming. And those dark brown eyes are just to die for. And his teeth…' She turned back to face Francesca. 'He's got a set of teeth that could appear in a television commercial. When I was doing his neuro obs in the middle of the night he got up for a shower. Now, that really was an eyeful.' She was off again, into her daydream-like state.

Francesca cringed. All the things that she'd noticed first about Gabriel. The kind of superficial things that shouldn't really matter. Looks were only skin deep. Words that she'd repeated over and over again to Jill.

And yet she'd done it herself. She'd seen him lying on the bottom of that boat and for a second had thought, Wow. Totally unprofessional. Thank goodness hearing his name had brought her back to her senses.

'Don't be fooled by his looks, Katherine. It's what's inside that counts. And I have it on good authority that his handsome looks don't penetrate beneath the surface.'

Katherine looked shocked. 'What does that mean?'

'He used to date one of my friends. And he didn't treat her particularly well.'

'Why, what happened?'

Francesca waved her hand. 'I don't want to get into it. Needless to say, the feelings are mutual. I'm not impressed to be working with him and he's not impressed to be working with me.' Francesca shook her head. 'And anyway, is it the handsome looks that are the attraction or is it the fact the man is practically dripping with diamonds?'

Katherine's pretty face turned into a frown. 'Now I really have no idea what you're talking about.'

'Gabriel Russo? Member of one of the richest families in Venice?'

Katherine shook her head. The name obviously meant nothing to her.

Francesca sighed and turned back to the computer, tapping into one of the internet search engines. 'I hadn't heard of him, either. But after he treated my friend so badly I looked him up. See?' She turned the screen to face Katherine.

Katherine leaned forward. 'Oh, wow!' Headline after headline. All about the Russo family and how they were one of the first printing families in Venice. Image after image appeared on the screen. Francesca drew in a sharp breath.

'What is it? Is it that one?' Katherine pointed to a brown, muscled, very well-endowed picture of Gabriel perched on the edge of a brilliant yacht in a pair of white swimming trunks. The picture left nothing to the imagination. It could have adorned the walls of teenage girls up and down the country.

'What? Yes... I mean, no.' Francesca sighed. 'That's my friend.' She pointed to a figure in the background of the picture, a young blonde in a turquoise bikini. 'I just didn't expect to see her online.'

Katherine read a few more of the headlines. 'It seems our new resident doc is dripping with diamonds. So what's he doing here?'

'It's a good question and I've no idea. I just know I won't be joining his fan club.'

'Look at that.'

'What?' Francesca really didn't want to look at another picture of Gabriel in his swim shorts. But Katherine was pointing at some professional journal articles, all with Gabriel's name attached, and all on paediatrics. So he specialised in paediatrics. The penny dropped. That explained his actions the other day. That was why he was so good with kids. How come he hadn't mentioned it?

Katherine pursed her lips. 'So what's he like?'

'What do you mean—what's he like? It wasn't me who used to date him.'

'No, I mean as a doctor. You worked with him last night—and I heard you didn't tell him about the cougar list, by the way, naughty, naughty.' She waggled her finger at Francesca. 'Was he any good?'

Francesca almost felt the words stick in her throat. Last night *had* bothered her. Whilst she knew someone who was a rat in real life could be professionally good at their job, it was more than that. She'd seen the compassion in Gabriel's eyes when he'd spoken to their patient. He'd been more than calm and competent in a situation in which others might have panicked. Especially when he was new on board. Especially now that she knew his speciality was paediatrics. He could have felt totally out of his depth and how much help would she have given him?

'He was fine.' Struck by the realisation of how well he'd performed the night before, it was as much as she could manage.

The look on Katherine's face said it all as she slid off the desk. 'He was fine? He diagnosed an ectopic pregnancy and organised an emergency airlift—probably saving a life on his first night on call. All from a guy who specialises in paediatrics, and "he was fine"?' She nodded her head sarcastically and disappeared out of the room.

Francesca felt overwhelmed. So much had happened in the last few days. She couldn't make sense of most of it. Most of the time she couldn't stand to be around Gabriel. But even that confused her. Everyone else thought he was charming, so why couldn't she?

It would be easy to say it was her extended knowledge of him. But there was something else. Something she hated.

The way she found her eyes following him around the room.

The way she believed the compassion in his eyes the night before had been real.

The admiration she'd felt for his skill while treating Elena.

The fact that if this was another life, another set of circumstances, she might actually be attracted to him.

A sense of loneliness swept over her, coupled with the feelings of inadequacy creeping up out of nowhere. The feeling of being under a microscope, her every move examined. Completely exposed.

She thought back to last night—automatically falling into self-preservation mode. She'd been right about Elena's condition. She'd made the right call. A new feeling of determination swept over her. Her mind was telling her one thing but her churning stomach telling her another. Why did she feel so unsure?

Katherine's words echoed in her brain. *He diagnosed an ectopic pregnancy and organised an emergency airlift— probably saving a life on his first night on call.*

Francesca was left staring at her screen. 'I diagnosed the ectopic pregnancy,' she whispered to the empty room.

Gabriel was furious. He'd gone back to raise a query with Francesca about a patient's medication and he'd caught the words 'dripping with diamonds'. They'd sent an icy chill down his spine.

He hadn't listened to much more—he didn't need to. Once more he'd been judged and valued on his bank balance rather than his clinical expertise.

He hated internet search engines with a passion. Wasn't a person allowed a modicum of privacy any more?

So now he was being judged on his money once again. His family name. How long before they found the word 'tragedy' attached to something and started to tiptoe round about him?

It was the overwhelming reason he'd chosen to work overseas—away from Italy and its close-knit gentry. Away from others who were aware of his family background.

It was bad enough that she hadn't told him about the cougar list. Yet another person sitting in judgement of him and believing the gossip.

For a second—just for a second last night—he'd seen a glimmer of hope in Francesca. She'd seemed an able and competent nurse. More than that, she'd shown good instincts. Even if she hadn't been sure of them herself, they had still been there. It would have been so easy for her not to ask for a consultation on their patient.

Some medical staff would have been content with the endometriosis diagnosis and assumed that some of the cells had spread, causing more pain and inflammation. Most would probably have given a stronger painkiller with instructions to come back if there was no improvement.

Might he have done that?

Last night he'd had respect for his prickly nurse—despite her poor choice of friend. Respect because she'd earned it.

Today she was back in the doldrums of disgust. Francesca had already told him she knew who he was and questioned his need to work. To earn his own salary.

But she knew nothing about his attempts to distance himself from the family business. About the general chaos he'd created as a teenager when he'd announced his intentions not to move into the well-paid position created for him but to follow the career of his heart. The one imprinted into his being years before.

He was the last remaining son—his father had been devastated by his decision. But Gabriel had been determined—nothing would change his mind. And his strong, intelligent and often overlooked sister was more than ready to step into his shoes, with a passion, drive and commitment to the family business that Gabriel could never have equalled.

Francesca knew none of this and probably would never understand. Not if she had the same mindset as her friend. One that could never look underneath the surface.

Jill had been horrified when she'd been caught with Gabriel's twenty-thousand-pound watch stuffed in her bag. He might have even believed the feeble story she'd started to spout if he hadn't seen her deliberately take it and hide it in the inside pocket. She was lucky he'd only flung her out on the street instead of calling the police.

Why did Francesca feel the need to tell all her colleagues about his wealth? He'd hoped to be part of a team that would judge him on his clinical competence, not the fact he was 'dripping with diamonds'.

How could he trust anyone now? Rich kids learned quickly that wealth attracted all sorts of insincere friends. It had never really been an issue at work before.

And now Francesca had made it an issue by gossiping.

He gritted his teeth. He wanted to hate her—he really did.

But he'd noticed something. Her happy, bubbly exterior with her colleagues was just that—an exterior. Scratch the surface and who knew what he might find? There had been a wistfulness in her eyes that had looked as if it reached down into her very soul. She genuinely hadn't trusted her instincts last night and he had to wonder why. She was a good nurse. She should have confidence in her abilities. Had something or someone taken her confidence away?

Whether he liked it or not, she was part of this team.

He wanted to work with competent, confident individuals. He liked to know their strengths—and their weaknesses—to get the best possible results for the patients they were serving. Here things would be no different.

It was why he'd taken some of her patients today. She seemed an able and competent nurse but he wanted to dig a little deeper.

So far, he'd found nothing to concern him. All the patients she'd seen had been well cared for. Her decision-making was sound. In fact, what he'd seen had given him even more confidence in her abilities.

Not that she'd ever know. She'd looked as if she was going to bite him when he'd said he wanted to check over her patients.

As a doctor he nearly always had staff to mentor, opportunities to increase their learning experience and instil confidence in their abilities. He just hadn't expected to find it here on a cruise ship. He'd almost expected the rest of the staff to be running circles around about him based on their longer experience. But it wasn't the case with Francesca. And whether he liked her or not, he was determined to find out why.

# CHAPTER FIVE

ONE week later Francesca felt as if she was still fighting to see her own patients. Gabriel had reviewed practically every staff member she'd ever seen. And for a man who'd spent the last six years in paediatrics he was a meticulous adult practitioner who missed nothing.

If she hadn't been so busy she would have been nervous. What if he did find something wrong? What if she'd mismanaged a patient?

Working with Gabriel was like walking a tightrope. Constantly teetering on the high wire, with him waiting to see her fall. There was no doubt he wouldn't be there to catch her. It was almost a certainty that he'd watch her splat on the ground like some fly on a windscreen.

He was constantly looking over her shoulder, asking her seemingly inane work-related questions. She was sure he was trying to catch her out and she felt like an amoeba under a microscope.

She almost wished he'd just come out and tell her that, rather than pussyfoot round about her. She preferred the direct approach rather than the wolf in sheep's clothing.

Everyone else around him was well and truly smitten. With the rest of the staff and the passengers, his Italian charm served him well. But the air between the two of them still crackled with animosity.

Francesca hated to admit it but there was something really intimidating about an insanely handsome man hating the ground you walked on. Sometimes she caught him looking at her with a strange expression on her face, as if he was trying to get the measure of her. She'd no idea why.

He could the see the practical examples of her work all over the ship. He could audit her written and electronic records until he was blue in the face. She was almost sure there was nothing for him to find.

But it was that little touch of uncertainty that made her nervous. No matter how well she performed there was almost always a tiny part of her wondering if she'd missed something. Wondering if she was about to make a mistake that would affect someone's life.

Before her father's death it had never been there. She'd been confident at her work and in her abilities. But no matter how hard she tried, she felt as if that confidence would never return.

It was always going to be there—that little voice in her head, telling her to guard herself and walk carefully. Questioning her abilities. Just the way Gabriel was constantly doing.

And worse still it was all her own fault.

There was nobody else to blame.

She'd allowed herself to be swept off her feet by a playboy doc just like Gabriel. A man with the attention span of a goldfish and the staying power of an ice cream on a sunny day.

But for a few months she'd been smitten. More important, she'd been distracted.

She'd spent less time with her father, too busy being swept from one date to the next by Dr Wonderful. Except he wasn't.

If only she'd paid attention. If only she'd spotted the signs of what her father had been planning. But she hadn't.

Now she had to live with the consequences. And Dr Wonderful? All the more reason to stay away from men like Gabriel. Turned out he hadn't been so wonderful after all. He'd dropped her like a hot brick when her father had died. Thank goodness for Jill.

How long could she work in this environment?

And what had happened to her Australian visa?

She looked down at the two lists in front of her—one for crew, one for passengers. Finally, a patient of her own to review. For a second she almost felt relief that he wasn't checking up on her today, then a glance at the passenger list made her realise that four children were waiting to be seen.

Gabriel always wanted to see the children himself. It was natural—he was a paediatrician after all. But he was almost a little too fastidious about it. To the point of being slightly obsessional. He'd even asked David Marsh to page him, whether he was on duty or not, to see any children requiring treatment.

Maybe the man was just a control freak. But she hadn't noticed it in anything else that he did. And it hadn't been on the list of complaints from Jill, either.

Jill. She still hadn't emailed Francesca back yet and Francesca was curious to know what her response would be. She couldn't quite decide whether Jill would send a rant about what a louse Gabriel was or a request for new pictures of her unrequited love. You could never tell with that girl.

Francesca gave a sigh and picked up the crew list. It was time to do some work. The waiting room already had a few customers.

'Roberto Franc, please.' Francesca smiled and ushered him into a nearby consulting room.

Roberto Franc was a twenty-year-old busboy on the ship. He had been diagnosed with diabetes mellitus a few weeks before and was struggling to control his condition. Diabetes mellitus was usually diagnosed in childhood and Roberto was older than the average new patient but Francesca was confident she could help him cope.

He settled into the chair opposite Francesca, pushing his diary across the desk towards her.

'How are you?' she asked.

'Not bad,' he muttered. She took the diary from him and glanced at its contents. Newly diagnosed diabetics were taught to monitor their blood-sugar results regularly and record them in a diary. It helped give an accurate picture of how they were coping on insulin injections, and if the injections were controlling their blood sugars accordingly.

'I can see you've been testing frequently,' Francesca said. 'Sometimes six times a day—how are your fingers?'

'Sore.' He lifted his hands and placed them palms upward on the desk in front of her.

She could see the little marks on his fingertips where the tiny lancet had pierced his fingers. The little dots appeared all over his fingertips, with some fingers looking slightly swollen. 'I think we can help with that,' she said. 'What type of meter do you have?'

He pulled a black package from the back pocket of his trousers. It was little bigger than a wallet, but when opened contained his testing strips, blood glucose meter and lancet holder. Francesca smiled, recognising the type of meter. She pulled the instruction card from inside the front pocket. 'I know it's hard initially, but until we have your blood sugars completely under control it is important that you keep testing. There are other sites you can take blood from—it doesn't always have to be from your fingertips.' She showed him on the instruction leaflet. 'You could try the forearm.'

He nodded slowly. 'I hadn't really thought of that.'

'It would give your fingers a few days to recover—you might find it useful to try.' She was still studying his diary carefully. 'I think we need to adjust some of your insulin doses,' she continued slowly. 'Your injection that you take at night—the long-lasting insulin that gives you a backdrop throughout the day—it needs to go up a little.' She pointed at the diary 'For the last week your blood-sugar levels have been quite high in the mornings when you wake up, that tells us we need to adjust the insulin you take last thing at night. We will put it up by two units initially and review it again in another week.'

He nodded thoughtfully. 'What about the dinnertime dose?'

'I notice that you've had a few hypoglycaemic attacks around 7:00 p.m. When have you been having lunch?'

'About three o'clock, after all the passengers have finished.' Francesca was aware that as a busboy Roberto would be expected to be on duty during lunch and dinner service times. It made it more difficult to control his own eating times. He wouldn't be having lunch till three and dinner till around nine. Hypos—or hypoglycaemic attacks—happened when a person's blood sugar fell too low. It didn't just affect people with diabetes. Lots of people could become tired, lack concentration or become cranky if they didn't eat for a while and, as a result, their blood sugar became low. For Roberto however, it was more serious. Diabetics' blood-sugar levels could fall so low that they could lose consciousness.

'How did you feel when you had the hypos? Did you have any warning signs?'

Roberto raised his hands and shrugged his shoulders. 'On a few occasions I was trembling and sweaty, and at those times I knew to sit down and have something to eat. On other occasions I haven't noticed so much, especially when it's busy during service. I dropped some plates the other night and one of the other busboys came and told me to sit down as I was a terrible colour. I checked my blood sugar then and it was low.'

'Okay.' Francesca nodded reassuringly. 'It takes time to recognise the signs of a hypoglycaemic attack—and they can be different in every person with diabetes. I realise it's even more difficult if you're busy and thinking about other things. It's good that your colleagues know what is wrong with you and can point out if you're not looking so good.'

His face twisted in frustration. 'But I hate that. I want to be able to control this myself.'

'I know all about how frustrating diabetes is. My dad was diabetic for years. Sometimes he struggled to control it, too. You've just been diagnosed and you need to give it a little time.' She patted his hand. 'We will get this under control. I think you need to reduce the insulin dose you're taking at three o'clock when you're having your lunch. It's a short-acting insulin and could be contributing to the hypos you've been having around 7:00 p.m. It could still be lasting in your body, particularly if you haven't eaten enough, or if your physical activity levels have been raised.

'We'll reduce it just by a few units, two would be best. I would also suggest that you need to have a think about how long you go between meals. I think you should have an extra snack around six. It's a long time until nine when you actually eat your evening meal.'

'But that's right when service starts for evening meals so we're really busy then.'

'I know that. But if you eat just before the doors open at six o'clock, then you'll probably be fine throughout service. I can speak to the dining room manager if it helps.'

'Thanks, you'll probably have to. I don't want him to think I'm shirking off.'

Francesca made a little note in his file. 'That's no problem. I'll speak to him today. Keep doing your blood-sugar readings and make the adjustments to your insulin as we've discussed. I've written a little note of them inside your diary. I'll give you an appointment for the same time next week and we'll see how you're doing.'

Roberto stood up from his chair and put his diary and meter back in his pockets. 'That's great, thanks, Nurse Cruz.'

'My pleasure.'

She showed him out to the door, and then headed back to put some more notes in his file and record his appointment in the book for next week.

Gabriel was standing at the doorway, his arms folded across his chest, watching her intently. He'd obviously finished seeing his four children in record time.

'That's quite a gift you've got.'

Her head snapped up from the appointment book. She realised that he must have been listening to her from the consulting-room door. She had been so focused on her patient that she hadn't noticed. A pink tinge of embarrassment flushed her cheeks. 'What do you mean?'

'You dealt with him like a real expert—as if you really understood.'

She could feel the adrenaline cursing through her veins.

*Fight or flight syndrome.* Gabriel was being nice to her—should she be suspicious right now or not? 'I do.'

'So I gathered. How long was your dad diabetic?'

'From around the same age. He was actually really well controlled, but I grew up recognising any signs of hypo in him and knew how to deal with it. Later in life, when things were a little more difficult for him, I helped adjust his insulin when he needed it.'

'It must have been a distinct advantage, having a daughter who was a nurse.'

Francesca shook her head and he could almost see her cringe. 'To be honest, most of the things I learned about diabetes I already knew before I started my nursing. But it made it easier for me when looking after patients with diabetes, and for dealing with the families.'

'You seemed to cover everything. Even how he must be feeling and coping with his fears and anxieties. You're good.'

It was a compliment but as soon as he'd said the words a shadow passed over her face. 'Not that good.' The words were quiet, almost whispered.

'What?'

He sensed her take a deep breath and saw her straighten, pushing her shoulders back. 'All nurses are supposed to practice holistic care,' she said, as if she was quoting straight from a textbook. 'But don't kid yourself. I'm not a mental health nurse. Experience has taught me I'm not good at any of that kind of stuff.'

Gabriel stopped his mouth from automatically opening in response. It would be so easy to pursue this. It would be so easy to ask her exactly what she meant by that. But Gabriel didn't pry. If she wanted to tell him she would. Was this the reason she had no confidence at work?

She tried to change the subject quickly to deflect what was obviously on his mind. 'I guess you could say diabetes was one of my "babies". We all have them. What's yours?'

'Paediatrics. It was the only reason I came into medicine. I always wanted to work with children.'

She tilted her head to the side. 'But yet you don't have any of your own. Makes me wonder about you, Gabriel. Too much playboy, not enough family man. Maybe it's time for you to settle down.' He had no idea how relieved she was right now to have moved the conversation away from her dad. The one person she didn't want to talk about. Not to anyone.

But Gabriel didn't look too happy now. His relaxed expression had disappeared. 'Having children has never been high on my agenda. Taking care of children has.'

There was finality in his words. Determination.

She wanted to reply, *But you've ended up on a cruise ship,* but the words stuck in her throat. Something told her not to respond that way. Not right now.

Katherine appeared at the door, her face pale and her hands on her stomach. It broke the instant tension in the room. He walked straight over and put his arm around her shoulders. 'What's wrong?'

'I'm not feeling so good.' She glanced between them. 'Do either of you mind if I go and lie down for a few hours?'

Francesca shook her head and Gabriel guided Katherine towards the door. 'Of course not. The clinics are finished for this morning and it's only emergency callouts this afternoon. Francesca and I can manage those. Go and lie down. And give me a page if you need anything.' He nodded at Francesca, who smiled in response.

'Thanks, you two. See you later.' Katherine practically bolted out the door.

Francesca bit her lip. 'Please let this be just an upset stomach. The last thing we need is a Norovirus outbreak.'

Gabriel's brow wrinkled as the realisation of her words hit him. There had been several cruise ships last year that had been affected by Norovirus. Cruises had had to be stopped and vessels berthed and deep-cleaned or sanitised before any new trips were started. It had been a nightmare for both crew and passengers.

He groaned. 'I hadn't even thought of that.' He shot her a quick smile as he leaned back in his chair. 'A Medevac, a near drowning and now a possible outbreak. I'm turning into the bad-luck fairy, aren't I?'

Francesca shook her head. 'There are always a few people aboard that become unwell. Katherine could just be unlucky. The next few hours will tell us if we need to put our public health hats on. Let's cross our fingers that we don't.'

She walked over to the side of the room, her eyes resting on a calendar in front of her. A tight fist was clenched around her heart as she realised the date. She felt physically sick. Almost instantly tears formed in her eyes. Was it the seventeenth already? How could she not have noticed?

She turned quickly to Gabriel. 'If you don't need me, I'm going up on deck to catch a little sun.' Before he had a chance to answer, she was gone.

Gabriel leaned back in his chair. For once the medical centre was empty.

He felt frustrated. Just when he thought he might have had an opportunity to talk to Francesca. To try and dig a little deeper, to try and find out what was going on in her head. But she'd dashed out of here like a startled rabbit.

He was sure she'd brushed a tear from her face as she'd left out the room. What on earth was wrong with her?

Should he go after her?

He looked around him, trying to figure out why. What on earth could have made her cry?

Nothing stood out. The conversation about Norovirus had been totally work related and entirely unremarkable. There was no reason for her reaction.

He was torn. The last thing he wanted to do was unintentionally upset another member of staff, even if the atmosphere between them had been prickly. Even if her actions at times had annoyed him.

He'd tried to brush aside the playboy comments. He didn't want to go down that road. What was the point in finding a wife and settling down? He'd seen what happened to families. There were some things that you could never recover from.

And although he'd never courted the media, being labelled a playboy wasn't so bad. It meant that most women had no illusions about him. No expectations.

His father had been furious at his decision to become a doctor. The printing business was their legacy, their mark on the world. Who was going to continue that now?

The reminder that Gabriel was the last remaining male was clear and it had stung. He could still picture his father's face—red with anger and glistening with sweat.

But even as a teenager Gabriel had been clear that saving lives was more important than a family business. Saving lives like Dante's. Surely his father had to be rational? Had to see the reasoning behind Gabriel's decision?

He'd dismissed him with the wave of a hand. And Gabriel had been furious with his father—at his lack of acknowledgement of Dante's lost life. At the way he'd focused on his work instead of his family, causing Gabriel to step into his shoes at far too young an age.

And now, with his increased frailty, it was happening again.

He looked over at the clock, calculating the time difference between Greece and Italy. He had an ideal opportunity to sort out of some of his father's day-to-day work duties. He could put this time to good use and maybe even fit in a phone call to find out how his father was feeling.

Whatever was wrong with Francesca would have to wait—even though it did leave his stomach churning.

He really didn't have time to waste on some nurse.

# CHAPTER SIX

FRANCESCA was feeling sick and it was nothing to do with a bug. She dashed along the corridor to her cabin. How could she not have noticed the date?

Eighteen months ago today. Eighteen months since her father had committed suicide and she'd found his body sitting in the armchair in his house, with a letter for her and a bottle of pills next to it.

It didn't matter where she was, or what she was doing. The seventeenth of the month was always a day where she felt in the doldrums. It was always a day she needed to clear her head.

It was also a day that was usually imprinted on her brain. What had happened to her?

She threw off her uniform and pulled on her swimming costume and matching red sarong. She needed to be out in the fresh air as the walls seemed to be closing in on her.

A few minutes later she reached the adults-only part of the ship. Away from the frantic swimming pools and happy families crowded onto sun loungers.

Up here in the adults-only section there were wicker pod sun loungers, the cocooned structures designed to give a little more comfort and a little shelter from the sun's rays. She flopped down into one and pulled her book from her bag.

There was a fantastic view of the sea from here. The beautiful blue sea that stretched on for miles and miles. The sun's rays licked at her toes and she could feel the cooling sea breezes through her hair. She always escaped up here when she needed to. The ship was huge, but still a confined environment, and it was often hard to get some time and space on your own.

She stared out ahead. The tears already prickling at her eyes. Why hadn't she noticed? Why hadn't she realised just how bad her dad had been feeling?

He'd taken the loss of her mum really hard. But that had been five years before and after a dark spell of depression he'd seemed to be making improvements. He'd started to go out more, eat a little better and socialise with friends again.

It was probably why she'd felt safe enough to allow distractions. To listen to the insincere words of flattery from the playboy doc and be fooled by them.

Her father's suicide had been like an absolute bolt from the blue.

And his handwritten letter had just broken her heart.

He couldn't face life any more without his beloved wife. And as much as he loved Francesca, he felt as if he was holding her back. It was time to go.

Did he think she'd found someone to love?

She'd taken a job back in Glasgow after her mum had died as she hadn't wanted to leave her dad on his own. The truth was, she *had* turned down other job opportunities so she could stay in Glasgow with her dad, but she'd never mentioned them. And after he was gone she'd flitted from job to job, gaining experience and building her portfolio.

But nowhere had felt like home. Nowhere had removed the ache of loneliness she always felt.

She closed her eyes. The padding inside the pod was wonderfully comfortable. The quiet sound of the sea was calming. The book slipped from her hands.

'So this is where you've been hiding. There's good news and there's bad news. What do you want first?'

There was a jolt as the weight of someone sitting at the entrance of her pod made the whole structure move. Gabriel's voice broke into her dream. A dream of her father reading her favourite bedtime stories, Rapunzel, Cinderella.

For an instant she wanted to be angry with him. But the truth was she was getting used to him. Gabriel Russo wasn't turning out to be the man she'd thought he was. The more she saw of him the less deplorable he became.

She groaned. 'You've just ruined my dream.'

He leaned forward, his body entering into the pod. It seemed like an intimate gesture and she pushed herself further back into the cushions.

'Was it a good dream?'

'It was perfect.'

'Was I in it?' He'd switched on his million-dollar smile. There was no way she was going to be affected by it.

'Not a chance.'

Other women would love this. A sheltered pod on a huge cruise ship with a handsome man. His face was only inches away from hers, his body seemed even closer. Whilst her red swimming costume and sarong were normal attire for most of the passengers, she automatically wanted to cover herself up. He had a pair of beach shorts on and those killer abs were visible again. Why couldn't he put them away around her?

She pushed herself up a little, moving her legs closer to

the pod entrance, the only route of escape. 'If you'd been in it Prince Charming would have turned into a slimy frog.'

'Ouch.' He sat up next to her at the pod entrance. 'What are you doing here?'

'I would have thought that was obvious. I'm being extremely lazy and lying here, reading a book.'

'What are you reading? Something pink and fluffy?' She raised her eyebrows at him.

'Or something, dark, dangerous and mysterious?'

'What do you care?'

'I'm interested. I like to know what people read.' He picked up her book and looked at the title, flipping it over and starting to read the back cover blurb.

A smile crept across her face as she waited and watched for the penny to drop. Any second now his face would go scarlet and he would drop the book as if it were on fire.

But no. Nothing. Just the tiniest twitch of his leg. He turned and handed it back to her.

She knew exactly what part of the body a blurb like that would have an effect on.

His face remained calm. 'So, hot and sexy, then?'

She nodded, 'Yeah, definitely hot and sexy.' She raised an eyebrow at him. 'A girl can dream, right?'

*What was she doing? She'd just flirted with him. The man she hated. The man who was watching her every move. Was she mad?*

Gabriel's dark brown eyes were getting even darker. He sat up straighter. 'About tonight…' he started.

'What about tonight? I'm off duty.'

'Yeah, I know.' He shrugged his shoulders. 'But Katherine's feeling really bad. She wondered if you'd mind covering for her.'

'Is that the good news or the bad news?'

'It depends entirely what you think of the next bit. Katherine was supposed to be on dining-room duty tonight, eating with some of the passengers.'

Francesca nodded. 'Yeah, that's fine. What else?' All officers on the ship had to take a turn in dining with the passengers.

Gabriel smiled. 'I'm on that duty, too.'

Francesca groaned and flopped back inside the pod. 'Am I ever going to get rid of you?'

The words were there but the atmosphere between them had changed. There wasn't the same tension. There wasn't the same angst. It was almost as if they'd reached a mutual plateau.

'You owe me.'

She narrowed her eyes at him. 'What?'

He shook his head at her. 'You know well that after the dinner we're supposed to go and watch the entertainment—be a visible presence amongst the passengers without officially being on duty.'

'And so?' The cogs in her brain were starting to turn. Dining-room duty was easy—eat dinner, make general conversation with the passengers.

After that she would be free to have a few drinks. She wouldn't be expected to respond to any patient queries—Kevin and David were on duty for those—so she could let her hair down. Try and forget about this bad day.

'There's no way I'm going out there alone. You'll have to watch the entertainment with me. You can rescue me from any cougars that may be about. You know—the ones you forgot to tell me about.'

She started to laugh and pushed herself up from the entrance to the pod. 'But you deserved that.' She lifted her book and pressed it close to her chest. 'As a professional courtesy I might agree to stay in your company.' She rolled her eyes at him. 'I'd hate it if our ship's doctor got caught in a compromising position.'

She turned to leave. 'But in that case it will cost you. I'm planning on having a few drinks tonight—and you're buying. See ya.' Francesca sashayed her way across the desk. She could almost feel his eyes burning a hole into her spine. One sentence at the forefront of her brain.

*What on earth are you doing, Fran?*

Francesca had managed to smile and nod her way through the eight p.m. dinner even though she hadn't been able to eat a bite. Her eyes had watched every minute tick past on the clock in the dining room.

Gabriel had been seated with a family at the table next to hers. Her eyes had kept straying in his direction and she'd watch him read *The Cat in the Hat* to one of the young kids as the adults ate their dinner.

He'd seemed totally at ease and relaxed sitting amongst the family. She'd even heard him laugh. Was that possible for Gabriel?

It was obvious why he was a paediatrician. He was great with kids, had a real affinity with them. It made her wonder why he didn't have any of his own.

This afternoon had been the most relaxed she'd seen him since he'd got here. He hadn't been staring at her with those disapproving eyes.

Maybe they were both tiring of the constant prickliness between them. The jagged edges that had been clashing together were finally being worn down. To be replaced by…what?

Because there was still something that crackled in the air between them. The animosity had been replaced by something else. An underlying current that had been there since they'd first met. That neither of them had acknowledged or acted on. Until now.

The tension had built inside her so much that it was a relief when dinner finally finished at nine p.m. and she was able to make her excuses and rush back to her cabin.

Her laptop pinged behind her and she pressed the button. An email.

From Jill.

Her hand hesitated over the keyboard. What did she want this email to say? That she was furious that Gabriel was there, and rant about how badly he'd treated her? Or something else entirely? The *do I have a chance of getting back in there* type email. You could never tell which way Jill was going to go.

She pressed the button, her eyes automatically skimming the page.

Hi honey!

Gabriel Russo—well there's a blast from the past! Is he still as dashing and gorgeous than ever? No, don't answer that. I might be tempted again.

What on earth happened? Why did you have to resuscitate him? Can't imagine someone as fit as Gabriel falling overboard, so there must be more to it than that. Do tell.

I'd love the thought of being trapped in an enclosed space with him. I'm sure I could find a way to while away the hours with Dr Delicious. Tell him hi from me.

Have to go. Meeting Ferdinand for lunch. He's a duke or something.

Try not to fall out with Gabriel on my account—he was really just another notch on my bedpost. Send me some pictures of him if you can. And remember to tell me all the details!

Love Jill xx

Francesca didn't know whether to breathe a sigh of relief or throw up her hands in frustration. *'Tell him hi from me.'* What was that supposed to mean? And if Jill wasn't in the least perturbed at her working with Gabriel, why was she so bothered?

She slammed the laptop shut. It had taken Jill over two weeks to answer her email. She could wait for a response.

She wrinkled her nose. What exactly had Jill told her about Gabriel? Now she thought back to that night, not a lot. Was there a chance she might have misjudged Gabriel? Maybe she should lower her defences—just a little—and give him a chance to be friends?

Her fingers were trembling as she unfastened her dress uniform and hung it carelessly back in the cupboard. She grabbed the nearest dress, navy blue, stared at it and then flung it back. For some reason she didn't want something boring and dull. Gabriel was a gorgeous man. She didn't want people to glance over thinking, *What's he doing with her?*

Something had changed in her brain. She pulled out a red dress that she'd bought for New Year; it was cut with a generous V-neckline to reveal her cleavage, and skirted just above her knees to show off her long legs. It sparkled with randomly placed sequins that added a little glamour to the colour of the dress. Francesca knew this dress showed off her curves well. Fashion rules said that you either revealed cleavage or legs but this dress made its own rules and showed a little of both—giving just a hint of what was underneath.

She picked up the gold filigree necklace she had bought in Venice a few months ago. It was the most expensive piece of jewellery that she owned—a gift to herself one year after her dad's funeral. He'd left her a little nest egg along with another amount that had instructions to buy something she would love for ever. So she'd wanted to buy something precious, something she could keep and remember him by.

She'd never really embraced her origins so an Italian necklace had seemed entirely appropriate. And somehow she knew he would approve. Especially today.

With its tiny beads of red murano glass it would go perfectly. She fastened the clasp around her neck. No other jewellery was necessary; the necklace was more than enough. She finished off her outfit with gold sandals and ran a quick brush through her chestnut locks. A flick of mascara and some ruby-coloured lipstick and she was ready. A glimpse out of the corner of her eye confirmed it was ten o'clock. A final squirt of perfume and she picked up her cabin card and left.

Gabriel was waiting in the Atlantis Bar. His brain was not entirely sure what he was doing there. Being one of the ship's doctors meant additional roles and responsibilities and he understood that. He'd invited Francesca merely as a means of self-protection. And if he kept telling himself that, he might actually grow to believe it. He eyed his watch nervously—what if she changed her mind and didn't come? The cougars were already circulating.

He looked at the drinks sitting on the bar. He had no idea what she drank, hadn't even thought to ask her beforehand, so he had thrown caution to the wind and decided to order something frivolous.

Seconds later he caught the scent of her perfume. He

was standing facing the main entrance, but she must have came in via the side entrance and crept up behind him. His head swam with the sensual fusion of woody, amber and floral essences with hints of orange blossom. He turned swiftly to find her standing directly behind him.

'Is this mine?' She picked up one of the cocktail glasses sitting on the bar and without waiting for an answer put her lips to the edge of the glass and took a sip. Gabriel stood transfixed, moving his gaze from her deep brown eyes to her ruby-coloured lips sipping from the glass, finally catching a sparkle of the intricate gold creation around her neck.

'Gabriel?'

Her face had broken into a wild smile. 'Don't tell me I've just stolen someone else's drink from the bar?'

He snapped out of his daze. 'Yes. Of course it's yours— I just wasn't sure what to order.'

But it was the gold filigree necklace that attracted his attention most. He recognised the design and the work-manship of the piece.

The necklace was a piece of art. A piece of art that he knew the value of. He was more than a little curious about who'd bought it for her.

Another little mystery about the woman who spoke so little about herself.

That afternoon he'd actually started to quite like her. He'd thought they might manage to have a working rela-tionship. The tension between them seemed to have disin-tegrated and things had seemed almost manageable.

The sight of Francesca in her red swimsuit and sarong had sent blood rushing to parts of his body. As for her taste in books…

He felt as if he was finally getting to know her a little. Finally scratching beneath her prickly surface.

But what now?

Another thought started to creep into his brain. Francesca hadn't mentioned a lover or a boyfriend. She didn't wear any rings. Did she have some sugar daddy who had given her such an expensive present?

'Gabriel, what's wrong?'

She was standing directly under his nose. Her cocktail glass already empty, her dark brown eyes staring up at him. 'You've got the permanent frown on your face again.' She shot a beaming smile at a passenger who said hello on the way past. 'Can't you lighten up a bit?' she muttered. 'This is going to be a long evening.' She waved her cocktail glass at him. 'And I'm going to need another of these. What is it anyway?'

She was positioned right under his nose. And as he looked downwards his eyes were drawn directly to her deep cleavage. She was a knockout in that dress. Not that he hadn't noticed she was a knockout anyway but he'd been too busy disapproving of her to step back and take a good look.

But she seemed on edge, jittery almost. She'd drunk that cocktail in two minutes flat. What was her story? The other team members were open about their home lives, sharing photos and tales of their families and friends. But Francesca remained tight-lipped. He hardly knew a thing about her. What made her tick?

Her nursing skills were impeccable. He'd reviewed every case she'd worked on, observed her, spoken to staff and crew alike—Francesca didn't have a thing to worry about. So why was she nervous?

The intricate goldwork and highly polished murano

glass of her necklace were shimmering under the neon lights of the Atlantis Bar. When she turned in certain directions the reflected light shone back on her face. And she was certainly attracting attention. If Gabriel had felt under scrutiny from the cougars earlier, it was nothing compared to the male reaction in the room to Francesca.

And she hadn't noticed. She flung back her head and laughed at something the man next to her said, her dark lustrous curls tossed over her shoulder. Her clingy red dress hugged her figure to perfection and the man had certainly noticed.

Gabriel was annoyed. He was *more* than annoyed. That guy should back off. Didn't he see that she was here with him?

He reached over and touched the necklace, circling his fingers around the droplet of red murano glass that skirted her cleavage. It might be a little forward but, hopefully, it would get rid of the man on the right.

'This is beautiful, Francesca. Where did you get it? Did a secret admirer buy it for you?'

Everything stopped. She'd been acutely conscious of standing next to him but not quite touching. Aware of his tall, broad frame and penetrating dark eyes. With his permanently knotted brow it was obvious that something was bothering him. He ought to be careful—if the wind changed his face could stay that way for ever. After watching him in the dining room tonight, she was beginning to think his frown was reserved solely for her.

Her eyes flickered up and down his body. He had changed from his dress uniform into dark trousers, a pale blue shirt and dark Italian shoes. It looked simple enough but was obviously expensive. Her eyes caught the several dark curled hairs revealed at the base of his throat. His

Mediterranean skin was bronzed and alluring and his obvious muscled and well-proportioned body seemed to be
attracting the attention of much of the female company
in the room.

But he was with her.

And she'd been desperately trying to put that out of
her mind.

And then he'd touched her, those fingertips unexpect-
edly brushing the swell of her breasts. Francesca froze. His
fingers were fastened around the biggest piece of glass on
her necklace and he was watching her. Waiting for an answer. Why couldn't she speak?

She shifted her weight on her feet. Right now she felt
like a starstruck teenager. But why? She didn't even like
this man so why on earth was he having this effect on her?

Maybe it was the email from Jill. It was strange that
she hadn't made any derogatory comments about him. She
hadn't been outraged at all. More interested in the details.
All of it sent tiny alarm bells ringing in Francesca's head.

Maybe she had misjudged him? What would Gabriel
say if she told him? Would he get that disapproving look
on his face at the mention of Jill's name? Why was that?
He was the one in the wrong.

Her stomach twisted, loyalty to Jill unsettling her.

His dark brown eyes were still staring at her. Watching every expression on her face. Did he know what she
was thinking?

She really didn't want to explain about the necklace. She
didn't want to tell him that her dad had left her money—
that would take the conversation down a road she wasn't
prepared to go.

He'd ask her how her father had died. It was only natural. And she didn't want to tell him about the suicide, particularly today—it was just too hard.

Then she'd have to admit she'd missed the signs and that if she'd paid more attention her beloved father might still be here.

Tonight her ambition was to drink herself into oblivion. And these strawberry-type cocktails were a good start. She had to steer this conversation away from the necklace as quickly as possible.

She gulped, struggling to find some words. 'Not so much a secret admirer,' she finally managed.

'No?'

His hand pulled her a little closer, the full length of her body coming into contact with his. What was he doing? She couldn't concentrate. 'I picked it myself. But it was a gift—to remind me of someone very dear to me.'

'Someone special?'

'More than you know.' She lowered her eyelids so he wouldn't see the tears threatening to pool there. Gabriel was a colleague, nothing more, nothing less. He wasn't interested in her. She would place bets he could have any woman in this room.

He'd ordered more drinks so she lifted her glass towards his. 'What is this? You didn't tell me.'

His eyes flitted from her necklace to her dress—was he looking at her cleavage?—and then back to her drink. 'A strawberry daiquiri.'

'Cheers,' she said, taking a long sip from the straw. 'It's almost as if you guessed what I'd be wearing.' She smiled as she tasted the strawberry daiquiri. 'Red to match my dress, and rum, my favourite flavour. Keep this up and I'll be expecting big things from the night ahead.'

She was holding her breath, hoping he wouldn't realise

she'd deflected the conversation. Hoping he'd just accept her answer and move on.

It seemed to take for ever for him to answer. He glanced at his watch. 'The show will start soon. Do you still want to go?'

Her face broke into a beaming smile. 'Absolutely—I've never seen it.'

'Why not? You've been on this boat for months.'

'I'm usually too tired to go and see a show that doesn't start until ten-thirty,' she admitted. 'But tonight I will make an exception, on the proviso, of course, that my boss doesn't give me trouble tomorrow for yawning while on duty!'

They walked along the corridor towards the Whisper Theatre. It was crowded with passengers who had all come to see the popular ten-thirty show. The theatre seated over eight hundred people and, although situated within the ship, its breadth and width covered three internal decks. Francesca and Gabriel filed into the nearest row of seats and sat in the velvet-covered chairs. The lights quickly dimmed and the audience immediately quietened. In the darkened theatre a juggler appeared at the side of the stage, but instead of the usual balls or skittles he was juggling fire-filled torches, which hissed and spat as he threw them in the air. The audience was mesmerised.

Francesca spent the whole time with her brain spinning. She had no idea what was going on. Whatever had shifted between her and Gabriel was terrifying her. She didn't want to be one of the millions blown away by his good looks and TV-star smile.

In the dark theatre, she was also acutely aware of how close she and Gabriel were sitting. Every time their arms brushed against one another she felt a little frisson of excitement tingle up her spine. When she went to change the position of her legs, her crossed leg touched his trouser-clad one and he turned in the darkness and gave her a brief smile. When the show finally finished and the lights came up slowly, Francesca was almost disappointed at being brought back to reality.

'Did you enjoy it?' Gabriel asked.

'It was wonderful.'

They stood back, waiting for the theatre to empty. As the crowd thinned he placed his arm lightly at her back. 'I'll walk you back to your cabin.' He smiled.

'Okay.' Francesca felt her heart dip in disappointment. He hadn't asked her to go back to the bar for another drink. She glanced at her watch. It wasn't that late—was he trying to get rid of her?

The corridor to her cabin was empty. Most people were either already in their cabins or drinking in one of the bars. She stopped outside her door.

'Thanks, Gabriel, that was lovely.' Her eyes were fixed on the floor. She felt awkward and uncomfortable, the ease and relaxation of earlier in the night having left her. Silence hung in the air and neither of them moved.

'So you gave me mouth to mouth?'

Her head shot upwards. Where had that come from? Was he flirting with her? Was he trying to unnerve her?

There was something there. Something hanging in the air between them. Something that kept bringing a smile to her face.

'I did.'

'I'm sorry I can't remember it.' His voice was low, barely loud enough for her to hear. But she did. And it sent a shiver down her spine. 'Shouldn't you have been wearing a red swimsuit for that?'

Her laugh was instantaneous. He'd obviously been having the same thoughts that she'd had. Funny how one TV show had made such a lasting impression.

'In my rush to do the mouth to mouth I forgot about the red swimsuit,' she quipped. 'But what does it matter? You've already seen it.'

'That I have,' he whispered, stepping forward and closing the gap between them. 'I can't remember if I ever thanked you.'

Then, with the lightest of touches, he bent forward and his hand lightly stroked under her chin. Automatically, she raised her head to meet his. He gave her a slow, sexy smile that sent her pulse racing. His eyes smouldered with fire.

'I can't remember, either,' she whispered. No one else was in the dimly lit corridor. All she could hear was the sound of her heart thudding in her ears. Suddenly he dipped forward and his mouth hovered just millimetres away from hers. She stepped forward as her body reacted unconsciously to his. She felt him hardening against her and as she moved even closer she felt a little groan escape from his lips. She could feel his breath on her cheek, tickling her skin.

*Now. Kiss me now.*

She closed her eyes. It was inevitable. Any moment now she would feel his lips devouring hers.

Instead his lips brushed against her ear. 'Thank you, Francesca,' he whispered.

He stepped back, his breathing shallow and ragged, his eyes burning.

His breathing slowed. 'Goodnight, *cara*.' His accent stroked across her skin and she watched as his lean, athletic body turned and disappeared down the corridor.

She collapsed back against her door. Wow! Her head was spinning.

She lifted her slightly trembling hand and pushed the cabin card into the slot on her door. The door swung open and she collapsed onto her nearby bed.

He'd almost kissed her but had then walked away. The sparks between them could have set the whole ship alight. She could already imagine the sensations of kissing him. A blow-your-mind, send-you-rocketing-off-into-space, turn-your-legs-to-jelly kind of kiss. She didn't know whether to laugh, cry or chase him along the corridor and drag him back to her room!

Everything was racing through her mind. The man she didn't want to like. The man who had treated her friend so poorly had nearly just kissed her. And she'd let him.

*Was she losing her mind?*

Gabriel wasn't someone she could ignore. She had to work with him every day. How on earth was she going to deal with this?

Kissing the boss could turn out to be an occupational hazard.

Gabriel stared at his inbox—forty-six emails, all having come in during the last few hours. He glanced at the clock. It was after midnight but he could already tell that sleep was going to elude him tonight. Payroll queries, exporters, poor-quality ink, complaints, late deliveries and a pile of other mundane details. Dealing with the day-to-day enquiries had seemed simple at first but the more he dealt with, the more seemed to come his way. He'd finished one long day and it looked like he'd have an even longer night ahead.

What on earth had he been thinking of? Kissing her. Was he mad?

If she was anything like her friend and money was her motivator then this time tomorrow he could be slapped with a sexual harassment lawsuit.

The thought made his blood run cold.

How well did he really know Francesca?

Not well at all.

Tonight she'd looked beautiful. He'd almost been blown away by how stunning she'd looked in that red dress, with her long hair falling about her shoulders. The few cocktails had certainly relaxed her and made her seem less guarded. Less unapproachable.

But it had been the reaction to his touch that had caught him by surprise. He hadn't been imagining things between them. The slightest brush of skin had electrified them both.

Her stolen glances towards him. The lingering looks between them, lasting just longer than was entirely natural. The way you felt when you couldn't tear your eyes off someone.

And in that darkened corridor, when it had just been the two of them, he'd acted entirely on instinct. And she'd responded, without a doubt.

A single lapse of concentration could result in a huge pile of trouble.

*What had he been thinking?*

Gabriel banged his hand off the desk. His laptop wobbled, teetering close to the edge of the desk. He pulled it closer, focusing on the unopened emails in front of him.

Work. That's what he would do.

Anything to get his mind off Francesca.

Anything at all.

# CHAPTER SEVEN

FRANCESCA stared at the duty roster and felt her stomach plummet. Gabriel had swapped shifts this morning. The sinking feeling of dread continued as her overactive brain sent a million signals all at once.

He'd only swapped a few hours ago. It was obvious he was trying to avoid her. He must be regretting almost kissing her. She cringed. This was a nightmare.

She was beginning to think it hadn't happened. Maybe it was all just a figment of her overactive imagination? So why did it feel like he was body-swerving her?

There was no way they could avoid each other on a cruise ship and with a medical crew as small as they had.

Talk about out of the frying pan and into the fire. They'd gone from one whole heap of tension between them to another entirely.

She hadn't slept a wink last night. No matter how hard she'd tried. Her brain just hadn't let her. She'd eventually got up and tried to compose an email to Jill but nothing had sounded right.

In fact, everything had sounded exactly the way she felt—guilty.

The first email hadn't mentioned Gabriel at all and had been a dead giveaway as complete avoidance.

The second had been too vague.

The third had been too over the top. Nothing had sounded normal. Nothing had sounded like she'd wanted it to. So she'd eventually given up, made herself a cup of coffee and watched the sun rise from the top deck.

She'd worry about the return email to Jill later.

She glanced over the clinic lists. The ship was due to dock in Ephesus, Turkey today and most of the passengers would probably disembark. Any passenger who needed medical attention would try and attend the medical centre early to avoid missing the coach trips ashore. Sure enough, the list for this morning was busy.

David appeared at her shoulder. 'Morning, Francesca. You okay? You're looking tired. Hope you're not coming down with the same bug as Katherine.'

Francesca shook her head fiercely. 'Just didn't get much sleep last night.'

'You as well?' He raised his eyebrow at her as if she'd just revealed a closely guarded secret.

'What do you mean?'

David shrugged his shoulders. 'Gabriel asked me to swap with him this morning as he didn't sleep last night, either. He said he'd be in around eleven to take over from me.'

'Gabriel didn't sleep, either?' She could barely keep the squeak out of her voice. What did that mean? That he wasn't really avoiding her? That last night had bothered him just as much as it had bothered her? For a second her spirits almost lifted.

David looked up from the chart he was marking. 'Yeah, he was up late into the night, doing some work for his father.'

Her spirits plummeted immediately again. Gabriel

hadn't been thinking about her last night at all. She'd probably been the last thing on his mind. He'd been busy doing other things. 'I didn't know he worked for his father,' she said lightly.

David leaned over and put a few ticks on the clinic list. 'Apparently that's why he came back from America. His dad's health isn't too good and Gabriel is taking over some of the day-to-day running of the company. Trying to ease the strain, so to speak.'

'Wouldn't it make more sense for him to stay in Venice?'

David wagged his finger. 'Aha. You'd think so. But apparently if he's too close to home they'll try and drag him into the family business. Strangely enough, they weren't too keen on him becoming a doctor. All right with you if I see these patients? A few of them are follow-ups from the other day and one is a patient in renal failure I'm familiar with.'

'What? Oh, of course.' She nodded absent-mindedly, lifting the list. Gabriel was helping his father? Why hadn't he mentioned it?

They hadn't wanted him to become a doctor? It seemed almost absurd. Most families would be delighted if their son or daughter became a doctor. What an odd reaction.

She cringed. Of course he hadn't mentioned it—she'd hardly rolled out the red carpet for him. He probably thought it was none of her business.

She looked at the first name on her list. The quicker she started, the quicker she could finish. There were a few crew members who'd managed to avoid their medicals for over a month. She could go and track them down. Thoughts around Gabriel's avoidance tactics would have to wait. And they would probably require another cocktail.

She pasted a smile on her face and walked into the waiting room. 'Eleanor Kennedy, please.'

A few hours later she was nearly finished. Just one child to see: a four-year-old who was feeling generally unwell.

Gabriel had swapped places with David half an hour ago but she hadn't set eyes on him as he'd remained locked in the doctor's office with a notorious staff member who was trying to get out of his duties.

'Carly Glencross, please.'

Carly was sitting on her mother's knee, her eyes red, her face flushed and looking generally miserable.

Carly's mother carried her into the treatment room. 'I'm sure it's nothing,' she said, 'probably just a virus, but she's been like this the last few days. She's been really irritable. Can you just check her over?'

'No problem.' Francesca bent down next to Carly. 'Hi, Carly, I'm Fran, the nurse. Is it okay if I take a little look at you?'

Carly eyed her suspiciously before eventually nodding.

Francesca picked up the tympanic thermometer and demonstrated it to Carly. 'I'm just going to put this in your ear to take your temperature. It only takes a second and I press this little button. Okay?'

Carly nodded again. Francesca got the impression she wasn't going to get a word out of her.

She checked her temperature. High. She knelt in front of Carly and checked her face, neck and chest. Her eyes were red and a little sticky—probably some kind of conjunctivitis. She had a blotchy rash over her chest. The lymph glands in her neck were swollen and so were her hands.

'Have you given her something for her fever?'

Mum nodded. 'I'm giving her paracetamol and ibuprofen alternately. It's not really having much effect and not helping with her other symptoms.'

Francesca made a few notes in the chart. Carly was like a hundred other children she'd seen on the cruise ship or in A and E in her previous role. No specific infection. Just some random virus that spiked a temperature and made the kid miserable for a few days.

'Is she eating anything?'

Mum shook her head. 'I've been feeding her ice lollies to keep her going.'

Francesca nodded. Viruses commonly put kids off their food and it was important to keep them hydrated, particularly when they had a temperature. If ice lollies worked, that was fine.

She was always a little nervous around children. Even though she'd had lots of experience with them in the past, she wasn't specifically trained as a paediatric nurse so she liked to make sure she hadn't missed something.

She walked over to the drawer to pull out a general advice sheet to give to the mother. Her eyes were drawn to Gabriel's door. He normally liked to see all the kids who came to the medical centre. Should she give him a shout?

Carly gave a little cough, so Francesca poured out some water into a cup. 'Do you want to have a little drink?'

Carly nodded, still not speaking, and opened her mouth to take a sip of the water.

Her lips were slightly chapped, with painful cracks at the corners, and her tongue looked slightly swollen.

Francesca took a deep breath. She'd been just about to send this little one away with instructions to come back if there was no improvement in a day or so. But now she wasn't so sure.

Even more than that, she wanted to see how he would

react to her. Would he be embarrassed or act as if nothing at all had happened? Her stomach was clenched in a knot. It was better to get this over and done with.

'If you don't mind, I'm going to get our doctor to take a quick look at Carly. He's a paediatrician, so it's probably best if he sees her, too.'

Just at that Gabriel's door opened. The crew member stormed off and Gabriel's face was like thunder. They'd obviously had words.

It was a shock seeing him after last night. For the first time she noticed every inch of his face—the tiny lines around his eyes, the furrows on his brow and the tense expression when he caught sight of her. It was just as she'd expected. He was dreading the thought of seeing her after last night. He probably had a million lines prepared to try and fob her off. As if she'd give him the chance.

'Dr Russo,' she said briskly, 'could you have a look at Carly Glencross, please?'

Gabriel seemed to snap to attention. He crossed the room in a few steps, the automatic smile appearing on his face at the sight of the little girl and her mother. If only he'd smiled like that for her.

'What have you got?'

Francesca handed over the chart with the notes she'd made. 'Carly's four and has been sick for the last few days. She has a temperature, conjunctivitis and a blotchy rash. The lymph glands are up in her neck. Mum just wondered if there was anything else we could do for her.'

Gabriel knelt down and spoke in a soft voice to Carly. 'Well, hello there, princess.'

Gabriel only took a few minutes to examine Carly carefully, listening to her heart and lungs, looking in her throat and examining her hands.

He ran his fingers across the palms of her hands. They were slightly oedematous with the skin particularly red on the palms and peeling slightly around her nails.

'What are you looking for?' Francesca felt uneasy. What did Gabriel suspect? Some of Carly's symptoms were a little out of the ordinary and for some reason they were now setting off alarm bells in her head.

He'd barely made eye contact with her since he'd left his room. Was this how it was going to be between them now? Avoidance and aloofness?

'Stick your tongue out for me, please, Carly.'

She did, with pleasure, pulling a face at Gabriel.

'Strawberry-coloured tongue. Get me some aspirin please, Francesca.'

'But kids can't have aspirin, Gabriel, it's dangerous for under twelves.' Her words were automatic. Surely, as a paediatrician, he should know that?

Francesca may not have been trained as a paediatric nurse and normally she coped well but right now she was feeling out of her depth. But there were some golden rules that had been drummed into her by the sister of the A and E department where she'd previously worked. Aspirin being dangerous for under twelves was one of them.

He shook his head. 'In these circumstances it's exactly what we need.'

Gabriel stood up and made a few notes. He touched the side of Carly's face and gave her a little smile. 'You have been the best patient I've seen today. Would you like a fairy sticker?'

He pulled some from a roll attached to the wall. 'You pick the one you like best.'

Carly bent over the roll of fairy stickers, examining their colourful dresses. The stickers were used widely for the kids that attended the medical centre—fairies for girls and dinosaurs for boys.

'Could you bring over the ECG machine, please, Francesca?'

An ECG for a kid? Did a child's ECG look different from an adult's? Francesca didn't even know.

Cardiac. He thought it was a cardiac condition. She had a mad flash.

He sat down next to Carly's mum. 'Have you heard of Kawasaki disease?'

The woman almost did a double-take at the strange-sounding disorder. Her face automatically paled and she shook her head. 'No. What on earth is that? Is that what's wrong with Carly?'

Gabriel nodded. 'It's not widely known. It's a kind of autoimmune disorder that causes inflammation, particularly around the blood vessels.' He touched Carly's palms. 'It has a whole set of classic symptoms. The red palms and peeling skin is one of them, as is the strawberry-coloured tongue, persistent temperature and cracked lips.'

Francesca had wheeled the ECG machine over and felt frozen at the bottom of the bed. Kawasaki disease? Oh, no.

She'd just remembered. A kid from one of her days in A and E. Just like this.

A kid where the key indicator had been peeling skin on the soles of his feet.

She automatically walked over to Carly and removed her socks. Sure enough, peeling skin on the soles of her feet.

She held one foot aloft.

'Gabriel?'

He nodded.

She should have caught this. Yes, it was unusual but she'd come across this before.

The sinking feeling in her stomach wasn't going to go away.

She'd done it again. The one thing she'd said she'd never do.

She'd been distracted by Gabriel.

And she'd missed something. She'd missed *this*. Her head had been too full of Gabriel and the night before to concentrate on the patient in front of her.

Distracted by the playboy doc.

It made her feel physically sick. The fallout from the last time had affected her father. The time it could have been a kid.

Gabriel swung Carly's legs up on to the bed and laid her back against the pillows. 'I'm just going to get a little tracing of your heart, Carly.' He held up the leads from the ECG machine. 'I just need to attach these onto your chest.'

It only took him a few seconds and Francesca pressed the buttons. The heart tracing spat out the other side of the machine a few moments later.

'What does this mean for Carly?' Mrs Glencross's voice was becoming higher.

'First, we give her some aspirin. That's the first line of treatment for Kawasaki disease. Carly should really have some bloods taken and a chest X-ray, too. I'm going to phone the local paediatric unit here and talk to their consultant. It might be better for her to have the rest of her tests done there.'

'We need to leave the ship?'

Gabriel nodded. 'Carly will need to be admitted to hospital. Kawasaki disease can cause complications in children.'

'What kind of complications?'

Francesca could see him bite his bottom lip, as if trying to decide how much information to give. 'Some kids can develop inflammation around the blood vessels at the heart. They need to be monitored closely. Carly will need to have a scan of her heart. There's also another drug treatment called gammoglobulin that can be given. But it's a treatment that needs to be administered in hospital.'

Carly's mother sagged back against the wall. 'I thought she just had a bit of a cold, or a virus. I'd no idea it could be anything like this.'

Gabriel reached over and took her hand. 'I'm going to give Carly some aspirin in the meantime. Let me make a call to the local hospital and then I'll tell you what happens next.'

Francesca rechecked Carly's observations and gave her the aspirin that Gabriel had prescribed.

She tried to make herself busy, making tea for Mrs Glencross and phoning her husband to come and join them in the medical unit. They had docked at Ephesus that morning with Kusadasi being the nearest large town. Francesca knew it had two large, well-equipped hospitals—one public and one private—but she had no idea about the paediatric facilities.

She walked into Gabriel's office just as he was replacing the phone.

'What kind of complications can Kawasaki disease cause?' She tried to keep the tremble from her voice. It had been obvious to her that he'd been trying to stick to the basics for Carly's shocked mother. She couldn't remember what had happened to her last patient.

That was the trouble with A and E, the patients came through so quickly with little or no chance of follow-up.

He leaned back in his chair. 'The ambulance will be here in half an hour to transport Carly to the paediatric unit.' His heavy eyelids lifted, meeting her gaze for the first time that day. He watched her for a few seconds before answering. 'The inflammation of the blood vessels can affect the coronary arteries. One in five kids with Kawasaki disease will develop inflammation of the coronary arteries. It can lead to an aneurysm.'

He picked a pencil from his desk, twiddling it through his fingers as if concentrating deeply. 'That's why we give aspirin—to try and reduce the inflammation. Even kids who have been treated can still develop an aneurysm. This is serious stuff. One per cent of kids with this disease die. And it can have lasting impacts. Carly will need to be monitored for the rest of her life.'

An aneurysm. Francesca's head spun around to the treatment room where Carly was sitting with her mum and newly arrived dad. That little girl could have a life-threatening condition. And she'd almost sent her back to her cabin with a basic child-with-a-viral-infection sheet.

She could have sentenced that child to death. All because she'd almost missed something essential.

Her legs felt like jelly underneath her.

'Francesca, are you okay? You're very pale.' Gabriel was standing next to her, his hand touching her shoulder.

She couldn't look at him. She couldn't look him in the eye.

After her earlier thoughts about him avoiding eye contact with her, the irony was that now *she* couldn't look at him.

If she did, he would see it. He would be able to read her like a book. He'd know the mistake she'd almost made.

She couldn't bear to look at him. She couldn't bear to

think she might have based her decision to get Carly a second opinion on the fact she'd wanted to see Gabriel.

It made her feel pathetic. And absolutely useless at her job.

*What if she'd sent that child back to her cabin? What if she'd developed an aneurysm that had ruptured at sea?*

She'd been so close to doing that. So very close…

'Francesca.' His voice was firm and he had a hand on either shoulder, standing in front of her and looking her square in the eye.

'Can you phone a ship's porter to help the family with their packing and luggage? We don't have a lot of time here.'

She nodded numbly. It was time to go on autopilot. She could do this. She could get through this.

Gabriel was still talking. 'The hospital is going to carry out her blood tests and chest X-ray. We just need to write a transfer.' He glanced over his shoulder. 'And I need to have another word with the parents.'

Francesca nodded again. Phone the porter, instruct him to pack up the cabin. She could do that.

She turned towards the office, ready to make the phone call.

'Good call, Francesca.'

The words stopped her in her tracks. 'What?' It was the last thing she'd expected.

Gabriel was giving her a knowing smile. 'It was a good pick-up. Lots of people would have missed that. You didn't.' He turned and walked back into the treatment room.

Francesca held her breath. He had no idea. No idea at all.

*But I almost did miss it.*

Her heart was pounding in her chest. It was making

her head swim and sending tingles down her arms—and not in a good way.

This could have held a very different outcome for that little girl. An outcome based on *her* poor instincts. It didn't matter how hard she tried to work at it. Her worst fear had been realised.

She really had lost her nursing instincts. They were dead. Gone.

Or maybe they weren't. Maybe it was all about distraction.

She'd allowed herself to get distracted by Gabriel instead of focusing on the job.

How could she admit the truth to anyone? That the reason she'd asked for a second opinion hadn't been based on the little girl's condition but her own selfish, misplaced desires. What kind of a person did that make her?

Everything about this had been a bad idea. From the second she'd set eyes on Gabriel she'd known he was going to be trouble. As for last night? That had been a joke. Something to push out of her mind and forget about.

She had to concentrate on her work. Concentrate on her duties as a nurse. This couldn't be about her. This had to about her patients.

She picked up the phone and dialled the porter automatically. She grabbed Carly's chart and transferred the written remarks into the electronic record, ready for Gabriel to print out for the transfer.

The porter was going to meet them portside with the family's luggage. There would be no room for it in the ambulance, so it would have to be transported in a taxi. Francesca made another quick call to the cruise company representatives to organise someone to meet the family locally and sort out accommodation for them.

There. That was everything she could do right now. So why were her hands still trembling?

She'd seen this condition with its unusual set of symptoms before. She should have picked it up. And she would have—if she hadn't been so distracted by Gabriel.

She stood up and walked back through to the treatment room. Gabriel had just lifted Carly and seated her in a wheelchair.

There was no getting away from it, the little girl and her family looked frightened. Gabriel was doing his best to put them at ease: he'd managed to find a book for Carly to read and was telling her about his favourite character as he tucked a blanket around her knees.

She still looked unwell, but no more unwell than dozens of other children Francesca had seen in her life as a nurse. How many other kids could she have sent home with this condition?

The thought sent a shiver down her spine and the hairs at the back of her neck tingling.

The phone next to her rang. 'Ambulance is here, Gabriel,' she said as she replaced the receiver. 'I've also spoken to the main office. Marie, a company rep, will meet Mr and Mrs Glencross at the hospital and sort out accommodation for them. The family luggage will be transferred by taxi.'

Gabriel gave her a nod. 'That's great, Francesca, I'd been so busy organising things with the hospital I hadn't considered that.'

He grabbed the handles of the wheelchair and turned to the parents. 'I'll walk you down to the ambulance. You can man the medical centre, can't you, Francesca?'

She nodded and he pushed the chair out the door. His voice drifted along the corridor, 'Dr Demir will be waiting for you, he's fully informed about Carly's condition and will be able to carry out the rest of her tests...'

Francesca sagged against the wall of the treatment room. The rest of the medical centre was empty and it was just as well as she didn't think she could cope with seeing anyone right now.

Tears pooled at the corners of her eyes. She sat down in front of the computer and opened one of the search engines. Kawasaki disease. A mediocre collection of symptoms that she could so easily have missed.

The temperature, rash, joint pains and sore throat and tongue could be attributed to just about any childhood ailment. Irritability, sore eyes, swollen lymph glands, going off food all seemed so run of the mill to her.

But the key indicators of the disease—the strawberry-coloured tongue, red palms and soles of feet and the peeling skin on hands or feet—were often used to help the diagnosis.

She'd missed them.

If she hadn't ever heard of this disease before, she could forgive herself.

But she *had* seen it before. And she couldn't forgive herself for missing it.

A handsome doctor was no excuse.

But Gabriel hadn't. He hadn't missed anything.

Her brain was ticking furiously. Would Katherine have made the same assumption? Would Kevin? Would David Marsh have picked it up? Or was it only the fact that Gabriel was a paediatrician that had gone in Carly's favour?

She couldn't even bear to think about it.

The tears started to trickle down her face.

Gabriel had praised her. He'd looked her straight in the eye and told her she'd done a good job.

But he'd had no idea she'd just wanted to see him. To see what his reaction to her would be.

He'd had no idea she had been wondering if he was as confused about the night before as she was.

She pulled herself up straight.

There was no way she could let this happen again.

She had to forget about Gabriel and just focus on her job.

She couldn't allow the slightest distraction—no matter how handsome.

# CHAPTER EIGHT

GABRIEL was relieved to wave the Glencross family off. Dr Demir at the local hospital had sounded confident he could deal with the condition. Carly would be in safe hands.

That was the second time Francesca had surprised him. The second time her instincts had been spot on.

Why was she so unsure of herself? She'd looked like a startled rabbit when he'd told her she'd made a good call.

But maybe that wasn't about her clinical abilities. Maybe it was about him.

In a sense he was relieved. He'd picked up something in a child that others might have missed—something that could have had devastating consequences.

Every time it happened he felt his stomach clench in endless knots at the thought of a child suffering—of something being missed. He was determined it would never happen on his watch.

He'd been there. He'd seen the effect on a family that losing a child could have. He'd experienced it firsthand.

His brother had only been a baby, not even a year old, when he'd died. And Gabriel had never forgotten his mother. She'd known something was wrong. Even when the local doctor had tried to fob her off and tell her Dante would be fine in a few days.

More than anything Gabriel remembered the scream. Dante's high-pitched scream—the scream of a baby with meningitis—had imprinted on him for life.

Once heard, never forgotten.

But by then it had been too late. A hasty trip to the hospital in the dead of night had resulted in some emergency treatment but it had all been in vain.

The day they had buried the little white coffin in the ground at the Isola di San Michele—Venice's cemetery— had haunted him.

For a six-year-old boy it had been hard to understand the impact on the family. He'd only known that nothing would ever be the same again. Over the years his mother had never lost the sadness in her eyes and his father had flung himself into the family business, as if immersing himself would dull the pain.

It hadn't helped that their family's loss had been widely reported in the media by nosy and intrusive reporters.

Dante had been their 'little blessing', their *piccola benedizione*. His mother had thought she couldn't have any more children after the birth of his younger sister, so the arrival of Dante had been greeted with much celebration.

And for years after Dante's death Gabriel and his sister had been afraid to mention his name. They'd kept a photograph of him in a locked cabinet in their room, taking it out and staring at the little smiling face on occasion.

He'd lost most of his childhood after that. His father had barely been in the house—only eating and sleeping there.

It had been obvious his father loved them but the house had held too many painful memories for him. So he'd spent more and more time at work. Long hours, stress and ignoring his physical health over the years had taken its toll.

It was no wonder he was a victim of heart disease—the disease that was slowly killing him.

Even as a child Gabriel had felt all the responsibility for his mother. Was it survivor's guilt? Trying to stick the family back together? Trying to distract her in any way possible to lessen the pain behind her eyes?

The only time he'd ever felt like a child again had been during the long summers they'd spent with his father's cousin and his family in Pisa. It had been the only time he'd ever felt relieved of the burden of family.

And for Gabriel every time a child came before him like this, every time a child with a vague set of symptoms appeared, he reminded himself why he did this job. No child should suffer the way Dante had. And no family should suffer the way they had.

Twenty-five years was a long time, but time didn't lessen the pain. Sometimes it only enhanced it. Only those who truly didn't understand thought that time could be a healer. Those who had suffered a similar loss knew the truth.

One of Gabriel's colleagues had lost a child some years before, and he was the only person Gabriel had ever confided in, sharing his pain as only a fellow sufferer could.

Frank had told him that every year was harder than the one before, particularly as the milestones of life approached. Time to start school, time to leave school, time to have girlfriends, special birthdays, time to make career choices—all things that his son and Gabriel's brother had missed out on.

And Gabriel had noticed little marks on the calendar that his mother kept. It had taken him a few years to work out what they were. Dante's birthday. The day of Dante's death. A star had marked the day he would have been eighteen. A little red triangle the day he would have graduated from school.

Gone but never forgotten.

Families. So much joy, but so much pain. That was why he never objected to the reputation the media had labelled him with. Millionaire playboy. Playboy doc. In a way it was easier for him. Women had fewer expectations of him. None of them were expecting a wedding band and a house with a white picket fence.

He'd made sure of that.

And spent most of his time focused on his work. A job that he usually relished.

But no matter how hard he tried to be relaxed in his role, there were always times it took him back to his childhood. And that's when it was essential for him to be in control.

That's when he got ratty. For some people being a doctor was just a job. But for Gabriel this was a chance for salvation. He might not have been able to save his brother but so far his decisions had probably saved the lives of over a hundred other children. A hundred children who had got to live another day with their families, to run around in the summer sunshine and enjoy a carefree existence instead of being buried in the cold, damp earth.

Precious, precious lives.

He was in charge now. Not some hopeless doctor who'd been more interested in getting back to his bed than caring for Gabriel's sick brother.

He always took the time with patients and their families. He always went that extra mile. No one should suffer the same fate as the Russo family. No one at all.

His phone buzzed in his pocket and he pulled it out to check the message. His father. Again.

Gabriel sighed. No rest for the wicked.

\* \* \*

Katherine had folded her arms across her chest. 'So spill.' She looked serious and she didn't normally take no for an answer.

Francesca tried her best to look innocent as she re-stocked one of the cupboards. The last thing she wanted to do was talk about Gabriel.

'I don't know what you're talking about.'

'Yes, you do, lady. I heard after the dinner the other night you and Dr Delicious went for drinks. What happened?'

*What happened?* It was a good question and one that she'd no idea how to answer.

'How did you end up going for drinks with him anyway? I thought you hated him?'

'I do. I mean…I did.'

'Aha.' Katherine slid along the counter towards her. 'Now that definitely sounds interesting.'

Francesca felt cornered. What was she going to say anyway? *I spent all night trying to decide if I liked him or not and then he gave me the most earth-shattering whisper of a kiss and walked away?*

She'd had butterflies in her stomach when he'd kissed her. She'd been too excited—like a pathetic teenager—to think any further ahead.

But the morning after she'd woken up with a terrible feeling in the pit of her stomach. *He'd walked away.*

What did that say about her? He wasn't interested? She wasn't interesting enough? She wasn't sexy enough?

The fact was she'd no idea why he'd walked away or what he was thinking.

Was he planning on doing it again? Or was she just going to have to spend the next few weeks working around him, wondering if anything would happen? Because that wasn't her style. Not at all.

And she'd no intention of being a shrinking violet, hanging around waiting to see if she could get a part of him.

Sure, he was handsome. Sure, he was sexy. Sure, for a few milliseconds she'd actually considered pulling him into her cabin and doing the midnight tango with him.

But he was also her boss.

And she had to work with him every day.

And most days she liked work. Or she used to. Her colleagues were a good team, they were a fun team and she didn't want to do anything to spoil that.

Besides, she was waiting for her visa for Australia, and surely—*surely*—it must be arriving any day now. She'd been repeating this mantra for the last six weeks. The last thing she needed was to have some mad fling with some Italian dreamboat.

Flings weren't her style. Flirting? Well, maybe. That she could control. Then she could decide when to back off and when to proceed.

Maybe things had just gone a little too far?

But she could sort that. She could talk to him. It would be fine.

So why was she talking to herself in her head?

Her eyes met Katherine's. The interrogator hadn't moved and Francesca felt her cheeks start to flush again.

'Nothing happened.'

Katherine raised her perfectly plucked eyebrows. 'Oh, really?' Her voice dripped with good-humoured sarcasm. 'And the band played "Believe it if you like".'

'No. Really, it didn't. We went to watch the show together, had a drink and that was it.'

Katherine nodded her head towards the computer. 'So,

in that case, you wouldn't be interested in anything I'd found online about our resident dreamy Italian?'

Francesca hesitated, just a fraction of a second. She could resist the temptation, couldn't she? She could feign disinterest convincingly.

Nope. She couldn't. Rats.

'What is it?' She crossed the tiny dispensing room in one second flat and sat down at the computer screen.

A gorgeous image of Gabriel in a tux glared back at her. Wow. This photo could rival the Mediterranean white-trunked Adonis that had adorned Jill's bedside cabinet.

But in this one he didn't look happy. And, wow—what about the woman surgically attached to his arm? Hanging on there like some piranha?

Beautiful, blonde, in an emerald-green to-die-for figure-hugging dress. The kind of woman who had the proportions of a Barbie doll, proportions no woman was supposed to obtain naturally. The woman was beautiful, perfectly formed, with exquisite features and wearing a dress that must have cost more than Francesca earned in a month.

Only problem was the ice-cold look on her face.

That face could have sunk the *Titanic*.

'Where on earth is this from?'

Katherine looked smug. 'Oh, so now you're interested, are you?' Her head shot down next to Francesca's, just inches away from her face. 'I thought nothing happened?'

Francesca stared her out, trying her absolute best to keep her face free from anything that might give away the stomach that was currently churning, probably giving her an ulcer as they spoke.

She shrugged her shoulders. 'Let's just say I'm as curious as the rest of the crew about our doctor.'

She read the caption under the photo: *'Heir to the Russo*

*printing fortune, Gabriel Russo, with Felice Audair at the
annual Venetian charity ball.'*

Katherine peered at the screen a little longer. 'Last
year's charity ball. I don't think you need to worry,' she
said assuredly. 'Look at their faces and their body language.'

'Do I have to?' Francesca's voice was becoming higher
pitched by the second.

'Yes,' said Katherine determinedly, 'you do.' She
pointed at the screen. 'He might have his arm around her
but look at his face, there's no affection there.' She glanced
at Francesca. 'And look at her eyes, they're like glass—she
isn't really interested in him.' She paused a few seconds
then added, 'You've nothing to worry about.'

'Who said I was worried?' Her self-defence mechanism had kicked in.

Francesca's eyes hadn't left the screen. 'Do you think
that could be a relative?' she asked half-heartedly, knowing the answer even before she heard the reply. Katherine
snorted. 'Not a chance—with those calculating looks I
would be more likely to call her a predator than anything
else.' She shrugged. 'At least the name matches the looks.
She sounds like a prime-time TV villain.'

Francesca sagged back into the chair. She clicked on
the links away from the photographs, her eyes scanning
the page that came up before her.

It seemed as if at one point Gabriel had been photographed wherever he went. It must have driven him nuts.
He seemed permanently surrounded by a bevy of beau-
ties. What did it feel like to have your life examined under
a microscope?

She'd no idea how famous he was in Italy. It appeared

he couldn't move without someone reporting it. It seemed almost obvious to her why he'd left.

So why come back?

And just how ill was his father?

Then there were all the listings for paediatric journal articles all with his name attached. Published papers. He was obviously dedicated to his job.

And a whole host of other, older headlines—mainly in Italian. Something about a tragedy. But she didn't have time to read because Katherine had clicked on another link.

She wrinkled her nose. 'I don't get it. He's a millionaire, with a whole host of specialist skills.' She turned to face Francesca. 'I mean, I'm glad that he's here but what *is* he doing here?'

Francesca felt herself bristle. David had mentioned his father being sick but maybe no one else knew. Maybe it was a secret. 'He must have his reasons.'

Katherine had her hand at her mouth. 'I wonder what they are.' She turned to face Francesca. 'Did you find out anything? You're the one who's been for drinks with him.'

Francesca shook her head. 'I was only there as a human shield. Guarding him from the circling bunch of cougars in the Atlantic Bar. He said I owed him after the week before.'

The answer seemed to placate Katherine. She shrugged. 'Yeah, you probably did. Did that family get away okay?'

'What family?'

'The kid, with the Kawa…whatever-it's-called disease, the potential heart condition.'

A chill crept down Francesca's spine. Of course Katherine would have heard about that. The medical unit was small so any unusual cases were always discussed.

'Yeah. She was admitted to the paediatric unit in the

hospital in Kusadasi.' She hesitated, wondering for a second if she should actually say the words. What would Katherine think?

'Did you have a look at the notes?'

Katherine was carrying a pile of boxes of rubber gloves ready to stock in the cupboard. 'Not yet. David said he would look over them later with me—just because it was such an unusual case.'

Francesca took a deep breath. 'Do you think you would have picked up on it?'

Katherine looked surprised. 'The Kawa-whatsit disease? Not a chance.' She shook her head. 'David wasn't sure he would have either. That's why we were going to discuss it later.'

'I almost missed it.' The words were out before she could stop them and the expression on her face must have said it all, because Katherine sat back down opposite her and put her hand on her shoulder.

'But you didn't.'

'But I've seen it before. I should have remembered. The symptoms are so remarkable—the strawberry tongue, cracked lips, peeling skin.'

Katherine stayed silent for a minute. 'How long since you've seen it?'

Francesca trawled her brain. 'A couple of years, in an A and E in Southampton.'

Katherine nodded, obviously choosing her words carefully. 'The symptoms are unusual and I hope I'll remember them. But I can't guarantee it. You've seen hundreds of patients since then. And everything's fine. You asked for a second opinion, that's what matters.' She squeezed Francesca's shoulder. 'And you won't miss it again.'

Francesca bit her tongue. She'd said enough. It wouldn't

do to tell her colleague the rest. That the real reason she'd missed it had been because her mind had been on a man. She couldn't let that happen again.

Francesca tried to appear calm. She gave a little smile and pushed herself up from the chair, away from the computer screen. 'I'm going to go and chase up some of the crew who have missed their medicals. They keep avoiding us, so I'm getting suspicious.'

Katherine nodded. 'Let's go up for a coffee first then I'll give you a hand. One of the engineers has steadily avoided us for over a month.' She gave Francesca a wink. 'I think it might be two-girl job.'

Ten minutes later they had just sat down to a well-deserved cappuccino in the Clipper Lounge when the piercing shrill of Francesca's emergency page sounded. '*Emergency Deck Five, Drake's Dining Room*'.

'Blooming typical.' Francesca sprang from her seat, leaving her steaming coffee untouched.

'Want help?' Katherine yelled after her.

'No, it's fine,' Francesca shouted over her shoulder. 'David or Gabriel will have the other on-call page. One of them will appear.'

She ran to the nearest stairwell and grabbed the emergency bag, which was stowed in a discreet hatch. Deck five was two decks beneath her and the dining room was immediately adjacent to the stairwell. She glanced at her watch as she reached the dining-room doors—ten to six, almost time for the first sitting. The dining room wasn't open yet to the passengers, which meant the incident had to involve a member of the crew. An anxious waiter was waiting to meet her at the doors. 'This way,' he said worriedly. 'I think he's having a seizure.'

Francesca hurried over to where the crewman was lying

on the floor, surrounded by a throng of worried colleagues. She pushed the onlookers out of her way. 'Let me through, please,' she ordered, her voice loud and commanding. They obediently stepped to one side to let her pass and she knelt on the floor next to the patient. Someone had had the good sense to attempt to put him in the recovery position, so he was lying on his side, but was still jerking and twitching, with his colleague's hands trying to steady him.

'Does anyone know what happened?' she asked the sea of surrounding faces. She bent her head over the patient and her heart lurched—it was Roberto Franc.

As soon as she'd identified him, it was obvious what was wrong.

But like any good nurse Francesca started with the obvious—airway, breathing and circulation. His airway was unobstructed and clear. He was definitely breathing, his chest rising and falling rapidly. Her fingers felt the pulse in his wrist, holding it firmly as his limbs continued to twitch intermittently.

'He was disorientated and muttering,' one of the fellow busboys started. 'I kept asking him what was wrong but his eyes were really glazed, it was if he couldn't hear me. Then he just dropped to the floor and started twitching'.

Francesca quickly checked him over. She wouldn't be able to get him to eat or drink anything as his consciousness level was too altered and he would risk choking. He didn't appear to have injured himself in the fall so she pulled the blood-testing meter out of the emergency bag and quickly tested his blood-sugar level. The meter only took five seconds to produce a result. One point four mmol/litre. His reading was way below normal. Francesca knew the average person had a blood glucose ranging between four and seven mmol/litre.

Roberto's blood glucose was so low it had caused him to lose consciousness.

A few seconds later Gabriel appeared at her side. He was obviously out of breath and she could feel the heat emanating from his body as he crouched beside her.

'Where on earth were you?' The medical centre was only one deck below; there was no way he could be so out of breath running up one flight of stairs.

He smiled and shrugged, 'The sports deck.'

'Deck Sixteen? Why didn't you use the lift?'

He gave a fake shudder. 'Too slow. Stops at every floor.' His eyes swept over their patient. 'Isn't this the young man you saw recently?'

She nodded and lifted the glucometer to show him the reading.

'Got any glucagon?'

She opened her nearby emergency bag and pulled out a bright orange box, flipping it open. The glucagon hydrochloride injection was only used in extreme circumstances and would help deliver glucose quickly to the body and bring Roberto out of his hypoglycaemic coma. The same injection was commonly carried by ambulances and used in accident and emergency departments.

'Want me to do that?'

Gabriel found a suitable bit of skin and administered the injection swiftly and waited for it to take effect.

'He's diabetic,' he said to the watching crowd. 'His blood sugar has dropped to a dangerously low level. This injection will bring him round but it takes a few minutes to work.'

'Diabetic? But he looked as if he was having a seizure,' said one of the confused waiters.

Francesca gave a rueful smile. 'It can look like that.

When a diabetic's blood sugar drops, the symptoms can vary from person to person. Some people shake, sweat and become confused, eventually all will lose consciousness, and sometimes their bodies can twitch or shake a little— it doesn't happen to everyone.'

She gave another quick look at Roberto. 'See? His twitching is starting to reduce as the glucose is beginning to take effect.'

'You must have done this a few times,' Gabriel murmured.

Francesca felt herself stiffen. She didn't want to talk about her dad. Her self-defence mechanism went onto autopilot. 'My dad was usually well controlled. He only ever needed glucogon a few times in his life.'

Gabriel looked puzzled for a second, then his face softened and he reached over and touched her hand, his warm skin encompassing hers.

'I wasn't talking about your dad, Fran. I was talking about being a nurse in general.'

Francesca held her breath. Of course. His brown eyes were fixed on hers, a barrage of questions stored in them. She swallowed and looked away quickly. She had a patient to treat and looked up at the staff around them. 'He was supposed to be allowed to take a break to eat before service started. Does anyone know what happened?'

A couple of the busboys shot each other uneasy looks.

Francesca shook her head impatiently. She didn't have time for this. 'Okay, tell me now what happened.'

'Well,' started one reluctantly, 'he asked earlier if he could stop for something, but the dining-room manager wouldn't let him.'

Francesca's face became thunderous. 'What?'

'Get back to work!' The dining-room manager stormed

up behind the crowd of onlookers, having obviously heard the preceding remark. Before the spectators could disperse, another voice cut through the air.

Gabriel was on his feet, his face furious. 'You and I are going to have words, sir.' His voice was louder, commanding, dripping with ice. He cut a path through the crowd of bystanders. He stopped directly in front of the manager. 'Your actions…' he squinted at the badge on his jacket '…Enzo, would make you directly responsible for this young man's condition.'

He pointed to Roberto, who now lay still on the floor. 'It would also make you directly answerable to me,' he continued sternly. 'I know that the medical centre had left strict instructions regarding Mr Franc's condition and the fact he needed extra breaks to allow him to eat.'

Gabriel was now directly face to face with Enzo, his arms folded firmly across his chest. There was no way he was going to allow his authority to be questioned. Enzo's face had turned a beetroot shade of red. 'We were too busy,' he spat. 'I have two members of staff off sick and I can't afford to babysit anybody!'

'When I give advice I expect it to be followed.' Gabriel's voice was low, menacing—the voice of a man getting ready to lose his temper.

Enzo waved his hand dismissively. 'I have a dining room to open and passengers waiting outside to be fed—when will you be ready to move him?' He turned his nose up disparagingly at Roberto.

Francesca could see the rage flaring in Gabriel's eyes. He stepped forward, his nose practically touching the other man's. 'You can open your dining room when *I* say so and not a second before that,' he hissed.

Francesca tugged at his trouser leg, anything to try

and diffuse the conflict. 'Dr Russo, can you give me a hand, please?'

Her words appeared to jolt Gabriel from his concentrated fury. He knelt down next to her. 'How is he?'

'He's going to be fine—but I'm not so sure I can say the same for you.' She was worried about him—he had looked as if he'd been about to erupt. 'I thought it best to distract you before you landed a punch on him.'

'I almost did. Stupid man. Medical orders stand, no matter what else is going on in the ship. He had no right to refuse Roberto time to eat. I'll be taking this up with the captain.'

His anger seemed to dissipate while he was talking to Francesca. She rested her hand on his forearm. 'Now you've calmed down a little, do you think you could give Kevin a call and ask him to bring a wheelchair up? Roberto's starting to come round now and I'd like to get him down to the medical centre.'

Gabriel leaned over Roberto, whose eyes had flickered open. 'What happened?' he groaned, clutching his forehead. He tried to sit up but couldn't quite get his balance. Gabriel put his arm around Roberto's shoulders and helped him straighten up.

'It's all right, Roberto. You had a hypoglycaemic attack. We had to give you a glucose injection to bring you round.'

'Oh, no.' He groaned, leaning forward and putting his head in his hand.

'I'm just going to arrange a wheelchair for you and we'll take you down to the medical centre for a few hours.' He gave Francesca a brief glance before striding off to the nearest phone.

Francesca caught the arm of the nearest waiter. 'Can you

go to the kitchen and get me some sandwiches for Roberto, please?' The waiter gave a quick nod and dashed off.

'How are you feeling, Roberto?'

'Sick. I feel really sick.'

'Unfortunately that's one of the side-effects of the injection we gave you. It can make some people feel nauseous. Once I've got you downstairs I'll start by giving you a cup of tea and see how you feel from there. The injection gives you a boost of glucose, but it would be better if I could get you to eat something.'

Now that Roberto had regained consciousness, some of the dining-room staff had started to disperse to prepare for the influx of passengers. Francesca could hear the voices of the passengers outside the main doors. They were obviously confused about why the dining room hadn't opened yet. A few seconds later she could hear Kevin's voice as he attempted to make his way through the throng. 'Excuse me, folks, can you let me through? We've got a bit of an emergency in the dining room—the sooner you let me through, the sooner I can deal with it.'

Seconds later he emerged red-faced through the dining room doors, pushing a wheelchair. 'Phew!' he said. 'That did the trick. For a minute there I thought they weren't going to move for me.' He parked the wheelchair next to Francesca and Roberto. 'Can I give you a hand?'

Together they helped a still shaky and slightly disorientated Roberto into the chair. 'Where's Gabriel?' asked Kevin as he started to push the wheelchair in the direction of the main doors.

Francesca indicated her head to the side. 'He's on the phone. I take it he's filling the captain in on his displeasure.' She caught hold of the nearest door and swung it open, balancing the plate of sandwiches for Roberto in the other. They were met by an array of anxious faces. 'Excuse me, please,' she said briskly, 'If you would let us past, I'm sure the dining room will be able to open in a few minutes.'

The crowd parted and they made their way over to the nearest lift. In a matter of minutes they were back at the medical centre.

Kevin and Francesca helped Roberto onto one of the nearest beds. 'I'll just start a chart,' said Francesca, lifting one down from above the bed.

'I'll check his blood-glucose level again,' said Kevin. 'What was it originally?'

'One point four.'

Kevin rolled his eyes. 'No wonder he hit the deck.'

The alarm sounded as Kevin checked the blood level. 'Well, it's up a bit. Three point nine. The injection must have started working.'

Roberto was pale and looked exhausted. Having a hypoglycaemic attack of this level often made patients feel very tired. Francesca knew that Roberto would be best if he was allowed to sleep for a while. She finished writing up his chart. 'I'm just going to get you a cup of tea.' She smiled at him. 'I know you're tired. I'll let you go to sleep once you've had something to eat. We'll keep an eye on your blood-glucose levels over the next few hours. Don't worry if you feel us stabbing your finger while you're sleeping.'

Kevin came and joined her in the nearby consulting room where the kettle was stored. 'Do you want me to do that? I don't mind, I'm due to be on duty anyway.'

'It's okay, Kevin, I don't mind waiting a bit longer. I've got some other patients that I should probably update you on before evening surgery.'

'By the way, there's mail for you.'

He pointed to an official-looking envelope with a tell-tale insignia on one of the worktops.

She drew a sharp breath. Her Australian visa—it had finally arrived. She stuffed the envelope into her pocket. 'Have you mentioned this to anyone?'

He shook his head and shrugged his shoulders. 'Your business, Francesca. No one else's.'

She gave him a smile. 'Thanks, Kevin.'

He gave her a nod and headed back out to Roberto. She finished making the tea and picked up the plate of sandwiches. She knew he was feeling sick but she would have to try and entice him to eat something before he went to sleep.

'Whoa!'

Gabriel let out the cry as Francesca walked out the door and almost crashed straight into him. He caught her hand to stop her spilling the tea.

'I see you're in a better mood. Did you manage to speak to the captain?'

'That's where I've just came from. All medical orders on this ship stand. Enzo will be spoken to this evening.

'I'll take those,' he went on, lifting the plate and mug from her hand. 'I want to speak to Roberto to reassure him that he won't have any more problems in the dining room.' He started walking back towards the door. 'Aren't you off duty now?'

She nodded. There she was being the dutiful nurse again, he thought. She'd handled the emergency situation just as well as he could have. Truth be told, she hadn't really needed him there. Her care and attention to Roberto had obviously been excellent.

It gave him the spur he needed. There was an underlying attraction between them but he still hadn't got to the bottom of what made her tick.

And there still hadn't been the opportunity to talk a little more about her friend. She seemed to get prickly whenever Jill's name was mentioned. Did she really not know what motivated Jill?

He needed to get to know her a little better. Thankfully, she didn't seem to be like her friend at all. And after that night he wanted to see if they could get along together. He wanted her to see the other side of him—away from internet rumours and newspaper headlines.

He needed a chance, outside this environment, to see how she reacted to him. And thanks to Kevin, their colleague, he knew exactly how to do it.

'Francesca?'

She jumped—she'd obviously been daydreaming. She looked at him a little self-consciously and tucked a loose tendril of hair behind her ear. 'Yes?'

'Ever been to Pisa?'

Her head tilted to the side. 'No.' She smiled curiously at him. 'Why do you ask?'

'Because the ship docks at Livorno tomorrow and if you are free I thought you might want to do some sightseeing with me.'

Whoa. Totally sideswiped. Where had this come from?

'Why Pisa?' she asked suspiciously, raising her eyebrows. 'Why not Florence?' Her brain was racing and she was trying her hardest to act as normally as possible. Both cities were accessible from the port of Livorno and it was usually a pretty even split between the passengers over which city they visited.

He crossed the room and put a hand on her waist, bending his head forward to hers. 'Because a little bird told me that you'd never managed to get there so I thought I might have the pleasure of showing you around.'

As his hand touched her waist she sucked in her breath. His movements were so easy, so casual. Almost as if he touched her that way every day. Was all this awkwardness just in her head?

The 'little bird' must have been Kevin as she'd told him the other day that even though she had done this cruise seven times, she had never managed to see Pisa. It was almost as if he'd read her mind.

'I would love to see Pisa.'

'How about we meet for breakfast tomorrow?' he asked. 'Get the day off to a good start?' There was a twinkle in his eye that made her heart flutter. Was he flirting with her? Or was she acting like some crazy hormonal teenager?

'I'll only meet you if you agree to meet at the Poseidon Lounge and not in the dining room. Who knows what Enzo might do to your food in there.'

He rolled his eyes. 'Doesn't even bear thinking about. Eight o'clock?'

'Eight o'clock is fine.' Francesca picked up her bag and headed to the door.

'Francesca?'

She turned back. 'Yes?'

'You won't need to bring your book. I'll keep you entertained.'

# CHAPTER NINE

Hi Jill

Sorry for the delay getting back to you. The ship has been busier than I expected.

Gabriel seems to have settled in fine. He's back here because his father isn't keeping too well. He certainly started off with a splash by rescuing a teenage boy who'd fallen into Venice harbour and was being swept out to sea. His first day was nearly his last as he rescued the boy then knocked himself out on the harbour wall. That's why I had to resuscitate him. Though, at the time, if I'd known who he was I doubt I would have bothered.

He hasn't talked about you, even though I told him how I recognised him. He doesn't say much of anything too personal. His doctoring skills, however, are another story and I've seen some impressive paediatric skills in the last few weeks. He caught a really unusual case in a child that could have resulted in her death if it had been missed.

The women seem to love him—all Italian charm, white teeth and Mediterranean skin. Very different from what I'm used to!

Hope things are going well with you. Have sent you a photo as you requested from one of our crew events.

Francesca

SEND. She sighed and leaned back from the computer. Six composed and deleted emails. There was no point in reading this one over and over like the rest of them. Then she'd just start tweaking it again and again.

And against her better judgement she'd sent the snapshot Jill had requested. If she hadn't it would only have resulted in a whole barrage of emails, so it was better to get it over and done with. Kevin had snapped it the other day when they'd been doing a crew training exercise and the photos had been uploaded to the medical centre computer, so it was easy to access without anyone asking difficult questions.

Would this mean that Jill would reply instantly, looking for more information about Gabriel? Because right now, Francesca wasn't sure how to answer any queries. She had no idea what was happening between them. All she knew was that *something* was.

And now she'd agreed to spend the day ashore with him.

The fact of the matter was this man was driving her crazy.

The sun was already streaming through her porthole when Francesca woke up. Her stomach gave a little lurch. A whole day with Gabriel. Half of her was dreading it, the other half...

She felt like a teenager going on a first date. Why?

Was it because he looked like an Italian film star? Or was it because she'd spent the last few weeks getting to know him? She'd seen him charm the most rambunctious child. He was thoughtful and kind with patients and their relatives. And every now and then she caught him looking at her through those hooded lids and it made her heart flutter.

There, she'd said it.

There was a definite attraction between them. One that neither of them seemed prepared to act on.

Ever since that night when he'd walked her back to her cabin and kissed her, she'd felt as if she was just waiting for something to happen. The kiss had been the briefest of touches but it had affected her in a way she'd never expected. How had Gabriel got under her skin?

And now she was going to spend the whole day with him…

Why had he asked her? Did he feel something, too? Maybe she was reading too much into it and he was just being courteous to a colleague, offering to show her around an area he was familiar with.

It wasn't like she'd never been kissed before. Actually, she'd been kissed quite a lot. Just not like *that*—and he hadn't even kissed her on the lips. Even when she'd spent time with the playboy doc he hadn't kissed her like that.

She'd had a number of boyfriends over the years but she'd never been broken-hearted when the relationships had ended. Sometimes she had actually felt relief. The truth was that since her parents had died Francesca had felt totally isolated.

No one had ever filled the gap that they had left. And nowhere had ever felt like home since.

Travelling had been the ideal way for her to try and cope. It gave her convenient blasé answers to difficult questions. *'I don't want to settle down—I want to see the world.'* No one really knew her well enough to ask questions about her family.

Australia was just the next port of call on her long list. After that it would be America—or maybe Hong Kong. Anywhere but Glasgow.

Her heartbeat quickened as she remembered the thick envelope inside her bedside cabinet—currently unopened.

She wasn't quite sure why she hadn't opened it straight away, even though she seemed to have been waiting for it for ever. But once she opened it, it would be time to move on again. And something about the cruise ship was starting to feel like home.

She showered quickly and dressed in white Capri pants, a red cotton blouse and some flat white shoes that would be comfortable to walk in. It only took a few seconds to pull her hair back with a clasp—she didn't want to be hot and uncomfortable today. She tossed sunscreen and lip gloss into her bag before picking it up and heading out the door.

Gabriel was sitting in the sunshine at the Poseidon Lounge, waiting for her. The food was served buffet style inside the lounge, which was surrounded by glass on all sides. Although some tables were inside, the majority were out on the deck, where passengers had the chance to eat breakfast in the early morning sun and watch the waves.

'It's kind of ironic, isn't it?'

'What is?'

Gabriel pointed to the sign above his head. 'That they named one of the restaurants after the greatest US disaster movies of all time.'

Francesca smiled. It was the kind of smile that had captured his attention right from the beginning. The kind that spread across her face and right up into her eyes. The kind she gave when she was relaxed, unguarded.

His eyes ran up and down her body. She looked as gorgeous as ever in her white trousers and red shirt, her chestnut curls swept back with a clip and sunglasses perched on top of her head.

'Somehow I don't think they named the restaurant after

a movie. It think it was named after the Greek god of the sea.'

Gabriel shrugged. 'Greek. I hear he was a bit of a rogue.'

'Poseidon?'

He nodded.

'And Italians aren't?' She raised her eyebrow as if waiting for him to take the bait. 'I think the expression you're looking for is, *It takes one to know one.*'

She had that little sparkle in her eyes. She grabbed his arm. 'Come on, let's eat. I'm starving.'

They walked through to the buffet and he watched while she piled her plate with scrambled eggs, toast and sausages before adding a pot of tea to the tray she was carrying. She turned around and stretched out her hands to add his plates to her tray.

A frown wrinkled her brow. 'What? That's it?'

He handed over his bowl of muesli as he filled up his coffee cup.

'I'm not a big eater in the morning.' His eyes caught her plate again and glinted with amusement. 'Unlike some other people.'

'I have a feeling I will need all the sustenance I can get,' she said with a smile on her face. She walked back out into the sunshine and sat down at the table.

They had arrived at Livorno at 7:00 a.m. This was the port for Florence and Pisa. Even though it was only a little after eight, the port was bustling with activity. Most of the passengers who were travelling to Florence would be leaving soon. The buses had already congregated near the ship and the tour guides were checking lists with passenger names. Gabriel looked at his watch. They still had plenty of time to eat breakfast. Pisa was closer to the port than Florence and the bus journey much shorter.

There it was again—that glint in her eye. She was in a really good mood this morning. Either that or she'd finally loosened up around him and stopped blaming him for what had happened with her friend.

She took a bite of her toast. 'So—just out of interest—think we would have got served in Drake's Dining Room this morning?'

Gabriel choked on his coffee. She was surprising him. Her sense of humour was coming out, the one that she only normally revealed to other people. He shook his head. 'I know the captain read the Riot Act to Enzo yesterday so in principle we should be fine. But in reality? I've no intention of setting foot in that dining room in the near future.' He gave a little fake shudder. 'As you said, who knows what he might do to our food?'

'Just as well we came here, then.' Francesca set her coffee cup down on the table and took in a deep breath of sea air. 'I much prefer it here anyway. There's nothing nicer than eating breakfast out on deck.'

Gabriel gazed out onto the dock. The buses laden with passengers heading for Florence had already started to leave. It would probably be best to get going.

'Have you finished?'

Francesca nodded. 'Do you want to go?'

He gestured his head towards the dock. 'We could catch one of the buses into Pisa. Do you need to get anything from your cabin?'

She shook her head and picked up her bag. 'I'm the kind of girl who travels light. I've got everything I need.'

Just for a second he hesitated, and then he held out his hand towards her. Would she take it? It seemed like the most natural instinct to him, but he didn't want to do anything that made her feel uncomfortable. He wanted to follow her lead.

This was nothing. This was just two colleagues on a day out.

It was harmless. So why was he having thoughts about Francesca that he never had about any other colleague?

Why—every time he closed his eyes—did he relive the feel of her warm body next to his, their lips almost brushing together, the sparks of electricity in the air?

Why did she continually invade his thoughts, no matter what he was doing?

He could see the fleeting expression on her face. As if she was trying to make up her mind.

Then she stretched out her hand and took his, allowing him to pull her up from her seat.

'Ready?'

She was poised right next to his hip. Any other time, any other woman, he would have slid his arm around her waist.

Under any other set of circumstances he would probably have kissed her, too.

But Francesca was different. This was the woman who had spent the first week on board glaring at him. The second week she'd begun to thaw. The third week they'd shared that moment in the corridor. And now? She'd only recently begun to look him in the eye and have normal conversations with him.

He had no idea how she felt. Was she trying to fight the natural attraction between them?

Because he wasn't imagining the chemistry between them. There was definitely something there. They'd both felt it. Especially that night in the Atlantis Bar when he'd walked her back to her cabin.

Those big brown eyes and plump red lips had almost

been the death of him. Not to mention the figure-hugging red dress.

The only thing that had stopped him had been the consequences. That—and the tiny niggling question at the back of his mind about her necklace.

Maybe this was nothing to do with Francesca. Maybe this was about the poor choices he'd made in the past when it came to women. Jill, the would-be reporter, and a number of others all more interested in Gabriel Russo the heir to the Russo fortune than Gabriel Russo the person. Every gold-digger under the sun, it seemed, had tried her hand with him. Maybe he should just get over it.

Because in the last few weeks he'd seen or heard nothing to make him suspicious of Francesca. Maybe she was just naturally quite reserved. Closed off to those she didn't know well. Maybe if he could get to the bottom of her lack of confidence at work, he could get to know her a little better. Maybe even enough to…

Time to get the day started. Gabriel grabbed her hand in his and pulled her towards the gangway. He spoke to one of the cruise stewards who pointed them in the direction of the next bus due to leave for Pisa. It was almost full and they grabbed the last two seats together moments before the doors closed. The bus set off and Gabriel turned to face her. 'So what do want to do in Pisa?'

'What do you think?'

He groaned and shook his head. 'No. I am *not* taking a photograph of you pretending to hold up the Leaning Tower!'

She folded her arms across her chest. 'Then I'm not getting out of this bus.'

'You're such a tourist.'

'I know. But that's why I've came here today. I've never

seen the Leaning Tower and I hear you can climb up it now, so I definitely want to do that. I don't care how many times you have done it before—you're doing it again today.'

'The Leaning Tower was closed for a spell when I was younger but it's been open for the last few years. We used to spend our summers in Pisa so I've been up it more times than I can count.'

'So, are you going to be a tourist, too, and climb the tower with me? Or are you just going to sit at one of the nearby cafés and wave from down below?'

'Anything else for us to do?'

She leaned back in her seat watching everything speed past. 'No, I just want to be a tourist today. Absolutely no medical dramas. No shopping. But definitely eating. You will buy me lunch today.'

He gave her a mysterious look. 'Ah, I've already made plans for that. But I won't need to buy you lunch.'

She looked at him in surprise. 'Don't even try to pass me off with a cruise-ship sandwich.'

He shook his head. 'No need. My father's cousin has a restaurant near the Piazza Dei Miracoli. Lunch is on him.'

Francesca felt her stomach lurch. 'So I get to meet a member of your family? No wonder they call it the Field of Miracles.'

'What do you mean by that?' He looked bewildered.

'Because no one knows that much about you. You don't give much away. You're a bit of an enigma, to be honest.'

'You mean you haven't read all about me on the internet?'

Her cheeks gave the hint of a flush and she had the good grace to look embarrassed. Part of him felt disappointed. 'Never mind.'

The bus pulled up in a large asphalt car park. The passengers disembarked and the tour guides started to put them into groups. 'Come on,' said Gabriel, 'we don't need to wait for this.'

He clasped her hand again and walked her along next to a high wall. The sun was already beating down and the heat could almost be seen rising from the ground. They walked a few hundred yards before they reached a large archway in the wall. They turned to walk through and Francesca stopped dead. 'Wow!'

There before them stood the Field of Miracles. On the left-hand side were the three white monuments. The sun was reflecting off the white marble, making it glisten in the bright light. The effect was startling.

Gabriel watched Francesca's face in amusement. He had wondered what she would think when she first saw this. Many people were taken aback by the initial glare coming off the buildings. That, along with the fact they were hidden behind the large wall and seemed to appear out of nowhere, made the sight all the more startling.

Gabriel could remember the first time he and his sister had come here. They had fallen in love instantly with the monuments and, because they had family here, had spent many hours playing on the grass in front. He gave her arm a little tug. 'You're blocking people's view,' he whispered as he pulled her to one side.

'Sorry.' She stepped to the left-hand side, nearest to the Baptistery.

'It's just astonishing.' Her eyes were alight with excitement. 'I honestly didn't expect that when we walked around the corner.' She watched the crooked smile that was bending up one corner of his mouth. 'You knew, didn't you?'

'Most people get a surprise when they turn the corner. I wondered what you'd say.'

She fumbled around in her bag to find her camera. 'Let's take some pictures.'

'Let's go and admire the monuments first,' said Gabriel. He stopped in front of one the cafés that lined the right-hand side of the square. 'And let's grab a coffee while we do it.'

'Just a coffee?' quipped Francesca. 'Or do you really plan on feeding me all day?'

He shot her a quick smile and came out of the café two minutes later with two steaming paper cups in his hands. He passed one over to her. 'Here you go, cappuccino with extra chocolate on top.'

'How did you know?'

He tapped the side of his nose. 'I know everything.' He handed over something else, a bag containing a pink box tied with a ribbon. 'Italian chocolates—but save them for later.'

They walked towards the Leaning Tower. 'I guess you want to admire this first,' he said, sweeping his hand towards the impressive structure in front of them.

'No,' she said determinedly. 'I don't just want to admire it, I want to *climb* it. Come on, let's go.' She turned him round and pushed him towards the bell tower. 'Now how many steps are there?'

Gabriel looked at the imposing tower. 'It depends which set of stairs you climb. The south-facing staircase has two hundred and ninety-six; the north-facing staircase has two hundred and ninety-four.'

Francesca gulped. She stood underneath and looked straight upwards at the tower. It really did look as if it could topple over at any moment. She had seen dozens of pictures and news reports about the Leaning Tower but here, seeing it in the flesh, so to speak, was entirely different.

She felt as if she could walk over and give it a push with her little finger. 'I should probably know this, but I've forgotten. What made it tilt like this?'

'Shallow foundations, set in weak, unstable subsoil. They tried many ways to stabilise it. They had tons of lead counterweights on the raised end of the base before finally removing soil from underneath. It's supposed to be stable now for at least two hundred years.'

'So it's safe enough to climb?'

'Definitely. Most people book in advance, though. You're usually given a scheduled time to climb the tower.'

Her face fell instantly. 'You're joking, right? Why didn't you tell me this before? You must have known about it.'

There it was again—that vulnerability about her. She looked like a child who had just had her sweeties snatched out of her hand. How could any man resist that?

She was making him see Pisa through a tourist's eyes. She was reminding him how much he used to love being here. Seeing her face as they'd walked through the archway in the wall had made him appreciate his surroundings all the more. What would she think when they reached the top of the Leaning Tower?

Time to find out.

'Because I came prepared.' He pulled two tickets from the back pocket of his jeans as they reached the entrance and stood at the bottom of the winding staircases.

She let out a squeal. 'You rat bag!' And swatted her hands at him. 'Right, that's it.' She put her hand on her hip and looked upwards. 'Tell you what, let's have a race.'

'What?'

'You climb one staircase and I'll climb the other. I'll race you to the top. Loser has to pay a forfeit.'

'What kind of forfeit?'

'Whatever the winner decides.'

'I like that,' he said. 'I'm sure I could think of something.'

Francesca took their paper cups to throw in the nearby rubbish bin. In an instant Gabriel had turned and started sprinting up the steps. Francesca was caught off guard by his quick getaway and dashed to keep up. She had been an excellent sprinter at school and was sure she could outrun him. Her heart was racing as she pounded up the uneven stairs, her legs thumping. She darted to one side to avoid some sightseers who had stopped on the third floor. She heard a yell from the other side of the tower and grinned to herself as she realised Gabriel must have run into some people.

Starting to pant for breath, she continued to charge up the steps, hearing the muttered apologies from the other side of the tower. Her legs were feeling heavy; running up stairs was definitely harder work than sprinting around a racetrack. By the time she reached the seventh floor she could feel the sweat trickling down her back in the warm air. Her face was flushed and her breathing ragged.

With a final spurt she dashed out towards the balcony that looked over the square. Gabriel was standing with his back to her, pretending to be nonchalant, as if he had been waiting for her for a while. She gasped her way over towards him, thudding her hands on the balcony. Although he looked incredibly sexy in his jeans and T-shirt, the small beads of perspiration on his forehead gave away his recent exertions.

'How on earth did you manage to beat me?' she panted. 'I can't believe it'.

He gave her a wide grin. 'What took you so long?'

She slapped his arm in frustration. 'I heard you banging into people on the way up. I was sure I was ahead of you.'

Her heart was thudding rapidly in her chest, but her breathing had started to slow. Gabriel leaned across and pulled her over to one side.

They stood together, looking out over the Field of Miracles. A welcome gentle wind was rippling against them. She leaned forward, looking down at the people in the square. 'This is a beautiful place, Gabriel. You were so lucky getting to spend time here as a child.' She wrinkled her nose, 'Rainy summers in Glasgow weren't quite the same.'

His arm brushed against hers as he leaned next to her. 'I don't think I appreciated it at the time. Everything about it seemed so ordinary. I thought all families did this. It's not till you go away and see the world from another perspective that you realise the importance of what's still at home.'

The words seemed so straightforward but there was a weight beneath them. What did he mean? She turned to face him, leaning back against the railing. 'So how come you spent your summers here when you lived in Venice?'

His eyes lowered, as if he was trying to figure out how to answer what should be a straightforward question. 'Things changed in our family. My mother…' he hesitated '…needed a little space. The summers were long and we had family here in Pisa. My sister and I were delighted to come and spend our summers with our uncle and our cousins.'

So much unsaid. Everybody had secrets—she knew that better than anyone. But what had happened in Gabriel's family? What about the tragedy referred to on the internet search engine? She hadn't read any of those articles.

It would be intrusive to just come right out and ask. But

curiosity was killing her. Time to try another tactic. 'So what about Venice? How is your father doing?'

He shrugged. '*Not what the doctors tell him* would be the most appropriate answer.'

'Isn't that the same as most folks?'

He sighed. 'My father is a law unto himself. I'm supposed to be taking over some of the day-to-day things for him—anything I can do electronically—to try and relieve the pressure. Trouble is, Dad just finds something else to do.'

She gave him a smile. 'Sometimes parents are worse than children.' Something curled inside her stomach, sending a lump to her throat.

Gabriel had moved a little closer, reaching up and catching a curl that had escaped from her clip. His fingers brushed her cheek as he tucked the curl behind her ear. His eyes had intensity she hadn't seen before. 'So what's your story, Francesca Cruz?' His body moved closer to hers as some people edged past them.

She could feel the heat pressing against her, but she didn't want to step away. It didn't feel intrusive. It felt natural. It felt comfortable. His other hand settled at the side of her waist.

'I don't know what you mean,' she whispered.

Then he moved even closer, his chest pressing against hers. 'You're one of the best nurses I've worked with, Francesca. Everyone in the team thinks really highly of you. But you seem to be the only person that doesn't think that. What's going on?'

She took a deep breath. If she told him the truth he would hate her. If she told him how she'd nearly sent Carly Glencross away he would be horrified.

She couldn't do that. She couldn't tell him about her

dad. She couldn't tell him she'd missed all the signs that could have indicated how low he'd been feeling.

Gabriel's breath was tickling her cheek. She was lost in those dark brown eyes. She didn't want to do anything to spoil this.

'What about our forfeit?' she whispered, a smile creeping across her face.

'Would you like to decide what your forfeit is, or should I?' His voice was husky, the implication clear.

She met his gaze and her stomach tightened. There was no way her heart was going to stop thudding now. At the top of the bell tower the light breeze cooled their heated skin. The beauty of Cathedral Square was just beneath them, but neither of them seemed to notice. He raised his fingers and captured another little chestnut curl that had stuck on her damp skin. He wound it round his finger slowly, never taking his eyes from hers. 'I think we might both have decided the same thing.'

She couldn't move. She couldn't breathe.

His lips bent to meet hers. His kiss was electrifying, the lightest, most delicate of touches. Nothing more, nothing less. With very little pressure his mouth teased the edges of hers. His hand brushed gently along her cheek, settling behind her ear and cradling her head in his hand. The kiss deepened slightly, the pressure increasing as he pushed forward then pulled away. Her first instinct was to grab him. To want more from this kiss. But he released his lips from hers and pressed his forehead against hers. It was perfect.

Their first proper kiss on top of one of the most famous monuments in the world. It could have been a moment from a movie. He might have kissed her outside her cabin. The air had been electric and atmosphere heavy, but it could never have matched this moment. A fleeting brush of his lips on her ear could never compare with this. She took a deep breath and stepped backwards.

He smiled at her, a thousand unspoken thoughts in his eyes. A promise of something else. Something for later.

Because she didn't need anything else right now. Her lips were tingling, the taste of him still there. The scent in her nostrils was that of his distinctive aftershave. The back of her head could still feel the warmth from his hand.

She'd thought everything about Gabriel would feel wrong. But it didn't. It felt very right.

A crowd of voices broke the silence seconds later as a horde of tourists reached the top of the stairs and joined them on the balcony, oblivious to what they had just interrupted.

Gabriel moved over to let some of them past. His hand rested on Francesca's waist. 'Do you want to take some photographs?' he asked, the lazy smile appearing on his face.

Francesca nodded. She wanted to capture this moment. She wanted to remember this. She pulled out her camera and was immediately accosted by a small grey-haired woman.

'Oh, let me, dear,' she said, grabbing the camera from Francesca's hand. 'You make a beautiful couple.'

Francesca looked over at him. Would he want to capture the moment, too? The enthusiastic woman gave them a prod to push them together again.

'Come on, then—give us a smile.'

They stepped together and both gave a smile. Gabriel's arm was still around her waist and he pulled her closer, nestling her beneath the crook of his arm. Her hand naturally lifted and rested on his firm chest. He smiled at her again, as if still reliving their secret moment.

Click.

'Perfect!'

The woman handed the camera back and wandered off.

Francesca felt her shoulders ease. She looked back over the balcony. 'Can we visit the *Duomo*?'

'Anything you want, Francesca.' His words sounded so simple, but she understood the hidden meaning. He was waiting for her lead.

'Great.' She turned and headed back down the winding staircase. It was becoming hotter now and getting busier. They walked across the crowded square towards the *Duomo*, the medieval cathedral at the heart of the square, his hand loosely grasping hers.

This felt different from this morning. Taking his hand, this morning had been a stepping stone. A starting point. What now?

An instant quiet fell on them as they stepped from the hot and bustling square through the massive bronze doors into the cooler air and hushed tones of the cathedral. Although it was filled with numerous tourists, there was a respectful silence and tranquil feeling inside. Francesca gave a little shudder as her body adjusted to the rapid change in temperature. The gorgeous gold-decorated ceiling gave a feeling of opulence and wealth, as did the decorated mosaics and the carved marble panels showing dramatic scenes from the New Testament.

Gabriel calmly kept her hand in his and walked with her in silence around the statues and elaborately carved pulpit. She was grateful for that silence. Even though she was wandering amongst some of the most beautiful artefacts in the world, Francesca felt as if she could hardly concentrate. She was conscious of him at her side. Of the dark curling hairs on his arm brushing against hers.

They had finished walking around the cathedral and had reached the bronze doors again. 'Are you ready for lunch yet?'

She gave a little nod. She was beginning to feel more relaxed and calm again. Lunch might be the perfect time to get to know the man she'd kissed a little better. They walked across the square and down a side street towards an Italian restaurant. Gabriel stopped just as they were about to enter the dark wood doors.

He shot her a smile. 'Prepare yourself,' he muttered as he pushed open the door.

Four hours later they stepped back out of the restaurant.

Gabriel had the noisiest and most welcoming family she'd ever met. The food and company had been delicious. The smells alone had been fantastic.

Her head was reeling. She'd barely caught a word of the rapid Italian. Her basic Italian was passable but so many regions of Italy had dialects and she struggled to follow the fast-paced words. Gabriel had flowed back into his native language with no hesitation whatsoever. His grasp of English was impeccable and she'd almost forgotten it wasn't his first language. But Gabriel, ever the gentleman, had obviously sensed her unease and had stopped time and time again to include her in the conversation.

Seeing the obvious affection he felt for his family had sent little pangs straight to her heart. It was at times like this she missed her mum and dad more than words could say. It made her realise what she'd lost.

'Francesca?'

The voice was a whisper in her ear, his warm hand touching her waist.

'I've something to ask you.'

A little shiver went down her spine. There was something about the way he was looking at her, the way he was touching her. All of a sudden her heart was beating furiously in her chest. Her breath seemed to have caught in her throat. They'd had a perfect day. Was it about to get better? Or was he going to spoil it? She held her breath.

'Want to do this again?'

# CHAPTER TEN

'WHAT you doing, gorgeous?'

The words danced over her skin like the warm afternoon sun. She was standing on the adults-only sunbathing deck again. But instead of hiding inside a pod and reading, she was leaning over the rail towards the swimming pool underneath, watching the children play with the entertainers.

She took a sip from her long, cool drink as she turned to face him. 'I like watching the kids. I like watching people who don't seem to have a care in the world.'

She wondered what he'd say as a frown seemed to hover around her brow. The guy was a paediatrician, surely he didn't have an aversion to kids?

He leaned on the rail next to her. 'Families,' he muttered quietly as his eyes swept over the scene below.

There was a whole host of children dancing in the sun with the entertainers. A younger bunch was in the paddling pool, throwing balls back and forwards. Families of all shapes and descriptions were scattered around the loungers next to the pool.

Francesca laughed as one toddler dumped her ice-cream cone onto her brother's back. He screamed at the top of his voice and ran away.

'I should go down there and talk about sunscreen. Some of those kids look red already.'

She gave him a sharp nudge. 'Stop thinking like a doctor, Gabriel, and start thinking like a normal person and have some fun.'

She couldn't see his eyes as they were hidden behind designer sunglasses. Just like the part of him he kept hidden from her.

But, then, they were both a little guilty of that.

'I like your family. Your father's cousin and his family were great. Think we can go back and visit again? The food in their restaurant was amazing.'

He gave the slightest nod. 'If only the rest of the family was like that.'

'What do you mean?' She pushed her sunglasses up onto her head. 'Aren't you and your dad close? I thought you were back to help him?'

She hoped it sounded like a casual enquiry with no ulterior motive. He'd hardly said a word about his mother or his father. He leaned further over the rail, focusing on the people below.

A classic avoidance tactic. One she'd used herself.

'Gabriel?'

She wasn't going to let this go. She'd shared a kiss with this man. Surely she was entitled to know a little bit more?

'I do what I can at night online. My sister is helping with the day-to-day running of things.'

'Your sister?' She could feel her eyebrows rise. He had barely even mentioned her before.

There was the tiniest moment's hesitation. 'Sofia could run my father's printing company with her eyes shut. She eats, breathes and sleeps the business. Whereas I...' His voice drifted off. 'But she's a girl—that's the problem.'

Francesca felt herself pull back a little. 'Is your father really that old-fashioned? In this day and age?'

She couldn't read him. She couldn't see his eyes at all and it was driving her crazy.

He shrugged, his arm curving around her waist. 'It's complicated,' he said as he bent towards her for a kiss, pressing his body up next to hers. A smile was starting to flicker across his face as if he had other, more pressing things on his mind.

'All family business is complicated,' she said as her arms crept around his neck and she lost herself in his kiss.

Whatever it was, it could wait.

The next two weeks passed by in a blur of ports, beautiful cities, sexy sightseeing and crackling electricity.

And, of course, passengers.

Sunburn and blistering seemed to be the common complaint amongst the children on board, parents misjudging the strength of the Mediterranean sun. For the older patients the trend seemed to be fractured wrists, with falls from the tour buses, slips on the open-air decks and tumbles on the stairwells.

But for Francesca and Gabriel all this was just background noise.

It seemed only natural that when they were apart they would seek each other out. If they weren't working together they were eating together, visiting ancient monuments or watching the entertainment.

The electricity between them seemed to be gaining momentum with every second they spent together.

He'd kissed her again, of course. Each one more tempting than the last. The increasing intensity was driving her crazy. It seemed only natural that things would progress between them. The only question was when. The lack of privacy on the cruise ship was definitely restricting their activities.

But, tonight, for the first time in two weeks, they were finally on call together.

'What are you doing, Gabriel?'

He sighed and leaned back in his chair. The rest of the lights in the medical centre were off and his face was lit up by the computer screen in front of him. 'I'm just typing up some notes for a patient I've just visited.'

'Anyone I know?'

He looked tired and he ran his hand through his hair. He handed her some notes. 'I don't think you've met him. Jackson King, seventy. Chest infection.' He ran his fingers through his dark hair, as if contemplating his thoughts. 'I should probably put him off at the next port but he's waited a year for this cruise and, to be honest, I don't think he'll make another. I might bring him down and try him on some IV antibiotics next.'

Francesca could feel herself getting flustered. In the past she'd dealt with lots of patients who had died. It was part of the element of being a nurse.

But since she'd lost her dad she found herself getting emotional and irrational about these sorts of things. She'd made a conscious decision to try and take herself out of these scenarios and cruise-ship nursing had been a pretty safe bet.

Most passengers who became unwell were transferred off the ship. It was only in really rare and unfortunate conditions that someone died on board.

Nothing like that had ever happened since Francesca had joined the crew.

A wave of fear swept over her body. 'Is it serious? Do you think he's going to die on board?'

She saw him bite at his bottom lip, his dark eyes fixed on hers. 'Hopefully not. I'd hate to put him off the ship and dump him into a local hospital if all they're going to do is put on him IV antibiotics for a few days and give him oxygen—we can do that here.'

'But maybe that's not in his best interests.' She could feel herself starting to twitter. 'I mean, we may have an X-ray machine but sometimes people are better off in a hospital. We can't deliver the kind of care he might need in here. We could ventilate someone for a few hours at most. And if he reached that stage, it would be even more risky to transfer him. I think it's best if you put him off at the next port, Gabriel.'

Gabriel reached over and took her hand. 'Sit down, Francesca.' His voice was calm but firm. He pulled her over towards the chair next to him. He was looking at her as if she had just sprouted horns.

'Wanna tell me what's going on?'

Her skin felt jittery, the tiny hairs on her arms standing on end. Her brain was working ten to the dozen, she was agitated and she couldn't hide it.

'It's not that I'm saying I can't look after him because obviously I could.' She swept her arm around the state-of-the-art treatment room. 'But it's best for the crew if we don't really have patients overnight. It puts extra pressure on us that we don't need. And we don't have everything we need here.'

He was staring at her with those big brown eyes. She could practically read his thoughts and it wasn't helping.

The *Silver Whisper* had every bit of equipment they could possibly need for a man with a chest infection. An X-ray machine to determine the extent of the infection, IV antibiotics to treat the infection expertly and efficiently, oxygen supplies, monitoring equipment, and an emergency ventilator if needed.

At least once a week they had someone who needed to stay in the medical centre overnight and be monitored. It was part and parcel of the job.

'What's the worst that could happen?' His voice was deep and even, perfectly controlled.

Silence hung in the air. There was the slightest rise of Gabriel's eyebrows.

Francesca could feel her heart thump against her chest. She couldn't breathe. Her chest was tight. She was struggling to pull in air.

She couldn't focus. She kept seeing her father's body sitting in front of her. The terrible colour and tone of his skin. That horrible deathly tinge of grey. It made her want to be sick.

All her nursing life she'd dealt with dead bodies. From the very old to the heartbreaking very young. She'd always treated them with reverence and respect, almost as if they had been members of her own family.

But the cold, harsh jolt of reality had been a terrible experience for her. She couldn't face it. She didn't think she could deal with a dead body again.

Everything had changed now.

'I really don't want to be around someone who's about to die,' she blurted out.

Gabriel was more than a little surprised by her reaction. She was freaking out. His normally calm, capable nurse had turned into a jittery wreck. Her hands were flapping all over the place, she was pacing up and down, talking nineteen to the dozen. What was this about?

She was a nurse. She was used to dealing with death. What on earth was wrong?

She'd helped pull him from the water and resuscitated him. Essentially, until she'd put her hands on his chest, he'd been dead. Until she'd given him mouth to mouth he hadn't been going to breathe again.

But she obviously wasn't thinking like that. This was something different. Her actions in an emergency were automatic—without thought. This was something else entirely.

He stood up and put his hands on her shoulders.

'Francesca, calm down.' She wasn't listening, she was still ranting. 'Francesca.' The volume of his voice increased, bringing her to a halt. There were tears glistening in her eyes, threatening to spill down her cheeks at any second.

This wasn't a normal reaction. This wasn't a professional response.

This was personal.

He guided her into the chair once again and knelt in front of her. The time his voice was quiet, almost a whisper. 'What is it, Francesca? What happened?'

Her shoulders started to shake and the dam burst. Whatever had been threatening to erupt inside her had just taken over. He put his arm around her shoulder as she sobbed, rubbing her back and letting her rest her head on his shoulder.

'My dad,' she sobbed. 'It was my dad.'

He ran his hand through her tangled hair, smoothing it down with the palm of his hand. The shoulder of his shirt was sodden with her tears but he didn't care. At last he was getting to the bottom of what was wrong with her.

'What happened to your dad, Francesca?' She hardly mentioned her parents. It had always seemed like a sensitive area. He knew both her parents had died, but had no idea of the circumstances. When he'd made tentative queries with the other staff, none of them seemed to know, either.

'I missed the signs. I should have known. I should have paid more attention.' He took a sharp intake of breath. Had her father died of a chest infection?

But Francesca wasn't finished. 'If I'd just understood how lonely he was then I would have known to pay more attention.' No. This didn't sound like a chest infection. This sounded like something else entirely.

Pieces of the jigsaw puzzle started to slot into place. 'How long ago did your mum die, Francesca?'

'Five years. I left London to come back home and help my dad.' Her eyes lifted to meet his. 'It was hard for us both and he was depressed after it.' She shook her head. 'But he was better, at least I *thought* he was getting better. He'd started to go out more, take care of his appearance. I thought the depression had lifted. I never would have left him alone otherwise. He was all I had left.' She doubled over, her body racked with sobs again and her head in her hands.

Gabriel took a deep breath. Everything was fitting together. 'Did your father commit suicide, Francesca?'

Through her sobs she nodded.

Everything seemed crystal clear to him now. That's why she struggled at work. That's why she didn't trust her instincts.

She'd missed something in the person who had meant the most to her in the world. She was crippled by guilt. Anyone would be.

He understood it well. He'd only been a child when Dante had died, but that didn't stop the feelings of guilt. That he should have known something was wrong with his brother. He should have tried to help his mother more. He should have chased after that obnoxious doctor when he'd left the house saying Dante would be fine in a few days.

He pushed a stray tendril of hair behind her ear and put his fingers under her chin, lifting her face to his.

'That wasn't your fault, Francesca.'

'Then whose fault was it?' Her voice was angry. She needed to vent.

He ran his hand along the length of her arm, stroking her skin. 'Francesca, often we can't see things in those we love most. You thought your dad was getting better. You were probably feeling relieved.' He shook his head, 'It's not till after the fact that you get to examine things. You must know by now that often people who are depressed seem to have a spell when they pick up, make improvements, and then something like this happens.' He clasped her hands in his.

'It's not your fault. This could never be your fault. I didn't know your father, or know his reasons. But he was an adult, Francesca. The decision to do that was his. It doesn't take away from how much he must have loved you.'

She was shaking her head slowly. 'But he was my responsibility, Gabriel. *Mine*. No one else's. I should have seen the signs.'

Gabriel nodded. 'I know that's what you believe. And I know that's what has been affecting your work. You think you've lost your instincts, you think you made a mistake.' Her eyes widened. 'But you haven't, Francesca. You're one of the most competent nurses I've ever worked with. And your instincts are spot on.'

A single tear dripped down her cheek and she lowered her gaze. 'I'm not, Gabriel. You have no idea,' she whispered.

'You're a nurse. I know you're scared. But you're going to have to learn to deal with death again. In this job, we have to be prepared. We have to be prepared for anything.'

He rubbed his hand over the top of hers. 'I'm going to tell you something that hardly anyone knows about me.'

Gabriel drew in a long, slow breath. He had to tell her. He had to share with her. She had to know she wasn't alone in feeling she'd let down her family. He had to be honest with her.

'I don't just have a sister.'

She tilted her head and looked confused.

'I used to have a brother, too. Dante died when he was a baby. I was six. Dante had meningitis—except we didn't know it at the time. My mother called for the doctor, but he was tired or drunk—or both. He was in and out of our house in less than five minutes, saying Dante would be fine in a few days. But my mother *knew*. My mother knew something was wrong. We all did. I've never heard a cry like that before. And by the time we took him to the hospital a few hours later it was too late.'

'Oh, Gabriel. I'm so sorry.' Her hand reached up and stroked the side of his face.

He caught her hand back in his. 'A mother's instinct is never wrong. It's the most valuable lesson I've ever learned. So I *know,* Francesca. I understand what it feels like to miss something in a family member. To question every day if there was something else—something different—you could have done.' He held her hand next to his chest. 'I understand in a way that other people can't. Because I feel guilty, too.'

Her reaction was instantaneous. She shook her head. 'But that's ridiculous. You were a child. You couldn't have done anything to save your brother. You know how it is with meningitis. It's so quick. It's so deadly. Even with all the technology in the world, we still can't save everyone.'

He pressed her hand closer to his chest. 'It doesn't matter what the logical explanation is, Francesca. It doesn't change what I feel in here. Just like it doesn't change what you feel in here.' He reached over and pressed his hand over her heart. He felt her pull her breath into her lungs, holding it in place, while she contemplated his words.

'Because our family was well known in Italy it was all over the press. Everywhere we went there were reporters following us, photographers snapping pictures. My mother was fragile enough as it was.' He shook his head. 'To add that into the equation…'

Now she would understand. He could see the realisation dawning on her of why he hadn't wanted any press intrusion about the incident in Venice harbour. Her hand pushed against him even more.

He was kneeling on the floor in front of her. In the dimly lit room she was beautiful, her eyes wide, her vulnerability shining through.

Did she know just how irresistible she was? Did she know how many times he'd wanted to kiss her? How much he wanted her?

'Sometimes we just need somebody.'

Her eyes met his. Dark brown, melting pools of chocolate.

'I need you, Gabriel.' Her voice had changed. This time there was no tremor—no vulnerability. This time it had a very determined edge.

Did she mean what he thought she did?

'Francesca?'

She moved from her chair. A decisive movement, kneeling on the floor to face him.

They were almost nose to nose, just inches apart.

She lifted her hand to touch the side of his face and ran her fingers through his hair.

He caught her hand in his. 'Are you sure?' The atmosphere in the room was so tense he could barely growl the words out.

'I'm sure.' There was no shred of doubt in her voice.

'Then not here.' It was all he could do not to push her onto the floor or up against the wall in the medical centre. But no matter how much he wanted her, he couldn't do that.

Anyone could walk in here at any time.

For Francesca he wanted uninterrupted time and pleasure.

He pulled her towards the door, striding down the quiet corridors of the ship towards his cabin—the two-minute journey had never seemed so long—fumbling in his pocket to find his card to open the door.

She could feel the electricity in the air between them; it felt as if any minute now a million fireworks could go off in a dazzling multicoloured display.

As the door sprung open she found herself slammed up against the wall, her hands above her head. His mouth was on hers in a second. Warm, scorching heat. His tongue probing, pressing her lips apart. This was no gentle kiss like the one on top of the Leaning Tower. This was pure passion.

She pressed herself against the blazing heat of his body, feeling his instant hardness across her taut stomach. Her fingers started tugging at the buttons on his shirt, struggling to unfasten them quickly. Her heart was thundering in her chest and her head was spinning. He pulled her over towards his bed and they crashed onto the mattress together. 'Tell me this is what you want,' he growled.

He bent forward and started leaving a trail of kisses behind her left ear, down the delicate, ticklish skin at the side of her neck and across her shoulder bone, carrying on downwards until he reached the skin between her breasts. Francesca squirmed in delight, feeling his breath on her electrified skin as he tantalised and teased her with his lighter-than-air kisses.

He reached up and wound his fingers around the strap of her bra, pulling it down roughly to release her swollen breast from the confines of her underwear. A wicked grin came over his face and he leaned over and flicked his tongue over the prize.

She groaned out aloud and her body reacted instinctively to his, arching her back towards him, thrusting her nipple further into his mouth. He devoured her endlessly before rising, brushing a kiss across her lips, and started his trail of butterfly kisses again under her other ear. She could barely stand the tension as she could feel the first involuntary tremors of arousal in her body. His hand lifted to move her second strap and release the other breast from its confines.

She pulled his shirt apart, pushing it down over his shoulders. She wanted to see him. She wanted to feel him. She didn't want anything between them.

His other hand wound its way downwards and inside her silk panties to find her moistness, stroking it with expert fingers. Francesca could stand the torment no longer. In his position astride her she could see and feel his erection brushing against her stomach.

'Don't play games with me, Gabriel,' she breathed. She wasn't waiting a second longer as she tugged at his trousers.

His reaction was instant as he fumbled from the bed

and threw his clothes across the floor. He stopped for a few seconds. There was a rustle of a wrapper before he was poised above her again.

Francesca used that time to push her silk panties over her legs to join his clothes in the puddle next to the bed.

Within seconds he was back on top of her on the bed. He gently pressed the length of his naked body next to hers. She responded immediately by opening her legs and winding them around his waist. 'Now, Gabriel,' she gasped. He was poised above her again and he hesitated, still waiting for her lead.

'Are you sure?'

'Come on, Gabriel.' She grabbed his shoulders. There was no doubt in her mind. If he stopped now, she would kill him.

She tilted her hips up towards him. Nothing else mattered. Nothing but right now and this moment. Nothing had ever felt this good.

He entered her in one powerful thrust sending shockwaves shooting through her body. The pressure increased with each stroke as his momentum increased, the tide of passion rising quickly. She wound her legs tighter around his body to pull him deeper into her as the first waves of ecstasy throbbed through her.

Making love had never felt like this before—everything about it was different. She'd never felt this kind of connection before.

Maybe it was because of what she'd shared with him? And what he'd shared with her?

She had never been able to do that before—to talk about her father and what he'd done.

She'd seen the hurt in his eyes, just as he must have

seen it in hers. It had given her this—the first time she'd felt truly connected to a man.

She was losing control. The sensations were sweeping over. Taking her to the place she wanted to go. Gabriel touched her face and whispered in her ear. Words of emotion. Words of tenderness. Words of passion.

And she let go.

She glanced at the clock on his bedside table; it was after midnight and Gabriel was already sleeping. She wondered what it would be like to wake up every morning next to this gorgeous man. A man who had spent the last few hours treating her as though she was the most important thing on earth.

She wondered what it would be like to share his bed every night.

The release of endorphins was obviously making her crazy because, in her head, she was picturing two dark-eyed children playing outside a beautiful house, with Gabriel and herself standing in the garden, watching.

Clearly, she was losing her mind.

She had never allowed herself to formulate dreams like this—she was so used to being alone. But Gabriel had evoked feelings in her that she could never have hoped for. His heat was enveloping her now like a warm blanket and ripples of fatigue were tugging at her. She dug her head into the feather pillow. This bed was much more comfortable than hers; she could get use to this.

It was almost as if a huge weight had been lifted off her shoulders. She'd hardly ever spoke to anyone about this.

She'd never known talking about it could have this effect.

But it wasn't just what she'd said. It was what *he'd* said that mattered.

He'd shared with her about his brother. How hard must it have been to dig up all those childhood emotions and memories? No wonder he never spoke about it. The pain had been etched on his heart, just like it was on hers.

Had she finally met someone who could understand? Really understand what this felt like?

Someone she could finally share with? Someone to take the aching feeling of loneliness away?

That could be too good to be true.

Her plans drifted through her mind, like feathers in the wind scattering aimlessly around.

Her letter from Australia? It might never be opened.

# CHAPTER ELEVEN

TIME was beginning to drift for Francesca. Her letter had sat unopened in her bedside cabinet for weeks.

She'd been very busy. Busy spending every moment with Gabriel.

Today they were on duty. The boat had docked at Mykonos in Greece, with most of the passengers visiting the nearby town with its maze of tiny streets and whitewashed-steps lanes. Things had been quiet.

But that was about to change.

They heard a cry from the corridor. It was the most distinctive cry she'd ever heard.

Gabriel was on his feet in an instant, not waiting for the patient to reach the medical centre but striding down the corridor at lightning speed.

Seconds later he returned with a toddler in his arms. The scream was like nothing Francesca had ever experienced before. Something was really wrong.

Gabriel laid the little one down on the one of the examination trolleys, listening as the parents joined him, both talking at once.

Francesca picked up fragments of the conversation as she connected the little one to a monitor. 'Temperature… fretful…not drinking…screaming.'

Gabriel was sounding his chest. Francesca lifted the tympanic thermometer and put it in his ear. 'High temp, Gabriel. Thirty-nine point eight.'

She lifted a nearby chart and touched the arm of the child's mother. 'Excuse me, what's your son's name?' In the speed and confusion she hadn't heard it.

'It's Jake. His name is Jake. Jake Peterson.'

Francesca nodded. 'Date of birth?' She wrote down the details; he was only fourteen months old. She watched as Gabriel finished sounding his chest, checked his blood pressure and checked his ears, nose and throat.

'He had an ear infection last week,' said his mother anxiously. 'He had antibiotics but I'm not sure if they've worked. We gave him paracetamol but his temperature won't come down. He won't drink. He's been vomiting.'

Francesca was still watching Gabriel. Was that a tremor in his hands? Did he suspect what she thought he did?

On autopilot she reached over and touched Jake's hands and feet. While his body temperature was high, his hands and feet were distinctly cold. An indicator of meningitis in children.

She gave Gabriel a little nod. He understood instantly. He took a few more moments, placing his hand behind Jake's head and lifting it while keeping his other hand on Jake's chest. The movement caused an involuntary reaction in Jake, flexing his hips and knees. 'Positive Brudzinki's.' He glanced over at Francesca. And she could see it.

The pain written all over his face.

Was Jake the same age that Dante had been?

He pointed to the phone on the nearby wall. 'Phone the captain, tell him we have a medical emergency. Tell him not to leave port.'

Francesca glanced at her watch. The ship was due to

leave Mykonos in the next few minutes. The engines had already started up and the anchor probably lifted. It was vital they stop this. Every minute in a meningitis case counted. An emergency sea evacuation would take up precious time. She spoke swiftly and quietly then hung up the phone. 'It's done.'

'What's happening? What's wrong with Jake?'

Gabriel put his hand on Jake's mums shoulder. 'Jake is showing signs of meningitis.'

She looked aghast. 'No. He can't be. He's had those vaccinations. He can't have meningitis.'

Her hand stroked the head of her son lying on the bed. The screaming had stopped. He was floppy and lethargic. His heart beating too fast, his colour pale.

Gabriel appeared calm. But she could hear it. The tiny tremor in his voice. The absolute control he was exercising over himself.

'Unfortunately there are lots of different types of meningitis. The vaccines only protect against the most common. Jake has obviously picked up another type. We won't be sure which type until we can do some tests, but in the meantime I'm going to give him some intravenous antibiotics.'

The woman gripped Gabriel's arm fiercely. 'What if you're wrong? What if it's not meningitis? Don't you need to do that horrible test on Jake to find out? The needle in his back?'

Gabriel shook his head. 'There's no time. I'm going to give him antibiotics and arrange immediate transfer to a children's hospital. He'll need some steroids, too. We can't wait. We have to act now.'

He was moving across the treatment room, opening cupboards, obviously searching for what he needed.

'What IV antibiotics have we got?'

Francesca was at his side in an instant. She glanced at the small, pale child over her shoulder. 'What do you want?'

'Vancomycin.'

She shook her head. They only had the most basic antibiotics on board. 'Benzylpenicillin or cefotaxime, then.'

'We've got both of them.' She waited while he scribbled his prescriptions.

'I'll take some bloods and insert the IV cannula while you make up the loading drugs.'

She nodded and got to work quickly. This must be his worst nightmare. She couldn't imagine how he must be feeling. Outwardly he seemed cool, calm and collected. An experienced paediatrician dealing with something he must have seen before.

Jake's mother had started to cry. 'But he doesn't even have a rash…'

Francesca touched her arm as she hung the bag of fluids up and ran the infusion through the IV line. 'It's probably best that he doesn't. A rash is a really critical sign of meningitis. The sooner we get these started the better.'

It had only taken Gabriel a few seconds to collect the blood samples and insert the cannula.

Francesca joined up the IV and set the electronic pump. It was important that these antibiotics were delivered as quickly and as safely as possible. She handed Gabriel a scrap of paper.

'Here are the nearest hospital's contact details. I'm not sure who the paediatrician is there.'

He nodded and walked swiftly over to his office, leaving the door open so he could continue to observe Jake as he made the call.

It was all over in a few minutes. 'Ambulance should be here soon. They're sending a doctor to do the transfer.'

Francesca started a new set of observations on Jake. There was no change. No improvement, no deterioration. Gabriel never left his side, writing his notes at the bedside and talking calmly and quietly to Jake's parents.

Ten minutes later the phone in the medical centre rang to say the ambulance was at port side. There had been no time to make any alternative arrangements, and the family's luggage was still on board as the stewards hadn't had enough time to pack up their cabin.

One of the pursers brought the family their passports and money from the safe in their cabin and promised to arrange the transport for their luggage. It was as much as they could do.

For Jake, time was of the essence. Everything else would have to wait.

Ten minutes later Jake and his parents were in the back of the ambulance, speeding off to the local children's unit in Mykonos.

Francesca and Gabriel walked back up the stairs to the medical centre in silence. She was watching him carefully.

He was clenching his fists and his jaw was firmly set. It was clear his frustration and anger was building. He strode ahead swiftly and she jumped as something crashed off the wall in front of her.

'We need to get better antibiotics in here! That child could have died!'

She froze. She'd never seen him like this before. His anger was frightening, even though it wasn't directed at her.

She turned to face him. 'You did a good job, Gabriel,'

she said quietly. It was a calm, measured response, hopefully one that would permeate across to him.

'What if we'd been at sea?' He was pacing now. His anger clearly had not abated. His hands were shaking.

She walked over to the worktop in front of her and started clearing up the remnants from earlier. Discarded vials, packaging from the IV line, the plastic cover for the bag of saline.

She'd no idea how to handle this. She knew he was angry. She knew he was frustrated. But the anger spike made her recoil.

Was that wrong? Shouldn't she be trying to support him, the way he had her?

He was a wreck.

Francesca walked across the room towards him.

She placed a hand gently on his arm. 'But he didn't, Gabriel.' She could feel a tremor in his arms.

It was her turn. He was one of the finest doctors she'd ever worked with.

If she hadn't known about his brother she would never have understood his reaction.

But he'd shared with her.

He'd told her something he didn't share with anyone and she loved him for it.

There. The words had finally formed in her head.

The man she'd started out hating was the man she'd finally bared her soul to. The one who was stealing a place in her heart.

She lifted her hands up onto his shoulders. 'You did good, Gabriel.'

'If we'd been at sea you would have started the antibiotics and the steroids and arranged the quickest air ambulance you could.' She paused, watching the frown that puckered his handsome face.

'Haven't you had to deal with a child with meningitis before?' It almost felt disloyal to ask the question. But she had to know. He was paediatrician. Surely he dealt with this before?

His reply was abrupt, snappy. 'Of course I've dealt with kids with meningitis. Just not in the middle of the sea before. I've always had the equipment and people around me that I needed.'

His words stung. Did he think she wasn't good enough to deal with a severely sick child? And they weren't in the middle of the sea. They were in a port, next to a reliable and capable children's hospital that would have dealt with this condition on a hundred other occasions. Jake was in good hands.

She picked up the item he'd flung at the wall. His wallet. It must have been the closest thing he'd had to hand. It fell open in her hands.

There, under a clear bit of plastic, was an old photograph. Two young children and a baby.

It wasn't quite old enough to be a black and white photo, but the colours had faded with age. The little girl's dress had probably been a vibrant pink. Now it was a paler version, her hair in dark curls about her shoulders. The boy was barely an inch taller than her, his dark hair and eyes unmistakeable.

But what made her stomach clench was the pride in their faces as they held their baby brother between them. The innocence of childhood. The joy of family, as they held him on their knees.

Dante. This was Dante.

The tears welled up her eyes.

She sensed him next to her. His finger ran across the battered plastic.

'It's a lovely photograph,' she whispered.

He took the wallet from her hand. 'Yes, yes, it is.' He closed it tightly and slipped it into his back pocket.

There was hesitation, as if he was about to say something. What should she do? Should she wrap her arms around him?

He seemed so closed. So self-contained. She wanted to reach out but couldn't bear the thought of him brushing her aside. Maybe he needed time. Maybe he needed a little space.

Yes, that was it.

She should give him a little time to process what had just happened. It must be so hard for him. It must have dredged up a whole host of difficult memories.

The aspect of feeling out of control must have been the most terrifying of all.

And she could relate. Because it was exactly how she'd felt about her father.

He was still watching her. The tension crackled in the air.

If only she could take that step.

If only she could cross the treatment room and put her arms around him.

But something was stopping her. Something was gluing her feet to the floor and her arms at her sides.

He hesitated. 'We need to discuss this case at the next staff meeting and review the drugs we have available.' He nodded and turned and swept out the door.

Leaving Francesca rooted to the spot.

The feeling of regret swept over her like an icy chill.

It was the last time he was alone with her for three days.

# CHAPTER TWELVE

GABRIEL looked furious.

And no wonder.

There, right in front of her, was the headline: *'Million-aire Doc Saves Drowning Teenager in Venice.'*

Her eyes swept over the newspaper thrust in front of her, a British tabloid that was prone to running scandalous stories of all descriptions.

And as she read the words her heart sank like a stone.

*Gorgeous Doc Gabriel Russo, thirty-one, heir to the Russo Printing fortune, saved the life of a British teenager the other day after he fell into the harbour at Venice and was swept out to sea.*

*Eyewitnesses reported that Gabriel didn't hesitate and dived straight in, swimming to the teenager and making several attempts to bring him to the surface. Unfortunately he then had to be rescued himself as they were swept by the tide into the harbour wall and the Italian millionaire was knocked out.*

*He was resuscitated by British nurse Francesca Cruz, who serves on the same cruise ship as him.*

*Ryan Hargreaves, age thirteen, from Sussex, on holiday with his parents and younger sister, was suc-*

*cessfully treated on board and managed to enjoy the rest of their holiday despite his ordeal. He is now safely at home.*

*Dr Russo had been working as a paediatrician in the States but recently came home to help out the family business after his father's health failed.*

*His skills haven't been wasted on the Italian cruise liner* Silver Whisper, *as he's reportedly saved the life of another child, diagnosing an unusual case that, if missed, could have resulted in the child's death.*

The accompanying photo made her heart turn to ice. It was the snapshot she'd sent to Jill, showing Gabriel dressed in his white uniform, directing the ship-to-ship transfer of a patient during a routine crew exercise.

Some of the words in the newspaper article were copied almost directly from her email. Why on earth had Jill done this?

Her brain was scrambled. She'd known that Gabriel had refused any publicity about the incident. She just hadn't exactly known why.

'How could you?' he hissed, before slamming the newspaper down on the table in front of her. 'After everything that's happened between us. You sold confidential patient details, Francesca. The first rule for any health-care professional—never break patient confidentiality. That's the first thing any medical student learns.' The volume of his voice was increasing on a par with his rage. His face was becoming redder and redder. She'd seen his rage before with the dining-room manager and over the antibiotics and that had been scary enough. But this?

Her head was spiralling. She tried to speak, 'Gabriel, wait—'

'Did you really need the money so badly? Did you? How much did they pay you? How much was it worth to sell me out? Do you know what this will do to the family business? My father is the patriarch of the family. He's the figurehead that everyone expects to see. This will ruin him. Share prices will plummet once people know he's been unwell. You've just ruined a business that's been in my family for generations—all because of your greed!'

*'Stop it!'* She thudded her hand down on the desk as she pushed herself up from her chair. She couldn't listen to this a second longer. He thought she'd sold this story? He thought she'd do something like this? Betray patient confidentiality?

How dared he? Surely he knew her well enough to know that she would never do anything like this?

'Stop it now!' She picked up the newspaper in disgust. 'I'm not responsible for this, Gabriel. I would never do something like this.'

'So who is their source, then, Francesca? Because they know things that shouldn't have left this cruise ship. And how the hell did they get their hands on that picture?'

She cringed. There was no hiding this. There was no getting away from any of this.

'I knew it,' he muttered furiously. 'I should have known you were just like your friend.'

*What did that mean?* She felt a cold chill wash over her skin. He thought she was a liar. The one thing in her life that she'd never been guilty of.

She couldn't stand this. She had to get things out in the open. 'Now…' She took a deep breath. 'Some of this I *am* responsible for.'

She pointed at the front of the newspaper. 'It was Jill. At least, I'm assuming it was Jill. She emailed a few weeks ago and I replied. I told her about the rescue and how I re-suscitated you. I also told her you'd saved another child's life. But I never, *never* revealed any patient details to her.' She shook her head fiercely. 'I would never do that. I don't know where they got Ryan's name from, but it certainly didn't come from me.'

Her fingers touched the paper. 'The picture, however, did come from me. She asked me what you looked like these days. And I sent it to her.' She lifted her eyes to meet his. 'And for that I'm truly sorry.'

She waited a few moments for them both to catch their breath.

'Now maybe you'll tell me what you meant about "being the same" as my friend Jill.' Her hands were shaking but she kept the tremor from her voice. Tiny jigsaw pieces were slotting together in her head—and she didn't like the picture they were forming.

He was trembling—still furious with her. It would be so easy to turn around and walk away. To storm off and open the Australian visa that was in the top drawer of her bedside cabinet. Book a flight and head off into the sunset.

But she didn't want to do any of that. She had to be grown up. She had to accept responsibility that some of this was her fault. Not the patient details but the Gabriel details.

For a few weeks life with Gabriel had almost crept into that dreamlike realm. The happy, blissful place where everything was tinged with pink. A few days of stolen kisses and secret moments.

But that had been before they'd looked after Jake. That had been before she'd seen his reaction to treating a child with meningitis.

Wearing rose-tinted glass was all very well but the reality check of life meant there would always be murky grey skirting around the edges.

And Francesca didn't want to walk away. Because for the first time in a long time she felt at home. At home with Gabriel.

It didn't matter that they were roaming the ocean on a cruise ship with no fixed abode. She felt relaxed and happy with Gabriel. And up until a few seconds ago she'd thought he felt the same with her.

For Francesca it was a revelation. It was the people that made the home, not the place.

She wanted to see this through. No matter where it would take her. She'd connected with him in a way she'd never experienced before and she wasn't about to let this slip through her fingers.

This was worth fighting for.

She took a deep breath. 'Tell me about Jill.'

His hands were fixed on the side of the desk, his knuckles white. His eyes met hers, his dark brown eyes almost black.

'Your friend is a thief. I threw her out when I discovered her hiding my watch in her bag. A few other things had gone missing and I'd had my suspicions. But this time I caught her—and her feet didn't touch the floor.'

She felt her throat close over. The hairs on her arms stood on end and an uneasy trickle crept down her spine.

There was no point in leaping to her defence. Jill had always been desperate for money. Francesca just hadn't known why. What's more, she hadn't *wanted* to know why.

'Do you know what, Gabriel? I'm sorry my friend did that. I have no idea why she did. It certainly wasn't anything that I knew about. But I have to be honest—to my knowledge, Jill never stole anything from me. Maybe I didn't have anything worth stealing. She was always diving from one get-rich-quick scheme to another but that didn't matter to me. What did matter was that when I really needed her, she was there for me. Just as I hope I will be for her. Particularly if she has problems.'

No one in life was perfect.

Not her. Not him. Not her father. And not Jill.

This was real life. Not some fairy-tale. Her father wasn't here to tell her those stories any more. He'd chosen a different path and it was time for Francesca to choose hers.

She reached her hand across the desk and touched Gabriel's cold skin.

Gabriel wasn't angry with her. He was angry at the set of circumstances he'd been dropped into. Things that were out of his control.

And she knew what that felt like.

Because she'd been there.

And so had he.

And what she wanted to do right now was help him. To prove to the man that she loved that she would stand by him through thick and thin.

She knew nothing about share prices. She didn't care about his money. Money had never been a factor in this relationship.

But what she did know was how it felt to have a family member to worry about. To want to ease the pressure and strain on them.

His hands were starting to loosen at the edge of the desk and she intertwined her warm fingers with his cool ones.

Hurt and confusion was written all over his face. And panic at the potential threat to his father's health and the family business.

This was it. This was the time to choose—between the dream job or the dream man. And she didn't hesitate.

'What can I do to help, Gabriel? Because I'm here for you. I'm not going anywhere.' She held his gaze and lifted his hand to her heart.

Gabriel was trying to control the anger he was feeling. Even as he'd shouted some of those words at Francesca he'd known couldn't be true.

Francesca could never be like Jill. The person he'd got to know over the last few weeks was warm and loving, not cold and desperate like her friend had been.

This was the woman who'd bared her soul to him and sobbed her heart out over her father's suicide.

She was one of the few people in his life he'd ever told about Dante. And he'd shared with her because he trusted her. Francesca Cruz was a good person. An honest person.

Even now, when he'd told her about Jill, she hadn't been reactive and angry. She'd immediately had some perspective and been rational about it.

He had to ask. He had to ask now. 'What are you running from, Francesca?'

He heard her sharp intake of breath.

'You've drifted from job to job, place to place. You hardly stay anywhere longer than six months. Hardly enough time to make friends—hardly enough time to get to know people. I heard that your next step will be Australia. When do you plan on going there? When do you plan on leaving?'

His head was swimming with how he felt about her. How he felt about everything. How he felt about his family.

'I'm not running, Gabriel,' she whispered as she tried to blink back tears. 'I'm just trying to find a place to call home.'

And it escaped. One single fat tear sliding down her perfect cheek.

But what would happen now? It would take the Italian press less than a few hours to pick up on the implication about his father's health.

Then it would be everywhere. He cringed. He had to get back home. He had to be with his family.

He'd come back to Venice to be near and to help his family, not to hinder it. There had to be a way to put this right.

'I need to go. I need to leave.'

He could see the expression on her face, the quiet determination masking the hurt in her eyes.

To him, she'd never looked so beautiful.

The next few days would be a nightmare.

And, as much as he wanted to, he couldn't possibly lead her into that.

It wouldn't be fair. They'd only really just met. They'd only spent one precious night together. He couldn't possibly ask her to…

'Just give me time to pack.'

He blinked. And in that moment he knew.

The person he'd always been looking for was standing right in front of him. She was prepared to come and walk into the lion's den with him—right by his side. Francesca had been searching for home.

And it was the one thing he could give her.

The words clogged in his throat. 'Are you sure?'

She looked as though she might cry again. Maybe she wasn't sure. Maybe she just wanted to walk away.

He looked across at the deep brown eyes as she tilted her chin up towards him. If he was lucky, it would be the face he'd spend the next fifty years looking at. A force to be reckoned with.

'I've never been surer.'

# EPILOGUE

EVERYTHING passed in a blur. A quick trip back to Venice followed by four more trips around the Med to see out their notice.

A press officer to deal with media enquiries.

A quiet phone call to a tearful friend who admitted she needed some help.

Gabriel's sister announced as the new, entirely capable CEO of the company.

Francesca fingered the still unopened envelope in her hand.

Australia. Her dream job—at least, that's what she'd thought.

She still hadn't told him—and she probably never would. Because everything she'd been looking for she'd found here, with him.

'What's your favourite fairy-tale?'

She smiled as she felt the warm breath at the back of her neck and his arms steal around her waist. She leaned back against his warm body, looking over at the city of Venice.

It was twilight and the twinkling scattered lights bobbed up and down on the inky-dark waters. Gabriel's penthouse with its gothic façade sat on the Misericordia canal. It was surrounded by gorgeous buildings and a fourteenth-century palace. Every girl's modern-day fairy-tale, with the gondolas slipping silently by at night. A perfect setting.

She sighed. 'I like a little bit from each of them. Snow White being kissed by the prince. Prince Charming sliding the shoe onto Cinderella's foot. Rapunzel throwing down her hair, and Sleeping Beauty being woken by a tender kiss.'

He smiled, showing his perfect white teeth. She turned around, her arms reaching up and twining around his neck.

This was her Gabriel. The tiny lines, caused by the worry and stress of the last few weeks, were dissipating. The tension was gone from his back and shoulders.

'You called me Sleeping Beauty once before.'

She pulled back in surprise. 'You remember? I thought you wouldn't remember any of that. Why didn't you tell me?'

He raised an eyebrow at her. 'And spoil all our fun?' He whispered in her ear. 'Do you know which part of the fairy-tales I like best?'

She shook her head.

'The happy ever after. Everyone deserves one of those.'

She felt herself freeze. The cool evening air danced over her skin, sending the hairs on her arms standing on end. Her breath caught in her throat.

It was just a moment because Gabriel had dropped to one knee and was holding a black velvet box out towards her.

His eyes were staring earnestly at her. 'Francesca Cruz, will you do me the honour of becoming my wife? In sickness and in health, through good times and bad, from here until the end of time? Because I've found my own fairy-tale, here, with you. And I can't imagine spending the rest of my life with anyone other than you.'

She couldn't speak. The words just wouldn't form.

It was perfect. Her own personal fairy-tale with her own perfect hero. Her mum and dad would have loved him. Of that, she had no doubt. Just as Gabriel's family had welcomed her with open arms, making her feel instantly at home.

He opened the box and she blinked. Then smiled.

He stood up and slipped the ring from the box. 'You know that money was no object. You know I could have bought the biggest diamond in the world. But I wanted to buy something that was about us. Something about where we met.'

The ring was flawless. An exquisite aquamarine—the colour of the Mediterranean Sea—surrounded by a host of sparkling diamonds.

'It's perfect,' she breathed.

'Is that a yes?'

'Yes!' she screamed as she jumped up on him. 'Yes, yes, yes!' She smothered him in kisses as he laughed and held her tightly.

Her feet touched the floor again as he took a second to slide the ring onto her finger.

A wicked gleam crossed her eyes. 'It's not just fairy-tales I like,' she said.

'What do you mean?'

'Do you remember what I was reading on the boat?'

He remembered instantly, blood flushing through his heated skin. 'I remember,' he said slowly.

'Then I think it's time to act out my favourite part.'

And she held her hand out to him and led him to the bedroom.

* * * * *

*A sneaky peek at next month...*

# Medical Romance™

**CAPTIVATING MEDICAL DRAMA—WITH HEART**

## My wish list for next month's titles...

In stores from 1st March 2013:

☐ NYC Angels: Redeeming The Playboy – Carol Marinelli

& NYC Angels: Heiress's Baby Scandal – Janice Lynn

☐ St Piran's: The Wedding! – Alison Roberts

& Sydney Harbour Hospital: Evie's Bombshell
— Amy Andrews

☐ The Prince Who Charmed Her – Fiona McArthur

& His Hidden American Beauty – Connie Cox

**Available at WHSmith, Tesco, Asda, Eason, Amazon and Apple**

*Just can't wait?*

0213/03

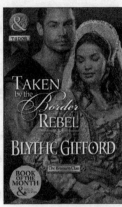

# MILLS & BOON® Book Club

## 2 Free Books!

## Get your free books now at
### www.millsandboon.co.uk/freebookoffer

---

## Or fill in the form below and post it back to us

**THE MILLS & BOON® BOOK CLUB™—HERE'S HOW IT WORKS:** Accepting your free books places you under no obligation to buy anything. You may keep the books and return the despatch note marked 'Cancel'. If we do not hear from you, about a month later we'll send you 5 brand-new stories from the Medical™ series, including two 2-in-1 books priced at £5.49 each and a single book priced at £3.49*. There is no extra charge for post and packaging. You may cancel at any time, otherwise we will send you 5 stories a month which you may purchase or return to us—the choice is yours. *Terms and prices subject to change without notice. Offer valid in UK only. Applicants must be 18 or over. Offer expires 31st July 2013. **For full terms and conditions, please go to www.millsandboon.co.uk/freebookoffer**

Mrs/Miss/Ms/Mr (please circle)
_____

First Name
_____

Surname
_____

Address
_____

_____

Postcode
_____

E-mail
_____

**Send this completed page to: Mills & Boon Book Club, Free Book Offer, FREEPOST NAT 10298, Richmond, Surrey, TW9 1BR**

Find out more at
**www.millsandboon.co.uk/freebookoffer**

*Visit us Online*

0712/M2YEA

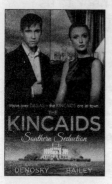